Moonlight and Magnolias

JESSICA LINDSEY

STARDUST
ROMANCE

STARDUST ROMANCE is an imprint of HYDRA PUBLICATIONS

Goshen, Kentucky 40026

www.stardustromancepub.com

Moonlight and Magnolias

Jessica Lindsey

Dedication

For Colin,
who gave me a pen.
Without it, I would have never written the first word.

Acknowledgments

First, let me start by saying thank you to you, dear reader, for picking up my book. There were so many people who came together to see this novel to completion so that you could have it in your hands. I would love to thank them all by mentioning them here.

To my husband, Greg, thank you for always being understanding and for all the times you cheered me on, helped me to defeat that ugly devil on my shoulder (aka imposter syndrome), thank you for the cheers and the happy tears, and for telling everyone you know how proud you are of me. But most importantly thank you for those fateful words; "I wish you would write a book." Look at me, I wrote a book!

To my best friend, Kadi. Thank you for listening to me babble on about my ideas and for all the times you manifested this dream of mine for me and for telling me to just do it. Your belief in me was unwavering. Thank you for never doubting me. You said you were holding out to read it until it was published. Well, here's your chance! Now go add it to your ever growing to be read pile.

To my Mother, Rita. Thank you for being so very supportive. No matter what it was I needed, you were ready to give it your all to help me achieve this goal. You're my number one fan in everything I do, no matter how hair brained it seems. From horses to vampires you've been my advocate to it all. Look Ma! I did it! Now, dry those eyes and let's move on to the next crazy scheme.

This whole thing couldn't have happened of course

without my son. So, here's to you Colin. I dedicated my first novel to you because you gave me the pen that I used to write the first chapter. You gave me the belief that I could do this. When you told me you were proud of me you made this momma's heart so happy. I'm proud that I made *you* proud. If I leave with nothing else, I at least have that.

Of course I couldn't forget my original cheerleaders. My work besties who so diligently and eagerly awaited the next chapter to be written. You endured my sloppy handwriting, crazy notes, raggedy notebooks, and constant ramblings all in the hopes of finding out what happens next. Sam, thank you for letting me talk you into reading a book about vampires and for actually enjoying it. Your T-shirt is on the way! Alex, thank you for believing in my little story even when I would often lose faith in it. Us rats must stick together!

To everyone at Stardust Romance, so many thanks goes to you for taking a chance with me and helping me see my book through to reality. Seriously, I'm still pinching myself.

Now I'm going to name drop a little bit, so bear with me. First I want to thank Lynn Tincher. Your advice, expertise, and guidance has been much appreciated. Not to mention your belief in me and my little novel. Your mentor program was a godsend to this author. Speaking of the mentor program, it is crucial that I thank the other mentors of From the Ground Up Books Mentorship Program. Tony Acree, Dan Klefstad, Dave Creek, Leagh Pugh, Erv Klein your sage wisdom and encouragement helped me get to where I am today. Many, many thanks. Oh, and by the way dear reader, if you haven't picked up any of their books, do it! Do it now!

And finally last but not least to all of my friends, family, and followers I may not have mentioned above (you know who you are). Thank you so much for believing in me. All the kind words and the encouragement did not go unnoticed. I took it all to heart and I return that love ten fold. Now, on to the next!

~

At the last it bites like a serpent
And stings like a viper
Proverbs 23:32

Prologue

AUGUST 1899

Diamond City, North Carolina

SILAS COULDN'T OPEN his eyes. Even if he could, there would be nothing but absolute black all around him. He didn't know how long he had been in the dark; it had felt like forever. There were no days or nights in the darkness. He couldn't see or move, but he could still hear and feel, not that there was much to listen to or feel where he was. The only sounds he heard were the slithering of worms in the moldering dirt outside of his coffin. Most days, he lay there in silence and tuned everything out, praying for the release death can bring. But death would never come for him; the constant burning pain in his chest from the damned stake in his heart was his reminder of that. It was the only thing keeping him pinned here in his prison of dirt. He was trying to ignore the pain on this particular day, when something changed.

Water began to slowly seep into his coffin. That wasn't too alarming;. It had happened before, but this time, it was differ-ent. The water began trickling in faster and faster until his body was nearly submerged and he began to hear muffled noises from the world above. Thunder crashed, and the wind was howling; it must have been a hell of a storm if he could hear it from his resting place.

Soon, the water had filled his enclosure completely, and he felt it begin to rise slowly until it emerged with a wet, sucking pop. His coffin began to float, bumping along as the wind and the rain beat at the wooden planks and nails that held it shut. One by one, the boards and the nails came loose as the flood waters dashed his coffin against God knew what.

Suddenly, Silas could feel the torrential rains as they sluiced down his cold gray skin. He was above ground now, he suddenly realized, and damn near free! He lay there for what seemed like hours, listening to the storm rage on until it finally diminished. He came to rest somewhere much farther away from his unmarked grave. It wasn't long before he felt the cruel sun on his face. Stinging and uncomfortable, but not quite burning.

———

At first, Silas welcomed the rays of the sun and the cool nights. Before long, though, the sun became irritating, and he was beginning to lose track of the days. He lay there, motionless and helpless, silently cursing his situation, when he began to hear voices. Two men, from the sound of it.

"I've got another one over here, Henry!" one voice called out.

The sound of hooves and wagon wheels plodding along in the mud filled the silence.

"Whoa, Bess," another voice sounded.

Silas assumed that must have been Henry. He could hear the jingle of a harness and the snorting and the sneezing of a horse as it came to a stop nearby.

"This one wasn't buried long before that hurricane came

through. Look, he hasn't even started to rot, and he doesn't stink yet," the first voice marveled.

There was more silence and the sound of heavy bootsteps as the second man approached Silas's coffin.

"Wait a minute, Tom, isn't that Callum Quinn's boy?" Henry asked in confusion.

Another beat of silence, and finally Tom chimed in. "Yeah, I believe it is. I wonder what they had done to the ol' boy for him to keep so well."

"You're right. He should be looking a lot worse after a year in the ground."

A year? Silas thought, *was that all?*

"Did they ever say what happened to him? I only know he went missing, and then nothing else was ever really said about it," Tom said.

"No, not really. Callum and Lottie were pretty mum about it. Callum only said his boy went off and killed himself after that girl turned down his proposal."

Was that the story they were feeding everyone? How convenient, Silas thought, wishing he could roll his eyes.

"He sure was a handsome devil, even now in death. Wonder why that girl said no." Tom tutted.

"Don't rightly know. Let's get him loaded up with the rest of these poor souls. We can notify the Quinns later so they can plan to have him reinterred," said Henry, sadly.

Silas felt himself being lifted and then roughly placed down in the wagon.

"What's this?" Tom asked, sounding shocked. "Looks like the storm sent a piece of something right through the poor lad."

"Crimany! It almost looks intentional. But there's no way Lottie would have let them bury him with that ugly thing sticking out of his chest." Henry paused a moment. "Just remove it and let's get going."

Silas felt one of the men place a firm hand on his chest.

Soon, a tugging sensation began to send wracking pain throughout his body as his senses came back to him with each tug on the stake.

The man whom he assumed was Tom grunted with the effort and eventually worked it free, tossing it aside when the job was done.

Silas heard the stake hit the ground and felt the wagon rock from one side and then the other as the men climbed aboard.

There was a snap of reins, and the wagon creaked as it lurched forward.

The men were quiet now, and Silas began to open his eyes for the first time in over a year. He squinted up at the blue sky above him, marveling at the feeling of the hole in his chest healing itself. He felt the skin and muscle work its way back together, stitching each sinewy piece back in place. The rest of Silas's muscles began to twitch back to life as he regained control of his body.

He took a slow, careful breath, taking in the scent of the air and his surroundings. He could smell the sea, and the foul rotten bodies in the wagon with him, but above all that, the smell of the two men overpowered it all. Silas was fully awake now, and he was hungry.

The men's scents smothered the stench of their macabre cargo. Silas sat up, salivating as he glanced around at the pile of bodies and bones in various stages of decay. He couldn't care less about any of it; all he could think about was the smell of the two men in front of him.

He silently crawled across the pile of putrid and fetid corpses. Their scattering bones tinkled and clinked like some kind of morbid wind chimes.

Silas zeroed in on the strong heartbeats and pumping blood of the men driving the wagon. Their heartbeats were like bass drums in his ears, loud and unrelenting.

He stood, shakily at first, but quickly gained his legs as his shadow fell across the men.

Tom and Henry didn't even have time to scream.

CHAPTER

One

PRESENT DAY

Ophidian Grove, North Carolina

I HAD A HEADACHE, but not just any headache. No, this was the kind that started behind the eyes and burned across your skull. The type of headache that makes you think there's a gremlin in your head, just kicking the crap out of the back of your eyeballs. My mouth began to water as nausea roiled in my stomach.

"Hold it together, Dani," I muttered to myself as I rubbed my temples. There was only one cure for a headache like this. Strong black coffee and apple pie *à la mode*.

I rested my head against the cool glass of the door as I locked it. I knew my forehead would leave a mark on the freshly cleaned surface, but I didn't care; it could wait until tomorrow. I turned the key to the dead bolt and heard it click into place.

Sighing, I reluctantly lifted my head and turned toward the parking lot behind the store. It was empty except for my own car, a sensible black Volkswagen Jetta.

I pressed the unlock button on my key fob and got in.

I glanced back at the business my family had owned and

operated for as long as I could remember, and I smiled, remembering how proud my parents were of their little boutique bookstore, Magnolia Tree Books. I took over managing it when they retired. However, running a bookstore was not what I wanted for my future. Sure, it provided a steady income and paid the bills, but I wanted more. Travel and adventure, romance and excitement; you know, the typical stuff.

I started my car and reached over to turn on the AC. I set it to full blast to battle the oppressive southern humidity and heat. It felt like there was a storm brewing. Even at 9:30 p.m. it felt like a sauna outside. Tonight's sticky climate was not helping my raging headache.

I reached into my bag and pulled out my bottle of Excedrin and swallowed a couple of pills. I gave a quick glance around me to make sure the path was clear and put my car into gear, pulling out of the parking lot and onto the road. The tiny town of Ophidian Grove, North Carolina was a blink-and-you'll-miss-it, one-red-light kind of town. It was situated on the outskirts of the Croatan National Forest and was on a scenic byway to The Outer Banks. The quaint little town square had a few shops and restaurants, a hardware store and a post office, as well as a bakery and a small home-town bank. All the buildings were old, and most had not been changed since the early 1900s. It gave the town charm and an air of antiquity. Just beyond the square was a little park that had a playground, a picnic pavilion, and a few walking trails. Ophidian Grove didn't have much in the way of public spaces, unless you counted the churches that dotted the land-scape, and most people drove out of town for any entertain-ment or major retail needs.

I didn't pay attention to any of that as I drove tonight; the fog of my headache wouldn't allow it. I had one destination in mind as I drove, and that was Lulu's Diner. As fate would have it, Lulu's was the only place to get my coffee and pie headache remedy at this hour.

Like a beacon, the flashing red neon arrow on the sign of the diner soon rose out of the darkness, guiding hungry, weary travelers in with the promise of southern-fried comfort food, milkshakes, and my personal favorite, apple pie.

I pulled into the lot and noticed Lulu's seemed particularly dead tonight. It was late and a Sunday, so I didn't think too much about it. There was only one other vehicle in the lot, a late '90s model blue Ford truck. Nothing strange about that in a small, rural town. I parked my car a couple spaces down from the truck, gathered my wallet and phone, and then headed inside.

The bell above the door gave a little jingle as I pushed it open. The cold AC and the sounds of a 1950's doo wop song washed over me.

Stepping into the tiny diner was like stepping back in time. Leanne Campbell, the owner of the diner and my best friend, designed Lulu's to look just like a '50s soda fountain shop. The floors were tiled in black and white checkerboard, the ceiling was lined with red neon light tubing, and there were retro hanging pendant lights above each booth. The booths were red vinyl and trimmed in chrome. But the best part about the diner was the soda fountain bar. It was almost the entire length of the diner, complete with soda fountains and a milkshake machine. The stools were round and could spin and were upholstered in the same red vinyl and chrome as the booths. Looking behind the bar, there was a swinging door to the kitchen and a large cut out window that had a counter for the cook to place the food orders. Leanne was a stickler for details, and it showed in her attention to all the nuances she chose for her diner.

I noticed Leanne at the corner of the bar, talking to a man partially hidden in shadow. She seemed agitated.

Leanne looked up when I walked in and flashed me a smile. It was her customer service smile, not a true one.

"Sit anywhere you like, Dani; I'll be right with you." She glanced back at the stranger in the corner and said in a low voice, "We're not finished; don't move."

I thought that was odd.

I sat down in a corner booth on the opposite end of the bar. I could feel the stranger's eyes on me as I fumbled with my menu. I don't know why, but it agitated me. My skin began to prickle, and I rubbed at the goosebumps. I held my menu up in front of me, trying to block his view. I didn't need the menu; I knew what I wanted. I just wanted a distraction from the feeling of being watched. I was grateful when Leanne approached my table stepping into his line of sight.

"Rough day?" she asked with a sympathetic smile as she placed a glass of ice water in front of me. "What can I get you?" Leanne was always meticulously dressed in a rockabilly style that suited her tall and slender frame. Her hair and makeup were always on point, too. Tonight, her jet-black hair was piled high in a red and white polka-dotted handkerchief. She looked like a '50s queen.

"Ugh, you have no idea, Leanne." I rolled my eyes and sank deeper into the red vinyl booth. I watched the beads of condensation roll down the glass in front of me.

I reached for it and said, "I really wish the parents around here wouldn't treat the summer reading program as a babysitting service. Half of those kids don't want to be there," I lamented, taking a sip of the water.

"Well, you and I both know that won't happen. Your parents started a good thing, and I think it's great you're keeping it going." She placed her hand on my shoulder and smiled.

I closed my eyes and groaned. "It's such a headache, though!"

Leanne giggled "Good thing I know the cure for

headaches. A big ol' slice of apple pie *à la mode* and a strong cup of coffee coming up!"

She truly was a mind reader. Leanne grinned and bounced on her heels then turned toward the kitchen.

On her way behind the bar, the stranger in the corner beckoned her over.

She huffed and stormed over to him. "What now?" she almost growled.

He spoke, softly.

I couldn't make out what he said; his voice was too low. I still couldn't see his face clearly; he was very good at keeping to the shadows. In fact, the whole diner seemed to be in shadow. Leanne must have dimmed the lights for the evening, or something.

Suddenly, I heard her slap the bar.

"Really?" she hissed, incredulously. "No, not her!" She tried to say that last part quietly, but I heard it, anyway. She glanced in my direction, and I quickly looked down at my phone and feigned interest in it. What could he have said about me to upset her?

Moments later, she came back with the coffee and the pie in tow. "Your tab has been paid," she said through gritted teeth and placed the food in front of me.

"Oh, okay. Um, you didn't have to do that." I was taken aback.

"I didn't." She looked over her shoulder toward the stranger, gave a tight-lipped smile, and abruptly walked away.

I lifted my coffee mug and nodded at the strange, shadowy man in the corner. I tried to give a friendly grin, but I'm pretty sure it came across awkward and weird.

I savored every bite and every sip until all that remained were a few crumbs and a small puddle of melted vanilla ice cream.

Leanne and the shadow man had talked in hushed voices

while I ate. Every so often, she would slide a glance my way, she eventually came back to collect my dishes.

"Leanne, is that man bothering you? Is there anything I can do?" My question seemed to startle her because she suddenly seemed nervous. The color drained out of her face, making her sun-tanned skin look pale and pallid. I hoped I had asked her quietly enough in case tall, dark, and shadowy was listening.

"Ha!" Leanne choked back a laugh, and the color returned to her face. "No, that's just my *cousin*. He's leaving soon." She said the word "cousin" with such venom it almost hurt *my* feelings. I've known Leanne since we were little girls, so I thought I knew all her cousins. She must have had a reason to have never spoken about this one.

I looked over at him.

This time, though, he had leaned forward into the light, and I locked eyes with the most handsome man I'd ever seen. I felt my face flush, and he grinned maniacally and tipped his coffee mug toward me before taking a sip.

Even from the distance, I could tell his eyes were an unnatural shade of green. They caught the lights in just a way that made them look animalistic, like the eyeshine of an animal at night. I couldn't look away. I became acutely aware someone had sat down across from me. Then came a snapping sound as if someone were snapping their fingers in front of my face.

"Dani?" Snap, snap. "Danica Jones? Hellooo?" It was Leanne. Apparently, I had dazed out and was staring hard at her cousin.

"Oh, um, yeah. Sorry about that; I don't know what happened there," I responded, rather flustered.

Talk about embarrassing. I was a grown woman, for Pete's sake, and I was ogling that strange man like a schoolgirl at a boy band concert.

I averted my eyes and looked at Leanne. I quickly looked

away and began gathering my things, reaching into my wallet for a few dollars to leave for Leanne's tip.

I placed the money on the table and looked up at Leanne.

"Call me later if you need to. I'll be up if you want to talk. I know how much fun family can be."

She smiled at me, but her smile faltered. Her pale green eyes brushed over me, and her face became worried. "Dani, do me a favor and make sure you lock up tight when you get home, okay?"

I cocked an eyebrow at her. "All right, any particular reason you're concerned for my safety tonight?"

Her face darkened, and her eyes shifted ever so slightly toward the man in the corner and quickly back to me. "Just promise me you'll lock up. Windows, too."

I promised, even though I thought it was a strange request.

I headed toward the exit, but not without one more look at Leanne's strange, handsome cousin.

He smiled, broadly, and waggled his fingers at me.

I quickly looked away. My heart began pounding, and I rushed out the door.

The summer night air was still and hit me like I had opened the door to an oven. The sudden onslaught of muggy air made me realize I had been holding my breath, and I exhaled. The night seemed darker and ominous with the moon hidden by storm clouds. The breeze kicked up suddenly, hot and heavy. It was scented with the sweet scent of honeysuckle, with the promise of rain, and of the cornfields close by.

Normally, I would have stood there and relished the smells of a hot summer night and the cool promise of a thunderstorm, but I couldn't shake the feeling of being watched. Goosebumps began creeping up my skin again as a low rumble of thunder sounded in the distance.

I rushed to get into my car and get it started. I gave a sigh of relief once I left the diner parking lot.

Leanne and I have been best friends since grade school, so seeing her so flummoxed by her cousin, if that's who he even really was, had me concerned. Why had I never heard her, nor any of her family, ever mention that guy before? He had to be distantly related, maybe a black sheep, or something. I tried to place him, searching my memory of family photos at Leanne's house and her parents', but I couldn't place his face. And believe me, that's a face you didn't forget.

———

I made it home before I knew it. Time flies when you're overthinking.

I hurriedly gathered my belongings and walked to the door. I still couldn't shake the feeling of being watched.

I clumsily put my key into the lock, almost dropping it a time or two. What was wrong with me? Did Leanne's demeanor really shake me up that badly?

I finally got my front door unlocked and rushed inside, throwing the door closed and locking it behind me. I immediately felt better after hearing the dead bolt slide into place.

I practically ran toward the back door to check it was locked.

Satisfied it was, I began drawing the blinds and checking the window locks on all the windows. My parents bought the renovated farmhouse when I was a little girl. The windows were old, but not quite as old as the house. They had been replaced at some point. My dad wanted exact replicas of the originals, so they still had old-fashioned window locks on them.

They all seemed secure, except for one, my bedroom window. There were two windows in my room, and the one closest to my bed had a broken sash lock. I began racking my brain about how to secure that window. Surely, it would be okay, considering my bedroom was on the second floor. Nevertheless, I couldn't just leave it. I settled for placing a baseball bat next to my bed, just in case someone happened to scale the side of my house and get my window open.

"Get yourself together, woman!" I said aloud while rubbing my temples. I needed to relax.

Just then, my phone buzzed in my pocket, making me jump. It was a text from Leanne.

Did you make it home okay?

Yes. Are you okay? I replied.

Yeah. My cousin and I do not get along, and I hate it when he visits. Glad you're home. TTYL.

He must have really been an asshole if Leanne didn't like him; she liked everyone.

I ran a bath, dropping a lavender bath bomb into it, and I eased myself into the warm water. I could feel the day melting away the longer I soaked.

I got myself ready for bed after my bath and I hoped I could sleep off what remained of my headache and the odd feelings I had. I was absolutely exhausted. I pulled back the covers and slipped into bed. Sleep came almost at once, and that night I dreamt of him, but it felt more like a nightmare.

CHAPTER
Two

I ARRIVED at the bookstore early the next morning. I had a little more cleaning up to do from the previous night.

After unlocking the door and switching the *CLOSED* sign to *OPEN*, I set a reminder on my phone to stop at the hardware store and pick up a new window lock for my bedroom window.

I walked around the store, straightening things as I went. I turned on the lights and the computers and readied the cash register. It's funny thinking back on how my parents were reluctant to have computers and internet access here. I had to practically drag them, kicking and screaming, into the twenty-first century.

They were so in love with their little bookstore. Mom spent hours dusting the shelves and arranging the knick-knacks and trinkets she sold. Dad manned the cash register and was oftentimes found in the office at the rear of the store on the phone ordering more inventory.

I helped after school and during summer vacation and came back after college to put my business degree to good use, making the store more profitable by adding online sales and tourist souvenirs. Our town was on the way to nearby

Shackleford Banks, so a lot of people stopped in town for last-minute supplies and to look around.

Mom and Dad's real pride and joy, however, was the summer reading program they put together for the local kids. It was their way of giving back to the community. Two Sundays a month from June to August, the store, which was normally closed on Sundays, would open from 6:00 p.m. to 8:00 p.m. to allow the local youths a chance to come in and take part in storytelling, writing workshops, and to discuss the books they chose to read. My parents kept a good collection of used and donated books that could be checked out for the kids to read for the program.

It started out strongly and was well-received, but during the last couple of years, many of the local families have used it as an inexpensive babysitting service. The reading program was basically free; we only charged a small fee for snacks or supplies, like notebooks and pencils. Sometimes, there was an extra charge if we asked a guest to come and speak to the kids.

I felt taken advantage of by many of the parents as they dropped their kids off and rushed out the door. Volunteer numbers had also begun to dwindle, down to just me and a couple other people, and most nights, like last night, it was only me. I wanted to end the program after Mom died, but I couldn't bring myself to do it. After last night and the mess those kids left behind, this just might be the last summer I will have it.

My parents doted on this little bookstore almost as much as they did me. We moved here when I was a tiny thing. Mom and Dad had big dreams of starting a successful boutique bookstore on the quiet and quaint town square. They were highly successful in the beginning, and when the summer months came, it brought tourists. Before we knew it, we were a well-loved and established business. My parents had realized their dream, and once I was old enough, they brought me on board as a co-owner.

Eventually, I became the sole owner upon their deaths. They left it all to me when they retired, and now, they were both gone. My father passed from a massive heart attack a few years ago, and I know it sounds cliché, but I'm pretty sure my mother died from a broken heart just a couple years later. She was never the same after Dad passed. I kept the bookstore open for them, to keep their memory alive, but truth be told, it wasn't easy. I did my best, but I thought about selling it often, especially as of late.

I made my way around the bookstore, bagging up garbage and dusting shelves. I also finished placing some books back where they belonged.

I stopped by the supply closet to grab the glass cleaner and the paper towels and then headed to the front door. I could hear my mom now tut tutting over the smudge I left on the door's glass.

I smiled at the thought and began cleaning the window, admiring the stained-glass magnolia blossom on the door.

It was about that time when my one and only employee showed up for the day. Jeff Mitchell was a local guy who began working here a couple of years ago. He had an all-American charm and good looks. He was tall and blonde with blue eyes, a quintessential guy next door type. Jeff was a good person and a hard worker, and I was happy to have him work for me.

"Mornin', boss." He smiled and watched me work.

I turned around and handed him the glass cleaner and towels. "Perfect timing. You can finish this, and I'll go inside and finish opening."

Jeff smiled, shook his head, and gestured for me to get inside.

I pushed the door open, the small chimes rattling as the door hit them. I stopped and straightened the family portrait in the entryway. It was one of my favorites. All three of us: Mom, Dad, and I standing in front of our bookstore on opening day. My parents looked ecstatic. My hand lingered on the edge of the frame.

I jumped a little when the door opened behind me.

Jeff came inside, wiping his brow as he closed the door. "Woo! It's going to be a hot one today. What's on today's agenda, boss?"

I rolled my eyes at him. He knew I disliked being called boss, but he did it, anyway, just to aggravate me. "Inventory. Today, we do inventory."

Jeff groaned but got to work.

I got busy checking the bestseller list and making sure we had enough copies in the store or on the way.

———

Soon enough, it was lunchtime, and still not one customer had come in. Mondays were always slow, but this one was exceptionally so.

"Hey, Jeff? Do you mind if I knock off early? I've got some errands to run and bookstore shipments to mail out. Can you handle closing this afternoon?"

"You got it, boss." He laughed. "I don't know why you bother asking."

I lightly punched his arm and said, "I ask because it's the decent thing to do, and that's what makes me a phenomenal boss."

"Sure, sure. Get out of here and try not to melt out there."

I thanked him and headed out.

Before crossing the street to Henderson's Hardware store, I paused and noticed Wenda Samuels sweeping the sidewalk in front of her deli next door. She and her husband owned it. She was in her early seventies and she had always treated me like one of her own grandchildren, even though she had plenty of her own.

I smiled and waved. "Hello, Mrs. Samuels."

"Hi, there, sugar!" She stopped sweeping and took out a hanky to wipe the sweat from her brow. A wide, friendly smile lit up her lovely brown face.

She began walking toward me. "We sure do miss your family at church;. You ought to come by sometime; we'd love to have you." She winked, conspiratorially. "Plenty of single young men there, too."

I smiled, uncomfortably, and looked for a way out of the conversation. I never could understand what it was with some of the older generation's need to fix up the single, young people.

Mrs. Samuels took my hand and patted it. "I just never have understood why some handsome young devil hasn't gobbled you up yet." She laughed.

I laughed, awkwardly, in return. "Just haven't run into the right one yet, I guess." I quickly changed the subject. "Your petunias are very lovely today."

"Thank you, baby. I've got some extra baskets if you'd like one to hang on your awning." She smiled, warmly, and wiped the sweat from her brow again. Mrs. Samuels was part of the Ladies Auxiliary at the First Baptist Church, and they always had petunia baskets for sale every summer to raise money for the congregation.

"Put me down for two. I'll send Jeff after them tomorrow." I waved as I left, and Mrs. Samuels beamed at me.

I headed across the street and made a beeline to the hardware store. I needed to get that replacement window lock and a few tools to get the job done. I wasn't quite sure what was involved, but it didn't seem like it would be too difficult.

The old hardware store hadn't changed much over the years, and it was about the only place I knew where I could find antique window locks to match the ones in my house.

Arthur Henderson was behind the counter. He had to be in his eighties, but he was just as spry and as quick-witted as ever. He and his sons ran the hardware store together and helped with minor household repairs around town.

Arthur helped me find everything I needed, rang me up, and bagged up my purchases.

Then, I was on my way. The post office was my next stop before I could go home.

I was not paying much attention as I stepped out onto the sidewalk. I was too busy, looking at my reminders on my phone and thinking about all I had to do today, when I stepped right into the path of another person.

We collided, and it felt like I hit a brick wall. My bag of hardware supplies spilled out onto the concrete sidewalk, and I dropped to my knees, without looking at who I ran into, to collect my things, apologizing the whole way down.

"Oh, my God!" I said, breathlessly. "I am so, so sorry. I'm such a klutz! I wasn't paying attention to where I was going at all."

A deep, unfamiliar voice chuckled and said, "You're quite all right. In fact, I was hoping to run into you, and here you are quite literally running into me." He knelt and started helping me gather my things.

I froze and then looked up and into the face of the stranger, Leanne's cousin, Mr. Shadowy himself.

"Oh!" I gasped.

"I'm pleasantly surprised, myself." He laughed as he handed me the box with the window lock.

His fingers grazed my hand as I took it, and I was shocked at how cold they were.

"Fixing a window lock?" he asked.

I could only nod in reply.

"You know, I'm pretty handy, and I'm somewhat of an expert on old houses." He smiled like he had told an inside joke. "Judging by that replacement lock, you've got quite an antique. I could help, if you'd like?"

I was flabbergasted. Just like the previous night, I couldn't look away. This time, though, I got a very good look at him.

He caught my elbow and helped me to stand.

Once again, I noticed the coolness of his hands. I never took my eyes off his face, even now that I had to look up at him.

He was tall and muscular, standing confidently; he exuded a magnetic presence I was undeniably drawn to. He wore a well-fitted black V-neck T-shirt, jeans, and an expensive-looking pair of rugged boots. His eyes were striking and held an air of mystery and danger. They were the most unusual shade of deep, dark emerald green I had ever seen. They reminded me of looking up at a forest canopy on a sunny day. He had a few smile lines around his eyes, the slightest hint of a five o'clock shadow across his strong, chiseled jawline, and his dimpled smile conveyed a sense of approachable charm. His skin was pale, but he didn't have an unhealthy look. There was a very slight blush on his skin, and he seemed to glow slightly from within. His tousled, dark hair seemed to frame his features perfectly and it fell effortlessly across his forehead.

I wanted to run my fingers through it, and my heart began to pound in reaction to that thought.

He stood there, grinning at me.

I finally came to my senses. "I don't even know your name," I said, breathlessly.

He laughed. "Silas. My name is Silas, and you are Danica Jones. My cousin speaks very highly of you."

"Mmm, I can't say the same about you, and it's Dani, by the way."

He smiled again, this time giving me a big grin. I could see his perfect white teeth. "Well, Dani, will you let me help you fix your window? I really don't mind."

I tilted my head and gave him a scrutinizing look. My heart was still pounding.

He just stood there, grinning like a madman. A perfect and beautiful madman.

"Sure," I said, slowly. "But first I need to stop at the post office. Meet me at my house in thirty?"

What was I doing? This was so wrong on so many levels! But on the other hand, he *was* Leanne's cousin, so how bad could he be?

"Excellent, I'll need an address, though." He handed me his phone, and I entered my address in the map application.

When he looked at his phone to read the address, there was a fleeting look of some sort. Was it recognition, or something else? It was so quick it was almost imperceptible. "See you in thirty." He winked and then walked away.

I really hoped I wasn't making a mistake.

CHAPTER
Three

I RACED home from the post office so I would have time to straighten up a bit.

I climbed the steps of my front porch, checking to make sure nothing was out of place. The rockers and the flowerpots were all in their designated spots on the covered porch, and it was neat and tidy, as usual.

I unlocked my door and stepped inside. I generally kept things pretty clean, so there wasn't much to do. I hadn't changed much to the old farmhouse since I inherited it from my parents. It was still basically the way my mother left it. I never felt like it was mine, even though it was. There was exposed shiplap in the foyer, and the rooms were still painted in soft pastels. It was an inviting home, warm and cozy, just like my parents were.

I ran up the wooden staircase to my bedroom to hastily make my bed and to make sure there was no dirty laundry on the floor.

As I was finishing up, I heard Silas pulling in. The low rumble of his truck announced his arrival as the tires crunched over the gravel drive. It soon became very quiet when his truck shut off and the door slammed shut.

I rushed down the stairs to meet him at the door.

I quickly opened the front door, and once again, the sight of him took my breath away. My heart was racing.

"Hi," I said, breathlessly.

He was grinning again, almost like he had a secret or something. It was annoying, and I needed to pull myself together.

I pushed the screen door open and stood to the side.

He hesitated at the threshold, and there was a brief look of annoyance on his face before it disappeared and was replaced with a smirk.

"Well, come on in," I said, inviting him in.

His smile was genuine this time, making the little lines at the corner of his eyes crinkle up. He passed so close by me on his way through the door I could smell him. He smelled like leather, clean linen, and bourbon. It was intoxicating.

I closed the door behind us and gestured to the stairs.

"The window is up here, in my bedroom." I could feel the heat rising in my face as I blushed.

"Your bedroom?" He was smirking again. "I do declare, Miss Jones, you wouldn't be trying to seduce me and steal my virtue, would you?"

"Hardly," I replied, shortly, blushing again.

He laughed. He seemed to do that easily. "Lead the way," he said.

I climbed the stairs with him following closely behind. The air seemed electrically charged and intense. My heart began to pound again.

I turned around at the top of the stairs, almost colliding with Silas as he stopped short behind me, and I pointed out my room. There was that goddamned smirk again. What was his deal?

"It's the window closest to the bed." I pointed toward it.

This time, I followed him, letting him enter my room first.

He looked around and seemed to be taking it all in. My

antique furniture, the blue flowered quilt on my bed, the framed photos of my trips to the mountains out west hanging on my walls. His eyes finally landed on the baseball bat next to my bed, and I saw his eyebrow raise.

"Do you play?" he asked, pointing at the bat.

"Not exactly." I shrugged, embarrassed. I grabbed the bat and swiftly put it in my closet.

"I see," he chuckled. "I feel sorry for the poor sap who tries getting in here."

This time, we both laughed, and the tension seemed to melt away.

I handed him the bag from the hardware store, and he got to work.

I quietly sat on the bed and watched.

His hands deftly and expertly removed the old, broken lock and replaced it with the new one. He gave it a few precursory locks and unlocks before finally locking it into place and trying the window.

"All set." He wiped his hands on his jeans, leaned against the window sill, and said, "Now what?"

"What do you mean?" I was curious as to what he had in mind.

"Well, do you have any other projects or are you free for the evening?"

It was my turn to smirk. "Are you asking me out?"

"Possibly, or maybe I just want to work on your house. You decide." He shrugged and crossed his arms.

"Well, I don't have any more home improvement projects, and I am free tonight, so dealers' choice?" I put the ball back in his court.

"Perfect, I'll pick you up at 8:00." He grinned like the Cheshire cat and left the room. "I can see myself out."

Now I've really gone and done it. Why did I so eagerly accept his invitation? What on Earth was I thinking?

CHAPTER

Four

IT WAS GETTING CLOSER to 8:00, and I still had not chosen anything to wear. I had showered, so I had that going for me. I stood in front of my open closet and just stared.

What should I wear? Where are we going? He gave me no clues as to what he had planned, just he would pick me up at 8:00. It was a tad after 7:00 now, so I needed to get a move on, unless I planned on wearing the towel I still had on.

Well, when in doubt, choose classy and comfortable. I picked a sundress I hadn't worn in ages, but I loved it, and there was no better excuse than a date to drag it out. It was teal with cap sleeves and a deep V neckline. I chose a simple silver necklace with a leaf charm and a pair of diamond stud earrings. The earrings were my mother's, and I had always adored them. I finished off the look with a couple of silver bangle bracelets and a pair of strappy sandals.

My hair decided to cooperate with me tonight; it fell in dark brown ringlets and waves down my sun-tanned, freckled shoulders. I scanned my reflection in the mirror, glancing at my heart-shaped face and wide-set brown eyes. Leanne always said I had bedroom eyes, whatever that meant, and cheekbones to die for. I puckered my lips and gave myself one last look over.

"Eh, you'll do," I told my reflection.

I didn't bother with much makeup; it was entirely too hot outside. I used a tinted lip gloss and some mascara, and that was about it.

I was fussing with my hair, when I heard the doorbell ring. I looked over at my alarm clock; it was 8:00 on the dot. That was annoyingly punctual.

I hurried down the stairs and opened the door.

He smiled when he saw me. "You look lovely. Are you ready to go?" He seemed eager to leave.

"Um, yeah, let me grab my purse."

I went to turn around, but he stopped me. He reached for my hand, and his cold fingers clasped mine, firmly. How could it feel one thousand degrees outside and his hands be that cold? He must have had awesomely frigid AC in that truck of his.

"No need for that. We won't be needing any money, and if we do, I've got it covered." He gave my arm a gentle tug toward the door before letting go.

I locked the door, and we walked side-by-side toward his truck in the driveway. It was the same Ford truck from the diner. I noticed he was looking around the yard, and his eyes fell on the huge magnolia tree out front.

"That is a very old tree." He said it with an air of nostalgia and started walking toward it.

"My dad always said he thought it was almost as old as the house," I replied.

"He wasn't far off." Silas said, quietly. He sounded a little sad.

He reached up, picked one of the smaller blossoms, and held it to his nose. Silas closed his eyes, looking wistful.

He turned and walked back toward me, holding the flower. "You know, magnolia blossom is one of my favorite scents." He was standing in front of me now. He looked me in the eyes and then reached toward my face with one hand.

I went rigid.

He took a lock of hair and tucked it behind my ear, pinning it in place with the flower. He hesitantly lowered his hand along my neck. He never took his eyes from mine, like he was waiting for me to protest so he could stop if he went too far. When I showed no objection he smiled tenderly and pushed my hair off my shoulder and let it fall through his fingers. His eyes lingered a bit too long and hungrily on my neck. He wet his lips, and a shadow seemed to fall across his face. He seemed to wake from some sort of reverie.

He let his hand fall to his side and said, "You smell like magnolias; I noticed it earlier."

Weird, I wasn't wearing any perfume, and my soap was not magnolia-scented. Maybe the smell of the flowers from the tree permeated the air more than I thought. My face began to flush; I could feel the blush heating up my skin.

I moved away from his touch, and he let his hand drop to his side. "I, I, guess I never noticed." I stammered.

Silas just smiled and headed us back toward his truck. He placed his hand on the small of my back, and it seemed to unfreeze me.

I took notice of how he was dressed. He wore a dark charcoal grey button-up shirt with the sleeves rolled up to his elbows and cuffed perfectly, a pair of expensive-looking tailored jeans, and a pair of western boots. His shirt was unbuttoned just enough to get a glimpse of the muscular chest underneath.

He caught me staring and grinned. "What?" he asked. "Do I not meet your approval?"

He opened my door and helped me in, making sure not to shut the door on my dress.

I watched him walk around the front of the truck.

He moved so gracefully and confidently. He hopped in and started his truck.

"Who are you?" I asked, dripping with suspicion.

His face darkened just a hair. He put his truck in reverse and without looking at me said, "That is a loaded question."

———

We drove in silence for a while; it got awkward and tense. Silas looked anxious and like he was trying not to breathe. His long pale fingers flexed tightly around the steering wheel, the leather cover squeaked in protest.

I couldn't take it any longer, so I said, "Where are we going? You never really said what you had in mind."

Silas smiled and seemed to relax slightly. "Nowhere in particular. It's just somewhere I like to go when I come for a visit. I felt like having some company tonight." The corner of his mouth raised, devilishly.

He glanced at me and then quickly looked away. The oncoming headlights of another car hit his eyes as he turned back toward the road, and his eyes seemed to flash, giving them that animalistic look they had in the diner last night. I tried to stifle a gasp but it escaped nevertheless. The whole thing was disconcerting.

He glanced sideways at me and caught me staring again. Silas just smiled nervously. After that, his expression seemed troubled; he did not smile, and he did not meet my eyes.

I wasn't sure what to say, so I just gave him a small smile and looked ahead. The surrounding countryside changed from farmland to forest.

It was getting darker. Silas switched on his headlights.

"I'm hoping to get there as the sun is setting. It's a beautiful place to watch the sunset." He seemed to be somewhere else in the moment, lost in thought, like he was trying to concentrate on anywhere but here.

I simply replied, "I can't wait to see it."

In that instant, I couldn't understand why Leanne had such a problem with this man or why she and her family had kept him a secret. Sure, I didn't know their history or anything about him really, but right now, he seemed sweet. A genuine, nice guy. A bit cocky sometimes, and he definitely had a few first date jitters, but he was nice. I mean, he fixed my window for free, has been polite, and enjoys watching sunsets and admiring magnolia trees. I was going to have to talk to Leanne about that.

We pulled off the road and onto a gravel drive that wound its way along a clearing in the woods.

We began a small climb up a hill, and soon Silas pulled off into the grass of a rolling pasture. We bumped along the open field until we reached the top of the hill.

He put the truck in park and got out.

I began to unbuckle my seat belt, and he opened my door, stepping back a few paces as I got out.

I stepped forward to close the gap between us, and he quickly turned around and headed toward the bed of his truck. He had an odd expression on his face, but he quickly covered it with a small smile.

I decided to ignore that new behavior and looked out at the rolling fields around us. There was a gentle breeze, and it stirred the air with the smell of honeysuckle and clover. The cicadas and crickets were beginning their night songs, and occasionally the sound of a whippoorwill and spring peepers could be heard from the nearby woods.

I stretched my arms above my head, delighting in the cool night air. The breeze blew my hair softly across my face, and I gathered it up in my hands, pushing it back behind my ears. I had forgotten about the magnolia flower. I removed it and held it to my nose.

At the same time, I heard Silas take a sudden intake of breath, almost as if he were hissing.

I turned to look at him, letting my hands fall slowly to my sides. Silas's eyes had taken on that preternatural glow I saw briefly in the diner.

He squeezed his eyes shut quickly, wincing with effort. He had a death grip on the two lawn chairs he was dragging out of the bed of his truck. He looked disturbed. His smooth features were pinched in a grimace, almost like he was in pain.

"Is everything okay?" I asked, slowly. "Can I help?" I took a step toward him.

"No," he growled. "Just stay where you are; don't move." His voice was clipped and menacing.

I subconsciously stepped away from the truck. His demeanor had changed so rapidly it was a bit unnerving. I crossed my arms over my chest and turned back to look out at the field, trying to take my mind off his sudden change in attitude. I heard Silas exhale slowly, and then he looked up and smiled, uncomfortably, at me.

"I just pinched my finger on this old tailgate. I'm fine." Another tight-lipped smile as he shut the tailgate. "They're not fancy, but they're comfortable." His movements were stiff and uneasy. The confidence and swagger from earlier were gone as he placed the chairs alongside the truck several feet apart. He offered me one before sitting down himself.

I thought it was odd he placed the chairs so far apart from each other. Come to think of it, he was suddenly keeping his distance from me all together. Maybe he was just being polite.

I took a seat, looked out at the setting sun and tried not to think about it. The sky was a riot of colors: pink, purple, orange, and blue. The clouds were the most striking; they seemed to be dyed red as the sun sank lower in the sky.

"Red skies at night, sailors' delight," he remarked.

"Red skies in morning, sailors take warning," I replied.

He laughed at my response. "You know the saying?"

"Well, yeah." I shrugged. "You can't live close to the ocean and not know it."

He looked thoughtful and asked, "What do you think? And be careful how you answer." He chuckled. "This is one of my favorite places."

"It's nice. I like how peaceful it is." That seemed to please him.

He smiled and nodded. "Me, too. It's a good place to think. We're also far enough away from any lights, so we should start seeing stars soon if the clouds clear out a bit more."

———

We sat like that for a couple hours, just chatting and watching the lightning bugs dance on the gentle evening breeze. He asked me about my life in the small town of Ophidian Grove, about the bookstore, and my parents. I answered his questions and told him my dreams of heading out west one day to see the mountains again and how absolutely stuck in place I felt here. He sat there and listened to every word, like it was the most interesting conversation he'd had in years. The more I spoke and answered his questions the more he seemed to visibly relax. His face became less drawn and he looked as comfortable now as he had been earlier in the night. At some point I swear I saw him move his chair closer to mine, but it happened so fast I thought I must have imagined it. Whatever had brought on the earlier sudden change in his disposition had now disappeared. Silas would hardly let me ask about him at all and would only answer cryptically when I got a question in.

"I feel like you know all about me now." I laughed. "What about you? Tell me your story."

He let out a sigh and seemed reticent. "Another time, perhaps. I should probably get you home, you know, before the monsters come out tonight." A mischievous smile spread across his face.

"Ooh, scary." I placed my hands on my cheeks in an insincere attempt at shock. "I think the only monsters out here are the mosquitos." I swatted at one on my arm and it left a tiny smear of bright red blood behind. "Gross little bloodsuckers."

Silas laughed out loud, but it seemed a tad strained. "C'mon, let's get you home," he said.

The night brightened a bit as the clouds moved away from the moon, allowing it to cast its silvery light across the field and making the woods seem a lot darker. I looked up at the sky to watch the moon appear from behind the clouds, when a shadow fell over me.

Suddenly, Silas was standing over me. His jaw was clenched, and his face looked like he was struggling with something again. The moon shone brightly behind him, casting him in an eerie glow, and it threw a dark shadow over his face.

I withdrew into my chair slightly, and he held his hand out to me.

I took it, hesitantly. His skin was smooth and cold. It reminded me of a snake, for some reason.

I stood with his help, and I shivered slightly when his fingers closed gently around my hand, bringing it to his cool lips, kissing it, softly.

We were standing close, very close, in fact. His eyes were smoldering as he looked over my face his own face had softened once more. His eyes settled on my neck for a fleeting second before finally alighting hungrily on my lips.

I swallowed the lump rising in my throat. I couldn't tell if he was going to kiss me or bite me.

I slid my hand from his and stepped back, breaking the moment. I shivered again.

"Cold?" he said, softly, with an edge of a smirk on his lips.

"No, I'm fine." I let out a shuddering breath and tried to

get my heart rate under control. "Just getting a bit tired; I think I'm ready to go home."

Silas was beginning to unsettle me a bit, but I couldn't figure out why. I disregarded it as first date jitters and shook it off by the time I was settled back inside the cab of his truck.

We drove back toward my place in companionable silence.

I snuck a few glances over at him and caught him doing the same in the dashboard lights. I felt like a teenager again, giddy with the idea of a new crush.

———

On the way back through town, we passed Lulu's Diner, and I saw Leanne walking through the parking lot after closing up. It was late. Lulu's closed at midnight, so that meant it must have been at least 12:30, or later.

Silas honked his horn at her and waved out his window. There was no way she didn't see me; the diner was on my side of the road.

I tried to sink lower in my seat, but I knew she saw me. I could feel the daggers her eyes were throwing at me.

"What did you do that for?" I groaned.

"Just having a bit of fun. I can't drive past my dear cousin and not greet her. His face looked impish and malevolent as he laughed.

I placed a hand over my face. Leanne was going to murder me.

We drove in silence for several minutes. I was inwardly cringing at the thought of what Leanne would say to me. Silas sat there smirking stupidly. I wanted to be angry with him but it was hard, he had such a devil-may-care attitude. He began to chuckle when he noticed me watching him.

"What's so funny?" I asked

"You're angry with me." He shrugged

It was a statement, not a question.

"And that's funny?" I crossed my arms and glared at him.

"Not exactly." He looked at me as we came to a stop at the red light. "I'm laughing because I know both of us are going to receive an earful from Leanne."

"Oh." I replied, relaxing a bit. He had me there.

The light turned green and we continued to sit there. Silas was still watching me. He smiled again and it lit up his face. He shook his head as he smiled to himself.

"What now?" I asked again, laughing. I couldn't help it, his smile was infectious.

"I've just made a decision." Silas answered. His eyes were ablaze with mischief and delight. There was something else there too, I couldn't quite put my finger on it. His face softened as he continued to gaze at me.

"I'm sorry if I seemed a bit distant at times earlier this evening."

"No worries." I answered softly.

He inhaled deeply, "I was just being," he paused while he thought of which word to use next. "careful." He finished.

"I see." I looked away reluctantly. "I barely noticed." I shrugged cooly but my insides were in turmoil. My pulse pounded in my brain and a new nervous energy took over my body. What was this decision, did it have to do with me? In some way I hoped it did. There was something about Silas that piqued my interest and something about him that definitely piqued my body's interest. I shifted in my seat, pretending to adjust my seat belt.

He chuckled again.

"Light's green." I nodded at the light.

"Indeed it is, indeed it is." He smirked.

CHAPTER
Five

THE FOLLOWING MORNING, I awoke before the sun. I slept terribly, tossing and turning all night. I know Leanne saw me, and she hadn't hidden her feelings about Silas. I knew she was going to be pissed, and I'm sure I was going to hear about it. I was making coffee in the kitchen, when I heard a knock at my door.

"Who on Earth could that be this early in the morning?" I said out loud.

I smoothed down my hair with my hands and glanced down at my pajamas and my bare feet. At least those pajamas weren't holey. I took a deep breath and headed to the front door, not sure who or what I was going to find. I recognized Leanne's silhouette in the frosted glass.

"Here we go," I said under my breath.

I opened the door, reluctantly, and waited for the berating that was sure to follow.

She didn't even give me a chance to say anything or even plaster a fake smile on my face. She barged right in, almost knocking the door out of my hand, and said, "We need to talk. Right now!" She sounded both angry and terrified at once.

I closed the door, fighting the urge to glare at her, when she stopped me.

"Lock it!" she practically growled.

I did as she asked, mocking her tone as screwed up my face and mouthed, *lock it*, to myself while my back was to her. I took a steadying breath before turning back around and pointing to the kitchen. "Coffee?"

"Sure," she replied.

She sat down at the table, and I poured her a cup of coffee, grabbed one of my own, and sat down opposite her and waited.

Leanne was grasping her mug like it was going to run away. She looked like she hadn't slept much, either. She was bouncing her leg in agitation. "Dani, what were you doing with Silas last night?" She got right to it.

"Oh, um, we went to watch the sunset, and we talked. He dropped me off here a little before 1:00 a.m. We hugged, and I gave him my number, and then he left. Nothing happened; we barely even sat close to one another."

I tried to sound assuring and decided it was best not to tell her how long we spent on the porch together, how often our eyes met, and what thrills it sent through me when they did. She still looked perturbed, nevertheless.

"How did that even come about? When did you even talk to him?"

"I literally ran into him outside the hardware store. He noticed what I had bought when I dropped my bag on the sidewalk and the things inside fell out. He offered to help me." I shrugged. "I figured it would be okay, him being your cousin and all. He asked me out after repairing my window sash."

I took a sip of coffee, trying to look and sound as casual as I could.

She placed her hand on her forehead and squeezed her temples. "You invited him into your house?"

"Well, yeah. How else was he going to fix my window?"

"Oh, Dani, how could you?" She was almost in tears. Why did Silas have that effect on her? What did he do to deserve her ire?

"Leanne, will you please tell me what's going on? Why have you never mentioned him before? I thought I knew almost all your family. What am I missing? Silas seems to be a perfectly nice human being—" I was rambling when she cut me off.

"There's where you're wrong!" She stood, abruptly, her face began to turn red. "You need to look beyond his handsome face; he is not what he seems!"

Leanne paced back and forth a couple times before wheeling on me. She grasped the back of her chair so tightly her knuckles were turning white. Her cobalt blue eyes were furious and sad at the same time. "There's a reason you don't know about him and a reason why my family has never mentioned him! He's bad news, and I really wish you'd stay away from him."

I bristled at that, but was she right? If he were unattractive, would we even be having this conversation? I would like to think I wasn't that shallow. "I'm an adult, Leanne. I can make my own decisions about who I want in my home and who I want to date."

"Ugh!" She sat down again and leaned back heavily in her chair, rolling her eyes. "I know, Dani, but Silas is different. Tell me, did he take you somewhere where you two were completely alone?"

I answered, slowly. How could she have known that? "Yes, he did. We went to an open field close to the forest. He said it was a favorite spot of his to watch the sunset."

"Goddammit! I cannot believe him!" She pounded the table with a fist. Leanne was really pissed now; she rarely cussed.

"What is going on? Have I done something? Has *he* done

something?" Leanne's caginess about Silas was beginning to really irritate me.

"Dani, look, I know Silas seems like an all right guy, but he…" She paused, seeming to choose her next words carefully. "He has secrets, and they are his secrets to tell. Not mine."

I noticed her eyes shift to take a glance at my throat. What was that about?

"I stopped by this morning to make sure you were okay and to tell you if you pursue this, if you pursue him, be careful. Silas is more than the black sheep in our family; he's a snake in the grass, fangs and all."

She pushed her coffee mug to the side and grabbed my hand across the table. "Your parents built a life here; you have a life here. Don't let Silas and his charms tempt you away from that." She gave my hand a squeeze. "Believe me, he's not the romantic adventure you read about in all those books of yours. He'll be the death of you; mark my words."

What the hell did that mean? I looked away from Leanne, taking my hand out from under hers, and looked out the window behind her. Something was very odd here, and I needed to know what was going on. I took a contemplative sip of my coffee and noticed the rising sun had turned the sky an alarming shade of red.

Red skies in morning, sailors take warning.

CHAPTER
Six

MY PHONE BEGAN TO BUZZ. I picked it up from my desk, where I was going over invoices, and looked at the caller ID. It was a new number. Was it Silas? I answered, nervously. My heart was racing.

"Hello?"

"Hey," his voice sounded deeper over the phone. "Are you busy?"

"Oh, hey, Silas. No, not really. What's up?" I tried to act nonchalant, considering my conversation with Leanne earlier this morning.

"I'd like to see you again, if that's okay?" I could hear the smile in his voice.

"Sure, I'd like that. Anything in particular you have in mind?" This was perfect. I could see him again, and I was going to get to the bottom of this whole Leanne/Silas animosity thing.

"Would it be too forward to ask to come over to your house? I enjoyed talking last night and would like to continue our conversation."

This was working out splendidly. I would be able to talk

to him in private. "Sure, Silas, that sounds nice. I get off work at 6:00. Is 7:00 good for you?"

"7:00 is fine. See you soon, Dani." He hung up the phone. Silas had a lot of talking to do if things were going to progress any further.

———

I finished up my day at the bookstore, and Jeff helped me close.

I stopped at the grocery store to buy a few things before going home. I picked up a bottle of wine and one of those rotisserie chickens. I had the makings for a light salad at home. No sense in us going hungry over conversation.

I pulled in the driveway and sent Silas a text before going in. **The door is unlocked. I'll be in the kitchen. Please come on in when you arrive.**

I freshened up a bit and changed out of my work clothes into something more casual. A pair of denim shorts and my favorite band T-shirt.

I set the food on the table with a couple of plates and some silverware and poured two glasses of wine.

As I was pouring the second glass, I heard a voice from the kitchen entry way behind me.

"Mmm, a sweet red, my favorite."

I jumped and almost dropped the bottle and nearly sloshed the wine in the glass all over the table.

Somehow, he rushed to my side. He closed his hand around mine on the wine glass and then took the bottle from my other hand.

I looked up at him, eyes wide, and glanced over his shoulder at the doorway. How did he cover that distance so swiftly and quietly?

"You told me to let myself in." His eyes met mine, and I

became all too aware at how close we were standing to one another. His stare was consuming. My mind went blank.

"Did I scare you? That wasn't my intention." His hand was still over mine on the wine glass; it was cold against my skin.

"Yeah," I laughed. "I guess you did. I didn't hear you come in." I placed my free hand over my chest and tried to calm my heart. Silas was still holding the hand with the wine glass.

"I didn't mean to frighten you, I promise. You seemed rather lost in thought. Is something on your mind?" He stepped back from me, letting my hand go, and leaned against the counter. Instantly, I felt empty without his hand in mine.

Was it that obvious? *I guess I better just rip this bandage off and come out with it.* "Yeah, you could say that. Leanne stopped by this morning, and she was less than happy."

"Oh, really?" He didn't seem concerned. "And what did my *dear* cousin have to say?"

"A lot, honestly. She really doesn't care for you, does she?" I gestured toward the table. "Why don't we sit down?"

Silas took a deep breath as he pulled out his chair and sat down. "Our relationship is...difficult." He thought for a moment and then said, "She sometimes feels responsible for me, and my actions, and she feels like it's an unfair liability bestowed upon her." A slow, secret smile spread across his face. "She's held a bit of a grudge against me for years and refuses to see my good qualities. She only focuses on the bad." He winked at me, his tongue flicking out slightly to lick his upper lip as he grinned.

I ignored his flirtatious smile. "Leanne said you were dangerous and bad news and I should stay away from you. She also mentioned you had secrets. How did she say it?"

I placed my finger to my lips while I thought. "Oh, yeah,

you have secrets that weren't hers to tell." I decided to leave out the part about how she thought he'd be the death of me.

He looked unsettled, and then it seemed like a shadow fell across his face, his eyes darkening. "She's not wrong, but there's something about you that tells me I can trust you." he said as he lifted the wine glass to his lips and took a drink.

When he lowered the glass, the dark red wine had somewhat stained his mouth. His wine-red lips against his pale skin reminded me of blood.

I shivered as I felt goosebumps rise on my skin.

"Are you cold?" he asked.

"No, just got a cold chill. Someone must have walked over my grave."

That made him laugh. "My mother used to say that."

"Mine, too." I smiled, the tension in the room abated. "Are you hungry? I've got food."

"No, thank you. I already ate." There was that infuriating smirk of his, like he was laughing at some inside joke again. "But don't let me stop you. Please, go ahead." He made a motion at the food on the table.

I made myself a plate as he sat across from me. I took a good look at him. His skin seemed to be a bit more flushed today. He had a healthy pink glow to him. It looked nice. He must have gotten some sun.

I pierced a piece of chicken with my fork and ate it, all the while watching my present company, scrutinizing him.

He sat in his chair, arm resting on the table and holding his wine glass. He was impeccably dressed again. Were all his clothes tailor made just for him?

Our eyes met, and I stared him down.

"I'm guessing you have questions," he said before taking another sip of wine.

I drank from my own glass, swallowed, and said, "Definitely."

"Be careful; you might not like the answers you receive.

Curiosity killed the cat, you know." He smiled, darkly. If I didn't know any better, I'd think he was trying to be sinister.

"Yes, but satisfaction brought it back."

His expression changed to amusement and mild surprise at my comeback. "Most people don't know the second half of that saying." He laughed.

I took another quick swig of my wine. No more games; I got right to the point. "So are you going to answer my questions honestly? Leanne is my best friend. I feel like I deserve an explanation as to why she's so adamant I stay away from you."

I didn't want to stay away from him, so there had better be a darn good reason for me to do so. I waited for his response.

He took another drink of wine. This time, he drained the glass.

"I'd be concerned if her feelings about me didn't bother you." He turned his intense green eyes on me, and it took all I had not to squirm under his stare. "I don't want to hide anything. I'm not ashamed of who and what I am, and to be fair," he smiled, "I was also told to stay away from you and to not let you in on my secret." He leaned back in his chair and crossed his arms, looking smug. "Obviously, I didn't listen."

"Okay, then, let's have it. No more guarded answers; no more mystery. The way Leanne was acting, I'm beginning to wonder what you've done in the past. Are you a murderer, or something?"

He gave me a knowing smile and placed both hands on the table, interlocking his fingers.

He just looked at me for a long time. His stare was curious, and it felt like he could see into my soul. His eyes were such an unnatural shade of green. I started to get anxious, and my heart began to race.

Finally, he broke the silence. "I make you nervous sometimes, don't I?"

I nodded. Was he a mind reader?

He laughed. "I should. I really don't think you'll like the whole truth."

"Try me." I was going to get my answers.

He sat, silently, for several moments. The tension in the room was thickening once more. He was thinking.

I watched him at war with his emotions. His eyes never left mine, and I began to squirm, uncomfortably, under his gaze.

Finally, after what seemed like eons, but was in fact only seconds, his face softened, and he seemed to come to a decision.

"Are you sure you want the whole ugly truth?" Silas seemed to be the nervous one this time. He was looking at his hands and began twisting the wine glass stem between his fingers.

Heart pounding, I answered him. "Yes, warts and all."

His eyes never left his fingers as they played with the stem of his glass. "I need you to understand something."

He looked up at me through his dark lashes, and I sat back in my chair, arms crossed, and an eyebrow arched, waiting for him to continue.

When he saw I made no plans to say anything, he continued. With a sigh he said, "I am neither a hero nor a villain. More monster than anything, really. I have done some awful things in my past, things that cannot be forgiven."

"Okay," I said, hesitantly.

"I am not a man, at least in the human sense." His eyes dropped from mine and back to his hands.

I swallowed the lump forming in my throat and sat there, silently, waiting for him to say what he wanted to say. My arms were no longer crossed; I had gone to hugging myself as goose bumps rose on my skin. What was he trying to say?

I watched as Silas stood up, walked to the counter, and grabbed the bottle of wine.

He poured me another glass and set the bottle to the side.

He walked toward me, slowly, silently, and placed my wine glass in front of me. He was still battling with something. Maybe he was just trying to figure out how to say it, and then he did.

"I'm a vampire."

"What?" I almost started giggling. What did he mean he was a vampire? I was expecting him to tell me just about anything, but not that. *Figures, I meet the man of my dreams and he's insane. Batshit crazy, delusionally insane!* No wonder Leanne had never spoken about him.

"Come on." I rolled my eyes and abruptly stood up, almost toppling my chair in the process. "If you're not going to take me seriously, you can leave." I waved my hand toward the door.

"Oh, but I am serious. It feels good to say that out loud to someone other than Leanne." He looked and sounded sincere. "I haven't told anyone else that in a long time." He finished, quietly. He believed his own delusion.

"I don't even know how to respond to you right now. You're neurotic, you know that?" I narrowed my eyes at him.

"Look, just let me explain."

He tried, but I cut him off. "What's to explain? It's the twenty-first century, for Christ's sake! Everyone knows monsters aren't real. Nothing about you screams *vampire*. This is crazy; you're crazy!"

"You said you wanted the truth, so I told you the truth. I do not want to hide anything from you. What more do you want?" Silas stood. "Shall I prove it to you next?" His voice was a low growl.

His eyes flashed, and they looked like they had changed for just a moment. It must have been a trick of the light. His face was strained, several emotions flickered across his features: anger, malice, confusion, and maybe even a touch of sadness and fear.

His face seemed to contort and shift minutely before he

pulled himself together. He looked rather sinister for just a moment.

I swallowed hard and shook my head. "Look, if you don't want to take me seriously, then I think you should go."

I began clearing the dishes away and turned my back to him.

When I turned back around, he was gone. I never heard him leave.

CHAPTER
Seven

IT WAS two whole weeks before I heard anything from Silas. I had been avoiding Leanne, too. I mean, all she had to do was tell me her cousin was crazy! Instead, *she* acted all cuckoo for Cocoa Puffs. She said things like, "I can't believe he flat out told you" and "What is he trying to prove?" I couldn't believe she was playing along with his fantasy.

I decided I wanted to be as far away from crazy as I could get for a while. I thought a lot about that night and the previous two before it. Silas seemed so normal, and like a nice guy. *Who on Earth believes they're a vampire? I'll tell you who, Silas does.*

When he tried contacting me again, I was at home on my couch, channel surfing.

"Silas," I said, coldly, as I answered the phone.

"Hello, Dani. Are you busy tonight?" He sounded apprehensive.

"No, I'm not busy; I'll be home all night." I kept my voice flat, trying to hide my irritation.

"I feel like I need to explain myself."

I scoffed and rolled my eyes "I'll say, but this is the only chance I'm giving you."

"I would rather have this conversation in person. Would it be okay if I came over?"

There was a pause on both ends as I considered.

"Please, it's important," he pleaded.

"Fine," I relented, "but no crazy talk. I want the actual truth, the whole truth."

There was silence from his end for a second, and then he said, "I'll be there soon." He hung up.

———

He must have been speeding or closer than I thought because he was standing on my front porch fewer than fifteen minutes later.

I opened my door and scowled at him.

Silas tried to smile, but it came across as a grimace. The light in his eyes had dulled. "It's such a nice night; let's sit out here instead."

I walked out the door and joined him on the rocking chairs that sat on the porch.

A cool breeze rustled the leaves of the magnolia tree, encasing us in its heady, sweet scent.

I looked at him, Silas's pallor had changed. His skin had a gray sallow, unhealthy tinge to it, and his eyes had large dark circles under them. He looked like death warmed over.

"Are you feeling all right?" I asked.

He laughed, softly. "I'm fine. I've just been skipping some meals. Haven't had much of an appetite." There was that secret smile again.

I felt bad for him; he looked terrible. "Can I get you something?"

"No, thank you." He smiled, but it was a small smile, and he seemed a tad nervous. "Just let me tell you what I came here to say, please." He ran a hand through his hair, nervously, and avoided looking at me. "The last time blew up in my face spectacularly."

"You think?" I crossed my arms and watched him. He was clearly mulling over what to say.

As much as I hated to admit it, for whatever reason, it felt nice having him here. I got comfortable and told him to go on. It was odd seeing him so serious. I know I had known Silas only for a very short time, but he was always so happy and so flirtatious. Seeing the dark side of him was weird.

"I'm sorry for the way things went the other night," he began, "but what I said is the truth."

"Silas, please don't—"

He stopped me and looked me square in the eyes. "Please, Dani, just listen. I want to tell my story. I need to tell you." His eyes bored into mine, and they were so solemn it nearly undid me.

He took a deep breath and looked away from me. "I understand what I said sounds ridiculous, especially in this day and age—"

"That's the understatement of the century," I interrupted him.

He was quiet for a moment, so I let him gather his thoughts.

"Leanne and part of her family are the only other humans who know what I'm about to tell you."

"Humans?" I said with an air of skepticism. "So you're not human?"

Silas shook his head. "I was, but now I'm not. I already told you what I am, and now I'm here to see if I can make you believe it." He turned those green eyes upon me again and smiled, thinly.

"Leanne is the Keeper of my secret, but telling you is going to lighten her load. At least, I hope it will. It all depends on how you react and whether you choose to believe me." He sighed, "I really need you to believe me." Silas sounded so serious, the usual carefree and joking tone he had was gone. It was replaced with a yearning that nearly broke my heart in two.

"I'll listen." I said, quietly. Despite my irritation at him for weaving this web of delusions he believed, I wanted to keep him talking. I needed to know why he and Leanne believed the lie.

He leaned forward, clasped his hands together, took a deep breath, and said, "I was born in April of 1863."

I scoffed. Wow, this guy was really committed! He gave me a look that said even he knew how ridiculous that sounded.

"My parents were Callum and Lottie Quinn. I had an older brother and a sister, Jonas and Sarah. My mother christened me Silas Matthew Quinn. My father was deeply religious, and my mother was too, though she also held fast to a lot of superstitions and old-world beliefs. She was a wonderful mother who loved her family unconditionally. My father was a hard man from his service in the Civil War. My mother said he used to be so happy and quick to smile; she said I was a lot like him. She told me I inherited my father's quick wit, humour, and unfortunately part of his temper. I don't remember him being witty and humerous, sadly. After the horrors of war, he was dark and morose. He believed only hard work, prayer, and God were Who and what would get his family through. He had no time for frivolity anymore."

Silas sat back in his chair and glanced at me to see if I was still listening. When it was clear I was, he continued.

"My father was a fisherman and was bringing my brother and I up in his trade. We lived in Diamond City. It was a settlement on the eastern end of Shackleford Banks. If you know the history of this area, then you know about the hurricane of 1899 and that it is no longer there. We grew up happy and healthy. We had a good life. My brother met and married a young lady from our hometown when I was fifteen, and he moved away. My sister married, as well, but she stayed close to home.

"With my brother gone, I helped my father with the fishing. He was hard on me, and extremely short-tempered but my mother saw to it he kept his temper in check. As I grew into a young man, I met a girl named Katie Young. Her father was another fisherman from the area. We were young. She was seventeen; I was eighteen. We planned to marry, but she succumbed to scarlet fever. I was heartbroken, and I swore off love and the thought of marriage and family. My mother and sister tried to convince me otherwise, but I wasn't interested." His eyes held a faraway gaze as he recounted the story.

"I've been in love twice." He quickly glanced at me, and a small smile crept across his face. "Or what I thought was love, anyway. First was Katie. And seventeen years later, Eliza Novak came into my life. She took my breath away. Raven-haired and fair-skinned and eyes as blue as the summer sky."

He chuckled, lightly. "Eliza also had a silver tongue; she held me captive the moment we first spoke. Eliza was exotic, with her Eastern European accent and strange ways. She was new in town, she and her brothers were only passing through, but I knew instantly I had to have her. It was love at first sight for me. I courted her, and we would go for nightly walks along the beach. I knew I wanted to marry her. I told my family, and they were elated. But Eliza was not what she appeared to be. Mysterious injuries, deaths, and disappearances began to happen when she and her brothers arrived, but I had not put two and two together yet."

Silas paused in reminiscing, clearly remembering something only he could see.

For whatever reason, a small pang of jealousy began to grow deep in my chest.

I crossed my arms and looked out into the yard.

Silas came back to the present, looked at my posture, and smiled. He began to tell his story again.

"I proposed after knowing her only a couple of weeks. She said, 'No,' at first. I was devastated and poured myself into my work to take my mind off her. We hadn't seen each other for several days after my failed proposal. I was repairing one of our boats in the boathouse, when she came to me.

"She seemed distraught. She told me she had not been truthful with me, and she had something to confess. She confessed to being a vampire and told me about her and her brother's quest to find perfect individuals to transform into vampires themselves. They were creating their own master race of vampires, and she wanted me.

"She hadn't planned on falling in love with me, but she had. I was just so overjoyed she had returned to me I told her I didn't care about her past, what story she told, or anything else for that matter; I just wanted her. That's when she kissed me. We had stolen kisses before, but they were nothing like this."

Silas paused and looked down at his hands. "I'm sure you can surmise what happened next. I'll spare you the details."

He cleared his throat, nervously, wiping his hands on his jeans.

Silas and looked at me. He was grinning, sheepishly.

I huffed and turned my head away from him.

"We fell asleep afterward, or at least I did. She had pretended to be asleep and waited to make sure I was completely out. That's when she made her move. I awoke to a stabbing, burning pain in my neck, and I was burning throughout my body. I tried to move, but I couldn't. Eliza was on top of me, and she had bitten my neck. She was so strong. But it wasn't her strength that held me.

"When you are bitten by a vampire, they release venom that incapacitates their victim, making them go limp and motionless. Every fiber of your being is screaming at you to fight, causing your adrenaline to rush, but there's nothing you can do. Eliza didn't feed, though. She had only bitten me, emptying her venom into my rushing bloodstream.

"When she lifted her face from my neck, I didn't recognize her. She was monstrous. Her face was stretched, her once-full lips were pulled thin across her gums, and sharp fangs dripping with my blood protruded from her upper jaw. Her eyes had changed, too. They were reptilian, and if she would have sprouted scales at that moment I wouldn't have been surprised."

Silas paused for a long time.

I watched him as he leaned forward in his chair again.

He placed his elbows on his knees and hung his head.

I wasn't sure what to think so far. He told the story with such fervor it was hard not to believe every word he spoke.

I cleared my throat. "What happened next?" I asked. My voice was barely a whisper.

Silas didn't look at me. He lifted his eyes toward the magnolia tree in the yard and spoke. "Eliza could sense my fear, and her face reverted to the beautiful one I had known. She stroked my face as I lay burning and in pain and said if I truly wanted to be with her, it was the only way. I needed to be immortal like her, and in order to do so, I needed to drink.

"Eliza bit her own wrist, opening the veins, and then held the open wound to my lips. I swallowed, not realizing in doing so I had sealed my fate. She stayed with me that night as the change took place. I was angry; she had given me no choice. But there was nothing I could do, not until the transformation was complete. I burned for almost twelve hours."

Silas scrubbed a hand over his face as if he could wipe the memory away. "When the agony of my metamorphosis was over, I sat up and just stared at her in disbelief. 'What have you done to me?' I asked her through my gritted teeth. She told me we could be together forever because I was a vampire, like her, but we couldn't stay because my beginning bloodlust would put us in danger of being found out.

"We ran away to what is now the Croatan Forest, where she explained everything. She told me that I had been chosen because of my strength and because of the temper they had watched me keep in check while around my father. She explained that they had been watching me for weeks before they finally decided to make their move, sending her in to act as bait." He grimaced and shook his head, "We hid there for several weeks, and she brought me victims to feed upon as she taught me. I was brutally viscious at first. The bloodlust caused quite a change in me, it brought out a side of me I was careful to contain as a human. Once again, I'll spare you, and myself for that matter, the details. She had no problem murdering humans, but I did. I wasn't happy about the accruing dead and told her as much.

"Reluctantly, she taught me to feed without killing and how to enthrall the person whom I had fed upon into thinking they had injured themselves or to believe just about anything I told them, within reason, or to just forget what happened completely. I can't make people do whatever I say. I can only do a type of hypnosis while they're in that incapacitated state and take over their subconscious and influence them to believe something other than what just happened.

"Meanwhile, during the weeks when I had been missing, my family was worried sick. They had no idea where I had gone. Eliza was bold and ventured back into Diamond City, where she was spotted by my father. He followed her one evening while she convinced one of the townsfolk to come with her. He followed her to our hiding spot, and when my father came upon us, he hid and saw what we were. He didn't do anything that night; he waited and sent for my brother the next day. They planned to catch and kill us."

Silas's mood darkened, and his voice became gravelly. "They caught Eliza first. We were getting brazen, and I was in full bloodlust. I was beginning to relish and embrace what I had become, now that I could do it without killing. Eliza was enjoying herself, as well, and we were getting careless. We were no longer concerned with getting caught. My father called out to Eliza one night when he saw her in town again and asked if she knew my whereabouts. Not wanting to destroy our ruse, she approached him under the guise of the concerned ex-fiancé. It was enough of a distraction for my brother to come from behind and stake her through the back as my father held her attention. She was taken by surprise, not expecting they knew what she was. She never stood a chance.

"I had grown restless while I waited for her outside of town and decided to try and find her. I hid in the shadows when I spotted them talking to her. I was afraid to show myself to them and could only watch as it all happened. I followed my father and my brother as they carried her off. They placed her in a small rowboat and tied a rope from it to a larger skiff we sometimes used. I watched in stunned silence, hiding in the tall grasses on the shore.

"My father and my brother took her out past the breakers and toward the ocean beyond the Banks. They had become tiny specks upon the horizon, but even from where I stood, I could see what they did. A figure stood up in the rear of the skiff and pushed the tiny rowboat away from their craft, and all at once the tiny boat where Eliza lay became engulfed in flames. They watched the rowboat float aimlessly as it burned and then they turned around and came back for me."

Silas was silent for several moments, and so was I.

He stood up and leaned against one of the porch pillars and stared out into the yard before beginning again. "I didn't run from them. In fact, I went home. I wanted to see my mother and my sister one last time. I knew my father was going to kill me and I knew my brother would help. My mother was so happy to see me, but one look at me was all she needed to know something had changed. She welcomed me home, anyway. We sat down, and I told them everything, right up to the point of my father and Jonas dispatching Eliza. I wanted to scream, cry, rage out, but I just sat there and hung my head instead.

"That's when my father came home. He was surprised to see me. My brother walked in shortly after, and an evil smile spread across his face. My father called me a demon spawn of Satan and said I was no son of his. I didn't fight them when they began to beat and bind me. My mother and Sarah screamed for them to show me mercy, but they wouldn't. I could have fought back and easily won, but they were my family, and I couldn't hurt them in front of my mother. I refused to be the monster they feared I was.

"They made me stand and took me outside. The last thing I remember from that night is my mother begging my father to give me a Christian burial, to at least allow her that. I looked at my mother during those last moments and watched the tears streaming down her face as she stood by, helplessly. Jonas held me up while my father drove a stake deep into my chest with a look of pure rage and hatred on his face. There was a moment of pain and then everything went black."

Silas stood there, silently staring out into the yard at nothing. The pain written on his face was clear. I wanted to reach out to him. I was surprised at my reaction.

I shifted in my seat, and my movement seemed to bring Silas out of his revelry.

He returned to his chair and finished his story.

"They buried me in a crude coffin in an unmarked grave at the local cemetery. I was buried for almost a year, in a sort of stasis mode."

Silas sat back in his chair and looked at me, his jaw clenched, and a pained smile curled his lips as he snorted a laugh. "Do you know what my father told people about what happened to me?"

I shook my head, unable to look away from him.

"He told them I killed myself after Eliza had turned down my proposal and left town." His hand clenched the end of the armrest on his chair, almost angrily. I could have sworn I heard a small crack.

"Anyway, it's a common misconception a stake through the heart will kill a vampire. You must behead them and burn the body to be sure of a complete death. As I mentioned before, a hurricane tore through the area on August 17th, 1899. The destruction was immense. The flooding and storm surge was so bad it had unearthed the cemetery. Caskets, bodies, and bones were strewn everywhere amongst the other wreckage on the island, including mine.

"There was a group of people who were cleaning up the aftermath when two of the men happened upon my casket. The floodwaters had torn away the lid, and I lay there, exposed for all the world to see. One of the men must have spotted the stake in my chest and thought it was shrapnel from the storm because he removed it. The two men placed my open casket into the back of a wagon loaded down with other unfortunate unburied souls, but I was the only one of them who awakened. I rose with such a ferocious thirst I couldn't help myself. I slaughtered two men that day."

He slumped in his chair and dragged a hand over his face as if, once again, trying to erase the memory of what he had done. "I changed out of my grave-stained clothes and stole the clothes from one of the men I had just killed. I promised those men they were the last innocent lives I would take."

Silas hung his head, the pain of the memory clearly etched in his mind. He gave a small sad shake of his head and continued. "I knew I needed to find my mother next. I found her and Sarah and what remained of our home a short while later. My mother was shocked to see me. She was apprehensive at first but threw caution to the wind and embraced me. I don't remember a time I've ever felt happier than I did in that moment. Sarah came forward next and hugged me, as well. They knew I was no threat to them.

My mother warned me I couldn't linger there. My father was still around, and he would find a way to destroy me. She told me they were all moving inland to live with my now pregnant sister and her husband, John. I asked about Jonas. My mother looked sad; tears were welling in her eyes as she told me he was killed in the hurricane. Several vessels were lost that day, and he was on board one of them. I hugged my mother again, and she called me her Lazarus."

Silas rubbed the back of his neck with his hand and smiled. He chuckled, lightly, and shook his head.

He picked up where he left off. "She promised to figure something out, to find a way for me to stay connected. She told me to find somewhere to lay low for a while and to write to her when I had found such a place. She also made me promise not to kill anyone else. I'm pretty sure she knew I had killed a person or two when I woke, given what I am.

"I wrote to my mother several months later, once I felt the coast was clear. She and Sarah came at once. They told me my father had passed recently, and Sarah and John had bought a home in Ophidian Grove, so now my mother was staying with them. I couldn't say I was sad to hear of my father's death; I've never fully forgiven him for what he did. I've forgiven Jonas. He was only following father's orders, and he was an obedient son. My mother and sister had devised a plan while they waited to hear from me." Silas paused his story and turned to look at me. "Are you familiar with the story of Cain and Abel?"

I nodded. "For the most part."

Silas nodded and continued. "When Cain killed Abel and God asked where Abel was, Cain said to Him, 'Am I my brother's keeper?' God knew he was lying and marked him so he could not be killed by anyone who found him, and he was cursed to wander the Earth. My mother drew inspiration from the Bible story and told me to roam and to never stay in one place too long. I was to play the part of Cain in this story. How better to be marked an immortal, unkillable murderer than to be a vampire. She told me to come back here every few years to check in and to write to her, of course.

"She made my sister my Keeper. Sarah was charged with helping to keep my secret safe and to send help when I needed it. I was to be held accountable for my actions, and any blood spilled in death would also be blood on my sister's hands. If I failed, it would mean my death. My mother also knew I was an immortal now, and she had made Sarah make a promise to safeguard my secret and to pass the duty of 'my brother's Keeper' on to her children and their children after that. We sealed that promise with a signature in blood. We each pricked our fingers and let the drops of blood fall into an inkwell. We both signed a ledger; Sarah's was the first signature under the oath of Keeper, and my signature came after. She would help me, and I couldn't kill anyone. I have done that with all her descendants, including Leanne, ever since."

Silas turned to look at me, his green eyes pleading for me to say something, anything. I wasn't sure what to do or say. The story he just told me was beyond belief, and he told it with such resoluteness I was almost a believer. Almost.

"I don't know what you want me to say to that. It's an incredible story, but I don't know what to believe or why you chose to tell me. I need some time to think." I shifted in my chair and looked away from him.

"That's fine, take all the time you need. I'm immortal, after all." He gave me that playful smirk I had grown so accustomed to. "I chose to let you in because I like you, a lot. You've stirred things inside of me I haven't felt in a very long time." He laughed. "It sounds funny, but when you look at me, I feel compelled to spill all my secrets."

I blinked, stupidly, at him, my eyes going wide for a

moment. I could only watch him in silence as he stood and walked toward the porch steps.

He turned when he reached the bottom of the stairs. "I think you should talk to Leanne. She knows you're avoiding her."

With that, he walked down the gravel driveway, got into his truck, and drove away.

CHAPTER

Eight

I WAITED a couple days before calling Leanne. I had to figure out what to say. How do you talk to someone about their delusional cousin? I had to know where the story came from, why he believed his own lies, and most importantly, why he was telling me all of that. I called Leanne and invited her over for coffee.

When she arrived, she seemed cautious and slightly irritated. I couldn't help but feel a bit awkward. It was not a normal conversation we were about to have.

We sat down at the kitchen table, and I just got right to it. "Silas stopped by a couple nights ago."

Leanne lowered her coffee cup from her mouth and just sat there and looked at me, waiting for me to go on, so I did.

"He told me a very interesting story."

"Is that so?" Leanne crossed her arms and sat back in her chair. "What did he tell you?"

"He said he was born in 1863, grew up around Shackleford Banks, met a girl who wasn't a girl, but a vampire, and she then turned him into one." I stopped talking and looked at Leanne, waiting for a reaction or anything, but instead she picked up where I left off.

"Then, his father and brother killed her, came for him, thought they killed him, but he was unearthed by a hurricane a year later. Mommy dearest devised a plan, created all the My Brother's Keeper crap, and here we are!"

She smiled at me, grimly, narrowing her eyes.

I wasn't totally surprised by her reaction; she had probably heard the story a few times. "Yeah, that's pretty much it in a nutshell. He has quite the imagination."

I took a sip of my coffee, and I almost choked on it when Leanne spoke.

"It's true. Every word. I don't know what game he's playing at telling you, though."

I looked at her in disbelief. "So does crazy run in the family or..." I trailed off, not knowing exactly how to finish that statement.

"I'm surprised he wanted to tell you, but no, we are not crazy." Leanne adjusted her stance in her chair, uncrossing her arms and relaxing a little.

She ran a finger around the rim of her coffee mug as she thought.

"Leanne, what are you not telling me?" I prompted her.

Leanne sighed, heavily, and rolled her eyes. "I tried so hard to talk him out of all this." She waved a hand vaguely in the air, seeming to gesture to me and everything else all at once.

"But he insisted. He said and I quote," Leanne did a poor impression of Silas's voice, "Dani is unlike anyone I've ever been around. Something draws me to her. Something about her makes me want to share all my secrets.' "

I snorted. "What does that even mean?"

"I told him I knew exactly what drew him to you, and he just about flipped out on me!" She crossed her arms again. "He said it wasn't that trivial. It wasn't about your blood."

"Then, what was it?" I asked, quietly, thankful Leanne couldn't hear my heart thundering in my chest.

"Silas said you make him happy. He told me he hasn't been able to get you out of hs head. That for the first time in many, many, *many* years he felt truly happy and to be thinking about something other than, well..." Leanne began playing with her mug again, avoiding eye contact. "His next meal." She finally finished

"I couldn't help but give in and be okay with his decision to tell you. I had never seen that side of him, ever. He was so vulnerable and besotted when he spoke of you."

She looked at me now, a million questions written on her face. "I don't know what happened on that date of yours, but you sure shook him up."

"Oh." I said, dumbly. "I mean, nothing happened. We literally just talked."

"Well, whatever y'all talked about worked on him. Like I said, I've never seen him this way. He was just so...happy." She wrinkled her nose and winced slightly.

"It was weird." She began to laugh lightly, and instantly the mood in the room lightened.

I laughed along with her before saying, almost in a whisper, "He makes me happy, too. That is, before all this vampire nonsense." I looked down and stared into the steam rising from my coffee cup. The truth was, despite our awkwardness, at times he was genuinely fun to be around. I wanted to be with him and I often found my mind wandering to thoughts of him. If there was truth in this vampire mumbo-jumbo it could explain away a lot.

Leanne looked at me for a long time. Apparently, intense staring ran in the family. She seemed to make up her mind about something, and finally began speaking. "Well, who am I to stop this happy union, then? Here goes nothing." She groaned.

"Silas isn't really my cousin; he's actually my uncle, my great, great..." She started ticking greats off with her fingers before giving up. "You get the picture. It's easier to tell people he's my cousin since we look so similar in age." She paused and took a deep breath. "I'm telling you the truth, and so did he." She looked so sincere when she said that.

I've known Leanne a long time and could tell when she was lying. She seemed to be telling the truth now, or she believed it as truth, anyway.

I sat for a moment, quietly, letting everything sink in.

That's when Leanne turned and grabbed her bag off the back of her chair and placed it in front of her on the table.

"I knew he was going to tell you, despite my wishes. I didn't want you caught up in this world at all; I've tried to shield you from it for as long as I could, only allowing him to meet me late at night at Lulu's or at his house on the outskirts of town. But of course, fate intervened in the form of a headache and a craving for coffee and pie, so now here we are!"

She tossed her hands up in exasperation. "I tried so hard to talk him out of it, and I almost did, but he must think you're something special if he's letting you in."

She was going through her bag while manically saying all of that. Leanne's face became stoic as she took out a book. It was old and leather-bound, a true antique. The leather looked soft and was worn around the edges.

"Here, just look at this." Leanne slid the book across the table to me.

I opened it to see handwritten pages of names and descriptions of duties performed and gifts received. I rifled through the pages quickly before coming back to the beginning. The first page had an oath written across the top. The ink had faded over time, but it was legible.

The oath read, *I solemnly swear to uphold the secret of Silas Matthew Quinn and to speak to no one about what he is without his consent. I will answer his calls for help, acquire what he needs to survive in the human world, and remain loyal to him. In return, Silas M. Quinn must not take the lives of those he takes nourish-*

ment in, lest their blood be on all our hands. If I fail, Silas has my consent to erase my memories of him. If Silas fails, he understands it will mean his death by beheading.

It began in September of 1899, with the name Sarah Rose, and it ended in May 2007 with the name Leanne Grace. Next to each name was the exact same signature, Silas Quinn. It had to be the ledger Silas spoke about. No last names were used for the Keepers, only first and middle.

I closed the book, and now I had more questions than answers.

"What is this?" I asked, even though I already knew, I just needed to hear it from Leanne.

"It's the book of Silas's Keepers. It started with his sister in 1899 and passes on to her descendants. She was his Keeper for fifty years before passing the torch onto her own daughter and so on and so forth, until it got to me."

"But what does being his Keeper mean? He told me he signed an oath, or whatever."

"Yes, we all did. I am the current Keeper. He's dead, or undead, for all intents and purposes, so technically he can't have a bank account, or property, or anything like that. We help him with the human side of life by placing certain things in our name and stuff like that and he in turn helps us."

"So that's what these gifts are?"

"Yes. He has put kids through college, bought homes and cars. He even bought Lulu's for me. He's loaded, you know." She gave a small laugh.

I furrowed my brow in confusion. "What keeps your family members from cutting him off and taking his wealth? It seems like it would be so easy. I mean, everything is in your name."

Leanne laughed. "We're not thieves. And besides, he is family, after all. He does so much good for our family it would be terribly unfair and hateful to do such a thing. Not that no one's thought of it."

She shrugged. "We just have to trust each other, and besides, he has ways of making people forget and do what he wants." She paused to take a sip of her coffee.

I nodded in agreement. I guess it made sense. "But if he does these nice things for you and your family, why does he get under your skin so much?"

Leanne pushed back in her chair abruptly. "Because of what he is, Dani! He's a monster who has taken human lives!"

I nodded, slowly, and kept my tone even. "He admitted as much, but the way he talked, he knew how to keep people alive and has been leaving them alive ever since his mother told him he had to." I thought back to the tale Silas told and swallowed, hard.

"He can, and he's supposed to, according to the oath. He's still a monster, though, and I don't know if I can abide by this oath much longer. Just knowing what he's doing to those people and now possibly to you."

She shivered. "I'm just bound to it because of the threat of mind manipulation and the sense of family obligation." She became quiet and looked down at her hands holding her mug.

I didn't know what to say. She was obviously torn by her duties to the oath, her family, and her morals.

I broke the silence a few moments later. "Would he let you out of it if you asked?"

Leanne shrugged. "Dunno, I never thought about it, honestly. It's just something my family has always done."

"Might be worth a conversation. You never know."

"Right, and then I'd have to put the burden on someone else. I'll deal; I've done it this long." She sighed and smiled, weakly.

"You said he's not supposed to kill, right? And he said himself he hasn't taken any lives since the day he rose from his grave, so that must mean something. What happens if he breaks his oath?"

"He's still a monster!" She banged her fist on the table. "He still hurts people! How can I continue to go along with this? I almost wish he would break his oath! If he did, then that means we kill him. Chop off his head and burn him to ash. Then I, nor anyone else for that matter, wouldn't have to do this any longer." Leanne seemed so tired and conflicted.

"I still don't understand, though. If all you have to do is help provide him a human life by putting things in your name and using his money to do so, and all he has to do is uphold his end of the bargain, I'm not sure I understand the problem."

She looked at me like I had grown another head. "The problem is you're involved now, it complicates things and it's not the *if*, it's the *when*. There will come a day when he slips up, when he takes a life. If that day comes under my watch, how do I live with that? Their blood is on my hands, too. Now that he's taken an interest in you, that blood could be yours."

Leanne's eyes began to well with tears. "Do you know he's the reason I've never married, the reason I do not have children? How can I pass this off to someone else? It's more than unethical."

I really didn't know what to say now. I stared at my hands instead.

She gathered her thoughts and began again. "I sometimes help him find his victims."

She placed her head in her hands and took a deep, but shuddering, breath. "That night you first saw him in the diner, when you walked in, he wanted you."

Leanne looked at me to see how I would take it.

I was shocked, to say the least. That must have been what he was saying to her that night to upset her so much.

"But you didn't let him," I tried to console her.

Leanne looked frantic. Her eyes went wide, and she began speaking in rapid fire. "Yes, but he went against my wishes and tried, anyway. It was no coincidence he found you at the hardware store. He was hunting you! And you invited him into your home! He can get in anytime he likes now. Vampires have to be invited in. I don't know why he didn't make his move here. That's why he took you to that field in the middle of nowhere. He must have been planning to feed on you! That's why I was able to guess he took you somewhere you were alone. Oh, God, Dani! I'm so sorry! I had no idea he was going to do that. I could have lost you!"

I sat there, shocked at first, but then I took her hand.

I softly and calmly said, "But you didn't lose me and nothing happened."

I still had so many questions and absolutely no proof what Silas and Leanne were telling me was true.

Leanne left her ledger book with me so I could look it over. There were names listed from daughters to great-grandsons and granddaughters and on down to Leanne. There were lists of bank accounts, properties bought and sold, cars and trucks, and so on and so forth. There were also smaller lists of names of family members charged with getting Silas any of the documentation he might need. No questions asked, I assumed. Passports and driver's licenses, medical records, and even birth certificates. It was all managed by the Keepers. No wonder Leanne seemed so overwhelmed. I'm certain Silas had a lot of say because it was his money. But still, the fact was that book wasn't proof of anything. It was just a list of names and duties performed, as well as gifts received in return. I still needed solid proof and answers.

———

I fell asleep on the couch with the Keepers' book in my arms. When a storm blew in later that night, I was awakened by the sound of thunder and driving rain hitting the windows. The lights began to flicker and then they went out.

"Great," I groaned.

I got up to find a flashlight.

A deafening thunderclap made me jump; it was followed by a flash of lightning. I could have sworn I saw a man's silhouette standing at my doorway.

"Is someone there?" I called out.

Another flash of lightning, and the dark shape was gone. I went to the door, afraid to open it, but the need to know was stronger.

I unlocked the door and stepped outside.

The wind whipped my hair around my face as I stepped farther out onto the covered porch.

"Hello?" There was no way anyone could hear me over the storm. I took a chance. "Silas?"

There was no answer.

Mostly satisfied no one was creeping about, I went back inside and locked the door. It must have been my imagination or my mind playing tricks on me. I found a flashlight and went to bed; it was getting late.

I lay there, my thoughts running rampant. I rested fitfully until finally falling asleep, listening to the storm rage outside.

I dreamt of Silas again that night, and much like before, it was a nightmare filled with fangs and blood. My blood.

CHAPTER
Nine

"SHIT! I'M LATE!" I said after I awoke with a start. Sometime during the night, the power came back on. My alarm clock never rang, and I never set an alarm on my phone, so I overslept. I was late to work.

I jumped out of bed, hastily dressed, yanked my hair back into a ponytail, brushed my teeth, and rushed out the door.

I sent Jeff a quick text, apologizing for being late and for not being there to help open.

I was locking my door, when I noticed a lone magnolia flower on the welcome mat. It must have blown off the tree during last night's storm. I bent down and picked it up. One of the petals was steeped in something reddish brown, almost rust-colored.

That's strange. I thought. *Oh, well, no time to worry about that now.*

I tossed the flower to the side and made my way to my car.

I opened the car door and just happened to look up at my neighbor, Jerry Williams', house across the street. He was cleaning up some branches from the tree in his yard. He had a large bandage on his neck. I stopped and looked closely at his house and noticed a window was broken. "Hi, Jerry." I waved. "Is everything all right?"

Jerry looked up and seemed a bit disoriented. "Oh, hi, Danica. Yes, yes, everything's fine. Just doing a bit of cleaning up after last night's storm. A darn tree limb broke off and went through my window." He absentmindedly scratched his bandaged neck.

I walked away from my car and toward Jerry. He was an older man who lived alone, and he just seemed so confused. He kept looking at his broken window and back to the old oak tree across the yard.

I glanced toward the tree with him, measuring the distance in my mind. The tree seemed so far away from the house. I know it was windy last night, but that distance seemed almost impossible. I shook my head in disbelief, trying to get it to make sense.

"Did the glass from the window cut your neck?" I didn't notice any other scratches or injuries on him, other than some small bruises on his arms.

Jerry's eyes glazed over. He stared at me, and he slowly answered, almost hypnotically. "Yes, the glass from the shattered window cut my neck." He just kept staring, blankly, at me.

"Mr. Williams, I'm going to call your daughter so she can come to help you. Would that be all right? Will you be okay on your own until someone gets here?"

I already had my phone in my hand and began searching for her name in my contacts.

Jerry seemed to snap out of his trance, and he shook his head. "Oh," he said, slowly. "Yes, my dear, I'll be just fine. Thank you." He smiled at me, wanly, and turned back toward his yard and got back to work.

I walked back to my car and left a message for Jerry's daughter. Hopefully, she would check her messages soon and come to check on her father.

I started my car and sped to the bookstore, trying not to think about befuddled ol' Jerry as I drove.

———

When I got there, Jeff was behind the counter. He smiled when I came in, but something was off. Was he upset I was late?

"Hi, Jeff; sorry I'm late."

"It's no biggie." He shrugged. "There's a customer here asking for you. I told him you were running late and he could come back later."

He had an odd tone to his voice; it was very unlike Jeff.

"Oh? Where is he? What did he need?" I was curious. Who would be asking for me?

"Yeah, he never left. He said he didn't mind waiting. In fact, he said he had all the time in the world. Whatever that means." Jeff turned away, and I swear I saw him roll his eyes.

What was that all about?

I started to head toward my office to put my stuff away, when Silas walked around the bookcase and into my path. He looked better today. There was a slight blush on his skin, and the dark circles under his eyes were gone.

I gulped, considering what that probably signified if the stories were true.

"Silas, I wasn't expecting to see you," I stammered, failing miserably to hide the anxiousness in my voice.

He smiled at me, wickedly. "I'm sorry to bother you at work, but I really wanted to see you again. Have you thought about our conversation the other night?"

I could feel Jeff's eyes on us as we spoke. I hoped he wouldn't hear us.

"I have, and I've decided I need more answers, more proof, to believe what I've heard. Let's go to my office to talk."

Silas glanced up toward Jeff, and a look of amusement lit up his face. "After you."

He put his hand on the small of my back.

I heard a book slam shut and then the jingling of keys. I resisted the urge to look back at Jeff.

Silas followed me toward the rear of the bookstore to my office.

I sat down behind my desk, and Silas leaned casually against the window casing.

I was about to begin talking to Silas, when Jeff rapped on the office door and then poked his head in.

He looked at Silas, inhospitably.

Then, he said to me, "Hey, boss, I'm stepping out for an early lunch. Do you want anything?"

"No, thank you, Jeff. Enjoy your lunch break." I gave him a smile and hoped that was the end of it.

"You sure? I don't mind." He looked at Silas again, a slight sneer on his face.

Silas grinned and looked at Jeff. "I could eat." His eyes flashed, and something about his face changed, but only slightly.

I butted in before any more testosterone was wasted. "Really, Jeff, I'm fine. Take an extra thirty today and go to Lulu's. Tell Leanne to put it on my tab. It's the least I can do for being so late."

Jeff gave me a close-lipped smile and left.

"If I didn't know any better, I'd say that boy has a crush on you," Silas said as he walked over to the chair across from my desk and sat down.

"Jeff?" I laughed. "He's like a brother to me, and he's a great employee. I'm lucky to have him."

"I'm sure you are, but he has it bad." Silas gave a hearty laugh.

I rolled my eyes and said, "I'm pretty sure he doesn't; you've never seen the way he looks at Leanne."

I smiled. "Anyway, why are you here?"

"I told you. I wanted to see you again, and I'm certain you have a lot more questions than answers at this point. I want to lay it all out there for you. Leanne thinks it's a good idea too." He leaned back in his chair and crossed an ankle over his knee, looking at me, smugly.

"She does?" I was astounded.

"Yes, she does. Your place again, say around 7:30 or 8:00?"

"Do you mind if Leanne is there, too? I don't know if I want to be alone with you. No offense."

"None taken, but you're alone with me now." That sly grin of his spread across his face.

"Yes, but there's cameras here." I pointed my pen at the camera in the corner.

Silas gave the cameras a furtive glance and turned his attention back at me. "I'll see you this evening, Dani."

He smiled, got up, and walked away.

I watched him leave and waited to hear the chimes over the front door sound, signaling his departure. Now, I had to call Leanne.

———

Leanne arrived first, carrying two bottles of wine.

"I have a feeling I'm going to need one of these all to myself tonight," she said as I held the door open for her.

She seemed to be in a decent mood. So far so good.

Leanne placed the wine bottles in the kitchen and returned to the living room.

We were sitting on the couch, just talking and catching up, when Silas's truck pulled into the driveway. I heard the engine cut off and the door slam and soon his footsteps were echoing across the porch.

"I'm going to get that glass of wine now," Leanne said, hopping up and heading to the kitchen.

There was a light knock on the door.

I stood and slowly made my way to the door, watching his silhouette as he stood a polite distance away.

I opened the door, and there he was, grinning from ear to ear.

"Hello, Dani." He smiled at me. "Are you going to invite me in?"

"We both know it's too late for that; come on in."

Silas passed by me closely, making sure to brush his hand against mine as he did.

It sent chills through me. "Why do you need to be invited in? Why can't you just enter someone's home?"

"A person's home is where they feel safe." Silas held up his hands and did finger quotes for the word 'safe.'

"That safety net provides a type of protection, a barrier, so to speak, you know, since all vampires are inherently evil."

He stepped uncomfortably close and grinned, wickedly, at me, making my heart race. "A vampire cannot enter unless explicitly invited in by an inhabitant of the home, whether their intentions are good or not."

Another agonizingly wicked smile spread across his face. "The longer a family has lived in the home, the stronger the barrier is, and if ownership of the house changes, a vampire can't get back in unless invited again. But once a vampire is invited in, they can enter as they wish."

Silas looked at me, staring intently into my eyes. "I have no intention of hurting you or bringing you harm in any way." His eyes were smoldering, liquid green and warm. "I hope to prove that to you."

I nodded and smiled, weakly.

Suddenly, I was very aware of how closely we were standing to one another. I must have subconsciously taken a step or two toward him. I took a step back so I could get around him and was trying my damnedest to calm my nerves.

Walking farther into the house, he began looking around. "I never told you about this house." He was observing the foyer and running his fingers across the shiplap. "It belonged to my sister, Sarah, and her husband, John. They moved here just before the hurricane in 1899. My parents came to live here after their home was destroyed, and little Maggie was born a short time later, in 1900. Your bedroom was Maggie's."

He stopped and picked up the family portrait of my parents and I in front of the magnolia tree out front.

"I planted that tree for Maggie's tenth birthday." He smiled at the memory and then looked at me as if he hadn't just said something completely strange. "I'm ready when you are."

I led him to the living room. I wasn't sure what to say, so I didn't say anything. How could any of what he told me have been true?

Leanne was back. She had three glasses of wine poured and set out on the coffee table.

Leanne sat on one end of the couch, and I took the other.

Silas chose an armchair diagonal from me by the window.

Leanne and Silas looked at me, expectantly.

I puffed my cheeks up and blew out. "Where do I begin?"

Leanne shrugged and sipped her wine.

Silas sat silently and then said, "Wherever you like."

I thought back to mine and Leanne's conversation; something she had told me was cause for some major concern. "Let's start with the elephant in the room, Silas."

He raised an eyebrow at me, and one side of his mouth twitched up into a smirk.

"Leanne told me the night I came into the diner you placed an off-the-menu order." I swallowed. "She said you wanted me."

I stopped speaking to gauge his reaction; he just sat there with one eyebrow raised and a smirk on his face.

I exhaled and began speaking again. "Leanne also said

you went against her wishes and came after me, anyway. The sunset date was a ruse to get me alone so you could feed." I met his gaze. "Why?"

Leanne downed her glass of wine, jumped up, and said, "I think we're going to need that other bottle."

We watched her go, and Silas started speaking. "I think Leanne talks too much." He said that rather loudly, obviously making sure Leanne heard him.

She came back in, sat the bottle of wine on the table, shrugged, and sat down, kicking off her flip-flops and tucking a leg underneath her.

"Well, Silas," Leanne said, "are you going to answer her or not?"

"It's true. I did tell Leanne I wanted you, but it wasn't for any reason in particular. You just happened to be the first person to come in, and I was hungry." He shrugged and spread his hands out in an apologetic manner. "But her reaction to my request told me you were important to her so I bought you a snack instead of making you mine."

His smile told me he thought he was very clever. I chose to ignore his comment.

"I see. So if it would have been anyone else?"

"Soup's on." He narrowed his eyes and smiled, sinisterly.

I had to fight the urge not to look slack-jawed at him.

"Gross." Leanne retched and put down her glass.

"Well, tell her about the date. Are you going to tell her how you gained her trust just so you could lure her out to the middle of nowhere so no one could hear her scream?"

I looked at Leanne, then at Silas, and back to Leanne. "Is that true?"

"Ask him." She was glaring at Silas, daring him to lie.

"Initially yes, that was the plan." He looked a little sheepish, but only a little, and then it was gone.

"At least you're honest," I said. "But what stopped you? Why didn't you attack, or whatever?" Was I really having this conversation right now? Did I just get someone to confess to wanting to eat me?

"If you must know, I just couldn't bring myself to do it. Leanne has always smelled faintly of magnolias for the past few years. I couldn't figure out why; it was maddening. I wanted to find the source, and it's not like Leanne could tell me. She wouldn't have known you smell like magnolias. When you left the diner the breeze blew your scent towards me as you closed the door and that's when I had a moment of recognition."

He leaned forward in his seat. "It wasn't until I ran into you at the hardware store when I figured it out. Your scent had intermingled with hers all those times before. I was intrigued now that I had pinpointed the source. I knew I had to have you, but just in a different way now."

Silas grinned and continued. "It also doesn't hurt you live in my sister's old house."

I could feel the heat rise in my face as I turned red from his admission. The scent thing made sense, I guess. After my parents died, I spent a lot of time with Leanne. I didn't like to be alone in the house.

"So you didn't attack me because I smell like magnolias?"

Silas reached forward and took up his wineglass. He took a drink, swallowed it and said, "There's more to it than that. I'm not exactly sure how to describe it."

Another sip of wine. "It's my favorite scent above all others, and when I smelled it coming from you, something snapped inside me. All I could think about was you and the thought of being near you made me happy at just the notion, but at the back of my mind was the nagging thought of what it would mean to taste you."

He downed the last of his wine glass in one swift gulp.

That must have been why he began acting so strangely that night in the field. He was struggling to keep his distance from me and at the same time wanting to be near me but afraid of doing something he might have regretted.

Leanne had been rather quiet during the exchange. She cleared her throat, and the tension between Silas and I broke.

"I'm glad to hear your need to get to know her was stronger than your need to taste her." Leanne leaned forward and grabbed the wine bottle.

"I need more wine." She refilled her wine glass and then topped off ours.

We sat in silence for a few minutes. Leanne was nursing her wine. Silas was casting glances in my direction, and I was trying to think of something else to say or ask.

"I'm really having a hard time believing this," I said, bewilderedly. "I mean, if you're truly a vampire, where's your fangs? How do you walk in the sunlight? Do you turn into a bat? Are you superhumanly strong or have powers or super abilities? I'm so confused."

He laughed and shared a look with Leanne.

She topped off his glass of wine again, even though it didn't really need to be, and said, "I think you're going to need this."

Silas had a large drink before beginning.

"I am truly a vampire, but my fangs only come out when I need them. My fangs fit into a sort of pocket in my jaw. It gives them somewhere to go when I'm not using them."

"Can you show me?" I leaned slightly forward, eager to see if he would show me his fangs.

Silas laughed, licked his lips, and said, "I'd love to show you how they work, but I'm pretty sure Leanne would kill me."

Leanne nodded.

"Okay then, how do you not burst into flames in the sunlight?"

"Another common misconception about vampires. It's…"

He looked away toward the darkening window, as if the

answer he was looking for would appear there somehow. "Uncomfortable. It's like the beginning of a sunburn, just painful enough to let me know it's there, weakening me slightly just to remind me I don't belong in the sunlight. Reminding me I am a creature of the night."

I nodded along, my eyes narrowing on him in slight disbelief.

Silas's lips curled into a small smile at the face I was making. "The truly ancient ones are the only ones who seem to burn in the sunlight. From what I've gathered, because they are the purest form of vampire, they seem to have the most problems with the sun. As the eons went on and vampire blood became more diluted, we began to have an easier time in the light."

He shrugged. "Besides all that, it is easier to hunt at night. It's less crowded, allowing us the chance to stay in darkness as not to be seen, to snatch a person without causing a panic, and to be comfortable while feeding" .

"We're physically stronger at night beacuase our bodies are not focused on the discomfort the sun brings us and our eyesight is much more suited for the dark. Humans came up with the whole sunlight thing to explain why vampire attacks only happened at night. Nowadays, feeding is rather easy. All I really need to do is run an ad saying, *Spend the night with a vampire,* and people come running. I have Hollywood to thank for that with your hunky, brooding, glittery, teenage vampires." He laughed darkly at his own joke.

"Fair enough, but what about the other stuff?"

"Superhuman abilities, you mean? No, not exactly. There are tales of vampires with better abilities than most, but I've never really seen them. I can enthrall a person while they're incapacitated with my venom; it's a type of hypnotism, but that's about as magical as it gets. As far as everything else goes, I am stronger and faster and have better senses than humans; I liken it to how a lion or a tiger relates to their prey. I am a predator, after all."

He smirked. "For example, I can hear your heart racing every time I make you nervous or draw too close. I find it amusing and a little endearing."

I could feel the heat of a traitorous blush creeping up my face. So that was why he was always smirking. I was going to have to learn to control that.

He continued. "I also can't read minds or tell the future or any of that nonsense. I'm just exceptionally good at using my assets to either hunt down or beguile my next meal. Oh, and I absolutely cannot turn into a bat." Silas rolled his eyes.

"No bats, got it." Could I actually believe any of this? He seemed so sure of his answers to my questions. There was no hesitation to answer anything so far.

I kept up my barrage of inquiries. "What about your blood or venom or whatever; does it have healing properties? I know I've seen somewhere it does. It was probably on TV, or something."

Silas shifted in his seat. "Not exactly. Vampire venom cannot heal humans, and neither can our blood. The only healing properties it has is during transformation. If you are sick or injured when you start the transformation into a vampire, you will be cured or healed of most, but not all, human ailments or frailty. Vampires are extremely hard to injure, even though we can be."

He paused, reflecting on something only he could remember. "We heal rapidly, and we do not suffer from human illnesses. There are injuries that even we cannot heal from. Fire destroys us. If we get burned and survive, we live with those scars for eternity. And if we get staked, depending on how long the stake remains, well..."

Silas pulled at the collar of his shirt and lowered it just enough so that i could see the top of a round scar above his heart. My eyes widened in shock and I quickly took a sip of wine to mask my face. It didn't work. Silas smiled slyly and readjusted his shirt.

"If our venom or blood were a cure, I'm pretty sure some lab out there would have us corralled like cattle and taken full advantage of that."

Silas laughed, cynically. "Besides, it's not just the venom that does the transformation. Otherwise, everyone I've bitten would be like me."

I cocked an eyebrow. "So you don't just bite to transform someone?"

Silas leaned forward in his seat just a bit. "No, you must ingest the blood of your creator to complete the transition."

I felt the color leave my face and suppressed a shiver. It didn't go unnoticed.

Silas smirked, wickedly, and winked as he sat back in his chair again.

"Speaking of transforming, are all vampires beautiful? Does changing alter your appearance? I know you said Eliza was beautiful, and I'm sure you've seen yourself in a mirror."

Leanne pretended to gag.

I waited for her to be done with her theatrics. "Hold on, do you even have a reflection in a mirror?"

Silas was getting a kick out of this. "For someone who is only on the verge of believing, you sure know your lore." He laughed and then answered my questions. "Not all vampires are beautiful. If you were an ugly son of a bitch in life, then you would also be an ugly son of a bitch as a vampire. It makes hunting harder for those who aren't as blessed as this." He gestured to himself.

Leanne's eyes rolled so hard I wasn't sure if they'd come back around.

"The mirror thing is also a myth, along with garlic, the fear of Christian symbols, and all that other stuff."

He waved his hand, vapidly, in the air. "Stupidity, fear,

and overactive imaginations created a lot of lore surrounding vampires, and a lot of innocent lives were lost in the beginning. They got a few things right, though. They were correct in their notion to behead a vampire or to stake it to its grave."

All three of us sat in silence for a moment while I contemplated everything I'd heard so far.

Silas began again. "For as long as there have been humans, there have been vampires. We have gone by many names throughout history: Draugr, Wearh, Strigoi, Upyr, Revenant, Nosferatu." He ticked them off with his fingers. "Just to name a few."

Silas watched me for a moment before speaking again. "Most vampires are not bloodthirsty beasts; we can assimilate quite easily within the human world. Those who want to, anyway. There are some who cling to the old monstrous ways, though. Many of us can control our bloodlust. It's not like I would go berserk if you got a small cut or something."

His face turned serious just then as he carried on. "But even I can be a monster at times. I've killed and severely hurt people over my past 100 something years as a vampire. It's a lot like trying to keep a tiger as a pet. Sure, a domesticated tiger can seem docile, but they still have that killer instinct and ability to turn at any moment. I'm thankful to my mother for setting up a way for me to be held accountable for my actions and I do not want to lose touch with my humanity. Even still, I do not completely trust myself."

He sighed, morosely. "I was never given a chance to choose this life for myself; it was forced upon me. No matter how good Eliza thought her intentions were, it was still selfish. I would never make that decision for someone else."

Silas looked at me, intently; his face was drawn and sad. He blinked and turned to look out the window again.

I gave him a moment to reflect before saying, "This is a lot to take in. All my life I've known stuff like this wasn't real.

Even some of the local lore like the Lost Colony of Roanoke, Blackbeard's treasure, and even the Bladenboro Vampire Beast is easier to believe than this."

At the mention of the Bladenboro Beast, Silas sucked in air, sharply, through his teeth. "Yeah, so that whole vampire beast thing was my fault."

Leanne almost spit her wine out. She choked slightly and coughed a few times.

"What?" I cried in open-mouthed surprise.

"Yeah," he laughed. "I was bored and curious one day. I wanted to know what would happen if I bit and tried to turn a bobcat. I had been watching one in the woods one day. I chased it down, tackled it, and managed to turn it, and voila, vampire beast."

He looked back and forth between Leanne and I, waiting for a reaction.

We both looked at him like he had a third eyeball.

"That thing caused a lot of trouble in '53 and '54."

Silas ran his hand through his hair, seemingly embarrassed by that admission. "I took care of it, though. No more experiments for me."

We all laughed at his embarrassment.

I stood up and began pacing the room, trying to let all that new information sink in.

I stopped at the window and toyed with the curtains before speaking. "I can't believe you've kept all this hidden from me for all this time, Leanne."

I turned to look at them both. I knew all families had a skeleton or two in their closets, but it seemed my best friend's family had a vampire in theirs.

Leanne opened her mouth to say something, but Silas held up his hand, silencing her. "To be fair, she kept you a secret from me, as well. I was always curious why she would smell faintly of magnolias from time to time, and now I know it was from spending time with you."

He tilted his head and smiled, flirtatiously, at me. "But I digress, my secrecy is very important to me. I pay very well to have my secrets kept, and I intend for them to remain that way. I only reveal what I am to those whom I know I can trust."

He stood and joined me at the window; he was standing excruciatingly close.

I wanted to hate how my body reacted to him, how I was so attracted to him. It took everything in my power not to step closer to him.

His face became serious, his eyes darkened, and his voice lowered. "As I'm sure Leanne has told you, I have ways to make people forget."

I swallowed, hard. "She may have mentioned it."

Silas's face softened and he began grinning again.

I swept past him to get out of the intensity of his gaze and joined Leanne on the couch.

Leanne took a sip of her wine and shrugged. "Like I said before, his secrets are not mine to tell."

We sat in the living room, talking about his life, and he answered my questions without fail.

———

It was getting late before we noticed Leanne softly snoring on the couch.

"Too much wine, I think," Silas said, standing up.

I stood up, too and grabbed the blanket off the back of the couch.

Silas took hold of Leanne's legs and gently lifted them to the sofa, helping me to lay her down. I covered Leanne with the blanket and turned off the lamp.

"I should go," Silas said, softly, but unconvincingly. He had moved to my side as I straightened. He was peering down at me through his long, dark lashes;. His eyes were warm and sensual.

I was achingly aware of how close he was to me. I wanted to reach out and touch his skin, run a finger down the curve of his arm. I crossed my arms to keep from doing just that.

"I'll see you out," I whispered, fighting the urge to finish closing the small gap between us, turning instead to walk toward the door. The air seemed charged with electricity as he followed me out the front door and onto the porch.

Silas walked to the steps, turned to look at me, and said, "Tonight was fun."

He grinned and went on, "I really do enjoy talking to you, Dani. Spending time with you is a joy as well. I'd like to do it more often if you'll allow it."

The look in his eyes disrupted my concentration and it took a lot to hold my thoughts together. I inhaled deeply and looked down at my feet, pretending to scuff at a patch of peeling paint with the toe of my shoe.

"Me, too, I mean, talking to you, that is. Even though you did admit to wanting to eat me. Talk about a red flag." I tried to act coy, but my heart was thrumming.

Silas smirked that irritating little smirk of his and stepped closer to me. "No hard feelings, I hope?" he asked, softly.

I smiled and shook my head. "No." I laughed, softly. "I am having the hardest time figuring you out."

"Is that so?" He took another step closer. We were mere inches from one another.

"Mmmhmm," I mumbled. "I've been going over everything for days, trying to make it make sense."

Silas smiled, and it sent my heart into cartwheels.

"Days, you say? It's good to know you've been thinking of me." His voice was low and playful as he took another step toward me, finally closing the gap between us.

Now, my heart was hammering.

Our eyes were locked on each other's.

He smiled, warmly, and brought his long, cold fingers up to my chin. There was no way he couldn't hear my heart pounding, even I could hear it.

Silas lifted my face to his and softly kissed my lips.

CHAPTER
Ten

I WENT to work the next day with everything that happened last night buzzing around in my thoughts.

"You seem really distracted today, boss. Is something on your mind?" Jeff looked concerned as he spoke to me.

"You could say that, I guess." I tried to give him a reassuring smile. "I'll be okay; I've just got a lot to sort out."

"If you need someone to talk to, I'll be right here." He smiled and patted my shoulder and then let it linger there for a moment.

"Thanks, Jeff, but, really, I'm all right." I placed my hand over his and gave it a gentle squeeze.

As we spoke, someone came into the bookstore, the chimes above the door alerting us to their entrance.

"Looks like we have a customer," Jeff said. "I've got it."

He walked around the counter and toward the front of the store.

I heard him say "Hi, welcome to...Oh, it's you."

Jeff came back to the counter, visibly agitated.

He was followed by a very visibly amused Silas.

"You have a visitor." Jeff said, smarmily.

He came back behind the counter with me and pretended

to be busy placing clearance stickers on some books, but I knew he was listening.

Silas began speaking before I had a chance to say anything. "Hello, Dani, I don't think I've had the pleasure of being introduced to your charming coworker yet."

I stifled a laugh and introduced them. "Silas, this is Jeff. Jeff, Silas."

Jeff looked up and blandly said, "That's an odd name. What kind of name is Silas, anyway?"

Silas looked at me, and I could see him coming up with something clever and smart aleck to say. "An old one." He chuckled.

I tried not to laugh again as I said, "It's practically an antique." I winked at Silas.

Jeff looked back and forth between us, obviously annoyed with our inside joke.

"I see. Well, I've got work to do. It was nice meeting you, Silas," he said, coldly, sliding past us as he headed to the storage room.

Once he was out of earshot, Silas leaned across the counter and took my hand. His fingers were cold, as always.

He lifted my hand to his face and kissed it. "I want to show you something. Are you available this evening?"

My heart seemed to skip a beat, and Silas grinned at me, knowingly. "Um, yeah. I don't have anything going on tonight. I'm not sure if we should be alone together, though, considering what you are."

Silas looked at me, clearly amused. He still had hold of my hand and was tracing small circles along the back of it with his finger. "Understandable."

He paused to smile at me. "It's a bit of a surprise, if that makes any difference."

"What kind of a surprise?" My breath hitched, and it came out in a breathless whisper. I couldn't believe the visceral reaction I was having to his fingers tracing over my skin.

"If I tell you, it'll spoil the fun."

He looked me in the face, and his eyes changed momentarily. The dark green of his irises seemed to spread as his pupils constricted and changed from black round circles into vertical slits and instantly back again.

I gasped, and he laughed.

"Pick you up at six?"

I was still trying to understand what I had just seen as I answered him. "Sure, sounds good."

As an afterthought, I added, "This isn't anything dangerous, is it?"

"Hmm," he purred, "only if you want it to be." He ran his fingers up my wrist, finding my pulse, and stopped there.

I swallowed and said, "See you at six."

———

It was Jeff's turn to close the bookstore tonight, so that meant I had plenty of time to get home before 6:00.

As I was finishing a few last-minute things and gathering my stuff to leave, Jeff stopped to talk me.

"Are you going out with that guy?" He had a disgruntled look on his face.

"Silas? Yes, he's taking me somewhere tonight, but he didn't say where. Why do you ask?"

"I don't know about him, boss; he gives me the creeps. Something seems off about him." His face looked like he had caught a whiff of something extremely smelly.

I laughed. "He's mostly harmless. I promise, I'll be okay. I can handle myself."

I snatched my keys off the counter and gave Jeff a wink.

"I'm sure you can, but still, just be careful, all right?"

He shuddered "He doesn't seem..." He paused. "Human."

"What do you mean by that?" I laughed, nervously.

"I don't know." Jeff scratched his head, seemingly uncomfortable. "He just seems unnatural to me, almost predatory."

He shrugged and laughed. "Besides, no one should be allowed to be that good-looking. And those eyes of his are weird, man."

He violently shivered this time. Jeff's instincts had caught on to Silas, so I wondered why mine didn't. And if they had, why was I ignoring them?

"I'll be fine, promise." I gave Jeff my best reassuring smile and headed to the door.

"See you tomorrow." I waved goodbye and Jeff gave me a small nod as I walked out.

———

Six o'clock got here quickly, and I found myself eager to get going. What did he want to show me, and why would he be keeping it a surprise?

Silas was running late and pulled up around 6:15.

"You're late," I chided him.

"Sorry about that. I wanted to make sure everything was ready before I left to pick you up." He met me at the front porch stairs and offered me his hand.

I took it and noticed the coolness of his fingers against my own skin.

"Your hands are always so cold," I commented.

"One of the perks of being undead, I suppose. You know what they say; cold hands, warm heart." He pulled me around to face him and lifted my hand to his chest.

I couldn't feel a heartbeat.

We stood there, facing each other for a moment. It was always so intense when he looked into my eyes, like he could see past them and into my soul.

I tore myself away from his gaze and got into his truck.

"Do you even have a heart?"

Silas smiled. His arm was resting on the top of the door frame, and he leaned his head against it, which brought his face closer to mine.

He gave me a quizzical look. "Of course, I do; it just doesn't beat quite like yours."

"There's so much to learn. I feel like I should be taking notes."

Silas stroked my cheek and let his hand come to rest on my neck. I know he could feel my pulse quickening.

He laughed again and then walked to his side of the vehicle.

We left my driveway and started heading out of town. I began to get a tad nervous.

Silas immediately picked up on it. "Nervous?" he asked, smirking.

"Maybe. The last time I went this way with you, I was almost on the menu."

"Mmm, I see how that could be a problem." He reached over and grabbed my hand, intertwining his cold fingers with mine. "None of that this time, scout's honor. Unless you want to, I'd be happy to oblige."

"Tempting, but no. You'll have to keep your fangs inside that pretty head of yours tonight."

Silas laughed, ominously. "You may change your mind eventually."

"Doubt it." I rolled my eyes.

———

A few moments later, we pulled into the same gravel drive from the night when we watched the sunset.

"Why did you bring me back here?" I asked, anxiously.

"Relax, I own this place. I wanted to show you where I live while I'm in town."

We drove right on up and over the little hill and clearing where we had parked only a few short weeks ago.

The driveway wound in and out of wooded patches before finally ending in front of a two-story log cabin. It had a wraparound porch and dormers up top. There was a small, detached garage to the right of the cabin, and the whole thing overlooked a rolling green pasture with a small pond and was edged with woods.

"Rustic," I said getting out of the truck, "and quiet."

"Do you like it? I've had it since late 1899. This was the abandoned cabin I sought refuge in after leaving my mother and sister. I've done some renovations along the way."

"It's beautiful, Silas. I can see why you wanted to stay."

We walked up the steps of the porch, and I turned around to admire the view of the land surrounding the cabin.

The grass waved gently in the summer breeze and was dotted here and there with colorful wildflowers. The small pond reflected the sky like a giant mirror. Puffy white clouds floated in the sky and in its reflection below. The forest just beyond the pond and rolling pasture was a mix of pines, beech, and oak trees. A beautiful, large dogwood tree stood along the banks of the pond on one side.

It was tranquil. I took a deep breath as I soaked it in.

Silas leaned against the porch railing, watching me as I took it all in. "I had Sarah inquire about it, and we were able to purchase it. The house and the property have been 'passed down' from Keeper to Keeper ever since. I allow their families use of it when I'm not here." He straightened, walked to the door, and opened it. "Would you like to come inside?"

"Are you inviting me in?" I asked, ironically.

Silas chuckled at my joke and said, "I guess I am."

I didn't know what to expect walking into Silas's cabin, but I don't think it was what greeted me.

It was simple and sparsely decorated. The main floor was one large room. There was a large wood stove in the corner, a big brown leather couch and armchair, a couple of side tables with lamps, a large, colorful woven rug on the floor, and a flat screen TV hung on the wall. Off to the side sat a plain farmhouse table and chairs, and behind that was a small kitchen and a powder room.

A set of stairs led up to what I assumed were the bedrooms. There weren't a lot of pictures or decorations on the walls, but the large windows made up enough for that. The view of the rolling pastures and surrounding forests was beautiful.

Silas was silently watching me again.

"It's come a long way from the single room, one story cabin it started out as," he finally said.

"It's wonderful," I breathed.

He was clearly pleased, but I was wondering if seeing his home was the surprise, or if he had more in mind. He seemed to have read my thoughts.

"Here, I want to show you something else." He led me out the back door and down a set of stairs toward the garage. "I keep something really special in here."

He opened the walkthrough door and flipped on the light switch. One bay was empty; I assumed that was where he parked his truck. The other bay had a car in it. I couldn't tell what it was because it was covered.

"I haven't kept much through my many years on this Earth. The cabin, my truck, a few family mementos, and this..." He slid the cover off the car and underneath was the most beautiful classic car I'd ever seen. It was sleek and shiny and a deep candy apple red. "I bought her new in 1968. I've done some upgrades and modifications, but she's still mostly original."

I got closer to it to take a better look.

Silas continued to tell me about it. "It's a 1968 Cardinal Edition Mustang. There were a limited number made for Virginia and North Carolina."

"It's gorgeous. Is it fast?" I asked with a smile.

"Only one way to find out." Silas was practically chomping at the bit.

He opened my door, and I climbed in. The black leather interior was just as clean as the outside. It truly was a beautiful car.

He opened the garage door and then got into the car.

Silas hit the key, and the engine roared to life.

He took it easy down the gravel drive, but as soon as we hit the asphalt, we were gone!

We sped down the back country roads, windows down, the air whipping our hair around our smiling faces. The fields and the trees flew by in a blur. It was exhilarating!

Silas slowed down as we neared the river.

He pulled over, and we got out, both of us grinning like fools.

We gravitated toward each other and met at the front of the car.

"That was incredible!" I said, breathlessly, smoothing down my hair.

"Yeah, she's a lot of fun to drive, especially with good company."

Silas had taken hold of my hands and pulled me closer. He was looking down at me. His wind-tousled hair had fallen slightly across his forehead.

He cupped my chin in his fingers and gazed into my eyes. His stare was smoldering. Silas lowered his lips to mine. His lips were cool and supple against my own, but this time, though, there was an eagerness to his kiss. It wasn't soft and gentle; it was something else. It was fire and ice, and I gave in.

I opened my mouth, inviting him in, and began winding my hands around his neck and then up through his silken hair.

A low groan escaped him as his tongue slipped over mine. His icy fingers left my skin burning wherever he touched me.

His hands eventually found their way into my hair, and he tangled his fingers in it, angling my head to deepen the kiss.

We held fast to one another, neither of us wanting to pull away first.

We slowly parted, and I looked into his eyes. They had changed. The green of his irises had spread; there was no white to be seen. And his pupils were slits, just like earlier in the bookstore. Only, this time, they stayed that way. They looked reptilian, almost snakelike.

"Silas, your eyes! They're…"

"Yeah, they do that sometimes." He chuckled, darkly.

"It's when the fangs come out when you should worry." He winked at me, and already his eyes were shifting back.

He pulled me back into him, and we stood there in an embrace.

My head nestled into his chest and his head upon mine, we listened to the river rush by as the night songs of the forest played, quietly. Tonight, I got my first manifestation of proof Silas was something supernatural. So why wasn't I afraid?

CHAPTER
Eleven

WE DROVE BACK to Silas's that evening with the kiss lingering between us.

Pulling into the garage, he turned to me and asked, "Are you hungry?"

I looked at him in slight surprise. "Are you?"

His signature smirk lit up his face. "Always."

I sat there, silently, for a moment and then asked, "Do you even have human food in there? Or is it all body parts, brains, and bags of blood?"

Silas laughed, lightheartedly, and answered, "Vampire, remember? Not a zombie. And yes, I do have food. That's part of the reason I was late. I asked Leanne to help me with groceries. I knew she would know what you like to eat, and I'm curious to know if I can still cook."

I laughed. "Been a while since you've fired up the stove?"

"You could say that, but at one time, I was pretty handy in the kitchen."

"I'm sure you were; let's see what you remember."

We went inside, and he began rummaging around.

I watched him as he gathered dishes and silverware and other kitchen utensils.

He seemed frustrated as he looked at everything in front of him.

"What exactly did Leanne tell you I liked to eat?" I asked, hesitantly.

Silas looked up, scratching his chin. "Leanne recommended I make you fish with an onion and garlic sauce."

I burst out laughing. "Oh, she got you good! You do realize she told you to cook the three smelliest things?"

I was laughing so hard now I almost couldn't breathe. "Oh, man, she is primeval! It's so simple, yet diabolical. Could you imagine what my breath would smell like after eating that? There's no way you'd get close to me!"

I was absolutely rolling now, especially after seeing Silas's pitiful face. Poor thing, he was so confused.

Then, I absolutely mortified myself. I laughed so hard at him I snorted.

Silas's face broke into a bright smile, and we were both cracking up now.

I was in tears as I stood up and went to the kitchen.

"Surely, she didn't intend for me to go hungry."

I began looking through the fridge and freezer, when I found a frozen pizza. "Here we go. I knew she would have provided a fail-safe."

Silas was still chuckling as he watched me prepare the frozen pizza.

"Well, I know I did one thing right." He grabbed a bottle of wine from the counter and poured two glasses.

We sat on the couch while I waited for the pizza to finish.

Silas shook his head and looked at me. "I can't believe I fell for that. What a conniving little minx!"

He took a sip of his wine.

I was curious about something.

I didn't know if it was the wine that emboldened me, or if it was the new comfortability we had, but I just came right out and asked. "How can you drink wine and coffee and other human drinks? Do you eat human food, too?"

Silas set his glass down and ran a hand through his hair before saying, "I enjoy wine, and bourbon for that matter, because my sense of taste is so strong, I can pick out the individual notes and the complexities of the drinks. I can't get drunk; I just enjoy the taste. I like to drink coffee because it makes me warm, and just for the briefest moment, I can remember what that used to feel like."

He thought for a minute, trying to figure out how to answer my second question. "I do not eat human food, although I can. It doesn't really do anything for me. The flavor of human food is still good, but it's nothing compared to the taste of..." Silas looked away from me and sighed.

He didn't need to finish; I knew what he was going to say.

The silence hung heavy between us, and I wanted desperately to say something, anything at all, but I didn't get to. The oven timer went off, breaking the tension the unspoken words left behind. My pizza was done.

We moved to the kitchen table.

He was obviously relieved not to have to talk about his eating habits anymore. Instead, he told me stories of his early life and of his sister, Sarah, and her family while I ate.

"It sounds like your sister and her daughter were very important to you."

"Yes, Sarah and Maggie were deeply loved. My sister was my closest ally and my best friend through everything. Sarah was only two years older than me, so we were very close from childhood on. Maggie came at a dark point in our lives; she was the rainbow after the storm. My mother had lost her oldest son, her home, and her husband. I guess that's why she clung so tenaciously to the idea I could still be good, despite what I am."

Silas took a deep breath and let it out as a long sigh. "My sister struggled to conceive and had some miscarriages, so little Maggie was a miracle in more ways than one. She was the reason I truly chose the no-kill method of feeding. I didn't want the blood on my hands to become hers.

"Sarah and I never hid what I was from her, so she grew up loving me for who I was, her weird, never-changing uncle who adored her. Maggie was the closest I would ever get to having my own child. Sarah's husband, John, wasn't my biggest fan and never fully trusted me, but he turned a blind eye to me out of love for Sarah."

I began clearing the dishes away and took them to the kitchen sink to wash.

Silas came up behind me and slid his arms around me.

He planted a cool kiss on my neck and said, "You wash, I'll dry."

We stood there, just mundanely washing dishes. It was both the most normal and the most abnormal thing I've ever done. I began to giggle.

"What's so funny?" Silas asked.

"Nothing. It's just so surreal, isn't it?" I dried my hands and turned to look at him.

"What is?" The corner of his mouth turned up in a half smile.

"I'm doing dishes with a vampire." I giggled again. "You're just so..." I fumbled around, trying to find the right thing to say.

"Human?" Silas found the word for me.

"Yeah, you're just so human. Even more so than some actual humans I know."

Silas smiled. "I do my best to hang onto my humanity. Like I've said before, I didn't choose this life, so it is important to me to hang onto my human side. My mother and my sister gave me motivation to stay as human as possible. Now, I believe I have a reason."

He looked me in the eyes. "I didn't ask to become a monster."

Looking at his face, it was hard to imagine him ever being a monster.

"I don't think you're a monster," I said, quietly.

Silas reached up and brushed a loose lock of my hair behind my ear.

He let his hand linger on my cheek. "Maybe not now, hopefully not ever, but you must know there is a monster hiding underneath."

He lowered his hand and then placed both hands in his pockets as he leaned against the counter. "As I've mentioned before, not all vampires are like me. There are a few, but many more are dangerous and a lot worse than any monsters in your worst nightmares."

I swallowed, hard, and just nodded.

I turned back toward the sink to finish cleaning up. The silence was deafening, and a new tension opened up between us.

"I didn't intend to dampen the mood with my talk of monsters," Silas said, awkwardly.

"I know." I smiled at him, and he visibly relaxed. "It's just given me more to think about, I suppose."

Silas squeezed my hand. There was a slight touch of sadness behind his eyes.

When we were finished and the dishes were put away, Silas opened a small broom closet under the stairs and took down an old, dusty box.

He sat it on the table and removed the lid. Inside was a very large, very old photo album.

"Would you like to see some pictures?" Silas asked.

How could I refuse?

We moved to the couch, but not before Silas poured me another glass of wine.

I sat closely to him and snuggled in. It was odd not feeling any body heat, but it was nice all the same.

He opened the album and showed me pictures of his

family. The pictures were old. There was one of Silas and Sarah together. She was beautiful, like him. If I hadn't already known she was older than him, I would have thought they were twins.

Every picture from that point on just got stranger and stranger. In each photo, I could see the changes that come with age, but not on Silas. He was the same in every picture. There was one picture in particular Silas seemed to linger on.

"Is that Maggie?" I asked. The little girl in the picture wore a white Jacquard lace dress with a bow in her dark hair. I was amazed at how much she looked like Leanne at that age.

"Yes, that's her. This was taken on her tenth birthday. I had just planted her magnolia tree. She had told me all she wanted for her birthday was a tree to climb. I planted that tree for her and told her not only could she climb it but it would give her beautiful blooms to enjoy in the summer. I've never been hugged so tight as she hugged me that day." His lips pulled upward in a soft smile that slightly dimpled his cheeks.

"It's so big, though. How on Earth did you get it planted?"

"I'm stronger than an average human, remember?" He laughed. "I found the tree growing wild and spent the whole night digging it up. I loaded it into a wagon and took it to Sarah's house and had it planted before Maggie woke up. She wanted a tree to climb, so I gave her one."

We sat there on the couch, looking through the old photo album at pictures of his family.

Silas was telling me stories of his past and about his family. It was just another piece of evidence Silas was more than he seemed; he was telling the truth. The book contained over 100 years of photographs, and in each one he was unchanging, frozen in time while everyone and everything around him changed.

I listened to his stories and before I knew it, I had dozed off and was fast asleep.

CHAPTER
Twelve

I AWOKE the next morning in a strange bed looking out an unfamiliar, sunlit window. It took a moment to register what had happened and where I was. I had a small panic attack and peeked under the covers. My pants were still on, so that was a good sign. I slapped a hand to my neck checking for any signs of a bite mark. Nothing.

My phone was sitting on the nightstand. I picked it up to check the time. It was early, so I still had plenty of time to get home and get ready for work.

I sat up and stretched.

Silas walked past the door at that moment, and I was startled to see him there. Shirtless, wearing a pair of pajama bottoms, and a towel draped around his neck. He had clearly just gotten out of the shower; his hair was slicked back and wet. He looked like a statue of a Greek God. Perfect, absolutely perfect. Except for the scar right above his heart that marred his chest. It was round and about half the size of my fist.

Silas leaned against the doorframe, his eyes full of want and hunger as he grinned at me. He was looking at me like I was the most beautiful thing he'd ever seen.

He crossed his arms against his muscular chest and said, "Good morning."

He looked flushed and luminous. Did he go out to feed while I was asleep?

My heart began to race, and I looked away.

He walked over and pulled me up off the bed and into his arms.

I tensed, bracing against the smooth, cold planes of his chest.

Silas noticed and held me at arm's length.

"Is everything all right? Did you sleep okay?" he asked, worriedly. He was looking over my face, watching for some kind of sign I might be perturbed.

"I didn't want to wake you last night, so I carried you up here to bed. I hope you're not upset with me."

"No, you're fine; I just need to get home. I have to be at work in a few." I glanced down at my feet, twisting my fingers together, anxiously. I was resisting the urge to step back into his embrace and let my hands wander over his ivory chest.

His wicked smirk crooked up one corner of his mouth. "Call off for the day." He sighed. "Spend it with me. I don't think I'm ready for this to end." He smiled down at me and kissed my forehead.

It was tempting, and it was another chance to get some questions answered. Surely, Jeff would be all right for one day.

I smiled, weakly. "I still need to go home," I told him.

"Okay," he laughed, "give me five minutes."

I watched him go down the hallway and disappear into one of the other bedrooms.

I then took that chance to find the bathroom.

Looking at myself in the mirror, I was shocked at my appearance. My hair was a mess, and my clothes were completely crumpled and wrinkled. I laughed and wondered how Silas kept from cracking up when he saw me.

I freshened up the best I could and did other normal human things. I tried to smooth out my hair and began thinking back over last night.

I contemplated my reflection in the mirror and soon found myself daydreaming, remembering the easy way Silas laughed, the gentleness in his eyes when he spoke of his niece, and just the thought of us together and the kiss we shared.

I smiled to myself, shook my head in disbelief, and washed my hands.

As I was drying my hands on the bathroom towel, I noticed Silas's clothes in the hamper. The shirt he was wearing last night was on top, and there seemed to be something on the collar.

I picked it up and held it out in front of me. The stain was already dry, and it was a dark, rusty brownish red color. There was only a spot or two, and I knew instantly what it was.

I quickly dropped the shirt back into the hamper and tried to push what I had just seen out of my mind, not wanting to let it ruin the daydream.

I rushed out of the bathroom and found Silas waiting for me by the stairs. I tried to compose myself the best I could and gave him another weak smile. He was wearing a dark pair of jeans and a rugged-looking pair of boots. His fitted T-shirt clung to him in all the right ways. It was dark green and made his eyes look brighter.

He smiled at me, but his smile faltered when he saw my face. "Are you okay? You look like you've seen a ghost."

I was holding my breath and let it all out in one exhalation. I nodded and smiled brighter.

He quizzically raised an eyebrow at me, turned, and went down the stairs.

I followed him down and out the door.

We got in his truck, and we were off.

We didn't talk much on the way to my house, but there were a few stolen glances, and Silas insisted on holding my hand the whole way.

———

When we arrived in my driveway, I disentangled our fingers and ran inside to change.

I pulled my hair back into a ponytail, washed my face, and brushed my teeth. The whole time thinking about what we would do today and trying hard not to think about the stain on his shirt.

Silas was waiting for me on the porch. "I thought I would take you to Lulu's for breakfast." He looked me over, appraisingly. He smiled, apparently liking what he saw.

I made a face and said, "Do you think that's a good idea?"

"It's an excellent idea. I can't have Leanne thinking she's successfully sabotaged our evening." He winked and held his hand out to me.

I laughed placing my hand in his. "True, I guess not."

———

We arrived at Lulu's just after the breakfast rush. There were still a few customers inside, and they all turned to stare at us when we walked in.

Silas took my hand and led me to the first available booth away from everyone else.

I tried slouching in the seat and hiding behind my menu to get away from their stares.

"Why are they staring?" I asked under my breath.

Silas was getting a kick out of the attention. "I think they're staring at me; I am the new, handsome stranger in town preying on the innocent and sweet bookshop owner, after all."

He leaned back in his seat and sat a little straighter. He grinned at me. "I hear the whispers."

Before I had time to react, Leanne walked over, practically fuming. "What are you doing here?" she hissed at Silas.

"My lovely Dani needed breakfast, so I brought her to the best joint in town." Silas was being smug.

"*Your* Dani?" Leanne was glaring at him. "What do you mean *your* Dani?"

She turned to me. "What does he mean?" she snapped.

"He's trying to rile you up, Leanne. Can we talk about this later? I really am hungry." I tried changing the subject.

Leanne huffed and took out her pad and pen. "What do you want?" She only directed the question at me.

"I'll take the strawberry stack, please, and a coffee."

Leanne wrote that down and started to walk away, but Silas stopped her, placing his cold white hand on her tanned arm.

She looked down at his hand as if it were something disgustingly slimy and revolting.

"Make that two coffees, dear cousin. Nothing to eat for me, I've already eaten." His voice was rife with mockery.

Leanne turned her seething gaze on me and raked me over with her eyes.

"Relax," Silas said, coolly. "I had my breakfast elsewhere."

She curled her lip at him, menacingly, and walked away.

"Take it easy on her," I admonished him.

"She should take it easy on me. I haven't done anything." He spread his hands wide across the table.

"I know she battles with her duties and with what I am, but if she's going to dish it out, then she better be able to take it in return." He was trying not to laugh.

I rolled my eyes. "You should turn the other cheek."

"Believe me, I'm all out of cheeks. The only ones I have left I'm sitting on, and I'm sure she'd love to kick those."

Leanne arrived a few moments later with our order, and I dug in. My pancakes looked delicious. They were stacked high with lots of strawberry syrup that flowed over the top of the pancakes in sticky red rivers to pool in crimson puddles on the plate. The whole thing was topped off with mounds of whipped cream and freshly sliced strawberries.

Silas sat smiling with his hands wrapped around his coffee mug and watched me eat.

"What?" I asked, licking whipped cream off my fork.

"Nothing." Silas smiled. "You really seem to be enjoying that." He took a sip of his coffee.

"I was hungry." I shrugged. "And, yeah, it's good; Lulu's has the best pancakes."

"Oh, I have no doubts about that." Silas reached across the table and wiped whipped cream off the corner of my mouth, letting his thumb linger on my lip a little too long, and laughed.

I could feel Leanne's murderous glare from across the diner. I tried to ignore it. "What can I say? I love to eat."

"I can relate," Silas said, unapologetically licking away the whipped cream from his thumb.

I blanched, but recovered quickly. It didn't go unnoticed.

"You have nothing to fear from me. You know that, don't you?"

"I want to believe it, but you said yourself it's like keeping a tiger as a pet, and you admitted to wanting to have me for dinner." I shrugged and popped the last red strawberry into my mouth.

He smiled widely in a toothy grin and then finished his coffee. "Are you ready to leave? I have something planned for us today."

"Sure, I'm ready when you are."

Silas retrieved his wallet and slid some money under my plate.

I looked at him, questionably.

"Don't worry, it's more than enough to cover it." He grinned.

We left without saying our farewells to Leanne.

Leaving Lulu's parking lot, we headed outside of town.

———

Silas turned down a gravel, one-lane road and stopped in front of an old church. It was small and white with multicolored stained-glass windows and red double doors. The steeple stood tall and proud and even had a bell inside it. The historical marker out front stated it was called Oak Chapel Church of God and had been established during the mid-1800s. The cemetery next to it was where many of Ophidian Grove's early inhabitants had been laid to rest.

We parked next to the marker, and he led me through the cemetery gates.

"Wait, can you even go in? Isn't this consecrated ground, or whatever?" I had stopped just outside the gate.

Silas smiled and gave a small laugh. "I can. Another myth created by authors and the like."

With that, he lithely stepped through the gate and turned to face me with an ostentatious bow. "See, I didn't burst into flames."

He held out his hand to me, and I took it.

We began walking amongst the older graves. The old tombstones jutted up from the ground like broken teeth in the shadows of the old oak and hickory trees.

A fenced off section of the cemetery came into view. It was surrounded by a low stone wall, and the sunlight filtered through the trees, hitting the small group of headstones with gossamer-like beams.

"It's a family plot."

He opened the gate, and we entered.

"My immediate family is all buried here." He began pointing out their graves.

"My mother and father, my sister, Sarah, and her husband. Even Maggie and her husband are buried here. My brother should have been buried here, but his body was never found after the hurricane. My parents placed a tombstone here for him, anyway."

I counted them as he spoke and noticed an extra grave. "Who is that?"

Silas placed his hands in his pockets and looked over to where I was pointing. "That one is mine," he said in a hushed voice.

We walked over to it, and sure enough it read, *Silas Matthew Quinn April 21st, 1863 - July 15th, 1898, Beloved son and brother*.

"But why? I mean, you're still here."

"It was all part of my mother's plan. There's nobody in the grave, of course, just an empty coffin. I think it also gave my mother some closure. Even though I'm still here, I'm not exactly the same. Sure, I'm still her son, but not really."

I leaned against the fence and watched Silas meticulously take care of the graves.

He brushed away dirt and grass and pulled the tall weeds that had grown up around the headstones.

Looking around, I noticed several patches of wildflowers growing nearby.

Leaving him to his work, I picked an armful. I gathered the flowers into three smaller bundles and bound them with long blades of grass to make small bouquets.

I walked slowly to Silas's mother's headstone and placed one on the ground in front of it. I could feel Silas watching me as I placed the other two on Sarah's and Maggie's graves.

When I stood up, Silas walked over and took my hand.

"Thank you," he said. It was almost a whisper. He seemed touched by my gesture.

I smiled up at him and leaned my head on his shoulder. "You're welcome." I squeezed his cold hand. "Missing them must be so hard for you. I know I miss my parents every day. I feel so out of place without them sometimes. I can't imagine having to deal with that ache for as long as you have."

"You get numb to it after a while. It's all part of the gig. I'll stay frozen just like this for eternity and watch everyone I know and love grow old and die. After a while, you just learn to manage and find new ways to cope with the loss. I mostly try not to get too close to anyone; it saves on the heartbreak. Of course, I've tried convincing a few people over the years to let me change them, but so far, no takers."

He smiled, darkly, and looked at me. "Not yet, anyway."

I gave him a reproachful look. "Keep trying."

We left the little cemetery and drove back to Silas's house.

―――――

When we arrived, we sat on the porch swing, and I asked him what else he had planned for the day.

"I'm yours for the day, so what do you want to do?"

He gave me that infamous smirk and said, "Oh, I can think of a few things, but you may not agree with them."

"Are you trying to scare me, or tempt me? It's not working, whatever you're doing."

He laughed and took my hand, lacing his icy fingers between mine "Today is ours. We can do whatever you want."

I was quiet; lost in thought. There were still questions I wanted answered, but I wasn't sure how to go about it. I still wasn't sure what exactly it was we were doing. Relationship wise, that is, or if I could trust him completely yet. So far, he hadn't given me any reason to be afraid of him.

The image of the stain on his shirt from this morning came to mind, and I quickly pushed it away.

I drew my legs up beside me on the swing and laid my head on his shoulder, trying my best to forget it.

"This is nice. Let's just do this for a while." It came out stiffer than I wanted it to.

Silas wrapped his arm around me, and we sat there on the swing, enjoying the rest of the morning.

After a while, he withdrew his arm, and I sat up.

"Dani, is something on your mind? You look relaxed, but I can tell your brain is going a thousand miles an hour. I can practically hear it buzzing."

"There's just so much I still want to know, I guess."

"Ask me; I'm not hiding anything."

"It's just so awkward," I mused.

"Let me be the judge of that."

I drew a deep breath and asked, "Did you feed last night after I fell asleep? Where did you go?"

"Ah, I knew this was coming. Yes, I fed last night. I left after making sure you were completely asleep. Being around you, around humans, for an extended amount of time can be difficult. The more satiated I am makes it easier to prolong my time with you."

I noticed he had avoided my other question.

"So by hanging out with you I'm putting people in danger?" I asked, quietly.

"Yes and no. I'm not killing anyone, and my feeding practices are relatively painless. The people I choose wake up feeling a bit groggy and weak, but they do wake up."

"Are you going somewhere outside of town? I haven't heard or noticed anyone saying they've felt weird or bad or anything."

"Yes, I have been feeding on the outskirts of town. That's all I'm going to tell you. I don't need you following me, after all." There was an edge of warning to his voice.

"Duly noted." My mind was racing. Was being with Silas worth the risk? How much was I really endangering other people's lives? Could I live with myself if he took it too far?

"Dani, there's more, isn't there? Go ahead and ask me. Talk to me; I'm an open book today."

"Okay, then. I've noticed on some days your skin and complexion look healthy, glowing and flush, actually. But on others, you've seemed pale, almost gray. Is that a result of how often you feed?"

"Yes, exactly. The more I feed, the more human or healthy I look. Everything about me functions like it should, as long as I'm well-fed."

He grinned. "If I go without, just like you, I grow weaker, and my pallor becomes sickly. I'm also more likely to give in to the bloodlust if I am overly hungry."

"Can you supplement with animals? Or feed only on animals?"

Silas made a face of slight disgust. "I can, and I have, but it's not the same. Animals will do in a pinch, but the taste is lacking and gamey, not to mention the fur gets caught in my teeth." He was watching me to see my reaction.

When I didn't react, he continued. "The act of feeding and the taste of human blood is euphoric. It's an excessive thirst finally quenched. It's intimate and frightening all at once." He licked his lips and closed his eyes. Was he fighting an urge right now?

I kept him going. "But how does it work? I mean, what happens to you?"

He was quiet, thinking of how best to answer. "I change. My face contorts to make room for my fangs, and my eyes transform. You've already witnessed the eyes. I choose where I want to bite, and I feed. I can control my venom, allowing just enough to incapacitate or I can do without, relying on my strength to subdue someone long enough. I don't often do that, though, because it makes things more difficult for both of us."

I swallowed, hard. Shakily, I asked, "Where do you bite?"

Silas sat up a little straighter and smiled, playfully.

He leaned in closer to me, his lips parted, and he brought his hand to my throat.

Silas began lightly tracing my neck with a cool finger. His face was close enough for me to feel his cool breath on my skin.

"This is the most efficient spot."

He bent his head to my neck and kissed it, I could feel his lips part as he lightly trailed kisses up and down my throat, allowing his tongue to delicately graze my skin in places.

My heart began to race.

He then picked up my arm, one hand under my elbow and the other under my wrist.

Silas slowly turned my palm upward and exposed my wrist. The blue veins visible beneath my thin white skin. "

This spot will do, but the flow isn't as quick; it's not one of my go-tos." He brought my wrist to his lips and kissed it, as well, inhaling deeply.

He placed my hand upon my thigh and continued. "Then, there is this one."

He moved his hand just above my inner thigh and ran his finger along the top and then down, stopping at my knee.

I shivered, and he turned his face up to mine; his eyes were wild with hunger. The green of his irises had swallowed all the white of his eyes, and his pupils were reduced to snakelike slits.

Silas came even closer, bringing his forehead to rest on mine. He inhaled, raggedly, and brought his hand up to caress my cheek.

His cold fingers were tracing my jaw line.

Then, he brought his hand to rest at the nape of my neck.

I was frozen.

His eyes fell to my mouth before he whispered, "I crave you, all of you Dani. Your mind, your heart, your thoughts. I crave the way your hair falls through my fingers, how your eyes light up when you see something you love. I crave your scent when your'e not around. You fill my thoughts more than anything else."

Silas met my eyes, they were still snakelike and on fire with an intensity I had never seen.

"I want to keep you, to have you, to make you mine." His voice was throaty and low.

My heart leapt into my throat, and I tried to swallow it down, but I couldn't. I knew he was no longer talking about feeding. We were way past that now. This was moving so fast, but deep down I felt the same. Silas also filled my thoughts and I too craved his presence. I wanted him much more than I had come to realize until this moment.

My mouth parted slightly, and I whispered, "I'm yours."

Silas locked his gaze to mine.

I couldn't move.

He chuckled; it was breathy and deep. He licked his lips again and brought them closer to mine and then kissed me deeply.

I had never felt so scared and so alive as I did in that moment.

I melted into the kiss, and soon the fear and the thoughts of danger went away. Isn't this exactly what I wanted? He *was* romance and adventure. He was an escape from my reality. I realized I was falling hard for him. I was his. It didn't matter to me what Silas was or had been. To hell with the risks; this was what I wanted. Silas was what I wanted.

CHAPTER
Thirteen

THE REST of the summer went by in a blur. Silas and I had become closer than ever. The fall started to show signs of an early arrival. Things were going great. Leanne and Silas had seemed to come to some sort of amiable agreement and were being civil to one another. Leanne had even gone so far as to say she thought I was good for him and she had never seen the softer side he exhibited with me. Silas and Jeff were even getting along. Jeff had told me he was glad to see me happy and he actually liked Silas once he gave him a chance.

It all seemed too comfortable. I kept waiting for the other shoe to drop. I had come to terms with what Silas was and what he needed to survive. I had accepted it and trusted him not to make the ultimate mistake and take someone's life. I had also accepted the fact he was not going to show me his fangs or his feeding habits, not even if I offered myself for the taking, which, of course, I did. That upset him, but not too much. He almost took me up on it but changed his mind, saying it would scare me away, and he wasn't risking that.

We were watching the sunset on the hill, when I addressed him. "Silas?"

"Hmm?" He was absentmindedly playing with my hair

while I laid my head on his chest. We were in the bed of his truck. He had placed blankets and pillows in it so we could enjoy the sunset in comfort. The sky was alive with color as the sun sank lower on the horizon.

"I was thinking."

"Dangerous pastime, you know." I could hear the smile in his voice.

"What if you didn't have to leave to feed?"

"I'm not sure I follow, and if I am following correctly, I'm not sure I like it." He had stopped running his fingers through my hair and had become deathly still.

"But go on," he said.

"Well, I mean, it makes sense, doesn't it?" I sat up, releasing myself from his arms and looking at him.

"What does?" he asked, cautiously.

"Why couldn't you feed on me? You've said yourself you've had willing dinner dates."

Silas laughed at my choice of words. "That's true, but I've always made them forget. I can't, and won't, do that to you."

"I'm not naïve; I know you've had human lovers and relationships. Did you ever feed on them?"

Silas looked serious for a moment before replying. "You're right. I haven't exactly been chaste in the many years I've been a vampire, but the relationships I've had were never long and never serious. I always made them remember something different, or forget me entirely. They never recalled what I did to them."

He brought a hand to my face and cupped my cheek. "Dani, I don't think you know what you're asking."

"Don't I?" I challenged him. "You told me feeding was an intimate act. Why wouldn't you want to share that with me, if I'm willing?"

Silas sighed and ran his hand through his hair, pushing it back out of his face. "I did tell you that, and yes, it is intimate, but usually only for me. I know I tease you about it often enough, but once I'm ready to bite, to feed, the other person usually becomes rather frightened. I have to bite fast and release my venom to keep them quiet and cooperative. So many humans have romanticized the act they don't truly know what they're getting into. I believe that is what you're doing right now."

He scowled. "Even once they've been immobilized, their fear still causes their hearts to race, and their adrenaline kicks in. But it's not the bite that is the most frightening part. It's my face."

Silas looked away from me and toward the tree line. "I'm not ready to show you that side of me. I don't know I ever will be."

I laid back down beside him with my head on his shoulder.

He brought his arms around me and gave me a little squeeze "But don't think I've never thought about it," he said with a chuckle.

"So you admit you've thought about feeding on me?"

"Always." He was laughing. "I am a vampire, after all, and you're a delicious human." He gave my ribs a tickle.

I pushed his hand away and sat up again. "I'm serious Silas. Let me share this side of you."

He leaned his head back against the rear window of the truck. "No, Dani. Not now, anyway. Maybe not ever."

"What if I were to ask you to change me?" I was becoming sullen.

"Now that's something different entirely, and you know it!" he growled.

I had pushed a button and was toeing the line now.

"Dani, if you asked me to change you, I would in a heartbeat, but only after you've weighed every last choice and considered everything that would change for you. The choice is yours and yours alone. I'll never take that from you."

"But it's my choice to offer to let you feed. Aren't you taking that choice from me?"

"No, I'm not. It's my choice, too, and I'm choosing not to. I'm not talking about this anymore."

I knew the conversation was over, and I also knew better than to push it.

"Look, it's a beautiful night; let's just enjoy what's left of it, okay?" He held his arms out and smiled, but he didn't look into my eyes.

I might have gone too far.

As soon as I laid back down, he kissed the top of my head.

We lay there together, watching the stars come out one by one. The moon shone brightly down upon us with its pale light.

Silas brought his hand to my chin and tilted my face to look at him. "You know I love you, don't you?"

It was the first time he had ever said it.

I was silent, not sure what to do or say next, and then he kissed me.

I answered him without words and met his kiss with a new intensity. I knew he loved me, and I loved him, too.

CHAPTER
Fourteen

"YOU TOLD HIM WHAT?"

Well, now I had gone and done it. Leanne was furious.

"It's not as crazy as it sounds, Leanne. Will you please calm down?"

She was pacing my kitchen, one hand on her hip the other pinching the bridge of her nose.

"Calm down?" she snorted. "How can I when my best friend has offered herself up for dinner?"

"It makes perfect sense to me." I shrugged. "Just hear me out."

"No, no way! I've let this go on for long enough. You've lost your damn mind if you think I'll let you do this. I should have never gone along with this whole relationship thing you have going on with Silas!"

Leanne stopped pacing and turned to face me. "Do you know the huge risk you'd be taking?"

"I do, but you'll be happy to know he declined my offer."

"At least one of you has some freaking sense. I never thought it would be him, though."

She sat down across from me and let out a frustrated sigh.

"Why, Dani? Why would you put yourself in peril like that? If he lost control..."

She turned away from me.

"I just thought if he fed from me that's less people he needs to hurt."

"Do you even hear yourself? You can't trust him with something like that! It's a fine line between life and death when a vampire feeds. It would be so easy to slip. He doesn't know his victims when he chooses them, so if he hurts them badly, he doesn't really care. He just needs to leave them alive."

Our conversation was not going well, and I knew deep down it wasn't going to, but I had to talk to Leanne about it. If anyone were going to tell me the truth, the whole truth, it was her.

"Silas admitted to feeding on past lovers during their relationships. Why am I any different?" I had to know.

"Past relationships? Lovers? That's rich! He's had flings, Dani. I've never known him to keep a girl around longer than a day or so, a few weeks at most."

"Oh."

"Damn right, 'Oh.' You are not dinner, and that's final!"

Leanne reached across the table and grabbed my hand. "I know you care for him, and I can see he cares for you, too, believe it or not. But this is one thing Silas and I can agree on. The risk is too high and far outweighs the benefits."

We sat together, lost in our own thoughts for a moment.

I needed something to do before asking my next question, so I got up from the table, went into the kitchen, and grabbed a Coke from the fridge.

I cracked it open and took a long drink before asking, "Have you ever seen him feed?"

Leanne looked at me, but she didn't seem surprised by my question. In fact, it almost seemed like she was expecting it.

"Once," she said, "and I hope to never witness anything that horrifying again."

"Will you tell me about it?" I sat down next to her and hoped she would be willing to share.

"I've never talked about it. I'm not even sure Silas knows I saw him. If he does, he's never mentioned it."

She crossed her arms over her body, almost hugging herself, as she began telling me what she saw. "It was several years ago. Silas had dropped into Lulu's to see me. We spoke, and he left. It was almost closing time, so no one was in the diner. I was doing my rounds before closing for the night. I had some trash to take to the dumpster out back. I thought Silas was gone, but I thought wrong. I stepped to the door and saw him through the window in the back door. It was terrible, Dani."

She hesitated and looked me in the eye. Her own eyes were brimming with tears. "He had hold of a young woman who had been in the diner just moments before. He was behind her and had one arm around her. He looked like he was speaking in her ear, and then he moved her hair to the side, and his face changed. It distorted. His lips stretched thin over his gums, and two huge fangs lowered out of his upper jaw.

"He sank those awful things into her neck, and she went limp. I was too shocked and scared to move, but I couldn't look away. A few moments later, he lifted his face from her neck, his fangs dripping with blood, his lips and chin were stained red. Silas's features changed back, and he turned the girl around to face him. He said something softly to her. She nodded, got into her car, and drove away."

A tear had managed to escape and slipped down Leanne's cheek. "Just the thought of him doing that to you..."

I leaned forward and hugged her.

She reciprocated, fiercely.

"I'll drop it, Leanne. I had no idea; I'm sorry." I held on to my friend and let her cry. I don't think I had ever fully thought about what it meant to be with Silas. In fact, I know I hadn't. Was it selfish of me to continue seeing him? I clearly had a lot to think about.

CHAPTER
Fifteen

I HAD LET the feeding issue drop. I didn't bring it up again, and everyone seemed the better for it. I still couldn't let it go for myself, though. Silas was having to feed almost every night, every other night, at the least. How was he not getting caught, and how was he finding enough people to feed upon? If he weren't careful, a new vampire beast legend would soon be born. Something would have to give sooner or later.

I feared he had stayed too long in Ophidian Grove. People were starting to notice him, recognize him, even. Others might not have known him, but they knew me, and Silas was almost always around wherever I was anymore. Not that I cared, but I was concerned for his safety, for his secret.

"You're worried about me?" Silas gave me a sideways glance.

"Yes, I am. Is that so bad?"

He reached over and patted my leg. "No," he laughed. "It's not a bad thing; it's nice."

"Don't patronize me!" I said, crossing my arms.

"I'm not." He was trying so hard not to laugh; he was biting his lip.

"You are! You can't even keep a straight face!"

Silas laughed at me, and I turned in my seat to glare at him.

"You're cute when you're mad, you know that? Your nostrils do this little quiver and flare thing. It reminds me of a bunny."

He tapped the end of my nose, and I tried to swat his hand away.

"I don't understand why this is funny. A girlfriend can be concerned for her boyfriend." I was beginning to sulk.

Silas hugged me, and I tried to resist, but I ended up relaxing into it. He kissed me, gently, and said, "You're so much more to me than just a girlfriend."

"I know, which is why I have every right to be concerned about you." He wasn't going to get out of this so easily.

Silas threw his head back and laughed. "Look, I'll hear you out, okay? Let's just get going and you can express your concerns on the way."

Silas was taking me out on his boat today. He had planned a whole day just cruising the sound along nearby Shackleford Banks. I had packed a cooler with snacks and drinks for me and a bottle of wine for us to share.

"Fine!" I tried to act angry, but the promise of having a whole day on the water with Silas took that away.

"Okay, then." He smiled. "Let's go."

We had barely gotten out of my driveway before I started in on him. "We have to figure something else out for you. I'm scared to death you're going to get caught."

"Dani, I have over a century of practice. I think I know what I'm doing."

"Yes, but when was the last time you hung around this long?"

"It's been a while, but I never really had a reason to stay before."

He looked at me and smiled. "I've stayed in other places for a year or so, sometimes longer. I've always stuck to larger cities, though. It's easier to disappear and go unnoticed. I can be quite the recluse when I want to be."

He laughed. "People tend to notice more in small towns, unfortunately."

"And you've never stirred suspicion before? You're always that careful?" I was skeptical.

"Not that I'm aware of. I can usually read the room, so to speak. I know when I've worn out my welcome."

"So what happens when that day comes while you're here?"

I couldn't look at him. I stared at my hands in my lap. "What happens when someone in this small town notices something's off?"

He didn't answer me. His grip tightened on the steering wheel, and his brow furrowed.

"We'll cross that bridge when we get there." His mood had darkened, and he was quiet again.

I left him alone after that; I didn't want to push it.

———

We were quiet for the rest of the ride to the marina. I could tell Silas was mulling over something in his mind. I guess we both had a lot to think about. There was a new tension between us, with so many unspoken thoughts and fears.

What were we going to do when it came time for Silas to leave before he roused suspicion? I had never really thought about it until now; and now it was at the forefront of my mind. *How do we make this work? Do we make it work or call it quits? It's been fun, see you later, goodbye? He is perpetually thirty-five; I am not.* There weren't very many options here. The obvious, and by far the heaviest one, was allowing him to change me. Could I do it? Did I want to?

"We're here," Silas said, quietly.

He parked the truck, and we both got out.

There seemed to be a dark cloud hanging over him despite the sunny September day. A gentle breeze stirred the waters of the marina, making the boats rock languidly in their slips. Gulls floated on the breeze, looking for an easy meal.

The fresh ocean air seemed to clear my mind, and I inhaled the salty scent deeply and took Silas's hand.

He looked down at my hand in his and then brought it to his mouth and kissed it. "I love you," he said.

"I know." I smiled and leaned into him. "Now, are you taking me on a boat ride, or are we just going to stand here?"

Silas's mood lifted, and he gave my hand a squeeze. "The boat is down here."

He bent down and picked up the cooler, and I followed him down the dock past the slips filled with yachts, fishing boats, and other vessels.

We finally stopped in front of a small, but beautiful, cabin cruiser boat.

"This is us." He was smiling now.

He stepped lightly onto the boat and offered his hand to help me aboard.

I sat down in one of the seats behind the cockpit while Silas prepared the boat to leave. The interior of the boat was stunning. It had white upholstered seats, lounging areas fore and aft, teak decking, and there was even an entrance to what I assumed was a cabin below deck.

"Silas, this is beautiful," I said, taking it all in.

"Thank you. I had it brought out of storage for today. There's a refrigerator below deck; I'll put your drinks and things in there."

"Oh, fancy." I smiled.

Silas took the cooler below deck and then did one more walk through before untying the boat.

He took the controls and expertly backed us out of the slip entering the waters of the sound.

Once we were well past the marina, Silas picked up the pace, and we headed toward Shackleford Banks.

I noticed as we neared Shackleford Banks Silas glanced wistfully toward it.

"Have you ever gone back to where Diamond City once stood?" I asked.

He answered me, woefully. "Not for a very long time. There's nothing really left for me there but ghosts."

I didn't ask any more about it. I let the silence speak and turned my attention back to the water.

The breeze whipped my hair around my face. I lowered my sunglasses and leaned my head back, face upturned, and soaked it all up.

The boat took the gentle waves with ease as we cut across them, sending up the sea spray into the air and misting us in the salt water.

I pushed my sunglasses up on top of my head and watched Silas. He seemed so at home behind the controls of the boat. He had lowered his dark aviator glasses, his pale linen shirt was unbuttoned and billowed behind him in the breeze, his bare chest exposed to the salty air. The water was calm today, and the boat handled it like a dream. The turquoise water surrounded us on all sides.

We began to slow down and were coming to a stop just along the shoreline of Shackleford Banks.

We found a beach that was less crowded, and Silas dropped anchor just off shore.

He stood on the prow, turned back to me, and smiled.

"Are you ready to swim?" he asked as he removed his shirt. Silas didn't even wait for me to answer. He jumped off the front of the boat and into the water below.

I got up from my seat and went to the front, looking over the side to find him. He was bobbing in the waves and smiled up at me.

"Toss me our stuff and I'll take it to shore."

I tossed him a bag with our towels and other things inside.

He caught it easily, holding it above the water.

I watched as he waded the short distance to shore.

He placed the bag on the beach, returned to the water, and swam back to meet me.

I was removing my shorts and my tank top to reveal my swimsuit beneath. I could feel Silas watching me and became self-conscious for some unknown reason.

"Why are you watching me?" I laughed.

"Why wouldn't I?" he said, playfully. "Hurry up and get in here."

I placed my clothes neatly under the seats of the cockpit and then jumped in. The water was cool and pleasant.

We swam to shore, but not without playing in the waves for a bit first.

Silas took my hand, and we got out of the water.

"Would you like a tour?" he asked.

I had visited Shackleford Banks before and knew what was there, but this was my chance to hear about it from someone who had been here when it was the small settlement called Diamond City.

I nodded, and Silas grinned.

I then removed our shoes from the bag, and we put them on before beginning our walk.

He began pointing out different places along the barrier island and telling me what once stood there. He regaled me with stories from his past as we walked along, telling me stories of growing up on the island, fishing with his father and his brother, and about life in general there.

His mood turned melancholy as we neared the end of our walk.

———

Silas and I turned around and headed back toward where the boat was anchored. We found a sprawling live oak tree, spread out our beach towels, and sat down in the shade of its branches.

The sand was warm, and I buried my toes in it, hugging my knees to my chest and resting my head on top of them.

Silas put his arm around me; his cool skin felt good against my sun-warmed shoulders.

I marveled at how his skin was still ice cold despite spending all day in the sun. Goosebumps started to rise on my arms, with the combination of Silas's cool skin against me and the breeze blowing in from the ocean.

He noticed, of course, and began to pull away.

"Don't," I said, quickly, and grabbed at his hand before he had the chance to pull his arm completely from around my shoulders.

He smiled, sadly. "But I'm making you cold."

"I'm all right, promise." I scooched over closer and pulled his arm back around me, holding onto his hand, tightly.

Silas sighed and looked out over the water. "That is one thing I've never grown accustomed to."

"What's that?" I asked.

"Being cold all the time. The cursed cold chill of death on my skin is a constant reminder I'm no longer a living being."

I wasn't sure what to say; he often rendered me speechless with revelations like that.

We sat quietly, watching the waves lick the sand while the seagulls and the sandpipers scurried along, looking for whatever the waves washed up. Off in the distance, the sky was beginning to gray with clouds.

Silas picked up a handful of sand and let it sift through his fingers, watching as the wind blew it away from him at an angle. He looked contemplative and sad.

I could tell it troubled him to be back here, but I was glad to share this with him, nonetheless. I was watching him, admiring the way the sun lit up his green eyes and the way the water sparkled on his skin.

Silas's head snapped to pay attention to something he heard off to his right.

"Shh." He held a finger to his lips. "There's a small herd of horses coming up the dunes over there."

He pointed to the direction they would be coming from, and sure enough, a small group of about six horses came up to the beach. They were sniffing the air and grazing on the coastal grasses and sea oats. They were all colors from dark russet browns, to gray, and black, and copper. They were beautiful.

Suddenly, the wind shifted, and one of the horses caught a scent of something she didn't like.

Her head shot up, and she snorted. The little mare turned and trotted toward the other horses tossing her head, pinning her ears, and nipping at their flanks to get them moving.

She moved to the head of the herd, and they galloped away from us down the beach, tails held high and streaming behind them.

"I wonder what got into them."

"They caught my scent," Silas said, sadly. "Animals recognize me for what I am, a predator."

"Oh," I said, dumbly. How was I supposed to respond to that?

I could feel the tension growing between us again. Something was changing, and I was pretty sure I knew what was coming.

"Dani, I've been meaning to talk to you. I've tried putting it off, but I don't think I can any longer."

"I think I know what you're going to say, and yeah, it's a conversation that's been a long time coming." I exhaled and prepared myself for the blow.

A rumble of thunder rolled in the distance. "We better

move this conversation back to the boat before we get rained on."

We swam back to the boat and sat together on the bench seat behind the cockpit with an oversized beach towel wrapped around us while the wind and the waves gently rocked the boat.

"You know my time here is limited. I can't stay here long before people start to notice I'm not aging or before I—"

"Don't finish that thought. I know feeding will become difficult for you." I sighed heavily, "I also know we can't keep this up."

We both sat there, looking out over the water, watching the rain roll in, and gathering our thoughts.

Silas went first. "The way I see it, there are only a few options."

"Which are? Because I only see two."

Silas smiled. "Ever the optimist, aren't you? Option one would be you come with me when I leave. We could travel, see places you've always wanted to see, and you'll always have the choice to come back home."

"Option two?" I asked.

"Option two is we try the long-distance thing. We could pick a destination to meet, and I would fly you there. We would spend some time together and then you go back home without me."

I thought for a moment about both options; there was something wrong with both. I come home without him, or I lose him to my old age and eventually my death.

"So what happens after ten years, fifteen, or twenty? When I'm old and gray and you still look young and gorgeous?"

He laughed, "You're still you, and I definitely don't mind dating a cougar."

He winked at me, and we both laughed, but the tension was still there. There was still that third and final option.

"What about option three?" I asked, nervously.

"Oh, well, option three is the most final." Silas wasn't joking anymore. In fact, he had become quite serious.

We looked at each other, and he said, "I change you."

But at the same time, I had said, "We break up."

"What?" we said in unison. We were both looking at each other like the other one was an alien.

Silas was visibly upset. "How could you go there? Why would you go there? I just told you I don't care if you age; I love you."

"So you won't mind watching me get older and eventually shrivel up and die? I just can't do that." I shook my head, vehemently. "I won't do that."

"That's your choice; it won't be easy, but I don't want to go with the nuclear option. We have time; we don't have to decide tonight. But personally, I like my option three the best." He gave me the smirk.

"How is that better?" I asked.

"It is for me!" He laughed. "I'm a selfish being, Dani. Changing you would be the answer to all my prayers. I would never be alone again."

He reached up and placed his hand on my cheek, and I leaned into it.

"Nothing would make me happier than to spend eternity with you, but ultimately, that is your decision. I'll never make that decision for you. I'll stand by you, no matter if you stay human or want to be immortal. Don't decide now, not tomorrow, or the next day, but take me up on my other options. Go away with me or come find me."

Silas looked up at me through his dark lashes. His hair had fallen into his face.

I reached forward and lifted his face from the stooped position he was sitting in and pushed his hair out of his eyes. "No decisions tonight," I whispered.

"No decisions tonight," he repeated.

The sky opened up around us and began to pelt us and the boat with a driving rain.

We were oblivious to it. We came together in a passionate kiss.

Silas stood us up and then led me below deck to the cabin beneath.

It was small and cozy, with a tiny galley kitchen, an even smaller seating area, and a large bed toward one end of the cabin. The bed was made up with crisp white linens.

I didn't have much time to look around before Silas pulled me close to him. He wound his hands around my back and pulled me in tight, resting his cool forehead against mine. His eyes were intense and troubled.

"Dani," his voice was barely more than a whisper, "I made up my mind about you long ago. That first night you agreed to go with me to watch the sunset, in fact."

His hand caressed my face, and he stared longingly into my eyes. A fresh new desire written in them. "I've seen thousands of beautiful sunsets, and you have eclipsed them all."

I was dumbstruck.

Silas's hands shifted, and he placed one on the small of my back; the chill of his fingers sent shivers through me. His other hand slowly slid down my face and then found the nape of my neck.

He twisted his fingers into my hair, and I raised my face to meet his.

My breath hitched as my hands found their way to his face and his neck.

I moved my fingers through his hair, and he began slowly running his hands over me, letting his fingers trail lightly over my skin, like he needed the touch of my skin just to survive.

He found the strings of my bathing suit top and untied them, letting it fall to the floor.

He pulled me in tight, crushing me against him. The skin

to skin contact was pure ecstasy. His coolness to my warmth sent waves of pleasure through me and raised the goose-bumps on my flesh. Silas's chest rumbled with a low moan that sounded almost like a growl, and he kissed me harder, letting his tongue wash over mine in icy delicious strokes. He began pushing me back gently and never breaking the kiss until we were inches from the bed.

That kiss was different than any other we had shared before. There was desperation in this kiss; it was a kiss that said, *I need you; I want you. I never want to let you go.* It said all the unspoken words between us.

Our lips only parted long enough for him to lay me down in the white linen sheets of the bed.

CHAPTER
Sixteen

LIFE SEEMINGLY WENT BACK to normal after our day at the Banks. There was a general unease in our relationship, however. I thought everything was going to come to an end, and Silas was being weird and overly protective. I noticed a change in some of the locals, as well. People were becoming jumpy, and the other day, I could have sworn I saw a customer in the bookstore with two marks that looked suspiciously like fang or bite marks. I pushed it out of my mind and blamed it on my own paranoia Silas was going to disappear at any moment. But mostly the options he had given me loomed heavily over my head. Which should I choose, and how could I be sure I was making the right choice?

The thought of leaving everything behind for a while and traveling with Silas was appealing. But it still left me with the decision to stay, leave, or change. Going away with Silas was only temporary, so was my second option of trying a long-distance relationship. And let's face it, those rarely work out. It seems there were only two true options left for me: break up, or allow him to change me.

How long could I truly ride this out before making a final

decision? Could I honestly stand to break both our hearts by ending what we have? On the other hand, could I stand to leave everything and everyone I know and love behind to start an immortal life with Silas? I was in turmoil, and I didn't have anyone to talk to about it.

I had just arrived home after working at the bookstore, when I spotted Silas, waiting for me on the front porch. That was a first; he usually waited for me to call him before coming over.

He got up from the rocker, hastily shoved something into his pocket, and then met me at the stairs with a smile. "Welcome home," he said, hugging me.

I buried my face into his chest and took in his scent, breathing deeply.

He hugged me tighter and kissed the top of my head.

"Thanks." My voice was muffled from being pressed against him.

He went to let go, and I wrapped my arms around him tightly. "Not yet."

Silas chuckled. "Not yet."

We stood like that for several moments before I finally let go.

"Is everything okay? You seem rather pensive this evening." Silas's brow was furrowed in concern.

"I've just got a lot on my plate, that's all." I kissed him, quickly, and went to the door. "Speaking of plates, I'm starving."

Silas put his hands in his pockets and leaned against the porch railing. "You're in luck, because I brought you dinner." He had that Cheshire Cat grin going on, and it lifted my spirits.

"Giving up on cooking?" I teased.

"Indeed. I stopped by Lulu's and had Leanne bag something up for you."

"Sounds amazing. Let me freshen up."

I ran up the stairs to my room to change out of my work clothes.

I heard Silas locking the door behind him. That was odd, he'd never bothered with that before.

I shrugged it off and went about my normal after-work routine. This was what I wanted, more days like this. Just a normal life and normal everyday living. But was that even possible with Silas?

I entered the kitchen, and he met me with a smile. His forest green eyes were twinkling, and his complexion was flush and healthy. He truly was beautiful, and he was mine. Could I give him up? Did I want to? No, I did not. Not now, maybe never. Turns out, I can be selfish, too.

The smell of the food was amazing, and my stomach began to growl.

Silas pulled out a chair and gestured for me to sit. "Here, let me serve you."

"Will I be expected to tip?" I taunted him.

Silas gave me his award-winning smirk and said, "Definitely."

He grabbed a takeout container from the bag and placed it in front of me and opened it with a flourish. I giggled and grabbed a fry and began nibbling as I watched him walk over to the fridge and retrieve a drink.

"A strawberry shake to wash down your burger and fries, madam."

"Mmm, my favorite." I smiled, broadly, at him.

"I know." He bent down and popped a kiss on my cheek.

Silas then walked over and took out the chair opposite from me and sat down while I ate.

After a few moments he said, "Come away with me."

I choked on my milkshake.

Coughing, I spluttered. "What?"

"Come away with me," he repeated.

I wiped my mouth and pushed the takeout container away from me. "Silas, I—"

He didn't let me finish. "Don't talk; just listen," he pleaded. "We both know I can't continue to stay here for long, but I can stay long enough for you to get your affairs in order. I'll help you."

He smiled. "Promote Jeff to general manager of the bookstore; he knows how to run things, and let him hire a new employee. Leanne can keep an eye on your place. Think about it, Dani. We can go anywhere. Take the boat up the coast or go west to see the mountains you love. The sky is the limit. Just go away with me for a year; stay with me. Please." If Silas could have cried, I believe his eyes would have been filled with tears.

"Silas, I don't know," I stammered.

"It's okay; just think about it. You don't have to answer me tonight. All you have to do tonight is finish your dinner and tell me all the places you'd love to visit." He reached across the table and placed his hand over mine.

"I can do that." I smiled.

I thoughtfully chewed my food and pondered all the places I'd love to see. "I'd love to go west and see more of the mountains or maybe go to the West Coast and see what the beaches are like out there."

Silas gave me a benevolent smile and said, "We can do that. The Rockies, the Tetons, Denali, all of them. I'll take you whale watching in Washington and sunbathing in Malibu. There's so much to see, Dani, and I can't wait to show you."

"So much to see and so little time to do it," I said, quietly.

"Not necessarily." Silas had a mischievous look in his eyes. "We could have all the time in the world, if you chose my option three."

I sat back in my chair "Is that so? Hmm. Maybe we ought

to travel to Transylvania to find a real and truly scary vampire to do it."

Silas made a show of acting offended. "I'm not scary enough for you? That hurts, Dani." He clutched at his chest and screwed up his face like he was going to cry.

"You're the least scary vampire I know."

"You want scary? I'll give you scary." He sneered at me and leaned on the table over his arms. He bowed his head slightly, and some of his dark hair fell forward across his forehead and his eyes.

He looked up at me through his lashes, and suddenly, his face began to change. First were his eyes; they took on that green snakelike appearance I was so used to by now.

"You're going to have to do better than that," I teased.

Silas laughed, darkly, and I noticed his facial structure had started to change. It was subtle at first, but soon he began to look completely different. He bared his teeth at me, and his lips stretched thin, exposing his teeth and his gums. His cheekbones and his jaw began to contort and lengthen like they were making room for something.

I could hear the muscles and the sinew sliding and stretching wetly over his jaws, as well as popping noises, as it seemed to dislocate and extend. He seemed to be dragging it out for the effect.

I gasped, My eyes widened in shock.

I gripped the table, realizing all that was left was for the fangs to come out. And then as quickly as it started, it was all over.

Silas sat back in his chair, running his hand back through his hair, and his features had returned to normal.

I must have still had a wide-eyed, shocked expression on my face judging by Silas's smirk. My heart was pounding like a terrified bird in a cage, and Silas looked like a cat who was about to pounce.

His smirk changed to a self-satisfied smile.

My brain was trying to make sense of what I had just seen, and it was incomprehensible. This was the first time I had been truly scared of Silas. He had always teased me, and just now he had given me the slightest glimpse of what he really was. But this time, he came dangerously close to showing me the face of what was beneath the beautiful human facade.

CHAPTER
Seventeen

THAT WAS the first time I didn't kiss Silas goodnight. When he went in for the kiss, I ducked my head to the side and offered my cheek instead.

He gave me an odd look but otherwise brushed it off.

"I can stay, if you'd like," he offered. He looked around the yard and out into the street before looking back at me.

I pretended to stifle a yawn. "No, I'm super tired. I think I just want to go to bed. See you tomorrow?"

Silas gave me another odd and injured look. "Okay, see you tomorrow. Lock up tight."

I nodded and didn't wait to see him get in his truck and leave. I went inside, locking the door behind me.

He must have stood on the porch for several moments because it was a while before I heard his truck start up and leave.

My plate was already full, and now it was overflowing. I was still in shock over the display Silas showed me at dinner. I know it was only a glimpse; he still hadn't shown me his fangs. I was so comfortable with him it was easy to forget what he truly was. He was so good at pretending. He was excellent at playing human. I had become complacent. And then there was the matter of him being here before me and letting himself into my house. Not that I cared; I had told him where the key was hidden, after all. But most importantly, I wondered what he had shoved into his pocket so quickly.

I needed time to think. I shouldn't have provoked Silas; it was stupid. Looking back, I'm not sure how playful he was actually being. He had seemed on edge all night. He tried to hide it from me, but I caught the anxious glances he threw out the window every time there was a sound outside. Was he really trying to scare me, or was he finally giving me a glimpse of what he hid so well from me?

I went back to the kitchen to clean up, ruminating over tonight's events.

Maybe he was just preparing me for what I might see if I went away with him. Whatever his reasons were behind the show, it gave me more to think about. I knew he was still holding back, though he said himself he hoped to never show me that side of him. But why hold back? If he truly intended to scare me, he needed to reveal that other side. He couldn't gauge my reaction from tonight; I was unprepared. How do you prepare yourself for something like that, though? It was all too much. I wanted to scream.

"Ugh!" I slammed the takeout container into the garbage can.

"I'm going to bed," I said to no one in particular. Maybe a good night's sleep would make things clearer.

I turned the lights off, headed up to my room, and got ready for bed.

Sleep came surprisingly easy that night, and so did the dreams.

———

I dreamt I was with Silas, and we were somewhere I didn't recognize. It was dark and gothic, like the inside of a medieval castle. There was a large gilded mirror hanging on the wall. Silas approached me and he was wearing a black cutaway morning coat with a red vest and a white collared shirt underneath. Around his neck, he wore a black Ascot knotted sophisticatedly. He also had on a pair of black trousers and some black leather lace up dress boots. He was the epitome of a gothic vampire.

Looking down at myself, I saw I was wearing a crimson ball gown. It had a bustle with a train and was made of taffeta silk. It was trimmed in black lace, and it was gorgeous.

Silas smiled at me and took my hand, leading me over to the mirror.

He stepped behind me and covered my eyes before placing me in front of it.

When he revealed my reflection, I didn't recognize the woman in the mirror. The face was wrong. It was pale, stretched, and contorted. Her teeth were bared, and fangs descended from her upper jaw. I drew my hand up to my mouth, and so did the woman in the mirror.

Silas moved my hair off of my neck and kissed it, revealing two tiny pricks still wet with blood.

I looked back into the face in the mirror to see my own staring back at me.

Silas leaned over my shoulder and whispered into my ear, "You make a beautiful vampire."

———

I woke with a start, grasping at my neck and feeling my face. Nothing had changed; I was safe in my bed.

I reached for my phone, turning the screen on to check the time. It was 3:00 a.m. I flipped through my contacts, searching for one name. I surprised myself at the one person I wanted in that moment.

Finding the number, I hit call.

The phone rang, and it was answered at once.

"Silas, can you please come over?"

CHAPTER
Eighteen

SILAS CAME OVER IN A HURRY; it was almost like he had never left.

He let himself in using the hidden key. All the lights were off in the house, except one, my bedroom.

He rushed up the stairs, calling my name as he went.

"Dani?" His voice was worried and thick with panic. "Dani, are you all right?"

"I'm in here, Silas," I answered.

He stood in the doorway; his brow was furrowed in concern.

Silas seemed hesitant to approach me, until I looked at him. I was sitting on the edge of the bed, clearly disheveled.

When I raised my head to look at him, all hesitation was lost.

He rushed to me.

Kneeling on the floor in front of me, he gathered both of my hands in his. "Dani, you're crying. What's wrong? Did something happen?"

He reached up and wiped the tears away. His fingers leaving cold, wet traces on my face.

"I had an odd dream," I said, tearfully.

"A nightmare?" Silas asked, sounding relieved.

"I don't know what you would call it." I shrugged and exhaled. "It was just odd, beautiful, and disturbing all at once."

Silas got up from the floor and sat next to me on the bed. He placed his hands in his lap, seemingly unsure what to do with them.

"I think I know what triggered that."

He looked at me, but I just hung my head, not wanting to look at him. I was afraid I would see the face from earlier.

"Dani, I'm so sorry." He put his head in his hands. "This is exactly what I was afraid of. I should have never shown you that."

"No, it's okay, Silas. I'm glad you did. I just wasn't prepared. I shouldn't have goaded you into it."

I placed my hand on his knee.

He removed his hands from his face and reached over to take my hand in one of his. "You have nothing to apologize for. I told you I never wanted you to see that side of me. I gave you a glimpse, and now you're having nightmares."

He squeezed his eyes shut and said, remorsefully, "*I* gave you nightmares."

"No, Silas, no you didn't."

He looked up at me with those penetrating green eyes.

And we just sat there, looking at each other, neither of us knowing what to say.

Finally, I leaned forward, placing my forehead against his. "I've had a lot to think about these past few days."

"Do you want to tell me about it? The dream, I mean?" Silas asked, quietly.

I lifted my head from his to see him more clearly. "I dreamt I was like you."

"Oh," he whispered.

"Yeah..." I looked at the floor, not knowing where to take the conversation next.

"Did I...Did I do it?" Silas asked, apprehensively.

"I didn't dream that part. I was already changed. We were dressed in Victorian clothing in a gothic castle, and you placed me in front of a beautiful mirror, and when I looked, my face was changed. It was..." I shook as a cold chill racked my body.

"Monstrous?" he interjected.

I was quiet, and Silas took that as a yes.

He bowed his head.

"You moved my hair, and there were bite marks on my neck fresh with blood." I reached up and rubbed the spot on my neck where the bite was in my dream. "You told me I was a beautiful vampire."

Silas made no attempt at a reply.

After several long minutes, he said, "What was the part that bothered you the most?"

He looked me dead in the eyes, daring me to answer truthfully, but probably hoping I wouldn't.

"I don't know, to be honest," I answered. "I think I'm just so overwhelmed with all of it. Staying, leaving, changing. My brain feels like it's being drawn and quartered."

I hugged myself and leaned forward onto my knees.

Silas placed his hand on my back and began rubbing it in methodical circles. It was soothing.

I relaxed into it and soon found myself leaning into him.

He put his arm around me, and I rested my head on his shoulder.

"Stay with me, please," I murmured.

"Always," Silas answered.

He kicked off his shoes and got into the bed, holding the blankets open for me.

I crawled in and laid my head on his chest.

He put his arms around me, and we lay there in the soft glow of the lamp's light.

"You don't have to carry the weight of any of these decisions by yourself. I will accept whatever you decide," Silas said, stoically.

"Thank you," I whispered against his chest. "I think the thought of changing scares me the most because I'm afraid I'll lose myself. I'm afraid the parts that make me, well, me, will be gone."

Silas didn't hesitate to reply. "You won't. I won't let you. You would still be you, just a little more parched than normal."

He chuckled.

I yawned, and Silas wrapped his arms around me tighter.

"Silas?" I said, sleepily.

"Yes?" he whispered.

"What did you put in your pocket earlier today?"

"Saw that, did you?" He chuckled, lightly. "It was nothing. Just the receipt from Lulu's."

He was lying; there was a slight quaver to his voice.

"Try and get some sleep." He kissed my head and began humming a tune.

It sounded familiar, but I wasn't quite sure. It was nice, though.

He began stroking my arm in time with the song.

Soon enough, I was asleep, but not before I heard him whisper, softly, "You would, you know, make a beautiful vampire."

CHAPTER
Nineteen

I PUT the dream and my fears behind me and decided to focus on the present instead. I was going to get to the bottom of whatever was in Silas's pocket. There was no sense in dwelling on the future of things that might never happen, not when there were new mysteries to solve.

I had chosen to live life day by day and enjoy each one I have with Silas, whether that meant a few more days, or months, or years, or forever. We were both a lot happier this way. I had also chosen to take Silas up on his offer to go away with him and travel. He had been very adamant about getting out of town lately.

"Where shall we go first?" Silas asked. He was still in my bed, sitting up against the pillows with his hands behind his head. He was grinning like he'd just won the lottery.

It had been several weeks since I caught a glimpse of Silas's vampiric face and had the dream, not to mention the whole pocket stuffing incident. I didn't bring any of it up again, and neither did he after a few awkward days.

We easily slid back into our old routine, and it felt great.

Last night, he was over the moon when I told him I had decided to leave with him for a while. He hilariously started rambling off plans and ideas and things to do before leaving. I told him to give me a few months to get things in order at home and with the bookstore and then maybe after the holidays we could start our new adventure. He was determined to get me to leave sooner than that.

I turned to look at Silas, his perfect form so out of place in my bed. I shook my head and laughed at him.

"First, I need to go to work. I have an employee to promote." I walked over to the bed and crawled across it to kiss him goodbye.

Silas grabbed me and, in a flash, he had me pinned to the bed under him.

"That's cheating," I said as he lowered his lips to mine.

"Is not," he mumbled against my lips.

I pushed him off me and got up, straightening my clothes. "Lock the door behind you when you leave, okay?" I said as I ran down the steps.

Silas was following closely behind and stopped me at the door.

He whirled me around to face him and kissed me, longingly.

It was one of those foot popping up in the air movie kisses. It took everything within me to break away.

"I love you," Silas said, stroking my cheek with the back of his hand.

"I love you, too," I answered back, breathlessly.

Silas stepped forward again, wrapping both arms around me and engulfing me in a hug.

I laughed and said, "I really need to go."

He loosened his grip and spun me away from him.

Leaving one arm around my front, he pulled me backward against him and lowered his face to my ear. "Then, you better get going before I change my mind." He opened his mouth and made like he was going to bite me.

I let out a strangled breath, and he released me.

I stumbled out of the door, and he laughingly said, "See you tonight."

I was still flustered, so I just smiled and waved, got into my car and left.

———

Surprisingly, I got to the bookstore before Jeff had arrived.

I was just starting to go through the process of opening up, when he walked in.

"Morning, boss," Jeff said, cheerily.

"Hi, Jeff."

Turning to face him, I saw he had a brown paper bag from Lulu's and two coffees.

"I brought breakfast," he said with a flourish, holding the bag up high and giving it a shake. "Lulu's famous muffins."

"Perfect!" I exclaimed, taking the bag and one of the coffees from him.

"Wait. Are you telling me you, Mr. Jogs-Every-Morning-At-Five-A.M., stopped at Lulu's for muffins?"

I was eyeing him, suspiciously. "Did you skip your protein shake this morning?" I laughed.

Jeff turned beet red and began to stutter. "I, uh, that is to say, I um, just wanted to do something nice." It sounded more like a question than a statement.

"Right." I winked at him, rescuing him from his own embarrassment. "Let's eat these in my office; I have something I want to talk to you about."

"Uh-oh." Jeff's face fell slightly.

"I promise, it's a good thing. C'mon."

We headed to my office, and I pointed to the chair across from my desk. "Have a seat."

I sat down in my chair and opened the bag of muffins. The smell of freshly baked blueberry muffins permeated the air. "My favorite! How did you know?" I asked.

"Just a hunch. Oh, and Leanne might have mentioned it." Jeff was blushing.

"How nice. Thank you, Jeff."

He smiled at me and said, "So you wanted to talk to me about something?"

"Yes, how would you like a promotion?"

"A promotion?" he stuttered. "What do you mean?"

"I mean a promotion." I laughed. "I want to promote you to general manager, and I think we need to hire an additional employee of your choosing."

I waited for a response.

He seemed dumbfounded. "I don't know what to say; this is a surprise!"

"I'll give you a raise, of course, and any additional training you think you need, but you already know the ins and the outs of this place. I can't think of anyone better suited to run it."

"What about you?" he asked.

"I'm going to be taking some time off after the holidays to do some traveling, and I need someone I can completely trust to manage things for me here."

"Oh, well. Okay, then. I mean, if you think I'm the right person for the job." He was beaming.

"I think you're perfect. Do you accept?"

There was no hesitation or second guessing this time. "Yes! 1,000 times yes! Thank you so much! I won't let you down!" he exclaimed. Jeff thrust his hand out and over the desk.

I took it, and we shook on it, heartily.

"I know you won't. Now, let's celebrate over muffins." I handed him one of the giant blueberry muffins, and we dug in, discussing plans to hire a new employee and about places to travel. That marked one thing off the list; so far, so good. I just hoped it went this well with Leanne.

Before we returned to work, Jeff brought something to my

attention. "I forgot to tell you about the creepers who stopped in yesterday before we closed."

"Creepers?" I said around a mouthful of blueberry muffin.

Jeff swallowed the last of his coffee. "Total creepers! They came in and looked around, not really looking for anything in particular. In fact, they seemed to be looking for *someone* rather than something."

He stood and gathered our empty cups and muffin wrappers. "I asked if I could help them find anything, and they just said they didn't see what they were looking for and left."

"How is that weird?" I asked, doubtfully.

"You didn't see them." Jeff screwed up his face in mild disgust. "They were super pale and greasy looking. Probably could have been decent-looking guys if they cleaned themselves up. One did all the talking in a thick accent while the other just grinned like a creep. And their eyes…"

Jeff shivered like he was trying to shake off the memory. "I swear I saw them change! They gave me the heebie-jeebies. I locked the door after they left."

"Well, hopefully they were just some eccentric tourists passing through and we won't have to see them again," I reassured him.

"I sure hope so. I don't remember ever being that creeped out by anyone before." Jeff shook all over again as if a cold chill went through him. "Not even Silas creeped me out that bad."

Jeff laughed and then left my office.

———

I called Leanne during my lunch break and invited her over for dinner. I told Silas to stay home. I figured it would be easier to talk to her about me leaving with him without Silas there.

I left the bookstore a little early so I could go home and prepare.

I was just finishing up dinner, when Leanne arrived.

"I brought pie," Leanne said as she walked through the door.

"Great." I took the pie from her and placed it on the counter.

"So what's up? You said you had something you wanted to talk to me about."

"I did, and I do. But first, let's eat." I sat a casserole dish of baked ziti on the table and turned around to pull the bread out of the oven.

"This looks and smells delicious, Dani." Leanne took a seat and poured us two glasses of wine from the bottle on the table.

I handed her a plate.

We served ourselves and began to eat.

Neither of us talked much. I was trying to think of the best way to bring up my leaving, and Leanne just kept looking at me with anticipation. I swallowed my bite of food and took a long drink of wine, draining my glass.

"I don't know any other way to say this, so I'm just going to come right out with it," I began.

Leanne sat back, placing her fork down on her plate. "Okay?"

I took a deep breath and blurted out, "Silas asked me to go away with him, and I said, "Yes.' "

"Oh, I think that's great, Dani!" She didn't hesitate with her reply, and she was smiling, genuinely smiling. She almost had a look of relief on her face, like the weight of the world had been lifted from her shoulders. What was up with that?

"Wait, really?" I asked, incredulously.

"Yeah, I do, Dani." She laughed. "I don't know; he's so much different with you. I honestly think he would never hurt you. Not intentionally, anyway. I've never seen this side of Silas before. I have to say, I'm actually starting to like him."

"Who are you and what have you done with Leanne?" I looked at her, suspiciously.

"I'm serious! I've seen the way he looks at you. As far as he's concerned, the sun rises and sets for you. He's one hundred percent in love with you." She picked up her fork and began eating again.

I was genuinely shocked, not to mention impressed, with Leanne's change of heart. "This really means a lot to me, Leanne. I'm glad you changed your mind about him."

She smiled and said, conspiratorially, "Just don't tell him that; I like making him squirm."

"Your secret is safe with me." I crossed my heart, and we both had a good laugh.

————

The rest of the evening went just like old times. We laughed and talked and had a genuinely good time.

I hugged her intensely before she left. "Thank you."

"For what?" she asked.

"For giving me your blessing on this. It means so much."

"Like you needed it." She rolled her eyes. "You would have done it, anyway."

She gathered me up in another hug and said, "I only have one condition."

"Anything."

"You call or text me every day and tell me where you are. Make sure you turn on your location sharing with me so I can travel vicariously through you, and I'm going to need pictures, lots of pictures."

"That's more than one," I laughed, "but you got it."

I waited for her to pull out of my driveway before calling Silas.

"You can come over now. We have a trip to plan."

CHAPTER

Twenty

I HAD DECIDED to let Jeff take the reins on the bookstore for the last few weeks. He was doing great, and I had to admit, I was enjoying getting to sleep in, especially since Silas always seemed to be there. He had turned into my constant shadow, not that I minded. It all just seemed so perfect, too perfect, honestly. I was still waiting for that other shoe to drop.

It was late morning when I got to the bookstore. Jeff had everything under control, no surprise there. I could hear him talking to someone in the back. He must have had an early morning customer.

There was laughter; I knew that laugh.

I walked around the corner of a row of bookshelves to see my best friend and Jeff sitting together in the reading nook.

"Leanne?" I asked, surprised to see her.

"Hey, Dani." She stood up, and Jeff followed suit.

He was blushing and looked like he had just been caught with his hand in the cookie jar.

Leanne was holding a stack of bright orange and purple papers. "I was just showing Jeff the flyers to my annual

Halloween party at Lulu's. He said it would be all right to leave a few here."

"Of course, Leanne. I wouldn't miss it for the world."

I smiled and glanced at Jeff.

He was looking at his shoes and rubbing the back of his neck. Was he embarrassed?

"Jeff, why don't you take those flyers up front and put them on the counter? We can tape one to the front door later."

"Sure thing, boss." He smiled brightly at Leanne as he took the flyers from her, and she returned the smile.

As Jeff headed to the front of the store Leanne's eyes followed him the whole way.

"Leanne, would you like to join me in my office? We can talk in there, if you'd like." I took her elbow.

She looked at me like I had just appeared out of nowhere and then laughed. "Oh, yes. That sounds good."

We both giggled, and she followed me into my office, closing the door behind her.

"What was that?" I asked, grinning like a fool.

"What?" She tried to act coy.

"Are you and Jeff…" I left the question open.

Leanne replied at once. "Oh, no. I mean, not yet. I don't know."

She flopped into the chair in front of my desk. "He's been coming by the diner a lot lately, and we have a lot in common, and he's fun to talk to, not to mention cute and charming. But I just don't know."

She was flustered, and it was hilarious.

"What's holding you back?" I asked, laughing. "He seems like quite a catch."

"I know. But he's younger than me. It's weird, isn't it?" She scrunched up her face and looked at me. Now, I really had to laugh.

"You're talking to me about age? My boyfriend is almost 160 years old!"

We both started giggling uncontrollably at that.

Once I caught my breath, I rolled my eyes and said, "A few years' difference hardly makes you a cougar."

"Yeah, I guess you're right. If it was the other way around, I wouldn't bat an eyelash at the difference."

"Exactly!" I smiled broadly at her.

"Do you think I should go for it?" she asked, dubiously.

"Absolutely!" I exclaimed. "Now, get out there and give that man your number before I do."

Leanne snatched a Post-it off my desk, wrote her number, and name and embellished it with a little heart.

Smiling at me, she got up and headed toward the front of the store.

I gave them a few minutes and waited to hear the chimes above the door signaling her departure.

When I arrived at the counter, Jeff was staring at the little yellow piece of paper in awe.

"Whatcha got there?" I asked with a sly smile.

He hid the paper in his palm and shoved it into his pocket. "Oh, um, it's nothing." He shrugged, but the smile on his face said otherwise.

"You should call her," I said as I gathered a stack of new arrival books off the counter.

"Yeah?" Jeff questioned.

"Yeah."

I winked at him and walked away with my stack of books. Seeing him quickly palm the note and shove it into his pocket reminded me of what Silas did just a few weeks ago. I never did find out what he was hiding. Truth be told, I had forgotten about it, until now.

The day passed by uneventfully. We had a few customers, and Jeff and I went about our duties as normal.

———

Several hours later, I was locking up after closing the bookstore. Jeff had already left, so I was alone.

I had my back to the parking lot, and my mind was elsewhere as I was locking the door.

Suddenly, there were two hands over my face covering my eyes. Two very cold hands.

"Guess who?" Silas whispered into my ear.

"How do you do that?" I shrieked. I never heard him approach.

"Years of practice," he said as he spun me around to face him.

"You're like a cat, or something," I said, reaching out to kiss him.

Silas raised an eyebrow and chuckled. "Thanks, I guess."

He leaned in for another kiss, when I noticed something behind me had caught his eye.

"What's this?" he asked, reaching behind me toward the bookstore door.

I turned my head to see what he was looking at. Silas was reading one of Leanne's flyers I had taped to the door.

"Leanne is having a Halloween party at Lulu's. She has one every year."

"I know," Silas said, smirking. "I've never attended one."

"Well, that changes this year. We are going," I said, resolutely.

"Is that so? Whatever shall I wear?" Silas asked, mockingly. A wide wolfish grin covered his face, making the smile lines around his eyes crinkle up.

He was up to something. Hopefully, he wasn't up to no good.

CHAPTER
Twenty-One

I SPENT the next several days and weeks leading up to the Halloween party helping Leanne. If I wasn't with Leanne, I was out with Silas. It seemed like I was never left alone for long. There were decorations to get out of storage, costumes to buy, and so much more. Jeff was offering to help as much as he could, and Leanne was loving it. She seemed so happy with Jeff, and I was happy for her.

Leanne had taken charge and decided on our costumes. She was going to be a 1950s carhop waitress, and I was going to be a '50s-style hot rod pinup girl. I wasn't surprised by her choice since she was a lover of all things '50s. I made sure to let Jeff in on the idea so his costume would go along with Leanne's. I tried to get Silas on board, but he wasn't having it. He told me his costume was already settled, and it was a surprise.

"He really won't tell you what his costume is?" Leanne asked while she unlocked her front door.

"Nope. Not a single clue." I shook my head. "He's clearly enjoying himself, though. He says it's perfect and for us not to worry."

"That's concerning." Leanne said, sarcastically.

We entered her house, and I made myself at home on her couch.

"Right? I don't know why he's being so secretive about it. He's cracking me up, though." I laughed at the thought of Silas, a vampire, getting dressed up for Halloween.

"Well, anyway, here's your costume. I just picked it up today." Leanne had gone down her hallway to her bedroom.

She came out and presented me with a garment bag and a shoe box.

I opened the bag, and inside was a pair of tight-looking, faux leather capri pants, matching gloves and a red-hot shirt that had a plunging neckline and capped sleeves. There was a black and white polka dotted scarf for my hair, and the shoes were black high heels. I made a face at the shoes.

"Get over the shoes, Dani." Leanne said, rolling her eyes. "I know you can walk in high heels. I've seen you do it."

"Yeah, yeah. Well, don't be surprised if I go barefoot the majority of the night." I stuck my tongue out at her.

"Nice, real mature." She giggled. "I'll stop by earlier in the day before the party to help you with your hair and makeup."

"I can't wait, Leanne. It's going to be fun."

I gathered my things and my costume and left Leanne's house. I was relieved to be almost finished with all of the party preparations.

I texted Silas before pulling out of Leanne's driveway. *I'm leaving now. See you in a minute.*

Silas almost instantly replied. *I'll be waiting.* He ended his text with the smiling vampire emoji.

"He thinks he's so clever," I thought out loud.

I drove home with a smile on my face, anticipating seeing him on my front porch, waiting for me.

———

When I pulled in, there he was, leaning nonchalantly against one of the porch pillars. He was wearing that dark green T-shirt I loved so much, the one that made his eyes look brighter. He also had on a dark pair of jeans and his favorite pair of rugged boots.

He walked lightly down the steps and met me at my car.

"Hello, lovely." He wrapped me in a hug and kissed my neck just below my ear. "I've missed you."

"I know. I've missed you, too. I'm sorry Leanne has kept me so busy lately." I pulled back and looked at his face. He must have recently fed because he looked downright radiant. That's when I noticed a dark speck of brownish red at the corner of his mouth.

"Silas?" I started to reach toward it to wipe it away but thought better of it. "You, uh, have a little something there." I pointed to the corner of his mouth.

Silas gave a little smirk and lifted the bottom of his T-shirt up to the corner of his mouth, allowing a flash of skin to peek out. "Sorry about that. I had a snack just a little bit ago."

He laughed wickedly and said, "You might even call it fast food."

I pushed him away. "Gross. I don't want to think about it. I hope you're being careful and vigilant," I scolded him. I couldn't risk him being found out.

"Of course, I am. That particular person was left believing they had been the victim of a couple of particularly nasty mosquitoes."

"Really? That's the best you could do?"

"Well, no, but I was pressed for time, and besides, those big ones can pack a nasty bite." He snapped his teeth at me and then reached in the car to retrieve my things.

"You don't think you're getting too close to town?" I narrowed my eyes at him.

"Nah, I was at the park on one of the hiking trails. Nowhere near town, technically."

He smiled and held up the garment bag. "Is this your costume? Can I see it?" He tried to change the subject.

I let it go, reluctantly.

"Yes, it's my costume. No, you may not see it. You won't let me see yours or even give me a hint at what you're planning. And frankly, it has Leanne and I nervous."

"Good. I promise you won't be let down. It's a riot, I swear."

The smile on his face was infectious, and I began to smile, as well.

"You better hope so, or Leanne will have your head."

We turned to walk inside, but I couldn't get the thought of that speck of blood on Silas's mouth out of my head. He couldn't afford to get sloppy now. We couldn't risk it.

CHAPTER
Twenty~Two

THE DAYS LEADING up to Halloween were filled with projects. Leanne had Jeff and I running in circles. Silas made sure to be scarce until it was all over. Leanne might have warmed up to him some over the past few months, but he still irked her, and he was not going to jeopardize his invitation to her party.

"You mean to tell me in all the years she has had Halloween parties you've never been to one?" I asked Silas.

"Not a single one, technically speaking. I've been on the outside of them, though." He was smiling as if he had told an inside joke.

"What's that supposed to mean?"

"Well, I've been on security detail, if you want to call it that." He laughed, darkly.

"I'm afraid to even ask," I responded.

"It's not that bad, honestly. I would hang out nearby or in the parking lot, and if Leanne had trouble, she would kick the troublemakers out, usually with some type of euphemism I could hear. Something like, 'Goodbye and goodnight; don't let the vampires bite.' That one was always my favorite."

He looked at me and grinned, hugely.

I rolled my eyes. "I can see why."

I waited for him to continue.

"Once I got my signal, I would follow the offenders and get them alone, and, well, I'm sure you can guess what happened next. Let's just say they weren't any trouble once I was done with them."

Silas had a good deep belly laugh at that.

"Yikes! I sure hope there's no scary vampires tomorrow night to follow me home." I gave him my best innocent look and batted my eyelashes at him, playfully.

Silas had a fleeting unsettled look and then said, darkly, "If there are, I'll protect you. There's only room for one scary vampire in this town." We had been sitting on my couch while I was finishing up the goodie bags for the party.

Silas turned in his seat and pounced on me, pinning me on the cushions beneath. He looked down at me as I laughed.

I told him to get off.

He opened his mouth and went for my neck, nipping me softly along my collarbone.

"My hero!" I said, gasping.

I pushed him off me and quietly said, "Silas, I feel like you're hiding something from me."

The mood in the room took a downturn.

"What do you mean?"

"I feel like you weren't telling me the truth a few weeks ago about the paper you hastily shoved into your pocket."

"This again?" He put his arm around me and hugged me close to him. "I told you; it was nothing. It's not even worth another moment's thought."

"You would tell me if it was something important, right?"

"Of course." He smiled, tightly. He really needed to work on his poker face.

"I just don't believe you." I narrowed my eyes and pushed away from him. "You and Leanne have been very overprotective of me lately, never leaving me alone for more than a few moments at a time. Silas, I need you to be honest with me."

Silas sighed, heavily, and ran his hand through his hair. "We didn't want to say anything to you because we have it handled. There's no need to scare you unnecessarily."

"What the hell is that supposed to mean?"

"Let me start at the beginning."

"Yeah, you do that." I was getting angry. He had been hiding something, and Leanne was in on it.

"That night a few weeks ago, when I came here early and you saw me put something in my pocket, it was a note."

"A note? What kind of a note?"

Silas stretched out one leg, reached into his pocket, pulled out a folded piece of paper.

He handed it to me. "It was under my windshield wiper that day. I had gone out to the forest for a bite to eat, and when I returned, the note was there."

I was so engrossed in the note I didn't even react to him saying he had gone out for a bite.

I carefully opened the note. It read, *We're watching her.*

"Me? This note is about me?" My hands began to shake, and the paper rattled as they did.

"That's what I'm assuming. I wasn't going to take a risk either way."

"Who would send you such a thing?"

I laid the note on the coffee table and stared at it.

"I have my theories. But in the meantime, I don't want you to worry about it. I'm hoping it was a prank or a mistake or something else of the sort." He reached out and took both my hands in his.

I looked into his eyes, and a single tear rolled down my cheek.

Silas reached up and wiped it away. "You're safe with me, Dani. You know that."

I tried to nod or respond in some way, but I couldn't.

Silas gently tipped my face up with his hand. "I've got you; you're safe." He leaned in and softly kissed me.

I finally found my voice and asked, "Has there been any more notes, or anything else?"

"No, not since that one, which is why I think it's nothing to worry about. But just to be safe, either me or Leanne will always be close by."

I tried to brush it aside and take solace in knowing everything was being handled. It was unsettling, to say the least. But I knew Silas would keep me safe, and I knew Leanne could hold her own. She had been taught how to kill vampires, after all. Lord knew she could handle whatever this was.

Speaking of keeping safe, I had to talk to Silas about one other thing.

"Silas, I need to ask you something." I said, nervously.

"Shoot."

"I need you to promise me you won't get caught, you'll be safe and not careless when you go out to feed."

"Is that all?" he laughed. "I will certainly do my best, but I don't know that I can make any promises."

"I'm serious, Silas! No more funny business and risky feeding practices. The other day in the park, you could have been caught. It was broad daylight, and the story you gave the person you fed on was flimsy."

I looked down at the coffee table and began toying with a piece of candy.

"It was one time, Dani. You know I can cover my tracks."

I raised my eyebrows, my eyes wide in shock at that statement. "It only takes one time. One time of being sloppy, and everything we have is gone! I've learned to accept what you are and what you need to do to survive, but I will not accept losing you to stupidity!"

"Okay, okay. I got it. No more shortcuts. I'll do better."

"And you have to be on your best behavior tomorrow

night. You'll be in the thick of it. No mistakes can be made." I looked at him, begging him to understand how important this was.

"I'll stay right beside you the whole night, I swear." He gave me the smirk and held up his right hand.

If I didn't know any better, I'd say his left hand was behind his back with his fingers crossed, but I could see it plain as day. I couldn't shake the feeling something bad was going to happen, and it was going to happen soon.

CHAPTER

Twenty~Three

IT WAS OFFICIALLY HALLOWEEN. We had decorated Lulu's, inside and out, in spooky regalia and pumpkins galore. There were fog machines and strobe lights and more candy bars than you could count. I had to hand it to Leanne, she knew how to throw a party.

I had not seen Silas since he left my house this morning, and I hadn't heard from him, either. I was trying not to think about the trouble he might, or might not be, getting into.

I stopped by Lulu's before going home from the bookstore to make sure Leanne didn't need anything else before the party.

"What are you doing here? Go, go! You need to be home, getting ready. I'm right behind you!" she said, shooing me out the door.

"Okay! All right! I'm leaving! It'll probably take me half an hour just to get into those leather pants you got me, anyway."

"Har, Har, Dani. Believe me, you'll be thanking me later. See you in a few." Leanne waved me off, and I got back in my car and headed home.

I half expected to see Silas waiting for me on the porch, but it was empty, and no lights were on in the house. I checked my phone once I parked the car. Still no calls or messages.

I couldn't take this; it was weird not hearing anything from him all day, especially since he had been glued to my side recently.

I texted Silas. *We're still on for tonight, right?*

Just a few moments later, he replied, *Wouldn't miss it. See you soon.* He ended his text with the vampire emoji once again.

I got out of my car, smiling, relieved to know he was still planning on coming.

I had barely got my door open, when I heard Leanne's car pull in.

She threw it in park and rushed toward the house, a bundle of clothes in her arms and her makeup kit dangling from one of her hands.

"Get up to your room! Go! Go! We've only got a little over an hour for me to work my magic!" Leanne smiled at me as she rushed past and up the stairs to my room.

I quickly followed, shaking my head at her. "I really wish you wouldn't go through all this trouble. I'm sure the costume will be enough," I said, trying to get out of the primping session.

"Nonsense. I'm going to make you an authentic pinup girl." Leanne puckered her lips at me and blew me a kiss.

"If you insist," I said, rolling my eyes. "I guess I'll get dressed first. Did you bring pliers so I can get the zipper up on these pants?" I teased her, holding up the pants, and wondering if I was really going to get into the tiny things.

"Shut up and get dressed." Leanne threw the top at me, and I went into the bathroom to change.

I shimmied into the black faux leather capris and couldn't

believe they fit me like a glove. I put the red top on next. It was a lot more revealing than anything I usually wore, but it fit me well.

I stepped out of the bathroom, and Leanne let out a wolf whistle.

"Wow, that outfit was made for you." She was clearly enjoying her fashion achievement. "Now for hair and makeup."

Leanne sat me down and got to work. She started by parting my hair, pinning it into sections, and pulling the rest into a ponytail. She curled my hair into three large curls and then began to tease, brush, and comb the curls into one big swoop at the front of my head. She then pinned it all in place and got started on my ponytail. She curled the hair in the ponytail into ringlets and then tied the polka dot scarf around it.

Leanne stood back and admired her handiwork. She chef kissed her fingers and began to work on my face. Luckily for me, she kept it simple. She gave me smokey eyes with winged eyeliner, bright red lipstick, and just a touch of color to my cheeks.

Leanne handed me a mirror, and I was astounded at what I saw.

"Wow, Leanne." I moved the mirror from side to side to see all the angles.

"I know, I know. I'm a miracle worker. Now, get those heels on and help me get ready."

Leanne's costume was a simple '50s carhop waitress dress. It was rosy pink and had a red collar and red trim on the sleeves. It came with a red-trimmed apron and a headband.

Once dressed, we both hurried down the stairs to look at ourselves in the big mirror in the foyer. Leanne's hair and makeup was always magazine perfect; she didn't need much more than a touch-up.

After admiring ourselves and her artistry, Leanne gathered her things to leave.

"I'll see you there," she said as she trotted out to her car.

I waved goodbye and closed the door behind me. Now, all I had to do was wait for Silas to get here. I couldn't wait to see what he had cooked up for a costume.

I sat down on the couch and absentmindedly scrolled through my phone. I was nervous and couldn't shake the feeling of butterflies in my stomach. It was an odd reaction to something, and I couldn't figure out what that something was. Could it be the party, or was it the note?

I was full of nervous energy, so I decided to get off the couch.

I started to pace. Why wasn't he here yet?

I looked at my phone again, no missed calls or messages. Was my anxiety from not knowing what Silas was up to or where he was? It had to be.

I took a deep breath and let it out, slowly, to help my nerves.

Out of nowhere, I heard someone walking up my front porch steps. My heart began to pound. Odd, I never heard a car pull in.

I went to the door and saw a dark shape through the glass. "What the?" I wondered aloud.

I opened the door, and there was Silas. He had his back to the door, and he was wearing a cape with a high collar.

"Silas?" I giggled.

He spun around with a flourish, holding the cape up over his face so only his bright green eyes could be seen. His dark hair was slicked back on his head. He still had not spoken.

"What are you doing?" I asked him, trying not to laugh.

That's when he dropped his arm and held the cape open wide like wings. He was dressed like Count Dracula from the 1930s film. He started to smile, and that's when I lost it.

I had to sit down I was laughing so hard.

He had a set of those cheap plastic vampire fangs in his mouth, and they fell out when he opened his mouth to speak.

He quickly caught them and shoved them back in his mouth.

In a thick accent he said, "Bleh! I vant to suck your blood!"

It was the worst Transylvanian accent I had ever heard and I was lost in a fit of giggles.

"You are too much," I said, wiping my eyes, carefully. "You're going to make me smudge my makeup."

Silas spit out the plastic fangs and helped me up off the stoop. "I'd much rather mess up your lipstick than your mascara."

He smiled at me, and I melted.

"You look amazing, by the way," he said as he bent down to kiss me. "If the girls looked as good as you do back then, I might have stayed in the 1950's."

I swatted at his chest playfully and tried to keep my blush to a minimum. Like all the other times it didn't go unnoticed. He smirked playfully and took a step back.

"And you look..." I gestured widely at his costume and laughed.

"Amazing, as well, I know." He smirked "Are you ready?"

"Yes, but what are we taking? Do I need to drive?" I asked, looking for his truck.

"I parked on the street about one house down. I was trying to surprise you."

We walked to the end of the driveway, and there was his Mustang, shiny and red and gorgeous.

"You drove the Mustang?" I didn't bother to hide my excitement.

"I did. I thought we'd arrive in style." He took my hand, led me to the passenger side, and opened the door for me to get in.

It was a sight watching Silas trying to get in the car around his cape.

He whirled it around and gathered it all up in a ball and got in. "I don't think there's an elegant way to do that at all," he said, laughing.

He started the car, and with a roar of the engine, we were off.

Pulling into Lulu's was a scene in itself. The car attracted plenty of attention, but the true spectacle was Lulu's. The diner had been transformed into a Halloween Wonderland. There were purple, orange, and green twinkling lights all around the parking lot and jack-o'-lanterns of all sizes and shapes. The fog machines were working overtime, keeping the entrance shrouded in a low gray mist. Party lights were flashing inside the diner, and music flooded the area.

Silas parked the car and said, "Let's party." He followed that with a wicked grin.

CHAPTER
Twenty~Four

THE PARTY WAS HUGE. It spilled out into the parking lot. There were people in costumes, milling around everywhere. Everyone seemed to be having a good time, and it looked like everyone had a drink in their hand.

We entered the diner, and Leanne was bouncing back and forth between guests. She hadn't seen us yet.

Jeff spotted us and made his way through the crowd toward us.

"Great costume, Jeff!" I shouted over the music. "Very James Dean."

"Thanks! That's what I was going for. You look terrific, as well."

Jeff paused and took in Silas. "Wow, Silas, that's really something. I don't know why, but your costume suits you."

Silas and I shared a look.

"Dani, would you like a drink?" Silas asked.

"No, not yet. I want to find Leanne." I craned my neck, trying to spot her.

Jeff and Silas tried to help.

"Good luck," Jeff said. "She's been running around all night. I've barely seen her."

Just then, Leanne came gliding into view, and I do mean gliding. She was wearing skates. How on Earth was she navigating that crowd while skating?

"Hey, guys! You all look amazing!"

She looked at Silas, and he beamed at her.

"Silas, you are perfect! How fitting."

She laughed. "Well, if you'll excuse me, I have more mingling to do. Jeff, would you care to join me?" She held her hand out to him.

Jeff's face lit up as he took her hand. "Later, guys!"

We watched them leave, and Silas asked, "Ready for that drink now?"

"Yes." I nodded, enthusiastically.

We made our way through the crowd of dancing bodies, hand-in-hand. I was leading the way toward the door. Leanne had collaborated with a local brewery, and they had a beer tent set up outside.

Silas and I were laughing and dodging people left and right as we headed out.

We were nearing the exit, when I noticed a scantily clad bunny heading straight toward us. She was a young twentysomething wearing a white bodysuit that was barely more than lingerie with white thigh highs and bunny ears on her platinum blonde head.

She was staring straight at Silas with a look of determination on her face.

I didn't even look at Silas; I just tried to steer us away from her.

She kept coming.

As she drew nearer, she finally took notice of me, and a superior look took over her face.

She turned her eyes back to Silas and smiled. "Cool costume. I love your contacts." She smiled again and bit her lip, seductively.

I huffed, irritably, and rolled my eyes. Of course, she

thought he was wearing contact lenses. She didn't know Silas was a real vampire.

"There are two other guys here with the same type of contacts. They're not nearly as hot as you are, though."

She purred as she ran her fingers down his arm and kept walking.

I tugged at Silas's hand, never taking my murderous glare off blondie. That chick was brazen!

I was still watching her and glaring, when I heard Silas clear his throat.

He was smirking.

I looked up into his face and noticed his eyes. "Hey!" I hissed. "Put those away!"

Silas laughed and shook his head like he was trying to clear his thoughts. "Sorry about that. I need to get some air. Too many bodies in here."

He grabbed me by my waist and ushered us toward the door all the while seriously scanning the crowd.

Once we were outside, we both took a deep breath of the crisp night air.

"Better?" I asked him.

"Much," he replied, taking my hand again. "Now, let's get you that drink."

I entered the tent and ordered a beer.

We took a walk around the parking lot, admiring the jack-o'-lanterns. Leanne had commissioned the locals to carve the pumpkins, and she displayed them all around the outside of the diner. The candlelight flickered inside each one, casting everything around them in a warm glow.

We found a bench and sat down.

"We can leave, if you want," I told him.

"No, I wouldn't dream of it. I was caught off guard; I'll be okay." He tried giving me a smile, but there was a touch of worry to his face.

"I like it out here better, anyway," I said as I sat closer to him, and he put his arm around me.

"Me, too," Silas said, quietly.

We sat and people watched, commenting on costumes and the music.

"Leanne outdid herself this year," I remarked.

"Yes, but she had help."

Silas stood up as the next song came on. It was a song by my favorite band, Lord Huron. It was called "Love Like Ghosts."

"Dance with me?" he held his hand out.

I placed my cup on the bench and took his hand. "I love this song."

"I know; that's why I wanted to dance." Silas intertwined his fingers with mine and placed his other hand on my waist, drawing me closer to him.

"I'm not a very good dancer," I admitted.

Silas laughed and said, "Just follow my lead."

We swayed to the music, and when the song hit a faster tempo, Silas spun me and then brought me back into him and dipped me, his strong arms holding me, firmly.

He lowered his lips to the hollow of my throat and gently kissed me.

Goosebumps rose on my skin, and I could feel Silas's lips draw back in a smile.

I heard the sound of stiletto heels tick tacking close by us.

Silas raised me up as the song ended, and I caught sight of Little Bunny Foo Foo from earlier.

She rolled her eyes at us and angrily said, "Get a room" as she sauntered past.

"Mmm, that's not a bad idea," Silas said, loud enough for her to hear.

I couldn't see her reaction because Silas had gathered me up in his arms and started to walk away. I was practically squealing with laughter.

He sat me down just outside the door of the diner. "Are you ready to go?" I asked him.

"Yeah, I've had enough human interaction for one night."

"Me, too. Let me find Leanne to say goodbye, and I need to find the ladies' room, as well." I squeezed his hand and said, "Be right back."

"Take your time; I'll be waiting right here." He kissed my cheek, pulled out his phone, and leaned against one of the Halloween decorations.

I found Leanne and Jeff almost immediately; they were sitting in a booth. She had pulled her skates off, and they were having an animated conversation.

Leanne was texting someone on her phone while they talked, and she hastily put it down when I approached.

I felt like I was interrupting something.

"Hey, guys. I think we're going to head out. We had a blast."

"Aww! Are you sure?" Leanne stood up and gave me a hug.

"Yeah, I'm sure. We're both pretty beat. The party was great, like always, Leanne."

"Thanks for your help, Dani. I'm so glad you came."

Leanne sat back down, but this time she sat in the same booth seat as Jeff, and he put his arm around her shoulders.

"Bye, Jeff. It was nice seeing you outside of work." I smiled, and he gave me a friendly wave.

I left the two new lovebirds alone. Not wanting to wear out my welcome any longer, I headed to the restroom. There was a line but it seemed to be moving quick enough. This would be an opportune time to be a vampire. I bet they never had to deal with stuff like this. As I washing up, I realized I was only gone for about ten minutes. I hoped Silas was still out front.

I made a beeline through the crowd and exited the diner. I

didn't see Silas where I had left him. Maybe he had gone to get the car.

I walked out toward our parking spot, and still there was no sign of Silas. Did he go inside to look for me?

I got my phone out and texted him. *I'm at your car. Where are you?*

While I waited for a reply, I took my shoes off. My feet were killing me.

I opened the door to the car to place my shoes inside and noticed Silas's phone sitting in the driver's seat.

That's odd, I thought. *Well, he has to be close by.*

I walked around the front of the Mustang to the driver's side to see if I could spot him.

Looking around, I couldn't see him in the crowd.

I was still searching through the faces in the throng of people, when I heard a crashing noise in the alleyway behind me.

I turned to look, but it was too dark to see.

There was movement, a flash of white, some raised voices, and the sounds of a scuffle.

I started down the alley, my curiosity getting the better of me. I wanted to be sure no one was in trouble, or making trouble for that matter.

I was trying hard to be quiet. I didn't know what I was walking into.

There was more movement, and that's when I noticed it was two people.

The larger of the two was crouched down, and the smaller person was sitting on the ground, leaning against the wall.

The larger person helped the smaller one to their feet.

That's when I noticed the smaller figure was a girl, and she was wearing bunny ears.

As the other figure stood, I could make out what looked like a high-collared cape, just like Silas's.

I crouched down behind some trash cans to try and get a

better look. Sure enough, it was Silas. I couldn't see his face, but I knew.

My hand flew to my mouth to keep me from crying out. The moon had come out from behind the clouds and washed the alleyway in an eerie silver light. It was just enough for me to see the fear in the girl's face; she was paralyzed. The only thing holding her up were Silas's arms. I still couldn't quite make out his face, the collar on that stupid cape hid most of it from me, but I knew that voice.

He turned the girl to face him, and he spoke to her in a hypnotic tone. "You drank too much."

"I drank too much," she repeated.

"You met someone; he gave you a nasty hickey," Silas continued, smiling at his own cleverness.

"Nasty hickey." Her voice was vacant of any emotion.

"You passed out in the back seat of your car. You're going to wake up hungover."

"My car, hungover." She sounded robotic.

"Now, go get into your car and go to sleep, like a good little bunny."

Silas spun her back around and sent her off.

She stumbled and lurched past me like a zombie, her eyes blank.

I saw her climb into the back of the car parked next to Silas's Mustang.

I quickly turned back to look toward the spot where Silas had been, but he was gone.

Instead, he was standing over top of me.

I slowly looked up into his terrible face.

He was unrecognizable. His once-handsome features were stretched and contorted into a horrific, animalistic, snakelike face. His eyes were bright green and reptilian, and his mouth was stretched, lips pulled back and thin across his gums. Then, there were the fangs. They were long and grotesque and descended from his upper jaw like those of a viper. This face was nothing like the one he had barely allowed me a glimpse of in my kitchen several weeks ago.

I wanted to scream, but I was frozen with fear. It felt like all the air had been sucked out of me.

Silas bent over and roughly grabbed my arms at the elbows, standing me up and pinning me against the wall at my back. The rough textrue of the bricks scratched at the exposed skin on my arms and right through the thin fabric of my top.

His face was inches from mine, and I could smell the acrid, metallic, copper tang of the girl's blood on his breath.

Silas looked furious, his eyes glinting in the moonlight.

"What are you doing back here? Why aren't you with Leanne?" His voice was guttural and thick around his fangs.

I couldn't speak; I was too terrified. My normally jovial Silas was replaced by a monster, the one he had kept hidden from me so well. I thought I knew what he was. I knew nothing.

"You're not safe here!" His eyes raked up and down my face.

My heart was jackhammering away in my chest, and I began to tremble.

"What did you see?" He made a growling sound in his throat, and he bared his teeth and fangs at me. "Did you think I didn't know you were there? I heard you coming down the alley; I could smell you, Dani."

He brought his face closer to mine and inhaled, deeply. "Do you know how close you came to death?"

I started to squirm, and his hold tightened on my shoulders.

He was looking me in the eyes now, and it was too intense.

My heart was pounding like a panicked bird in a cage. I had to look away.

I squeezed my eyes shut and turned my head.

"Can't bear to look upon my true face, can you? I warned you you wouldn't like it, and now here we are! You are too curious for your own good."

He smacked the wall behind my head with the flat of his palm, making me jump.

I whimpered.

"It's going to get you killed!"

Silas was quiet for a moment, and then I felt him move. His hair brushed my cheek.

I opened my eyes and saw he had lowered his face to my neck, just below my ear.

I felt his mouth brush the skin of my neck.

A fang grazed my throat. His cool breath was coming in waves.

When he spoke, his voice became a low rumble. "This was not what it looks like."

I tried to wiggle out of his grasp, and I found my voice. It came out shaky and fast.

"Well then, tell me what I saw, because it sure looked like you were feeding on that girl! I can smell her blood on your breath!"

I must have struck a nerve.

He hissed and stood up, rapidly.

When I looked at him this time, his features had begun to soften and return to normal.

Silas loosened his grip on my shoulders, and I was able to come away from the wall.

He looked at me with troubled eyes, and his face fell.

"Dani, I'm telling you, it's not what it seems."

His arms fell to his sides. He took a step back and hung his head.

When Silas let go of me, I didn't hesitate. I ran and never looked back.

CHAPTER
Twenty~Five

I HEADED STRAIGHT for the diner; I had to find Leanne.

She and Jeff were still sitting in the same booth.

I pushed my way through the crowd, tears streaming down my face, and my bare feet slapping the linoleum floor.

Leanne wasn't looking in my direction, but Jeff was. His smile left his face and changed instantly to shock and concern.

He said something to Leanne, and she turned.

She shot up out of the booth and hurried toward me.

I collided with her, and she wrapped me in a hug.

"Dani? My God, you're shaking! Are you hurt?" Leanne's voice was tense.

Jeff hung back, silently watching.

"I need to go. Can I borrow your car?" I was sobbing.

"Absolutely not! You're in no state to drive." Now, she was angry.

"I just want to go home," I sobbed.

"I'll drive you," Jeff piped up.

"Take her to my house and stay with her. I don't think she should be alone," Leanne said with concern.

Jeff nodded.

Leanne added, "I'll be home as soon as I shut things down here."

She hugged me.

Jeff put his hand on my back and asked if I was ready.

I followed him to the parking lot to find his car.

I glanced in the direction of where Silas's car was parked and noticed it was gone.

I breathed a sigh of relief, but there was also a pang of longing and an ache in my chest. I was completely confused.

I got into Jeff's car, and that's when it hit me; I was barefoot. I had left my shoes in Silas's car. I was so completely terrified and distraught I hadn't even realized my shoes were gone. It struck me as funny, and I gave an exasperated chuckle.

"Everything okay?" Jeff asked.

"Yeah, it will be. Just a lot to think about, I guess." I looked down at my dirty, bare feet on the floorboard.

————

We drove the rest of the way to Leanne's in awkward silence. Luckily, she didn't live far away from the diner.

We pulled in the drive.

"Do you have a key or something?" Jeff asked.

"I do. I can let us in."

I got out of the car and limped across the gravel driveway.

"Your shoes? Where are they?" Jeff asked, surprised.

"Oh, I must have left them in Silas's car. It's okay. I'm sure Leanne has a pair I can borrow."

I unlocked the door and flipped on the light.

Jeff followed me and locked the door behind us.

"Dani, what happened? Did Silas do something. Did he hurt you?" Jeff's questions were tinged with anger.

"No, not exactly. We, um, had a fight. I don't know if we'll be seeing each other again." I turned my back to him before he could see the tears.

I made my way to the bathroom, leaving Jeff standing in the doorway.

"I'm going to get cleaned up and probably just go to bed," I said as I walked away. "Thank you for staying with me until Leanne gets home."

I closed the bathroom door and leaned against it.

Jeff called out to me, "I'll be in the living room if you need anything."

A few moments later, I heard the TV turn on with the low murmur of voices from a late-night talk show, I assumed.

Jeff had really become a good friend over the last few months. Now he and Leanne were together, our friendship was even closer. I was glad of that friendship tonight.

I took a shower and tried to let the hot water wash everything away, but every time I closed my eyes, I saw Silas's terrible face.

I gave up on the shower and decided to just go to bed. I knew where Leanne kept most everything, so I wrapped myself in a towel and let myself into her room. I found an old T-shirt and a pair of cotton shorts. I put them on and made my way to the spare bedroom.

I turned on the bedside lamp because I didn't want to sleep in the dark.

I pulled back the covers and laid down.

The tears came as soon as my head hit the pillow. Was I crying out of fear, or loss, or both? Did I really think my relationship with Silas would work? I was dating a monster, a vampire, after all. We were doomed from the beginning. I came face-to-face with the reality of what Silas really was, and I didn't know what scared me more, the fact he truly was a monster or the fact we might be through because of it.

I was so exhausted as I watched the moon outside the window.

My tears began to fall again as I realized the same moonlight had revealed what was real only a short time ago.

Sleep came for me and drowned me in a black dreamless slumber on a tear-soaked pillow.

———

I was awakened a few hours later, when Leanne came home.

She came into the bedroom, quietly, to check on me. "Dani," she whispered, "are you awake?"

I rolled over and sat up, fresh tears rolling down my face.

Leanne sat on the bed beside me and hugged me. "Tell me what happened. Are you hurt?" I could tell by the tone of her voice she was angry.

I pulled away from her and grabbed a tissue from the box on the nightstand. "Is Jeff still here?" I asked.

"No, I sent him home. Now, tell me what happened."

I took a deep breath and exhaled, slowly, trying to think things through. I began playing with the tissue in my lap.

"Dani, please?" Leanne pleaded.

"I saw him, Leanne." I looked up and into her eyes. "I saw him feeding."

She turned away from me and said, "Are you sure that's what you saw?"

"What do you mean?" I asked, slowly.

Leanne stood up and began pacing. "Was it a girl in a slutty bunny costume?" she asked.

"Yes."

I threw back the covers and placed my legs over the side of the bed. "How did you know that?"

"I saw two creeps following her and asked Silas to check it out. If I had to guess, you walked up on Silas scaring them off."

I was dumbstruck. It must have been Silas whom she was texting when I went to find her at the party.

I sat back down on the bed.

Leanne started to explain.

"When I noticed you and Silas were not together for a moment, I texted him. You were never supposed to know. He was just supposed to make sure she got to her car all right and then come right back to you. Something must have been going on if you had time to find him and see anything at all."

She sat down next to me. "What did you see? Are you certain you saw him feeding on her?"

I looked at her, clearly baffled. "I could smell her blood on his breath."

"Oh," she said, quietly, cringing.

"He was awful, Leanne," I whispered. "How could I have been so naïve?"

Leanne was silent.

"He seemed so angry at me. He told me I wasn't safe and my curiosity would get me killed!"

Leanne's head snapped up. "He said what?"

"Yeah, he said I was too curious and it would get me killed. What did he mean by that? He was holding me so roughly against the wall, and his face was so, so..."

"It wasn't the Silas you thought you knew and loved," Leanne noted.

I nodded. "How can I love someone like that?"

I wasn't sure about anything anymore. I felt confused, angry, and heartbroken. There were a thousand emotions rolling through my mind. The biggest thought on my mind was, *How has Silas kept this from me so well?*

I needed to think; I needed to be alone.

Leanne remained quiet; she seemed almost ashamed of what had happened.

"I want to be alone," I said, climbing back under the covers. "Can you take me home first thing in the morning?"

"Sure, Dani," Leanne said, getting up from the bed and heading for the door.

She stopped in the doorway, her body silhouetted in the hallway light. "I didn't mean for any of this to happen. Truly, I didn't. And in some weird way, I know Silas didn't, either."

I didn't reply. Fresh, warm tears were streaming down my face.

Leanne hesitated and then turned to leave, closing the door behind her.

CHAPTER
Twenty-Six

LEANNE DROPPED me off early the next morning. The car ride home was awkward, to say the least. I didn't speak or look at Leanne. I just gazed out my window and tried not to think about what she had told me last night.

She stopped me before I got out of the car.

"I know you're upset, and you have every right to be, but you would have seen him like that eventually. Whether by accident, like last night, or on purpose because he—"

I stared at her, blankly, for several seconds before telling her off. "Don't! Just don't!" I exclaimed.

She held up her hands, placatingly.

"I don't want to talk about it! I know what I saw. And what I saw was a monster!" I was seething.

"That's not fair, or true!" she shot back.

"How would you know? You didn't see what I did!"

Leanne was still glaring, but I could tell she was also listening.

"He had the girl on the ground and was crouched over her. He stood her up and told her some bullcrap line about being drunk and receiving a nasty hickey and then sent her away to sleep it off in her car. She was paralyzed with fear!"

I got out of the car, and so did Leanne.

"I sure as hell didn't see two creepy guys with that girl. Only Silas!" I slammed the car door.

"Dani, I'm not questioning what you saw but I don't think you're seeing the whole picture."

"I saw enough," I said through gritted teeth. I was fighting back tears. Why was she defending him so adamantly?

We both stood in the driveway, staring each other down.

"I'm not so sure about that," Leanne said, sadly.

I couldn't believe her! Why was she taking his side on this? I turned my back on her and began walking, indignantly, up the sidewalk to my front porch.

"You can't just love the pretty parts of him, you know! It's not like he can change what he is!" She hurled that at me like a fastball. "You should really hear him out since you're obviously not going to listen to me!"

It caught me off guard and stopped me in my tracks.

I clenched my fists and squared my shoulders and refused to turn around. I didn't know what to say, so I did what I did last night when things got too real; I ran, like a scared little girl.

I left Leanne standing in the driveway as I launched myself up my porch steps and into my house, slamming the door behind me.

I headed upstairs to change. I needed to call Jeff. I needed a day off to get myself together.

Jeff must have been reading my mind because my phone began to buzz in my hand. The text read, **Hey, boss; I hope you're feeling better. I know last night was rough, and I won't pry, but just take the day to recoup. I got this.**

I really felt like he was the only friend I had right now.

I texted him back. **Thank you, Jeff. I appreciate it. See you tomorrow.**

I got changed and went to the kitchen for some coffee. I had to resist the urge to call or text Silas. His reaction to my being in the alleyway was frightening and overly aggres-sive. I still couldn't get the image of his face out of my mind.

Silas must have been a mind reader, too. There was a soft knock at my door.

I answered it, but I opened the door only a crack and left the screen door closed. I wasn't ready to see him, let alone talk to him.

He was dressed in the same outfit he wore on our first date. Coincidence? Probably not.

"Silas," I said, coldly. I could barely look at him.

"Cinderella left her shoes at the ball." He gave me an embarrassed smile and held my shoes out.

I didn't reach for them.

"Just set them there. I'll get them later." I gestured to the porch floor in front of him and went to close the door.

The smile melted away, and he took a step forward. "Wait, Dani. Please, let me explain," he implored.

"Silas, I can't. Not yet." I closed the door in his face and locked it.

I stepped back from the door and watched Silas through the frosted glass. He stood there, facing the door and then bent over, placing my shoes on the porch.

He stood up and walked away, stopping and turning to look at the door before going down steps and leaving.

My breath hitched, and fresh tears started to fall.

Once I heard his truck leave, I went to the door and opened it. There were my shoes, and underneath them was an envelope.

I stepped outside and picked them up. The outside of the envelope just said my name in Silas's elegant, tidy scrawl.

I took everything inside, dropping my shoes on the floor of the foyer.

I took the envelope into the living room and just stared at it. I was too afraid to open it.

———

The letter sat on my coffee table for a full day before I finally summoned the courage to open it.

It read,

My dearest Dani,

I'm writing this in case you have decided not to speak to me. My behavior last night was inexcusable. It was abhorrent and unforgiveable. I have put you in danger and have gotten too close. There are dangers out there that have come for you and the town of Ophidian Grove because of me. I see now I'm not good for you, not if your life is in danger. I have made a difficult choice. I am leaving, and I hope those dangers follow me. I never wanted you to be frightened of me, and yet that's exactly what I've done. It is as plain as day your opinion of me has changed, and it is my fault. Once again, I have become the stuff of nightmares. I believed I was doing the right thing by keeping that part of me hidden from you. I was wrong. I will no longer haunt your nightmares, or your life. I love you, and I hope you know that. I also love you enough to let you go.

Eternally yours,
Silas

I laid the letter down on the coffee table with a shaking hand. I thought I had everything figured out. I thought I knew what I wanted. I thought I knew who and what Silas was. I didn't know the vampire within and how to truly love him, monster and all.

CHAPTER
Twenty-Seven

A WEEK CAME AND WENT, and I did not go after Silas. I couldn't bring myself to. I was still struggling with my feelings after Halloween night. My sweet, gentle Silas, always smiling and laughing, had turned into a monster before my eyes. Sure, I knew what he was, but I didn't grasp the scope of it. It was all so natural, so easy for him. The ease with which he slipped into a monstrous vampire, the way he manipulated the girl, the fear in her eyes, and the vacant, hypnotic look she took on when he spoke to her. He seemed to revel in it.

Was that what he had been doing to people all along? How could I have been so blind? What hurt the most, and was by far the most frightening, was how easily he turned on me. All the warning signs had been there all along. The way he made me feel the first night I saw him, his back-and-forth emotions before he revealed what he was, Leanne's cagy warnings, my dreams, all the subtle clues were there and yet I chose to ignore them.

I went through the motions of normal daily life that week, and for the weeks after. Showing up to work and going home were my only activities. I hadn't talked to Leanne since she dropped me off the day after Halloween. Poor Jeff was walking on eggshells around me. He found ways to avoid being alone with me, so I eventually helped him out by keeping myself holed up in my office.

Jeff finally worked up his nerve to come talk to me one afternoon. He knocked on the office door before entering.

"Dani?" He must have been concerned; he didn't call me boss. "Can I talk to you?"

"Sure, Jeff. Come on in." I tried to smile, but it came across as a wince.

Jeff sat down. "Look, I don't know what happened Halloween night, and it's honestly none of my business, but I'm done seeing you and Leanne so damned mopey." He sat back in the chair and crossed his arms.

I glanced up from the invoice I was pretending to look over. "Oh, is that right?"

"Yeah, it is. Whatever happened between you and Silas, and you and Leanne has got her so upset she's just not the same. Frankly, neither are you. I'm not asking you two to apologize to one another because I don't know what's going on. I'm just asking for you to talk to each other."

Jeff stood up and went to leave. "I care for both of you. Hell, I think I might even love Leanne, but this is too much. As much as I care about you both, I know you two care about each other even more. Don't throw that away."

With that said, he walked out.

Jeff was right, and I couldn't even be irritated at him.

I pushed my stack of invoices away and sighed, heavily.

I looked at my phone sitting on the edge of my desk, gingerly picked it up, and unlocked the screen. The picture of Silas and I long since replaced with a boring screensaver. A twinge of regret wracked my heart.

I quickly stuffed it down and opened my text messages. I didn't even know what to say to Leanne. I felt bad, sure. We had never stayed angry at one another this long before. We'd been friends far too long to throw it away over a relationship of mine that was doomed, anyway.

I extended the olive branch and sent Leanne a text. *Can we talk?*

A few moments later, she replied. *I'd like that. Stop by tonight on your way home, if you'd like.*

So far so good.

———

I spent the rest of the afternoon working up my courage and trying to find the words to say to Leanne.

I finally decided on honesty and to just let her know exactly how I felt and what I was thinking.

Leanne was waiting for me on her front porch when I arrived. I was prepared for feelings of anger to overwhelm me again, like they did the day of our fight. Instead, I was overwhelmed with guilt.

Leanne looked at me with such remorse and sadness all anger was lost.

"Hey," I said, softly.

Leanne remained sitting and gave me a sad smile. "Care to join me?" She pointed to the chair next to her.

I sat down but didn't say anything, the awkward silence and tension growing between us.

Finally, Leanne spoke up. "I'm sorry. None of this was supposed to happen this way." She hung her head and shook it.

"Leanne, I—" I started, but she cut me off.

"Let me finish."

I shut my mouth and waited for her to finish.

"I just didn't want any trouble at my party. There were these two goons who were following that girl a little too closely, and they had such wolfish grins on their faces. They gave me the creeps. She might have been a troublemaker, but she still deserved to get home safe. I texted Silas when I saw you come inside the diner and asked him to keep an eye on her. He must have seen something that was off, or else he would have never left you to find him like that. I can't attest to what you saw because, as you pointed out, I wasn't there. But if you say you saw him feeding on her, then I'm inclined to believe you."

I was so startled by her confession I couldn't bring myself to say anything. Everything I had planned to say went right out of the window.

"Have you spoken to him at all?" Leanne asked, quietly.

I could only look at her. I had a million things to say, and not one would come out.

I just shook my head.

After several moments of poignant silence, I sighed and finally spoke. "What I don't understand is why he didn't stop. He said he knew the moment I stepped into the alley; he said he could smell me."

"Like I said before, I don't think you got the whole story. He never told me what happened; I've barely spoken to him since that night. I truly don't think he was given much of a choice." Leanne waited for me to respond.

I gave her a blank look. I wasn't sure I was following.

Leanne explained, "If those two men did something to her, he might have been trying to clean up their mess the best way he knows how."

"Do you mean by making her remember something else?" I wished that could be true; I wanted that to be true. But I know what I saw, and it was terrible.

"Exactly." Leanne looked me dead in the face, willing me to see another side to the debacle.

I turned away from her and leaned forward in my chair, resting my chin in my hands. "I know I loved Silas, and a big part of me still does, but I just don't know if I can do it. Knowing the monster he becomes, the fear he instills in people, or just how quickly he can turn it on or off. It's very Dr. Jekyll and Mr. Hyde." I sighed.

"How well can he actually control the monster that lurks just beneath the surface, Leanne?" I sat back in my seat again and rubbed at the stress knot forming in my neck. "I don't know; I guess I had this romantic notion we would work, but I don't see how."

We sat in silence, listening to the leaves rustling in the wind. Neither of us knowing what to say next.

"He is crazy about you, though," Leanne said. "He was so completely distraught when you wouldn't see him the day after. He knew he had messed up. He told me so. I just hope this doesn't drive him to do something reckless."

Leanne reached over and gave my hand a squeeze "I'm sure I'm worrying about nothing, though." Her smile was tight lipped, and I could tell she was hiding something from me.

"You don't think he'll try anything, do you?" I asked, warily.

Leanne wouldn't look at me. She shrugged. "I don't know, Dani; I really don't know."

CHAPTER
Twenty~Eight

LEANNE and I slowly got back to normal over the next few weeks. Our fight (if you could even call it that) put behind us, we moved on. I tried to move on from Silas; I needed to move on, but I was finding it increasingly difficult. I felt empty without Silas, and my smiles, which often felt forced, didn't come as easily as before. It was strange, but everything felt better when he was around. There was a void in my life now, and I tried to fill it any way I could. I tried new projects at the bookstore, did some home renovations I had been putting off, and I even offered to help cook at Thanksgiving with Leanne's family. But when I was alone at night with my thoughts, they wandered to Silas. What was he doing? Where did he go? I even dared to wonder if he was thinking about me.

I had planned to spend Thanksgiving and Christmas with Leanne's family, just like I had always done since my parents died. I hoped it would be enough distraction to keep my mind off Silas. Since Leanne refused my offer to help cook, I offered to do the shopping for her. She gladly accepted and sent me on the hunt for all things turkey dinner the weekend before Thanksgiving.

I decided to drive out of town a little way to one of the bigger cities so I could shop at a larger chain store. The drive out of town would do me some good, and it was an excuse to drive past Silas's place.

I was getting closer to his driveway and warring with the decision to pull in.

I pulled over a few feet away instead.

I turned my radio off and sat, staring at the mouth of his driveway. I couldn't see the house from here, of course; it sat too far back.

I don't know how long I stayed there before I finally made the decision to just drive away. What good would it have done me to see an empty house? Even if he were there, what would I say?

I turned my radio back on and caught the end of a song.

After that, the DJ began talking introducing the local news brief on the hour.

"Now, it's time for your local news. The Rangers at Croatan National Forest are asking hikers to be extra careful right now as they investigate a rash of attacks and missing hikers along several of the trails inside the park. They are asking people to be vigilant and aware of their surroundings. They also want people off the trails before sundown, to carry bear mace, and to not go out alone. The Park Rangers are unsure what is behind the attacks and are hopeful they can resolve it without closing the park. Now for the weather—"

I reached over and turned the radio off. Weird, what kind of wildlife would start attacking out of nowhere? I knew there were bears, but that was still unusual.

I continued to ponder the newscast on my way to the grocery store, refusing to think about what I really thought was going on. I needed to get to the bottom of the situation, and I hoped my initial thoughts weren't right.

I wanted the monotony of grocery shopping to take my mind off the news report. It wasn't working. It seemed everywhere I turned someone was talking about it. The ladies in the produce department, the two men in the deli, even the TVs I passed in the electronics department all seemed to be talking about the strange attacks happening in the forest.

I stopped and watched one of the display TVs. The news anchor warned of a disturbing image and then showed a picture of a woman's neck.

My hand flew to my mouth to stifle my cry of shock. There were two deep puncture wounds in her neck. In between the punctures was a broken line in an almost half-moon shape. It looked like it was viciously made. It was gruesome and seemed like the side of her throat had been nearly ripped out.

They went on to say the young woman, who didn't want her named aired, had survived the attack. But she couldn't remember anything about what happened, and there were no other marks on her body.

I hurried away from the TVs and rushed through the rest of my shopping. I had a sinking feeling in the pit of my stomach. Somewhere deep down, something was telling me that could have been Silas's work, but I didn't want to believe it. I needed to talk to Leanne.

I left the store and drove straight to her house.

———

She met me outside to help me carry the bags inside the house.

"Thanks again for getting all of this. It really saved me some time," Leanne said, grabbing a couple of bags from my back seat.

"It was no trouble."

I shut my car door and hurried to catch up to her as she entered the house.

"Have you seen the news today?" I asked, coolly. I wanted to see if she had the same thoughts I did.

"Yeah, I did. Weird stuff going on in the forest, huh?" She wasn't looking at me.

"What do you think it is? Bears, gators, escaped zoo animal, or…" I questioned her, letting my thought trail off.

She still wasn't looking at me and kept her back to me as she went through the bags on the counter.

"It's hard to say. Probably a bear." She shrugged but sounded unconvinced.

"A bear? Did you see the wound on that woman's neck?"

I walked over to where she stood, forcing her to look at me. "Why would a bear only bite her neck and not leave another scratch on her whatsoever?"

Leanne placed both hands on the counter and looked down, shaking her head. "I know what it looks like, Dani, but Silas is gone. Besides, he's not that sloppy. He knows better."

"How do we know he's gone? You said yourself he was distraught and you hoped he wouldn't do anything reckless. Well, this seems pretty reckless to me!" I exclaimed.

Leanne sighed and faced me, placing a hand on both my shoulders. "I'll keep an eye on it, promise. It's what I do. But right now, I see no reason to be concerned. This really doesn't look like anything Silas would do."

"And you'll let me know if it starts to *concern* you?" I asked, sardonically.

"Yes, of course. You'll be the first to know. But if you really wanted to know, you could just call him."

I looked at her, eyes wide in consternation. There was no way I was ready for that, was I?

CHAPTER
Twenty~Nine

I KEPT my eye on the news for the next several days. Someone needed to be concerned about it since Leanne wasn't. I was fairly certain she felt the same way I did but she didn't want to face the facts. I don't think Silas had ever given Leanne any trouble like that, and I wanted to believe it wasn't him.

I was sitting on my couch, watching the evening news, waiting to see if any new developments had come up about the attacks in the forest. The news was mostly quiet; same old stuff, as usual. They discussed the weather, the newest trending holiday gifts, a few political stories, and finally they got to the local news.

"Rangers at Croatan National Forest are still baffled by the recent attacks on visitors to the park. They have decided to close some of the camping areas in light of recent events."

The station broke away to show footage of a campground. It looked like a tornado had swept through. Tents were shredded. Picnic tables, chairs, and other items were overturned and strewn across the area.

But what caught my eye were the people. They were sickly pale and had bandaged necks; some were bruised along their arms. They all shared the same vacant look in their eyes, and when asked what happened to them, they all seemed confused and said they didn't remember. Except for one. She had spoken to the police, and they now had a sketch of a suspect. The news footage went away and panned back to the studio.

"Authorities are looking for this man. He is wanted for questioning. He is said to be a white male in his thirties with dark hair and green eyes."

They showed the police sketch.

A black and white sketch of a man filled my screen. It looked like Silas, but only slightly. Still, the resemblance was too strong.

"Park Rangers have closed most of the campgrounds and many trails that have access to the deeper forested areas. They have installed trail cameras and stepped-up patrols in the hope of finding and stopping whatever is happening here."

I turned the TV off; I had seen enough.

I sat there, shocked and uncertain about what to do next.

My cell phone was in my hand, and I jumped when it rang.

I answered without looking at who was calling.

"Hello?" I said, nervously.

"Dani, we have a problem," Leanne said. "Did you see the news?"

I breathed a sigh of relief. She had finally come around to my side of things.

"Yes, I just turned it off. What do we do?"

"If this is Silas, he has to be stopped."

"Do you really think it's him? If so, how can we stop him?" I asked.

"I really want to believe it's not him, but he's the only vampire I know who's been around. Not to mention he was feeling lost and desperate the day he left. I need to come up with a plan."

I was silent for so long, lost in thought.

Leanne had to make sure I hadn't hung up. "Dani, are you still there?"

"Yes, I'm here," I squeaked. "Tell me, what I can do?"

I heard Leanne exhale.

"You aren't going to do anything! Let me come up with something and we'll do it together. I just need to sleep on it."

"Okay," I answered. "Just let me know how I can help, and I'll be there."

"I'll call you tomorrow."

"Okay, Leanne, I'll talk to you tomorrow."

We hung up, and my brain went into overdrive. There was no time to wait. If it was Silas, he needed to be stopped, and quickly!

I couldn't wait for Leanne to devise a plan. I made up my mind I would leave first thing in the morning and find him myself. I needed to hear from him first, though. I needed to call him.

———

It was almost midnight before I summoned up the courage to call Silas.

I slowly took out my phone and scrolled through the contacts.

My heart was doing cartwheels in my chest. I suddenly had an image of all the times my heart raced around Silas for other reasons and how it made him smile. What would he think now?

I found his name, took a deep breath, and hit *call*.

The phone rang, once, twice, and then he answered.

"Dani?" Silas sounded rough and surprised.

"Hello, Silas," I stammered. There was a silence; it was long and drawn out.

Another deep breath. "Please, tell me you're not the one

behind these attacks. The police released a sketch, and it looks almost like you."

Silence again.

"Silas, are you still there?" I asked, apprehensively.

"Yes," was all he said.

"Please, Silas. If you're responsible, I beg you to stop."

He didn't say anything, just more silence on his end.

I kept going. "We can meet and talk, if you'd like. I want to see you."

I was quiet after saying that, waiting for a reply.

"No, it's not safe," he said, gruffly.

There was a barely audible click and the line went dead.

I just stared at my phone in disbelief. Something was off. I couldn't tell Leanne; she would instantly go on the warpath. And with Thanksgiving being only two days away, I didn't want to add any more to her plate. No, this was up to me. I needed to stop Silas, to save him from himself. If I had created the monster he had become, and if he was the one behind the terror, I was going to end it one way or another. Tomorrow, I was going to find Silas.

CHAPTER
Thirty

I WAS up before the sun the next morning. The sky was just beginning to turn a lighter shade of purple, and there were still a few small stars in the sky. If I was going to find Silas, I needed a head start.

I dressed in a T-shirt and a pair of jeans and grabbed a hoodie from my closet. The late November mornings could be chilly.

I laced up a pair of hiking boots and then headed to the kitchen to put some supplies in my backpack.

I drank a cup of coffee and ate a light breakfast while I worked.

Packing a few water bottles and some snacks, I planned to be gone all day. I hoped all the hiking would help wear off all my nervous energy, but I doubted it.

I slung my backpack over my shoulders and checked my appearance in the foyer mirror, ignoring the bags under my eyes from a sleepless night.

Satisfied with how I looked, I headed out. I knew Silas was probably hiding deep in the forest, away from the more crowded areas. The campground he had allegedly attacked was one of the few primitive ones deeper inside the forest. I planned to start there.

———

I parked close to the trailhead where the campsite was located. I grabbed my backpack and locked my doors and with a determination I didn't know I had, I headed into the forest. The sun had fully risen, and the morning chill and patchy fog had started to disperse.

I removed my hoodie, stopping along the trail to stuff it into my backpack.

I stood there for a moment, taking in my surroundings. There was a slight breeze, and it rustled the tree branches and leaves above me. I was pretty far into the forest at that point, and I noticed just how eerily quiet it was. No birdsong, no squirrels crashing through the underbrush. It was just the sound of the wind through the trees.

I looked up toward the forest canopy, searching for a sign of life, and found nothing, only the sunlight filtering through the leaves. I was reminded of the first time I really looked into Silas's eyes and how they made me think of the forest canopy on a sunny day. I tried not to think about his eyes or the absence of wildlife in the trees.

I took a drink from my water bottle and carried on.

It wasn't long before I came to the campsite. It had been cleaned up; all signs of chaos were removed. The only thing left behind were a couple of trail cams. I steered clear of them, hoping to remain unnoticed.

I circled the area and kept my eyes open for clues of Silas's presence.

Finding nothing, I headed farther in.

———

After another hour or so of hiking, I found myself in a truly remote part of the wilderness.

I checked my phone; it was nearly noon, and I had no cell signal. No wonder I hadn't heard from Leanne yet.

I decided to take a quick break before continuing down the trail.

I sat down on a tree stump and surveyed the woods. It was strangely quiet there, too. I wasn't sure if it was my mind playing tricks, but I began to get the feeling I was being watched.

I shook it off, gathered my pack, and soldiered on. The trees began to feel like they were pressing in on me. Their branches wove together in a sea of green, red, brown, and yellow that almost completely blocked out the blue of the sky above.

The feeling of being watched never left; it seemed to intensify with each step I took deeper into the trees.

The energy in the forest seemed to shift; the air felt heavy and thick. It was difficult to breathe and just felt wrong. My fight or flight instincts began to kick in, and I tried to make sense of the feelings I felt. My blood was pumping, my heart was pounding, and my hair began to stand on end.

I started to turn around and head back, when I heard a loud crack, like someone or something had stepped on a brittle stick on the forest floor. I jumped at the noise and turned to see what had disturbed the silence.

I saw movement in the woods.

A flash of red, and suddenly there was Silas appearing out of the tree line.

He stopped just at the edge, leaning heavily on the tree next to him, and he stared me down.

I was startled. My breathing stopped, and my heart skipped a beat.

He was dressed in a red and black flannel shirt, unbuttoned to show a black T-shirt underneath. He was wearing dark jeans and his favorite pair of boots. He seemed disheveled and dirty, and he was paler than usual. His skin was almost gray. He had dark purple circles under his eyes, and his cheeks were slightly sunken in. That was not the look of a vampire who had recently fed.

I couldn't tear my eyes away from his face; it was menacing.

His eyes narrowed. Was he angry to see me?

"Silas?" I gasped. I was shaking.

"Why are you here? I told you, it isn't safe!" he growled.

I took a step forward.

His head snapped up; nostrils flaring, and his eyes were wild.

I stopped. My heart was beating loudly in my ears, my brain was screaming at me to run, and I began to tremble.

But I stood my ground, ignoring my body's very sensible flight response.

"I needed to see you, to know you were okay and to warn you people are searching for you." My voice shook.

Silas gave me a smirk. "Nice to know you care."

I furrowed my brow. "I never stopped."

Silas laughed and took a step closer. "Is that so?" He chuckled, arrogantly.

He paused a moment before saying, "I admit, I made a mistake on Halloween night; I can't take that back. Seeing you so afraid of me, unable to even look at me, it broke my heart. No, it did more than that; it broke me."

His face was so full of pain, all arrogance lost. He scrubbed at the back of his neck, bowing his head, slightly. "You never gave me a chance to explain, to apologize. I knew I had made an irrevocable mistake."

He took another step closer; he was almost within reach. "You treated me like the monster I tried so hard to hide from you, and now you're out here checking to see if I am that monster."

His lips turned up in a sneer.

My shoulders slumped, and a tear escaped my eye. "I made a mistake, too; I see that now. But what was I supposed to think? You turned on me so quickly."

Silas's face softened, his lips parting as if to say something, but he remained silent.

"I never stopped thinking about you. Every day, I was miserable with the what ifs of it all. I came out here to find you, to tell you I'm the one who's sorry. I came out here after seeing the police sketch of you last night, to ask you to stop all this."

This time, we both stepped forward, closing the distance between us.

Silas looked outraged.

"You think I'm the one doing this? That I'm capable of this?" His voice was raised, angrily, and he waved his hands vaguely at the forest around us, but I knew he was talking about the attacks.

"Then, you believe me to be a bigger monster than I thought." He sneered again, trying to mask the pain he was feeling.

"Silas, I'm not sure what to think, especially after Halloween night. But I hoped against hope this wasn't you. When you spoke to me last night and said it wasn't safe to see you, I knew something had changed; I had to see for myself. What's happening? I can plainly see now you haven't fed, so clearly these attacks are not you. Who, or what, is it?"

Silas's face relaxed, and he sighed. He finished closing the gap between us and reached up to tuck a stray lock of hair behind my ear. His cold fingers, which were even icier than ever before, left traces on my skin.

"I have no right to be upset with you; how could you

know how to process all of this? I am angrier with myself."
He was trying to distract me and avoid my questions.

I took a small step back. "Answer my questions," I demanded.

Silas paused, never taking his eyes off me. He was thinking.

I could see the wheels turning in his mind.

He finally answered me. "It's a who. Two vampires, in fact. They have been the cause of all this. I couldn't leave, not with those two monsters lurking around. I couldn't leave you unprotected."

He stopped speaking and gazed into my eyes; they were pleading with me to understand.

I stood my ground and waited for him to continue his explanation.

"I'm pretty sure I've run them off, but not without severe consequences to myself. I have been so focused on getting rid of them and keeping you safe I haven't stopped to feed in a week. It doesn't matter now, though; they're gone, and you're safe with me."

He smiled, and my heart melted.

Silas reached out for me and stumbled, falling forward into me.

I caught him and lowered both of us rather clumsily to the ground.

"Silas!" I had never seen him like that, so weak and vulnerable. My hands fluttered about him before finally resting on his cheeks. "You need to feed! You're so weak."

It was at that moment I noticed the bruises on his body, all along the skin I could see. "What did they do to you?"

Silas chuckled, faintly. "You should see the other guys."

I couldn't believe he was kidding around as weak as he was, yet it was nice to see he still had his sense of humor.

I smiled at him. "This is no time for joking. We need to get you something..."

I stopped myself before I said it. I knew instantly what had to be done.

Silas seemed to know exactly what I was thinking. "Dani," he growled, "no."

"Well, I don't see anyone else around, and you're in no position to argue!"

"I could hurt you; I'm too far gone. It's too dangerous!"

"Oh, shut up! If you were that hungry and dangerous, you would have already done something by now!"

He was shocked at my boldness. I was, too, for that matter.

"Dani, I don't—"

My hands went to his face again. I smoothed out the lines of worry that drew his eyebrows and face into a frown. I smiled at him, as I took his arm and placed it around my shoulders. Slowly, steadily, I stood us both back up and I faced him.

I looked him deep in his eyes and spoke. "I'm yours, Silas Matthew Quinn. I know now I cannot have you without the darkness you've kept hidden from me. It's a part of you, just as much as this madness to love you is a part of me. I'm yours; I always have been."

I looked into his eyes, and he didn't hesitate.

He rushed forward and wrapped me in his arms and kissed me so longingly.

I felt whole again. The ache, the confusion, and the guilt I had been feeling were gone.

He kissed me with the promise of a million tomorrows, and I answered in kind.

Silas released me, his eyes wild and snakelike. He quickly began to change.

I watched, enraptured, but not afraid.

Then, he was on me.

He swiftly, but gently, pulled my head to the side, exposing my throat.

He placed his lips to my neck, and his fangs slid into my skin.

It happened so quickly I couldn't even gasp.

There was a burning in my veins, and a cooling numbness spread throughout my body.

I was aware of everything around me, until I wasn't. My vision went black, and I knew no more.

CHAPTER
Thirty-One

I AWOKE, feeling drained, quite literally. I hadn't opened my eyes just yet, but I could feel I was lying on something soft, and there were blankets on top of me.

I slowly opened my eyes, turned my head to the side, and noticed a window; it was familiar. I was in Silas's bedroom at his cabin. It was dark outside. How long was I out?

In an instant I remembered what happened to me. I went to feel my neck, and there were two small sores; they were already scabbed over. I felt so dizzy and weak I groaned.

Silas was sitting in a chair at the opposite end of the bedroom.

He quickly stood up and rushed to my side. "You're up! Thank God! I'm so sorry, Dani. I went too far."

I had never seen Silas so distressed.

"I got carried away, caught up in the moment, and when you said you were mine, I just..."

Silas sat on the bed and hung his head.

"I almost changed you," he said in a whisper. "I brought you back here after you lost consciousness. I'll never forgive myself for what I've done, and I won't blame you if you can't, either." He wouldn't look at me.

"So do you bring all the girls back home to your bed, or am I special?"

Silas turned to look at me, clearly astonished.

He took my hand. "You're not angry?"

I shook my head. "No, I'm not angry. I meant what I said, Silas." I laughed, lightly, and then patted his hand.

"When dating a vampire, it comes with the territory." I smiled at him.

Silas was still wide-eyed in shock at how I was taking all of it.

"I suppose it does," he said, slowly.

I sat up and hugged my knees. "Who were those other vampires you ran off?" I asked.

"No one of importance. They won't be back, not after the beating I gave them. If you saw the campground, then you have an idea. They thought they were smart by using my technique of having the victims forget what happened. They wanted this to look like I was to blame, which is why they let one person be a 'witness.'

"They showed her a picture of me, and that's how she was able to give the police a description. Luckily for me, it was a terrible picture, and a rather old one, at that." He laughed. "I guess they must have taken the photo I had given to Eliza in a locket back in 1898. If so, my hair was very different and it was from before I was changed, so the likeness was slightly off." He chuckled again, "I couldn't have them handing my description around, so I took care of it." He said it so seriously I knew it was the end of that conversation.

I nodded and looked down at my hands as I twisted the quilt between my fingers. "So were they the ones behind the note?"

"Notes, actually. There were more. Each one more menacing than the first."

I looked up at him, quickly. "Show me!"

Silas stood and walked to his dresser.

He opened the top drawer and retrieved a small stack of about five or six pieces of paper.

He handed them to me, and I snatched them out of his hand.

The one on top of the stack I had already seen.

The second read, *She reeks of magnolias, and so does her home.*

"They were in my house?" I asked, angrily, bunching the note in my fist.

"No, they were never in your house. They would have to be invited in, remember? That doesn't mean they weren't there, though." He turned back to the drawer and pulled out a wilted magnolia flower with one petal steeped in something rust-colored, now brown with age, and handed it to me.

The flower! I almost forgot about it. "Wait, I remember seeing this. It was on my doormat the morning after a storm. I just thought it blew off the tree."

I turned the flower around in my hand. "That means they were watching me well before I knew about it."

I stopped when I came to the stained petal. "Silas, what do you think this is?" I asked, fingering the petal, lightly.

Silas took the flower back and crushed it between his fingers. "You already know."

I blanched. I suddenly remembered seeing the silhouette of a man outside my door that night and the conversation I had with my neighbor, Jerry. I sharply recalled Jerry's bandaged neck, the broken window, and his confused state of mind. "Did they attack my neighbor?"

Silas flinched and nodded. "Yes. They were smart about it, too. They knew the rain and the wind would cover their scents. I'm certain they broke a limb off Jerry's tree and threw it into his window, which forced Jerry outside to survey the damage. That's when they struck."

Silas let the magnolia petals fall to the floor. "They were leaving me clues and staying just beyond my reach, toying with me to show me just how close they could get."

The anger rolled off him in waves, and his eyes flashed in the lamp light.

He ran a hand through his already tousled hair and took a steadying breath.

I was silent as I mulled things over, and Silas let me think. One of those two had attacked Jerry, and the stain on the flower was blood, Jerry's blood.

I clapped my hand to my mouth when I recalled how I stepped out into the storm to look for whom I thought was Silas.

He looked at me with understanding and took my trembling hand away from my mouth and held it.

I thought it might have been blood, but I didn't want to believe it. And now I realized just how close I came to it being my blood on that flower.

Silas sat down on the end of the bed.

I took back my hand and anxiously began reading the rest of the notes. The third note was just a printed picture of me unlocking the door of the bookstore.

The fourth said, *I'm sure she's delicious. We can't wait to sink our teeth into her!*

I threw that one away from myself and watched it flutter to the floor.

The fifth piece of paper was one of Leanne's Halloween party flyers. They wrote over the top of the information; *See you there!*

And the sixth note simply stated, *She's ours!*

"They were stalking me?"

Silas nodded. "Hunting you, actually. They were trying to get under my skin. I did my best to ignore them and just focused on keeping you safe. Their threats have always been idle ones, just enough to rile me up for a good fight if I could lure them out. That's why it took me so long to act."

Silas dropped his gaze to the floor. "I kept most of these away from Leanne, as well. I only let her know someone was watching you and threatening me with the notes about you."

"They were there Halloween night, at the party?" A silent tear escaped my eye.

"Yes, what you saw in the alleyway was me taking care of the mess they left behind. That's where they left the sixth and the final note in fact. In my car, under your shoes."

I shuddered. "Leanne kept trying to tell me there was more to what I saw. Did you tell her anything?"

"Only the two goons she had me follow were gone and the girl would be okay. I didn't want to worry her any more than was necessary."

"So what exactly did I see that night?" I asked, remorsefully.

"I wasn't feeding. I did bite her, but it was out of necessity. Those two barbarians fed on her and left her in pain and scared out of her wits. They fed without venom. Two strong vampiric men against one small twentysomething girl, she didn't stand a chance. I found them feeding on her and lost it. I was able to chase them off, but that was it. I couldn't leave that young lady bleeding and scared to death in that alley. I had to let them go."

Silas went quiet and shook his head. "I knelt beside her and sat her up, telling her I'd take it all away. I asked her to turn her head and look away from me. I bit her and released just enough venom to be able to influence her thoughts. I didn't feed on her. The blood you smelled on me was from the previous bite. Her neck was covered in it. I used my cape to clean her up the best I could and told her to forget about what had happened and then told her the story you undoubtedly heard as you tried sneaking up behind us. That's the truth."

We looked into each other's eyes for a long time. Me searching for the truth and him begging me to find it.

I nodded and quietly said, "I believe you."

"When I found that goddamned note under your shoes in

my car, I raced over to your house. I searched all around and found no trace of them. I called Leanne and asked where you were. She told me you were at her house with Jeff. I drove like a bat out of hell to her place and saw Jeff in the living room and then caught a glimpse of you as you drew the blinds for the night. I sat in my car across from Leanne's all night to make sure you were safe."

Silas laughed, lightheartedly. "I've been doing some stalking of my own lately. I couldn't leave you unprotected, not knowing where those two had gone. I just made sure you never knew I was around. Leanne knew, but I think she felt better knowing I was out there somewhere close by. That was their plan, to drive us apart so they could get you alone. It didn't work. I never left you alone, not really."

Everything he was saying struck a chord for me. It all started to make sense. Why Leanne was able to defend him so easily, why I always felt like I was being watched, and so on and so on. The puzzle was solved, and the final two pieces, Silas and I, were back in place.

Silas began speaking again, still trying to explain away the past few weeks. "When the attacks began in the forest, that was the final straw. I knew I had to do something. I took the fight to them. I found them easily enough, and when I did, I gave them hell. They fought back savagely, of course, but I had more to fight for. I should have killed them."

He growled, long and low. "But being the slippery little snakes they are, they tucked tail and ran before I could finish the job. I don't think they'll be back, but Lord help them if they return!"

Silas's face darkened, and another low growl came from somewhere deep in his chest.

I reached out and took his hand.

He jerked his head up and looked at me in surprise and immediately calmed.

I never flinched and just kept hold of his hand. He was

obviously worked up over the retelling of his story I must have surprised him. "I'm sorry it took me so long to try and find the truth and I never let you tell me your side. I shouldn't have waited so long."

Silas squeezed my hand and let it go.

He stood up, quickly, and spoke again.

"Dani," Silas ran his hand through his hair, pushing it back out of his face. "You're taking all this rather well. I'm having a hard time understanding the change of heart."

"Honestly, I am, too. I'm not going to lie; Halloween night terrified me. But Leanne said something to me the next day that made me second-guess everything. She said I couldn't only love the pretty parts of you. She was right, I'm just sorry it took me a month to realize it."

Silas leaned forward and kissed my forehead.

"I am the one who is sorry. I scared you and lashed out at you in anger at seeing what I am. I wanted to explain to you what had happened. And when you could barely look at me the next day, well, I knew that was the beginning of the end. I hoped so badly you would change your mind.

"Hell, I would have settled for a phone call, telling me we were through. When I didn't hear from you at all, I lost it. I did everything I could to keep myself from running back to you. But I knew I wouldn't be able to handle the way you looked at me that day. Not again. And then those filthy leeches showed back up and gave me plenty to do for a few days."

He laughed, but it was a pitiful little chuckle.

I took his hands in both of mine.

"I thought I had accepted who and what you are. I thought I knew you; I was wrong. I only knew what I wanted. I didn't truly accept what you are, not really, and when I was faced with the truth, well-

"I should have done things differently, stood my ground, but you were so angry and frightening I did what I do best; I ran. I have felt guilty for weeks for not letting you tell your side of the story, and I should have called as soon as Leanne told me what she thought had happened. It was pretty much right in line with what you told me, minus the vampire parts, since she didn't know those two were vampires. So for that, I'm sorry."

Silas sighed and laughed. "It sounds like we should have both picked up the phone."

"True." I didn't have the guts to tell him how close I came to stopping by here the day I went grocery shopping. To think, if I had, some of this could have been avoided.

"We're here now, though." I patted the bed beside me.

Silas laid down next to me.

I lay back down and put my back to him, allowing him to wrap an arm around me.

He nestled his face into the back of my neck and kissed it, softly.

"Why didn't you change me; what made you stop?" I whispered.

Silas was dead silent a long time before saying, "You didn't give me permission, and I told you I'd never do that unless you were 100% sure and had thought about it from every angle."

"Silas," I rolled over and we were lying face to face, "when I said I'm yours, that's exactly what I meant. I want to be like you."

CHAPTER
Thirty~Two

SILAS SHOT out of bed with a derisive snort.

"Your brain is still addled from the blood loss. There's no way you've thought this through!"

He began pacing the floor, running his hand through his hair and looking at me in disbelief. "Don't say things like that!"

"What do you mean? I thought you wanted me to be like you."

I sat up against the headboard and looked at him in confusion.

"Of course, I do! But there's no way you're rushing into this! I'm not ready for you to change." He stopped his pacing and looked down upon me from the foot of the bed.

"I see," I replied, looking down at the bedspread.

There was a stretch of silence between us for several minutes.

"How does that make you feel?"

Silas turned his back to me and sat down at the end of the bed. He looked up at my reflection in the dresser mirror.

I shrugged, locking eyes with his reflection. "I'm not sure. Sad, shocked, angry, relieved, disappointed."

Silas stood up and walked over to my side of the bed.

He took my chin in his hand, tilting my face up to look at him. "We have time to think about this, to see it from every angle. There's no need to rush."

He leaned forward and gave me a gentle kiss.

"Silas? Who were those other vampires?"

"Changing the subject, are we?" He smirked. God, how I missed that!

I nodded, and he sat down next to me.

"Like I said, no one of importance, just some old friends turned enemies. They like to show up from time to time and make my life hell for a few days."

Silas smiled tightly at me and then ran his hand over my hair. "Seriously, they're not worth thinking about."

I sat, silently, just looking at Silas. I knew he was leaving something out. Trying to protect me, as usual.

I let it go and smiled at him.

"You must be hungry by now," Silas declared.

I nodded. I was famished.

"I'll see what I've got."

He got up and went to the kitchen.

He came back with a bar of dark chocolate and a glass of water. "We'll start small and get something more substantial in a bit."

I smiled and took the snack.

"Thank you," I said, breaking off a square of chocolate then popping it into my mouth.

"There's so much I don't know about you," I said, quietly. "I honestly feel like I don't know you at all sometimes."

"You know me better than most," he said.

"I want to know more about you. You can't just tell me about two vampires who cause chaos in your life periodically and not expect to have to explain yourself. You can't keep all your secrets, not with me. No more hiding, and no more protecting me from the truth."

"I'd love to share my secrets with you, Dani. I want to share my life with you, and if that means showing you the skeletons in my closet, then so be it." His eyes held such fervor I knew he meant it.

"Me, too."

At that moment, I knew Silas was the one I was meant to be with. I felt so complete when he was near. I never wanted to be without him again. Monster or not, logic be damned, I wanted him and all his secrets.

We didn't talk anymore about the other vamps; I let it go, planning to bring it up again another time. Right now, all I wanted was rest.

———

I stayed the night with Silas in the cabin. It was peaceful, and I realized just how much I had missed him now that we were together again. My chest no longer had that ache, and the melancholy had lifted. The confusion I had felt while we were apart was gone, as well. It disappeared the moment he stepped out of the tree line. In that moment, I knew my future, and it was with Silas.

———

The following morning, Silas drove me back to where I had left my car. He insisted on following me home, afraid I was still too weak from last night's events.

I didn't argue.

We pulled our vehicles into my driveway.

As soon as I parked the car, I unbuckled my seatbelt and got out.

He followed suit and rushed out of his truck to help me into the house.

"I'm fine, really," I laughed, trying to brush his hands away.

"Maybe I'm just looking for a reason to hold onto you," Silas said, shrugging.

I stopped on the top step.

Silas was just behind me, one step lower. His face was almost even with mine.

I reached up and placed my hand on his cheek.

He leaned into it and placed his hand over mine, turning his head slightly and kissing my palm.

"I didn't realize just how much I actually missed you until last night," I said, softly.

Silas smiled, charmingly. "I'm glad you came to your senses."

I narrowed my eyes, playfully, and gave him a pursed-lipped smile. "And if I hadn't?" I asked, wrapping my hands around the back of his neck.

Silas cocked his head to the side and pretended to be thinking.

He turned suddenly to me.

His eyes started to change, his lips pulled back next, they thinned as his face contorted to allow his fangs to drop.

He quickly scooped me up and said, "I might have had to become a monster until you did."

Even though it happened quickly, I wasn't afraid.

He started to allow his features to soften as he held me up in his arms.

"Don't," I whispered, "Let me look at you."

Silas remained quiet and continued to hold me.

I took one hand and traced the features of his face. I really looked this time. I found him to be both alien and alluring, as well as exciting and altogether exotic. If I was going to love Silas, I needed to love this face, too.

I smiled, benignly, and placed my forehead against his. "I love you. I don't think I ever stopped."

I lifted my face and kissed his forehead.

Silas had returned his features, his eyes full of deep adoration.

He sat me down and drew me close, never taking his eyes off mine, he kissed me.

Gently at first, and then it changed to passion and hunger.

His hands found their way to the small of my back and the nape of my neck. Mine were wrapped around the back of his neck and through his hair.

Silas pulled away. "You don't know how much I wanted to hear those words. I love you, too, Dani. More than you'll ever know."

He embraced me, and I melted into him.

I took in his scent, breathing deeply.

He rested his head atop mine.

I let go first and began fumbling in my pocket for my house key.

When I found it, I turned around to unlock the door.

Silas stood behind me.

He brushed my hair off my neck and began kissing me, softly, behind my ear and down my neck until he reached the point where he had bitten me, and he lingered there.

I shivered as I got the door open and felt Silas smile against my skin.

He laughed, softly, and then swiftly scooped me up again, carrying me through the door, closing it with a swift backwards kick of his foot. He was rushing me up the stairs to my room before the door had time to click closed.

Silas gently placed me on the bed and lowered himself over me.

He kissed every inch of my skin he could reach.

His cold hands slid under my shirt and caressed my back, lifting me toward him as his lips found mine.

I held myself close to him, silently cursing the clothes that were between us, they were keeping me from feeling the chill of his skin against me.

As if sensing my need, Silas straightened, and I sat back against the headboard as I watched him pull his shirt over his head and finish undressing.

I quickly followed suit.

His eyes raked over me, adoringly. And then, hungrily, they went dark and morphed into the emerald green snake-like eyes I had come to love.

Once again, Silas lowered himself over me.

I wrapped my arms around him, pulling him down on top of me. The feel of his cold and silken skin sent chills through me.

Silas growled, long and low, as I wrapped myself around him and let him take me.

———

We lay in bed most of the morning, skin to skin, my head on his chest, his arms around me. It felt so normal, so natural; it felt like home.

"I missed this," Silas said, kissing the top of my head.

"Me, too," I sighed. "Can we make sure to never be apart again?"

"I think I can handle that." Silas grinned.

I raised up on one arm and looked at him.

Silas reached up and tucked my hair behind my ear and slowly ran his fingers down my cheek, my neck, my shoulder, and my arm. His hand was cold, like always, but it left me feeling warm.

"If we're going to do this, and I mean go all in, no more hiding things," I said. "You hid things from me before, only showing what you wanted me to see, but that's not going to work anymore."

We stared at each other; I wasn't backing down.

I was prepared for an argument, when suddenly, Silas smiled wide and sat up.

"I agree," he said. "Hiding my true nature from you didn't work, and it damn near cost me everything."

I smiled, relieved he agreed with me. "I wouldn't exactly call it your 'true nature', just..." I paused, trying to think of the right words. "One facet of your whole self."

Silas laughed, swinging his long legs over the side of the bed and standing up. "My whole self?"

"Yes, your whole self. I need to know everything."

Silas began to get dressed and asked, "What do you want to know?"

I watched him while he dressed, trying to think of what I wanted to ask.

"Well?" Silas picked up my shirt and threw it, playfully, at me.

I caught it and put it on. "What's it like?"

"What?" Silas replied.

"Being a vampire, of course."

Silas's face grew dark, and he smiled a wicked smile. "I thought you'd never ask. It would be easier just to show you."

CHAPTER
Thirty~Three

I WASN'T sure what Silas meant by saying it would be easier to show me. At first, I thought he meant to change me right then and there. I admit, I got a bit nervous and scared.

Silas picked up on my reaction at once. "Did I scare you?" he asked, laughing.

"A little." I tried to shrug it off.

"Judging by the sound of your heart, I'd say it was more than a little."

Silas sat back down on the bed, pulling me to him.

"I thought you meant to change me. Right here, right now," I said into his chest.

"Ah, I see." He chuckled. "And that right there is exactly why I wouldn't. You're not ready."

"Is anyone ever really ready for something like that?" I rebutted.

"Good point. I honestly wouldn't know. I've never changed anyone before."

"Never?" I asked, pulling away to look at him.

He shook his head. "Never."

He smiled, "Sure, I've offered to change a few people so I could have a companion, but they all backed out in the end."

"So you've been alone all this time?" I asked.

"I wouldn't say that, not exactly. I've had Leanne's family and her predecessors. I've also made some friends and a few enemies along the way."

He grinned and pulled me back into a hug. "Until you, I never realized just how lonely I actually was."

"That's kind of sad, actually. To go that long without knowing true friendship and love," I said, hugging myself to him tighter.

"That's why I want to do this right. If you truly want to do this, let me change you, then everything must be in order. You must be 100% sure, no doubts whatsoever."

"I am. I'm sure I want this. I want to be with you. But you're right; it can't be rushed."

"First things first. You need to learn all things vampire and lesson one starts tomorrow night." He winked at me.

"Tomorrow, why tomorrow?"

"Because tonight you have Thanksgiving dinner with Leanne and her family." He grinned.

I groaned. I had forgotten all about dinner with all the chaos of the past forty-eight hours.

Silas laughed, lightly. "Come to my house before sundown tomorrow. There's so much I want to show you."

———

Silas left, and I went about my day.

Jeff and Leanne both noticed the uptick in my demeanor, but I decided to leave them in the dark, for now. I needed to figure out the best way to tell them Silas and I were back together and I didn't think Thanksgiving dinner was the right time for that. I sat through dinner and dessert and shared in the lively conversation with Leanne's family, but my mind was elsewhere. I kept thinking about my plans with Silas tomorrow evening. I just wanted tonight to be over.

———

I tried keeping myself busy the following day to alleviate my anticipation for this evening's activities.

The bookstore was dead, and I hastily closed up shop and drove straight to Silas's. His truck was parked in front of the garage, so he must be here somewhere. I didn't see him waiting on the porch; he had to be inside.

I let myself in since the door was unlocked.

The lights were off, so I flipped the switch by the door, turning some on. The house was way too quiet. It was odd.

"Silas?" I called out. "Are you here?"

No one answered.

I walked from room to room, flipping on lights as I went. He was nowhere to be found.

I went back outside to see if maybe I just missed him. It was starting to get dark.

I walked to the garage and peered inside, still nothing.

I grabbed my phone out of my pocket and went back to the porch, sitting down on the swing.

I texted him. *I'm here. Where are you?*

No answer. I know he said to meet him here tonight. I was getting anxious and a little perturbed.

Suddenly, there was a voice in my ear. "Lesson one, stalking your prey."

A light kiss landed on my neck.

I jumped and whirled around, screaming. "Jesus Christ, Silas! Where the hell did you come from?" I was clutching my chest and trying to still my heart.

Silas was almost doubled over in laughter. "I was right behind you, or somewhere close by, from the time you pulled in to now."

I inhaled deeply and blew it out. "I never saw or heard anything."

"I know. That's the point. You only hear me if I want you

to." He was as proud as a cat who had just caught a mouse. "You'll be able to do that, too, once you're changed."

Silas rounded the porch swing and sat next to me.

"I knew you could be quiet, but I had no idea."

"It's a gift." He pretended to dust his shoulders off and smiled at me.

I rolled my eyes. "What other 'gifts' do you possess?"

"Allow me to demonstrate."

Silas's mood was infectious. He seemed so happy, like a weight had been lifted.

I couldn't help but laugh.

"Start running," Silas said, lazily pretending to inspect his nails.

"What?" I asked. I wasn't sure I had heard him correctly.

He responded slower this time. "Start. Running."

I stood up. "Where?"

He leaned forward, rested his elbows on his knees, and placed his chin in his hands. "It doesn't matter; just start running."

His eyes flashed in the porch light, and I took off.

I had never been known to be a strong runner, but I could hold my own.

I started running toward the field below the house in the direction of the pond.

I made the mistake of looking back to see where Silas was. He wasn't behind me.

I slowed down, trying to spot him, and all at once I was hauled up from the front and thrown over Silas's shoulder like I didn't weigh a thing.

"What the…" I tried to say as I was jostled around.

Silas had, once again, appeared out of nowhere. This time, he had grabbed me up and tossed me around like a sack of potatoes. He was laughing, maniacally.

"I'm glad you're enjoying yourself," I was finally able to say once he put me down.

"Lesson two, speed and strength."

He took off running again. He was faster than the fastest Olympic sprinter. He looked like he could outrun a cheetah. A mere human stood no chance of outrunning him.

Silas stopped at the edge of the pond.

I jogged over, breathlessly, to where he stood.

"See this rock?" he asked, pointing to a large boulder that was on the bank.

"Yeah, what about it?" I said, curiously.

"How much do you think it weighs?" He was smirking.

"A few hundred pounds, give or take." I shrugged.

Silas squatted down next to the rock and wrapped his arms around it. The small boulder had to have been at least three feet across and at least that tall. He stood up like it weighed nothing, palmed it in one hand, and hurled it into the center of the pond.

It landed with a spectacular splash.

Silas sauntered, cockily, over to me and wrapped his arms around me. "Close your eyes," he whispered.

I did as I was told.

"Now, tell me what you hear."

I listened, intently, trying to hear all the sounds I could. "I can hear birds, a few bugs, and the wind rustling the trees."

I strained to hear more, but there just wasn't much else.

Silas chuckled. "Open your eyes."

I did.

Silas was gazing lovingly down at me.

"I can hear all that and more. I can hear a cricket rubbing its legs together over there in that tree, I can hear the individual blades of grass rushing against each other as the breeze blows through them, and I can hear a small sports car driving down the road at the other end of my driveway. I can also hear the blood rushing in your veins and your heartbeat in your chest."

My eyes widened. "Doesn't that ever get too loud?"

He laughed again. "You learn to tune it out and focus on what you want to hear."

I nodded and cocked an eyebrow at him. "Well, I already know you have a super sense of smell, too, since you told me I have a smell all my own."

I laughed and looked toward the pond as I nestled my cheek against his chest. "My hero." I said, coyly.

"Stealth, speed, strength, super senses. All the makings of a superhero." I sighed, "My very own superhero."

"I'm far from a hero." Silas laughed. I enjoyed seeing that side of Silas. He seemed so much more carefree and open now.

"So I'll be capable of things like this?" I asked, looking up into his face.

"All this, and I have a feeling you'll be capable of so much more," he replied before giving me a kiss.

CHAPTER
Thirty~Four

SILAS and I had become inseparable over the next couple of weeks. We were like two teenagers experiencing our first love together. We couldn't get enough of one another. It seemed the old adage was true; absence does make the heart grow fonder. It was time to tell Leanne. Although, I was certain she already had a clue as to what was going on. I had gone to Leanne's for a visit. I made sure to keep a social life outside of Silas by hanging out with Leanne at least once a week. With Christmas just around the corner, we were having a Christmas movie night.

"Okay, spill," Leanne said as she flopped down on the couch next to me. "You've been in a fantastic mood for weeks. You are constantly texting someone on your phone; something or someone has come into your life."

"Or come back." I sat, quietly, staring into the bowl of popcorn in my lap.

"Come back?' Her eyebrows raised in comprehension as she took in what I said.

"Silas? You're back together?" Leanne didn't sound shocked or angry; she just sounded unsurprised.

"Yeah, a few weeks now. I thought you'd be upset. That's why I didn't say anything."

"I'm not upset."

She turned to look at me. "I'm not totally surprised, either."

She shrugged, grabbed some popcorn, and ate it, casually.

I looked at her with my eyebrow cocked and confusion written all over my face.

Leanne smiled, slyly. "There were clues." She shrugged again.

"Clues, what clues?" I demanded.

"The first clue was the attacks stopped. I figured you must have gotten through to him somehow. Then, shortly after, you were all giddy and wistful. Plus, Jeff told me he overheard you talking sweetly to Silas on the phone at work." She added that last part rather smugly.

"Tattletale," I said, scornfully.

"Maybe you should keep your office door closed if you want your phone conversations to be private." Leanne laughed.

I threw a piece of popcorn at her. "And maybe Jeff needs to learn not to eavesdrop."

We both were giggling.

I was relieved to know Leanne wasn't angry or upset with me for getting back together with Silas.

I waited for our fit of giggles to pass before saying, "There's something else you should know; the attacks weren't Silas."

"They weren't?" Leanne seemed genuinely surprised.

I shook my head. "Apparently, he has some enemies out there who like to mess with him in the worst ways possible."

"Interesting," Leanne replied, sarcastically. "I wonder why he has never said anything. That seems like something I should know!"

I shrugged. "Not sure. Maybe he felt like he could handle

it on his own. The two vamps were behind the creepy notes, as well."

"Notes? Silas never told me there were more!" Leanne exclaimed, angrily.

"Yeah, there were a few. He showed me."

"Well, I hate to admit it, but it sounds like he handled it since things are nice and quiet now. But Dani, I only have one question," Leanne said, getting serious.

"What's that?" I asked.

"Why did you forgive him so easily? You were so genuinely frightened and sure of what you saw."

How was I going to explain that one? It was the simplest and the most complicated thing I've ever done, to forgive Silas.

"I just did." I shrugged. "It was partly my fault, and it was what you said the day after Halloween that got me thinking. I can't love only some of Silas. I need to love all of him, vampiric monster and all."

"I see."

"It's complicated, but yes," I huffed.

"I've got time for complicated."

She reached over and took the bowl of popcorn from me.

"The night the police sketch was released, I knew I had to get in touch with Silas, so I called him. When he answered, he sounded rough and out of sorts. I asked if he were behind the attacks and told him to stop if he had been. He never said anything. I asked to see him, and he said it wasn't safe. Then, he hung up."

Leanne urged me to continue.

I took a breath. "I knew I couldn't tell you, so I decided to head out the next day and confront him myself."

"Typical Dani." Leanne rolled her eyes.

I ignored her remark and continued.

"I hiked the forest for hours before finally finding him. When I saw him, I could tell he hadn't fed in a long time. I instantly knew he wasn't behind the attacks. He was deathly pale with sunken cheeks, and there were bruises all over his body. He told me about the other two vampires and how he stopped them. We both spoke our piece. We forgave each other, and here we are."

I decided to leave out the part where he fed from me, but Leanne was sharp, and she knew I wasn't telling the whole truth.

She eyed me, sagely, and I knew I was caught.

"Why do I get the feeling you're leaving something out?" she asked, eyes narrowing.

I got quiet and looked down at my hands.

"Dani?" Leanne's voice had a threatening edge to it. "Tell me, or so help me..."

Boy, if Silas could hear my heart right now, he'd be smirking his head off. I took a deep breath and blurted it all out in one exhalation. "I let Silas feed on me."

Leanne stood up, rapidly, upending the popcorn bowl onto the floor. *"You did what?"* she screamed.

I winced, still not daring to look at her. "He was so weak, Leanne. He could barely stand; I had to do something!"

"How many times? Is this like your new kink, or something?"

She kicked the bowl out of her way and sat on the coffee table in front of me. "Dani, this is too much; this is too far!"

"It was just the one time," I said, stubbornly. "In fact, I wish it were more."

Leanne stood up, began pacing, and then she turned and glared at me. "You know he could kill you?"

"He won't. I can't explain it, but I know he won't," I argued back. "You don't have to accept it. In fact, I know you won't, but what's the difference between me and some stranger he hunts down in a dark alley?"

Leanne crossed her arms and continued to glare at me.

"Look, Leanne, just trust me on this. I love Silas, and that's not going to change. I'm in it for the long haul."

Leanne relaxed a bit and flopped into the recliner that was close to her. "That's exactly what I'm afraid of," she said, quietly.

She looked at me with tear-filled eyes. "Please, tell me you're not planning on letting him change you."

I didn't know how to answer that, so I just said, "No. Not yet, anyway."

Leanne looked at me, a tear escaping one of her eyes. "I'm not surprised about that, either."

She got up and went to her room, closing the door behind her.

I sat there on the couch for several silent minutes, staring at the popcorn on the floor and the unwatched movies on the coffee table.

I got up and got the broom and dustpan from the kitchen and cleaned up the popcorn.

After that, I started to head down the hall to Leanne's room then changed my mind. I figured she wanted to be alone.

It was time for me to go, so I headed to the door and let myself out.

The door clicked closed loudly behind me.

CHAPTER
Thirty~Five

I THOUGHT Leanne and I would be on the outs again, so I had planned on giving her some space and a few days' time before calling her.

She surprised me, however, by calling me the next evening.

I picked up on the second ring. "Hello?"

"Hey, Dani." Leanne sounded chagrined.

"Hi, Leanne. I've got to say, I'm surprised to hear from you."

"I know, I know. I called to apologize. Not for overreacting! I will not apologize for that because I think it's insanely stupid what you did, and I think it's just as insane to consider letting him change you!"

She paused and took a breath.

I stayed silent on my end; it was clear she wasn't finished.

"What I will apologize for is leaving and locking myself in my room instead of facing this like an adult and talking it out with you."

"I need to apologize, too. I'm sorry I didn't tell you about Silas and I sooner. I'm also sorry I divulged our secrets to you. I knew you probably wouldn't handle it well, but since Silas and I aren't hiding anything anymore, I figured I wouldn't hide anything from you, either."

Leanne and I were silent, both of us stubbornly set on our own sides of the argument.

"This isn't a conversation to be had over the phone, Leanne. Why don't you stop by after work tonight so we can hash this out?"

"All right, I'll see you a little after 8:00."

"I'm looking forward to it. Goodbye, Leanne."

I hung up before she could add anything else.

———

A few hours later, Leanne pulled in. She was still in her uniform, so I knew she had come straight from the diner.

I let her in, and we headed into the living room. You could have cut the awkward tension with a knife.

I spoke first just to get the ball rolling. "I don't want you to think Silas is feeding on me every day, because he's not. Like I told you, it was just that one time. I also don't want you to think I'm going to change in the next few days, either. Nor will it be in the next few weeks or months. But I do know I want to be with Silas, and to truly be with him, I need to become like him."

Leanne huffed. "Yeah, I guess ' 'til death do us part' is a bit different when one of you is immortal."

I laughed at her gibe, still trying to ease the tension. "Exactly."

Leanne inhaled deeply and exhaled slowly. "Look, I can get past the feeding, and I have finally come to terms with what Silas is because I can finally see the good in him because of you. But when my best friend wants to completely change who she is, what she is, to be with someone like," she gulped, "Silas...Well, I feel like I should get a say in that!"

"Is that so?" I asked, bitterly. "If you can see the good in Silas, why can't you do the same with me?"

"Silas wasn't given a choice to be who he is now. You still have a choice! I know you feel like you have no one left after your parents passed, but you have me. You will always have me."

She took my hands in hers and looked at me, her eyes pleading with me to understand.

"I know that, Leanne. You've always been like a sister to me. I'm not making this decision lightly, and neither is Silas. In fact, he is all for waiting as long as we can."

"So there's no definite date or timeline for this?" she asked.

"Nope." I shook my head. "Nothing is set in stone."

"Good." Leanne sighed. "There's still time to change your mind."

"Absolutely." I smiled, hopefully convincingly. I only said that to placate her.

I reached out and hugged her, thankful we had seemed to come to some sort of stalemate over this.

Leanne pulled away from our hug and said, "I gotta know, are you two still planning on your trip?"

I hadn't thought about it. I assumed it was off after the Halloween fiasco. "I...I don't know. We haven't talked about it."

Could our trip still happen? I mean, almost everything was already in place. Jeff was running the bookstore practically on his own now, and he had hired another employee. I just needed a house sitter, I guess.

"Well, let me know as soon as you make a decision," Leanne said. "My original offer still stands."

I was shocked she would still offer, considering the circumstances. "Thank you, Leanne. I certainly will."

She smiled at me, warmly, and said, "Now that's out of the way, we have Christmas to look forward to."

"Oh, yes, Christmas. I almost forgot." I rolled my eyes.

Leanne laughed. "As you know, my parents are going on a cruise for Christmas, so it will just be Jeff and me. So we were thinking about a double date Christmas. What do you think?"

"You actually want to spend Christmas in the same room as Silas?" I asked, doubtfully.

"Well, no, but if he's important to you, then he's welcome."

"I'm glad to see you in the generous Christmas spirit, Leanne." I laughed.

This was going to be a Christmas to remember.

CHAPTER
Thirty-Six

THERE WAS something fishy about Leanne's sudden forgiveness; she was hiding something from me. She seemed so concerned and upset I was even considering letting Silas change me. It was odd she would want me to leave for months on end with him, and it was especially odd she had invited him over for Christmas.

It wasn't long until I got some of the answers I was looking for.

Silas was waiting for me when I got home from work the following day.

He greeted me with a smile and a kiss.

"How was your visit with Leanne yesterday?" he asked as we walked through the door.

"Oh, you know, same old stuff we always argue about. To be a vampire or not to be a vampire."

I nudged into him with my shoulder, and he wrapped me in a hug.

"And what did she have to say about that?" Silas asked, chuckling.

"She's definitely not into it; that's for sure." I gave an exasperated laugh. "She did surprise me, though."

"Oh?" Silas asked, raising an eyebrow and giving me a mocking smile. "How so?"

"She asked if we were still planning on taking our trip and she offered to watch the house. How does that make any sense?"

I looked up at Silas. He had a mischievous grin on his face. "She also invited you to Christmas."

Silas's grin widened. "Yeah, I might have had something to do with that."

"I knew it! But how in the world did you convince her to do that, and to see about the trip? I've got to be honest with you, I haven't thought about it much since Halloween."

He laughed. "I needed to know if you were still interested in going, and I need Leanne's presence at Christmas for your gift. Once I laid it all out for her, she couldn't refuse. She only had one stipulation, funnily enough." Silas laughed. "You'll never guess what it was."

"Oh, do tell. I can't wait to hear this." I rolled my eyes.

Silas's eyes shimmered.

He smiled, darkly, and in a sinister voice he said, "She told me I had to return you in your original human form."

"Is that all?"

We both laughed, and Silas took my hand and led me to the couch in the living room.

I groaned as we sat down, suddenly realizing something.

"Oh, crap! I didn't even think about gifts. I haven't gotten anyone anything!" I sank lower into the couch cushions.

"We still have a few days. I'll go with you." He looked like a kid in a candy shop with his face lit up in a smile.

I was having a hard time imagining Silas in a crowded mall or a shop with all the other last-minute shoppers. The temptation would drive him crazy.

"Okay," I laughed, "this should be interesting."

"As for me, you don't need to get me anything. I have everything I need."

He took my hand and kissed it.

"Good to know. What do you buy a vampire for Christmas, anyway? A new coffin? Oh! How about your very own dark and spooky castle?" I waggled my fingers in front of his face and made a noise like a moaning ghost.

Silas snapped at my fingers with his teeth. "Clever, very clever."

"I thought so." I shrugged. "So now our trip is back on, what are the plans?"

"No plans. Not really, anyway." Silas began. "I figured we would just go where the road takes us."

"I like it." I smiled.

"The first leg of the trip is already planned, though. But you'll have to wait until Christmas to find that out." Silas winked.

"I can't wait." I said, excitedly. "Where will we be staying along the way?"

"We still have time to figure all of that out. I figured we'll spend our nights in different places along the open road."

Silas pulled me closer to him. "We'll stay in luxury hotels, or roadside vintage motels, if you like. We can sleep under a blanket of stars in a field of wildflowers. The choices are endless, and they are all yours to make."

He began running his fingers up my arm and then along my neck.

I had noticed earlier he seemed a bit paler than usual, and the dark circles were returning under his eyes.

I moved my hair to the side off my neck and leaned in closer to him.

Silas started to kiss my neck, lingering on the area just before my shoulder.

"Silas?" I said softly.

"Mmm?" he purred against my skin.

"When was the last time you ate?" I asked in a whisper.

Silas lifted away and brushed my neck with his fingers, back and forth.

I turned my face upward to look at him.

His eyes had changed, and it was all the answer I needed.

My pulse began to flutter.

Silas's fingers stopped, my vein pulsating beneath them.

"Are you sure?" he asked.

I nodded.

Silas lowered his mouth to my neck, and I felt his lips open against my skin. His teeth took hold of my throat, and then his fangs slipped sharply under my skin and into my vein.

There was a warm gush, and Silas began to drink.

He didn't release his venom, so I felt everything. The sharp sting of the bite, the warm flow of blood from my neck, but most of all I felt enraptured that I could do this for him. To know we craved each other so much my presence sustained him and he completed me in ways that were indescribable was more than enough proof of the bond we had created.

When Silas pulled away his lips, teeth, and his tongue, were now stained red with my blood.

CHAPTER
Thirty-Seven

I STARTED HAVING DREAMS AGAIN. Only this time, they were mostly about me being the vampire rather than Silas. I wasn't sure what had triggered them. It could have been my conversation with Leanne or the many conversations I'd had with Silas. The stress of Christmas and our upcoming trip didn't help, either. One thing was certain, though, they were no longer nightmares. In my dreams, I was strong and fast, wickedly beguiling, and most importantly, Silas and I were happy.

My last dream, however, was a bit odd. I had dreamt, no matter how much I tried to slake my vampiric thirst, I couldn't satisfy it.

I awoke with a start. My mouth and throat were parched, and my hair hung damply against my neck.

Silas sat up next to me as I rubbed my throat.

"Are you okay? Did you have a nightmare?" He began rubbing my back.

"Um, yeah, I suppose so," I said. My voice was raspy. "I'm going to get a drink of water."

I threw the covers back and started for the bedroom door.

Silas turned on the lamp and watched me, a worried look on his face.

I walked, slowly, down the stairs and into the kitchen.

I took a glass from the cabinet and filled it with cold water from the tap. My thoughts were going back to my dream with its piles of bodies and rivers of blood.

I downed one glass and then another.

My back was to the entrance of the kitchen, so I was startled when Silas entered.

"That must have been some dream if it made you that thirsty." Silas chuckled. He slid behind me, wrapping his arms around my waist.

I leaned back into him and let him hold me.

"Do you want to talk about it?" he asked.

"What's it like, the thirst?" No sense in beating around the bush.

I felt Silas tense, slightly, but he relaxed and turned me around to face him.

"I think I can surmise what you dreamt about," he said, his brow furrowing in thought. "It's not easy to describe, as it never really goes away."

"Is there no way to relieve it?"

"Sure, there's one. But it's only temporary and leaves you wanting more. You must learn to control it and not let it control you. Otherwise, you'll be a monster and lose touch with any humanity you have."

"Does it hurt?" I whispered.

"In the beginning, it's enough to drive you crazy, and for the most part, it does. It's an itch you can't scratch, a burn you can't relieve. After your first taste, you want more and more as the bloodlust takes hold. It's hard to stop, but not impossible."

"I don't want to be a monster!" I cried.

Silas lifted my face to look at him, wiping my tears with his thumbs.

"You won't be. The choice is still yours, and I'll stand by whatever decision you make. But if you choose my path, I'll stand behind you every step of the way. You will not lose yourself; I won't let you."

Silas wrapped me in a tight hug, and I buried my face in the hollow of his neck, breathing in the smell of his skin. I believed him. I somehow knew if I chose to go through with it Silas would not let me down. I wouldn't become the thing of my nightmares.

"I think I'm ready to go back to bed now." I yawned.

Silas smiled and kissed me, softly. "After you."

———

The next morning, we got up and decided to go shopping. I still needed to get gifts for Leanne's get-together.

We drove out of town into the closest big city. We found a department store and decided to try our luck.

It was crowded with last-minute shoppers, like me. The toy aisles were chaos.

Luckily, the home goods section was still relatively unscathed. Leanne had her eye on a reproduction vintage stand mixer, so I had decided to get it for her. That store was one of the places that still had a few available.

We were walking past the jewelry cases, when I noticed the girl behind the counter eyeing Silas.

He must have noticed, too, because he turned to me and grinned.

"Are you ready for another lesson?" he asked, conspiratorially.

I laughed and nodded.

Silas rubbed his hands together and said, "All right. Next lesson is all about charm and gaining someone's trust."

He winked at me. "Watch and learn."

I pretended to peruse the nearby clearance rack as I watched Silas saunter over to the counter.

The young girl with the roving eyeballs rushed to his aid, tripping over herself to get to him.

Silas turned on the charm.

He gave her his best heart-melting smile, and she practically swooned.

"C-can I help you?" she stuttered.

"Hello," he paused to read her name tag. "Yes, Stacy, I'd love your help."

Another flashy smile, and he began leaning on the counter, looking into her eyes. "I need to buy a gift for someone special, and I'm at a loss."

Little Stacy's face fell. "Oh, is this for your girlfriend?" She glanced quickly at his left hand, checking for a wedding ring.

"Something like that." He smirked and placed his elbows on the counter and rested his head in his hands.

"What would you like your boyfriend to get you?" He asked her, sweetly. Oh, good gravy, he was really laying it on thick.

I tried to stifle my laughter by feigning interest in a rack of shirts.

"Oh, um, I don't know. I don't have a boyfriend." She batted her eyelashes and blushed.

"Come now, you're joking." Silas gave her the smirk.

Stacy began to turn redder and shyly shook her head as she started to look through the glass cabinets.

I just knew Silas loved that. I wished I could see his face; I'm sure he had the smirkiest of smirks on his lips.

"Diamonds are always nice." She brought out a diamond tennis bracelet.

"Too mundane." He waved it away. "No, I need something special. This person is my whole world. She is the sun to my moon, and her eyes are more brilliant than the stars in the sky."

Stacy was practically melting at this point.

I was doing my best not to gag. Did that crap really work on people?

"Rubies are always lovely," she stammered. "Or how about emeralds? They match your…"

She stopped, her face turning redder as she looked at Silas.

"Yes? They match my what?" Silas said, demurely, leaning in a bit closer.

"I was going to say your eyes." Stacy quickly looked away from Silas's grinning face and grabbed an emerald and diamond tennis bracelet from the cabinet.

"Oh, that is lovely." Silas pretended to admire it. "Would you mind if I put it on you to see how it looks?"

"Oh, uh, not at all." Stacy was practically eating out of his hand.

Silas took her hand and fastened the delicate clasp, turning her wrist this way and that in the light.

"Lovely, absolutely lovely," he nearly purred. "I'll take it."

He winked at her, and Stacy almost fell over herself, once again, to get him rung up.

She placed the bracelet inside a gift box and then put it in a bag, but not before she slipped her card inside. "Call me, if you have any problems with it or anything."

"Thank you, Stacy, I will."

Silas turned on the full power of the smirk and then walked away.

She watched him leave and fell back against the counter, trying to recover.

Silas walked past me and winked. "Hook, line, and sinker."

I caught up with him and said, "You're incorrigible. I'm glad you never tried any of that with me."

"Didn't need to. The hook was set with you the night I bought your apple pie at Lulu's." He grinned.

He was right, of course.

———

We finished up our shopping and headed out to find my car in the parking lot.

We were laughing and joking with each other, when suddenly, Silas pulled me to him, protectively.

His arm tight around my shoulder, he leaned in close to my face and hissed, "Stay close to me and walk quickly. Don't look scared, keep smiling, and give me your keys."

I tried to look around, but Silas's arm wound tighter around me.

"Just walk; don't look!" he whispered out of the corner of his mouth.

I fished my keys out of my pocket and handed them to him.

"What is it?" I whispered.

"We have company." He growled while eyeing a black Camaro that had just started its engine.

I turned my face to him as we briskly walked along. "Company? Who?" My heart was pounding.

"Calm down. They won't try anything here. Just get in the car."

Silas unlocked the car, opened my door, and tossed our things in the back seat.

I got in, and he rushed to the driver's side.

Silas quickly opened the door and sat down in what seemed like one swift movement.

He brought the engine to life and barely put it in gear before he hit the gas.

We squealed tires, pulling out of the lot and running a red light in the process.

"Silas, tell me what's going on!" I screamed at him while hanging on to the "oh-shit" handle above my head.

He was driving like a maniac, weaving in and out of traffic.

"Remember those two vamps I told you about? The ones who caused the mess in the forest a few weeks ago? Well, they're back."

A low growl escaped his lips. "I should have killed them when I had the chance!"

He ran another red light.

"What do you mean they're back?" I screeched as I shut my eyes to not see the oncoming cars. I also began stomping my imaginary brake pedal as if I could slow us down by sheer will and determination.

"I guess they're back for more. Now, they're following us."

He glanced in the rearview mirror, and his eyes flashed in the lights of the oncoming traffic. His face was growing darker by the minute. If he got any angrier, he'd be in full-blown vamp mode before long.

I turned around in my seat to look behind us, and my stomach dropped.

Sure enough, there was another car weaving in and out of traffic, erratically. I couldn't see what type of car it was; I could only see it was a black sports car that looked suspiciously like the Camaro that was in the parking lot, and it was gaining on us, fast.

"Silas, they're getting closer!" Watching the fast-approaching car was more terrifying than any deranged driving Silas was doing.

"I can see that. I'll try to lose them."

He cut another driver off and quickly pulled off the next exit, merging into traffic and looking for our next escape.

I looked again and saw the black car taking the same exit. The driver had switched on the car's driving lights. They were red, and they looked like a pair of demon eyes staring us down.

"They're still following us!" I exclaimed.

This time, they got closer than either of us would have

liked. I could see now it was, indeed, the same Camaro from earlier.

Silas slammed the brakes and did a U-turn in the median.

I braced myself against the seat and the armrest.

My head was snapped back into the headrest as he punched the gas pedal with his foot. The engine in the car was whining with the extra effort Silas was asking of it.

We were heading the other way now, into oncoming traffic and back toward the interstate.

Chaos erupted in a cacophony of screaming brakes, screeching tires, and honking horns as we weaved in and out of the cars coming straight toward us.

Everyone around us tried to avoid a potential wreck, which caused a backup that trapped the demon-eyed Camaro in.

We got back on the interstate going the wrong way before Silas whipped my car around in a maneuver I'd only ever seen in the movies. Kicking it down again at a higher rate of speed than my poor little car has ever been driven.

I turned around to look behind us and didn't see anyone following.

"Do you think we lost them?" I was shaking from fear, and it wasn't Silas's driving I was afraid of.

"For now. But they know where you live, and they know where I live, too. Dani, I'm sorry, but we have to leave. Tonight!" I've never heard Silas sound so angry in all the time I've known him. His voice was low and gruff, mixed with venom and hate.

"Tonight?" I stammered.

"Yes! I don't know any other way to keep you safe! I have to lure them out of town, so Leanne and Jeff and the rest of the town are safe, as well."

I was quiet for a long time before I finally acquiesced. "Okay."

CHAPTER
Thirty-Eight

WE PULLED into my driveway at what felt like 100 miles per hour, gravel slinging everywhere.

Silas slammed the car into park and was out of his door and to mine faster than I could blink. He all but carried me to the house.

"Pack a bag, quickly! Whatever else you might need, I'll buy it later." Silas's voice was raised and frantic.

We rushed upstairs to my room, and I grabbed a large duffel bag out of the closet.

I threw a few days' worth of clothes and other things in it before I stopped what I was doing. "Silas, stop!"

He walked out of my bathroom with my toothbrush in his hand. "Stop? We can't stop! We have to go!"

"Not until you tell me what's really going on! Why are those two coming after me?"

I angrily zipped my bag, walked over to Silas, and snatched my toothbrush out of his hand. "Tell me, now!"

Silas's shoulders slumped, and he looked at me with a pained expression. "They're after you because they finally know they have something that can hurt me. I can't lose you, Dani; I won't!"

"What does that even mean? You have to tell me who these people are; I need to know what I'm running from."

We sat down on the end of the bed, and Silas began to tell me about our pursuers. "Their names are Kazamir and Garridan, and they blame me for their sister's death."

"Their sister being?"

"Eliza," Silas answered.

"But you didn't kill her," I attested.

"No, not directly. The way they see it, though, I might as well have. She never meant to care for me, but in her way, she did. Eliza was only meant to find a new recruit for their master race of vampires and failed when she began having feelings for me.

"The way her brothers see it, if she had never changed me, she'd still be here. They've hunted me down off and on for many, many years, making my life hell, but they've never been able to keep up with me or defeat me. But now I've given them all the ammunition they need to end me."

He looked at me with such sorrow and regret I had to look away.

I couldn't hold back my tears as they silently slid down my cheeks and fell to the floor.

"No, no, no, Dani; don't cry. None of this is your fault. It's mine. If I had just kept to my life as usual and not gotten involved, you wouldn't be in this mess. This is why I've been alone for so long."

"Are you saying you have regrets?" I asked, almost silently.

"No. I'm not saying that at all. I haven't felt this alive in almost two centuries. You make me feel more than I have in all my life, both alive and undead."

Silas grinned at me, but his face fell quickly. "My only regret is taking those two for granted and not keeping you safer."

Silas stood up. "This ends sooner rather than later."

I stood, scrubbing the tears from my eyes with the back of my hand.

I grabbed my duffel bag off the bed, slinging the strap over my shoulder.

"What are we waiting for? Let's get this over with!" I sounded braver than I felt.

CHAPTER
Thirty~Nine

BEFORE HEADING OUT OF TOWN, I made Silas take me to Leanne's. I couldn't leave without saying goodbye to her and explaining why we were leaving.

"You can't tell her verbally why we're leaving," Silas said.

"What do you mean? How else would I tell her?"

Silas sighed. "I mean, you're going to have to tell her without telling her."

"Okay, now I'm even more confused." I crossed my arms and huffed.

I began watching the houses go by with their cheerful Christmas lights and holiday decorations whizzing past. The weather had turned cold, and a sad, steady drizzle began to fall.

We passed a house that was decorated in red twinkling lights. The rain was running down the windows in streams and rivulets and had caught the red glowing reflection of the Christmas lights. For a moment, the water looked as if it had turned to blood.

It gave me chills, so I shut my eyes to block it out.

Silas reached over and placed his hand on my knee. "I'm saying we need to come up with a way to tell Leanne we're leaving, but silently tell her where we're going and why. If the brothers are anywhere close by, which I have a feeling they are, they could be listening. We don't want to give them any clues as to where we are going."

"I see, so you mean like write it down but in the meantime carry on a different conversation."

"Exactly."

We pulled into Leanne's driveway and swiftly got out. Her house was decorated in vintage multicolored Christmas string lights that bathed the yard in a soft kaleidoscope of color.

Leanne met us at the door.

"Dani, Silas? What are y'all doing here?" She was surprised to see us, and rightfully so. It was getting late, and I didn't call first to tell her we were coming.

"Hey, Leanne," I answered, cordially. "May we come in? We have something to talk to you about."

Leanne's face was wrought with confusion.

My face did not match my tone, and I'm sure Silas was scouring the yard, looking for any sign of trouble.

"Yeah, guys, come on in."

Leanne held the door for us, and we made our way to the living room once inside.

"What's up?" she asked.

I took out my phone and opened the notes app and began typing.

Some of what we need to say cannot be said out loud. We might have listeners. There are two vampires stalking Silas and I, and we need to leave town to draw them away from here. Just please, act casual and keep your tone light.

As I was typing my message, Silas began talking. "Leanne, we have decided we can't wait for Christmas to leave for our trip."

I showed Leanne the message I had typed out.

I don't know if her eyes widened in shock from my message or from what Silas said, but she played along.

"Oh. Oh! That's wonderful, guys! I think that's a great idea!" She angrily screwed up her face and grabbed my phone from me and began typing.

Is it the two creeps *from the forest? I thought Silas handled that.*
She showed the phone to us.

"Yes!" I nodded, emphatically, tapping the phone. "We think so, too, we're just so excited!"

This time, Silas snatched the phone from Leanne. *I did handle it, but they came back!*

"I wanted to swing by before we left to give you your gift since we won't be here for Christmas. Silas, can you be a dear and grab Leanne's gift from the car?"

Silas went back out to the car to grab her gift.

I took my phone from him and began typing.

We don't know what else to do. They almost killed us tonight in a high-speed car chase that only ended when Silas caused a mess in traffic, blocking them from getting out! We're hoping they follow us out of town and we can lose them somewhere along the way. Silas is prepared to kill them, if necessary. We'll be careful. We're doing this to keep you and Jeff and everyone else safe. They want me, and the only way to keep me safe is for me to be with Silas.

I handed Leanne the phone.

At the same time, Silas walked back in with her gift.

"Here's your present, Leanne. Sorry we didn't have time to wrap it," Silas said, quickly.

As she went to take her gift, Silas motioned for us to gather in closer.

He whispered his next few sentences. "I checked all around outside. I didn't see, hear, or smell anything out of the ordinary. I don't think they're here. We can speak freely, but keep your voices down. Maybe turn on the TV to muddle our voices, just in case."

Leanne turned on the TV and then turned to face us with a fierce look in her eyes. "This is nuts!" she hissed. "What am I supposed to do with this information?"

Her eyes began to well with tears.

I reached out and took her hands in mine.

"I don't think we have any other choice. Those two are hell-bent on wrecking Silas's life through me, and that means they could come for you, too. If we're gone and they follow us, then you are safe. Jeff is, too."

"How do you know they'll follow you?" Leanne asked, doubtfully, looking at Silas.

"They don't want anyone here; they want Dani."

He looked at me, sadly, and then quickly glanced back to Leanne. "They know she's what will hurt me the most to lose."

It suddenly felt like all the air had left the room.

"I don't like it, not one bit!" She pulled me into a hug so tight I thought I could hear my ribs cracking. "I don't understand any of this, but I guess I'm going to have to. I hate this; I'll be worried sick the whole time."

I returned her hug. "I know, Leanne. Silas will keep me safe."

"Yeah, well, he'd better." She scowled at Silas before letting me go.

Leanne got up from the couch and went into the next room.

I heard a drawer open and close, and Leanne returned with a small box. "I guess you'll be needing this."

She handed the box to me.

"What's this?" I asked, looking back and forth between Silas and Leanne.

Silas spoke for the first time in several minutes.

He came away from the window he was looking out of and placed his hand on my shoulder. "Open it and see. This is the only reason I was invited to Christmas."

He smiled at Leanne, and she rolled her eyes.

I lifted the lid off the box, and inside was what looked like a house key attached to a keychain that was a tiny version of the *Welcome to Colorful Colorado* sign. "Are we?"

Silas held his finger to his lips, to keep me from finishing my question. He tapped his ear and pointed outside. "That's the key to our next destination. We'll leave as soon as you say your goodbyes."

CHAPTER
Forty

WE WERE GOING TO COLORADO. It would take us two or three days to drive there, and once there, we hoped the roads would be clear of any snow so we could get to my surprise. It was the one silver lining in all this mess. Leanne and I said our goodbyes; it was tearful for us both. We've never been away from one another long, and given the circumstances, I knew she was worried. She made me promise to call her every day and reminded Silas of her one stipulation, as well.

We drove in silence for a bit, and I was trying to take in as much of the North Carolina scenery as I could, knowing it would be a while before I saw it again. The rural and the forested areas of Ophidian Grove began to give way to suburbs and cities and busy interstates.

I looked at Silas, and he met my gaze with a smile.

"Try not to worry, okay? It's all going to work out, you'll see." Silas's smile waivered, infinitesimally, which told me even he was worried.

He began humming a song. I'd heard him hum and whistle it numerous times before, but I never thought to ask about it.

"I've noticed sometimes you hum a song. It sounds so familiar, but I can't put my finger on it. What is it?"

" 'Scarborough Fair.' My mother sang it to us often when we were children, and she hummed the tune all the time while she was busy around the house. It's a permanent earworm."

He smiled, bemused. "I guess I got that habit from her."

"That's sweet. I'm still not sure why it sounds familiar, though." I pursed my lips in thought.

"It's been around for hundreds of years, but Simon and Garfunkel made it popular in the '60s. So it's not too far off base to think you've heard it while growing up."

I nodded. Silas had been alive, or undead, whichever way you wanted to look at it, for so long. To think about all the history he's seen was mind boggling.

"You're pretty amazing. You know that?" I said, admiringly.

"I'm glad you think so." He smirked "Otherwise, this relationship would be pretty one-sided because I think you're rather amazing yourself."

"Me? I'm nobody. You, on the other hand."

Silas scoffed.

"Seriously, Silas. Think about all you've seen. The end of the Civil War, the Roaring '20s, the Great Depression, both world wars, and so much more. You're a walking, talking history book."

"I guess that's cool, if you like that sort of stuff. Most people are intrigued by the whole being a vampire thing," he teased.

"Well, yeah, that's cool and all," I shot back. "But the stories you could tell, someone should write a book about you."

"They'd never believe it!" He laughed, loudly.

Our conversation was a nice break from the reality of our

situation. I just smiled at him, in awe that this creature, this beautiful being, called himself mine.

I began to laugh.

"What?" Silas asked, surprised.

"Nothing," I replied. "I was just thinking about how much of a trope we are."

Silas was quiet, and then his expression turned comical. "A trope? How's that?"

"Think about it. It's the classic vampire romance trope."

Silas just sat there, with that comical look on his face, waiting for me to explain.

"Tall, dark, mysterious stranger comes to town. That's you, by the way."

Silas nodded, going along with me. "He meets the small-town girl who's craving adventure and maybe a bit of romance in her life. That's me." I pointed to myself.

"I'm following; go on." Silas chuckled.

"Said vampire becomes conflicted about whether to take her to dinner or to have her for dinner. They like each other, so he holds off. She soon discovers the truth but doesn't care, and then they live happily ever after." I mimed a spreading rainbow with my hands.

Silas shook his head, and his smile had disappeared. "There's only one thing wrong with your trope theory."

"What's that?" I asked.

"We haven't reached the happily ever after moment just yet."

And just like that, the crushing weight of why we were on this road trip in the first place came roaring back to the present.

CHAPTER
Forty~One

WE DROVE for hours on end. Silas did almost all the driving. We only stopped for gas, grabbing snacks and drinks for me when we did and also allowing time for bathroom breaks. Otherwise, we drove non-stop, only stopping at a roadside motel so I could get at least one good night of sleep. There was no time to stop and take in any sights or enjoy the road trip, for that matter. If we were going to outrun and outsmart the brothers, we had to stay on course.

We arrived in Colorado by late afternoon two days later. It was cold, and there was snow, lots of snow, but the roads were passable. We passed the ski resort towns packed with winter tourists and locals alike. The snow-covered mountains were beautiful, and I couldn't wait to see our own little slice of mountain living. Silas had revealed to me during our long drive the key was to a cabin he had bought for us.

"Which mountain range is our cabin closest to?" I asked, excitedly.

"It's just outside of Silverton, in the San Juan mountains," Silas answered.

"I've never been to that part of Colorado. I've only been to the Rocky Mountain National Park. That feels like ages ago. I came with my parents after I graduated from college." I smiled, even though the memory was bittersweet.

I turned to look out my window at the breathtaking views Colorado had to offer.

Silas remained quiet, letting me silently reflect on my memories.

"I really think you'll like where the cabin is," Silas said after a while. "It's remote, but only about thirty minutes or so to the nearest town. The views are unbelievable."

"I'm sure I'll love it. Are we getting close?" I yawned.

"Just a couple hours away now," Silas said with a smile.

I tried to stifle another yawn, but I wasn't successful. Two days of driving and not a lot of sleep was starting to catch up.

"Why don't you try to catch a nap? I'll wake you when we get there," Silas offered.

"That's not a bad idea." I sat lower in my seat and reclined back as far as I could and got comfortable.

I was asleep in no time.

———

It only seemed like a few minutes before Silas gently woke me up.

"Dani, we're almost there. Wake up; I don't want you to miss anything."

I slowly opened my eyes and put my seat back up. I had a terrible crick in my neck, and I rubbed at it. We were stopped at a pull out on the side of the road.

My eyes went wide when I took in the scenery. The landscape was crisp and white in a blanket of snow. There were rolling hills and valleys which led to the San Juan mountains, and they were dotted with green groves of pine, fur, and spruce trees.

The Aspen trees stood in tight thickets, stark and skeletal, with their white trunks and spreading branches. There was movement along one of the hilltops that caught my eye. It was a herd of elk attempting to graze through the snow. It was almost too beautiful to be real.

Silas took my hand and kissed it. "Are you ready?"

I was still taking in the sights, so I merely nodded.

Silas chuckled and drove off.

A few minutes later, we turned off the main road and went down a recently cleared gravel drive.

"I called a local snow removal company to come and do the drive before we arrived," Silas remarked. "It's quite a long driveway."

I was too busy watching the scenery go by to reply. The property was mostly wooded and was nestled in a valley. No matter where you looked, you could see the mountains.

"How large is the property?" I asked.

"About 100 acres, give or take," Silas answered, smoothly.

I balked. "100 acres?"

"I didn't want us to be bothered." Silas laughed. "We are surrounded by nothing but forest, mountains, and nature."

It took us several minutes to reach the end of the driveway, and what was at the end of the drive made me cry out.

"Oh, my God, Silas!" I began to tear up. Standing before me in a little clearing was the most perfect A-frame cabin I had ever seen.

"It's perfect!"

Silas had a huge smile on his face. "Do you like it?"

"I love it," I whispered, choking back tears.

Silas parked the car and rushed to get out.

He opened my door and took my hand, leading me up to the cabin. There was a flagstone walk path, recently cleared of snow, from the driveway to the huge front porch that took up the entire length of the front of the cabin. The setting sun gleamed off the floor to ceiling windows on the facade. Even the front door was mostly glass. I was almost afraid to touch it.

Silas handed me the key. "Well, go on in!"

I took the key and unlocked the door. The interior was beautiful. It was completely open. The furnished living room was decorated in rustic, cozy furniture, and a floor-to-ceiling bookcase was filled with books. The wall of windows allowed for spectacular views of the mountains and the surrounding valley. There was a small, eat-in kitchen just behind the living room. There was a fireplace, and a set of stairs leading to the lofted bedroom above.

I turned around, expecting to find Silas, but he was still standing in the doorway.

"Aren't you coming in?" I asked, laughing.

Silas took out his phone and said, "Give me a second."

He scrolled through his phone and called someone. "Hello, Leanne, we've just arrived. Can you do what we discussed?"

Silas put the phone on speaker, and I heard Leanne.

"Dani? Are you there?" she asked.

"I'm here, Leanne. It's absolutely stunning! You wouldn't believe it!"

"I'm so glad you're happy with it and you've arrived safely. Did you notice if you had anyone following you? It's been quiet here."

"No. So far so good, Leanne." I smiled warmly at her concern for me.

Silas cleared his throat, a tad obnoxiously.

"All right, all right," Leanne responded, annoyed. "Silas, now you've arrived, please go on in and make yourself at home."

"Thank you, Leanne."

Silas stepped through the doorway. "Goodbye, Leanne," he said, smartly.

"Take care of her, keep her safe, and remember our agreement!" she exclaimed.

Silas hung up and rushed to my side.

He placed his hand on my cheek and stared into my eyes before drawing me in for a long, slow kiss.

"Welcome home." Silas said with a smile.

"Welcome home," I repeated. I still couldn't fathom the cabin was really ours. "Is this place in Leanne's name?"

"It is, along with many of my other possessions. Silas Quinn is supposed to be dead and buried six feet under, so I can't really put it in my name. It's possible, but I have my reasons for why I do what I do. I also couldn't put it in yours because it would have ruined the surprise."

We walked over to the couch and sat down.

"I plan to change all that soon and have it put in your name. It is yours, after all. Besides, it's safer when a house is in a human's name. Vampires can just walk right on into another vampire's home. Since they are not technically alive, it's not technically theirs, per say."

He put his arm around me and drew me closer to his side.

We sat on the sofa, watching the sunset behind the mountains. The sky turned from hues of red and orange and pink to darker shades of purple and blue and eventually black. It was so completely dark outside. The partially full moon reflected off the snow, giving everything an ethereal glow.

Silas stood up and turned off the lights.

"Come with me," he said, holding his hand out to me.

I grabbed my coat, and we went outside.

We walked to the rail of the porch, and Silas stood behind me, wrapping his arms around me.

"Look up," he said.

I turned my eyes to the sky, and it took my breath away. I had never seen the sky so brilliantly alive with so many stars.

I stepped away from Silas and walked around the porch, never taking my eyes off the night sky.

"It's so beautiful," I said, suddenly feeling wonderstruck.

"It certainly is," Silas whispered.

I turned around to look at him and found him watching me.

In that one perfect moment, all thoughts of any danger we might be in had vanished and were forgotten.

CHAPTER
Forty~Two

WE SPENT the next few days snowed in at the cabin. It was Christmas Eve, and I couldn't imagine anywhere else I would want to be. Silas and I sat on the couch by the light of the fire in the fireplace, sharing stories of our lives. His stories were admittedly much more interesting than mine.

"Tell me about the people you've met. I'm sure you've met some very interesting folks along the way."

I snuggled in closer, and Silas pulled the blanket up around my shoulders before he began.

"I have met both interesting and uninteresting people in my travels. But none have held my interest quite like you have," he said, giving me a squeeze.

"Over 100 years of existence and no one has piqued your interest enough to maintain a relationship?"

"Not really, but it's a little more than that. It wasn't safe for me to become attached to anyone." Silas began fiddling with a loose thread in the blanket.

"I think I already know why that is." We had spent the past several days being so happy and at peace I had almost forgotten we were in hiding.

"Those two made my life hell, chasing me and hunting me

down. They threatened my family and anyone I held close. I tried to stick around my family as close as I could to protect them. I hadn't seen those two in years, until last month. I have always been able to run them off."

Silas was quiet, thinking to himself. "They must have decided to try their luck with me again and found me with you at some point."

"I still don't understand why they blame you so much for Eliza's death. It wasn't your hand that drove that stake into her heart."

"I know, but to them, it might as well have been me, and when I came back from my grave, that infuriated them further."

"What did they do?"

"They chased me all over the place, but I was always able to stay ahead of their game, thanks to the friends I made on my journeys. When they couldn't catch up to me, they began threatening my family. The last time I saw them, they had threatened Maggie. She was in her twenties by then, and she was beautiful. They threatened to do the most vulgar things to her."

He clenched his fists and his jaw tensed. I could hear him gritting his teeth. "I couldn't have that, so I called them out."

"You called them out? You mean, you challenged them?" I asked, astonished.

"I did. I let them find me, and we fought. Well, I fought one of them, anyway. Kazamir doesn't like to get his hands dirty. I beat Garridan within an inch of his life, or unlife."

He laughed at his own joke.

"I took pity on him and let him live, but not before I ripped out his tongue and fed it to Kazamir. I told them I would do worse if I ever saw them again. I did what I did so they would no longer spew lies and threats. It has been decades since that run-in, so I'm not really sure what brought them back around. I should have killed them both back when they threatened Maggie."

"I wonder what their story is. Are they older than you?"

"They're much older than me. Some say their family were royalty or some type of nobility in medieval times and their mother and father made a deal with the devil himself to keep them safe from the Black Death. Whatever their story is, all three siblings were changed, and the rest is history."

I sat back against the sofa, pulling the blanket tighter around me. I watched the fire while trying to process Silas's story.

I started to ask another question, but Silas butted in.

He checked the time on his phone and stood up, saying, "It's almost midnight."

So much for no more hiding; he was clearly looking for a way out of this conversation. What wasn't he telling me?

Silas went to the kitchen and got a bottle of champagne and two glasses.

He expertly popped the top and poured us both a glass.

I checked the time.

"12:00 on the dot," I said, taking my glass.

"Merry Christmas," Silas said as we clinked our glasses together and then took a sip.

"Merry Christmas," I whispered as he leaned in for a kiss. His lips tasted like champagne, and the kiss was soft and full of love and unspoken words.

We sat close together on the couch and watched the fire dying down in the fireplace. The champagne went straight to my head, and I started to get sleepy.

I stretched out on the couch leaning against Silas, my champagne flute in one hand.

He shifted his seat so he could put both of his arms around me.

"Penny for your thoughts?" he asked, softly.

I sipped my champagne, trying to think of what to say.

"It's just been so quiet. I was just wondering if they've given up?"

Silas hugged me. "Who knows with those two? I'll be ready if they do show their faces again."

I breathed a sigh of relief. "Good to know."

I finished off my champagne.

Between the alcohol and the warm fire, it wasn't long before I was asleep nestled against Silas.

I might have been asleep, but my brain wouldn't let me rest. Why did I have such an uneasy feeling about everything? If the history of our relationship has taught me anything so far, it was this: when things seem to be coming up roses, something always comes along to rip us apart.

CHAPTER
Forty-Three

SEVERAL DAYS LATER, I was staring into the open refrigerator and taking stock of my dwindling supplies.

"We really need to go to town. I am low or nearly out of everything," I said, closing the refrigerator door.

"Let's go, then," Silas said. "I can check out the locals while you shop."

He had a devilish grin on his face. Silas had not been feeding like he should have, and it was showing in his face.

"Am I not what you are looking for anymore?" I teased him.

Silas grinned. "Can one desire too much of a good thing?"

"Quoting Shakespeare now, are we?" I asked, mockingly. I knew Silas was itching to get out of the cabin as much as I was.

I grabbed the car keys and tossed them to him. "Let me grab my coat."

"I'll be in the car; I'll get it warmed up for you," Silas said as he walked out the door.

I pulled my coat out of the closet and quickly put it on.

I walked into the kitchen and grabbed my wallet off the counter. I practically jogged to the front door, it was going to be good to get out of the cabin for a little while. The late afternoon sun was deceiving as I stepped outside into the cold Colorado winter air.

I pulled my coat tighter around me and hurried to the car.

————

The drive into town was slow. A fresh layer of snow had fallen during the last few days. The roads had been plowed, but there was still a layer of compacted snow and slush. It was late afternoon once we reached town. The sunset is early this time of year, so we only had a couple hours of daylight remaining. We would be driving home in the dark.

Silas pulled into the grocery store parking lot, parked the car, and handed me the keys. The lot was almost empty.

"Is this store even open?" I asked, doubtfully.

"Yes, for another hour or so. I looked up the hours before we left to be sure. Will that be enough time to get what you need?"

I nodded. "Should be."

Silas smiled. "I'll meet you back here shortly. If you finish your shopping before I get back, call me."

He reached over and kissed my cheek. "I won't be long."

"Behave," I told him, sternly.

"Always." He smirked.

Silas got out of the car and was gone.

I hurried through the parking lot and into the store.

I grabbed a cart and began shopping. I needed to make sure I bought enough food to last because I didn't want to leave the cabin again for a while.

As I was absentmindedly shopping, my mind began to wander to Silas and to what he was doing. I smiled to myself and shook my head at the absurdity of it all.

I came to the end of the coffee and tea aisle and almost crashed into a man as I exited.

"I'm so sorry, excuse me," I said, apologetically.

The man smiled a greasy smile and gestured for me to go ahead.

"No, please, excuse me," he said in a thick European accent. He wasn't much taller than me, but he was stocky. He could have been handsome, but his smile was creepy, and his skin was the color of the slush outside. He had his long black hair pulled back in a low ponytail. His eyes were an interesting shade of icy blue gray, and they were cold. Something about him gave me the creeps.

I gave him a half smile and a wide berth as I quickly walked away.

I finished up my shopping, pushing the strange encounter to the back of my mind.

While I was checking out, I sent Silas a text, telling him I was finished and would wait for him in the car.

The manager of the store approached the cashier. "Becky, she's the last customer. The store is clear. I'm heading back to my office if you need anything. Start closing up when you're finished."

The manager looked at me, briefly.

"Have a nice evening," he said before walking away.

I smiled and waited for him to walk away. "I apologize for holding you up. I'm sure you're ready to get out of here."

Becky flashed me a friendly smile. "It's no trouble at all."

She finished ringing me up and then helped me bag my groceries.

Becky followed me to the door and with a wave she locked the door behind me.

The sun had set, and it was dark out now. The parking lot was nearly deserted, except for my car and a couple others which I assumed had belonged to the employees.

Becky or her manager switched off the large, lighted sign, which plunged the parking lot into partial darkness. The only light was one measly street lamp in the lot, and it was nowhere near my car.

I began to get the eerie feeling I was being followed or watched, but I chalked it up to nerves and being alone in the dark. Silas and I had neither seen nor heard anything that made us believe the brothers were close by. Silas would have never left me alone if he thought they were.

I made it to my car without incident, despite my nerves, and began loading the grocery bags into the trunk.

There was a crunch of snow behind me, and I felt someone approaching.

Before I could turn around, I heard someone speak in a thick accent.

"It's no wonder Silas likes this one so much, Garridan. Up close, she reeks even worse of that horrid magnolia flower he loves so much."

Garridan? That meant the other one must have been Kazamir. I barely had time to make the connection before they were both on me.

Garridan struck me across the back of the head, and I was out.

Where are you, Silas? Was the last thing I remember thinking.

———

I came back to consciousness in a dark room. I had no idea where I was.

I tried to move but found myself bound to the chair they sat me in. I didn't want to alert my captors I was awake, so I silently took in my surroundings.

My eyes adjusted to the gloom, and I could just make out a small table and a chair at the opposite end of the room. There was one window, and it was boarded up. My chair was in a dark corner of the room farthest from the entrance. The door to the room was closed with what looked like a heavy, steel door.

I tried to move my arms and my hands, but to no avail. They were bound tight, and so were my feet.

I heard a muffled accented voice on the other side of the door but couldn't make out what it was saying. The voice had to belong to Kazamir.

My head was pounding from the blow I received from Garridan. I needed to get out of here, but how?

Just then, my phone rang. It was sitting on the table at the other end of the room. It had to be Silas calling.

The brothers must have heard it ringing because they came rushing into the room.

Kazamir picked up the phone and pushed *ignore*.

He looked at me staring right back at him. "Ah, she's awake, Garridan."

Garridan sneered and hissed through his teeth.

I glared at them both.

Kazamir casually walked over to me, waving my phone back and forth.

"This thing has been going off nonstop since we've arrived. Now you are awake, let's say we answer it the next time it rings."

As if on cue, my phone rang again, and Silas's name popped up on the screen.

Kazamir grinned, and Garridan laughed, gutturally.

Kazamir tapped the *answer* button.

"Hello, Silas, long time no see."

I could hear Silas ranting on the other end.

"Now, now, Silas; is that any way to speak to an old friend?"

Kazamir approached me and put his finger under my chin, lifting my face to look at him.

I jerked my head away.

"Don't touch me!" I spat.

"I like her, Silas; she's feisty."

Silas must have said something particularly nasty about that.

"Oh, my, Silas. Do you kiss your darling human pet with that mouth?" Kazamir cackled and grabbed me by the hair, jerking my head back.

I cried out in pain and heard Silas yelling on the phone.

"You'd better hurry and get here, lover boy. I'm afraid she won't last the night when we're through with her." Kazamir pressed the icon for the speakerphone, and I heard Silas frantically yelling.

"I'm coming, Dani! I'm—"

Kazamir pressed *end* and hung up the phone.

He looked down at me with a malevolent smile.

CHAPTER

Forty-Four

I WAS TERRIFIED, but I wasn't going to give the brothers that satisfaction. I tried putting on my best brave face, but I knew they could hear my heart pounding.

"Silas will never let you get away with this," I hissed.

Kazamir knelt in front of me, so we were face-to-face.

Garridan lit an oil lamp, and the room was filled with soft light.

I got a good look at Kazamir. His skin was pale and looked transparent, almost like wax paper, and his eyes were rimmed with dark circles. He must not have eaten in weeks. He smiled, broadly, at me, and I noticed his teeth were yellow.

When he spoke, his breath was rank.

"Silas isn't coming to save you. He doesn't even know where we are." Kazamir cackled.

"You underestimate him," I growled.

Garridan made a noise that sounded like a mixture of a scoff and choked laughter.

I didn't look at him; I never took my eyes away from Kazamir's pale gray, blue eyes.

"Oh, no, my dear; he underestimates us. His first mistake

was not killing us when he had the chance. Instead, he took pity and let us live."

Kazamir sneered. "But not before mutilating my brother and making me consume his ripped-out tongue."

Kazamir stood up and paced back and forth in front of me. "Silas had such promise to become a most formidable vampire. That's why Eliza chose him. He was strong, handsome, and had a violent streak that could be provoked." Kazamir sneered hostilely,"I'm sure he left that part out in all his stories about his past." He cackled. "Oh yes! Your dear gentle Silas lost control many times after he was changed. He was hotheaded like that blasted Father of his and when he was changed it amplified it." Kazimir clicked his tongue in a tsk tsk manner. "But instead, he chose to be moral, and push that part of him down, clinging to his humanity." He smiled, cruelly. "Instead of choosing to embrace the darkness, as we have."

"His humanity is what keeps him from being a monster like you!" I interrupted his monologue.

Kazamir spat at my feet. "Humanity! Bah! It holds him back!"

He knelt before me again. "Silas, the good vampire." He curled his lip. "A vampire with a conscience and a code to live by."

He grabbed my face with one long-fingered hand, his dirty nails digging into my skin.

"But Silas is a monster, and you'd better not forget that. He let my beautiful sister die at the hands of his family! He stood there and watched."

Kazamir threw my face away from him, leaving behind a long scratch on my cheek that began to bleed.

He stood and walked over to join his brother, and they both stared at me, hungrily.

"The same family staked him and left him for dead, too!" I argued back.

Garridan growled, and Kazamir said, "Yes, but Silas was able to come back. My poor sister is left to rot at the bottom of the sea. It's just not fair. Is it, Garridan?"

Kazamir looked at his brother and pretended to pout.

Garridan shook his head.

"But why take me? Why not just go after Silas?" I was trying to buy some time before the inevitable by keeping him talking.

"Why?"

Kazamir laughed as he approached me again. "It's just so simple. Silas's biggest mistake was falling in love with you. It made him blind and complacent, and most importantly, an easy target. When we heard he had fallen for a human woman, we had to see for ourselves. We found you eating breakfast in that tacky diner his niece operates, and the rumor was confirmed.

"We watched you two for a while before we made our first move. We needed to see just how *in love* he was. He never left you alone, even when you thought your relationship was through. Silas fought ferociously in the forest to protect you, but in the end, we slipped away. We knew it was only a matter of time before he felt safe enough to leave your side. We only needed a moment, and now we have you!"

Kazamir licked his lips and smiled, hungrily, at me.

He was close enough to touch me, and he did. He raked the nail of his pointer finger down my neck, opening another scratch.

It bled freely, and Kazamir shamelessly licked his finger.

I gasped in pain as I felt the blood flowing down my neck.

"If you kill me, he won't let you live. He will find you." I was trying to sound tough, but my voice betrayed me by trembling with fear.

Kazamir and Garridan hissed in unison.

"Enough talk!" Kazamir yelled, making me jump. "I'm growing weary of this. I can smell your fear, you know."

Kazamir looked at his brother. "Her fear makes her smell delectable, does it not, dear Brother?"

They both turned to look at me, simultaneously.

Garridan glared at me, hungrily. If he could have licked his lips, he would have.

Much like his brother, Garridan was pale and dark-haired, but his hair was cropped short. His eyes were blue but lacked the gray coloring of Kazamir's. He was taller than Kazamir, as well. Garridan was slender, whereas Kazamir was stocky. However, the family resemblance was there.

I started to panic. I wasn't going to survive this, and Silas was going to arrive to find my cold, lifeless body. I didn't want to imagine any of it.

Kazamir and Garridan looked at each other and then began slowly walking toward me.

I struggled with my bonds, but it was no use.

I heard them both laugh.

In horror, I lifted my face to watch their approach. The lamp threw their shadows across the wall, making them seem even more sinister. I couldn't tear my eyes away from their terrible faces.

Their jaws and faces began stretching to make space for their ghastly fangs, and their eyes were chilling. More dragonlike than anything.

I wanted to scream, but I was frozen with fear.

Kazamir reached out his hand and grabbed a fistful of my hair, wrenching my head to the side.

I could feel my hair ripping away from my scalp. I screamed as he sank his teeth and fangs into my neck, ripping into the muscles and tendons, shredding what was there.

He didn't just bite me, he ripped into me, opening the artery to let it flow freely.

Garridan had waited, hungrily, but suddenly decided he couldn't wait any longer. The smell of my blood was too much for him.

He went to his knees beside me and bit through my pants and into my thigh. His fangs reaching the artery he was aiming for.

He released me and began ripping away the section of my jeans he had bitten through. My blood was flowing freely now, and he latched back on.

I couldn't struggle or cry out as their venom coursed through my veins, incapacitating me. I was trapped as those two foul creatures drank away my life.

I began to cry, tears streaming down my face, and my thoughts went to Silas. *"You're too late,"* I thought.

My vision started to fade, and there was a ringing in my ears. *"Goodbye, Silas, I love you"* was the last thing I thought before everything went black.

CHAPTER
Forty~Five

I WAS in and out of consciousness and getting weaker by the moment. My neck and my leg were on fire with pain, despite the venom, and I clung to it to keep myself going. If I felt the pain, I was alive. I was too weak to move or even open my eyes, but I could hear everything.

Kazamir released me first, pulling away from my neck.

"Garridan, that's enough. I don't want to kill her just yet," Kazamir said, smugly.

I could still feel Garridan on my thigh; the nasty leech wasn't letting go.

"I said enough!"

There was a thud. Kazamir must have kicked Garridan away from me.

In doing so, his teeth tore more skin from my leg.

The pain made me open my eyes and cry out, but it was too much to bear. I lost consciousness again.

———

I came to moments later to the sound of crashing and metal screaming like someone had kicked a door in. There were sounds of scrambling and scuffling feet. Kazamir and Garridan sounded shocked. I heard a feral growl and immediately recognized it as Silas's.

I found the strength to open my eyes and saw Silas silhouetted in the doorway. The door he kicked in lay in ruins across the floor.

"Where is she?" His voice was loud and echoed off the walls with a growl.

"Silas, old friend," Kazamir cooed, menacingly. "Come to rescue your pet? I'm afraid you've only just made it in time to watch her die."

Silas didn't answer.

I watched him walk over to the table and chair that were next to the door. He was seething.

He picked up the chair and ripped off one of the legs. The sound of splintering wood echoed across the room.

All he had to do was look up to see me, but he never took his eyes off the brothers.

"Look, Garridan, I think he means to stake one of us." Kazamir was howling with villainous laughter. "I don't usually enjoy fighting, Silas, but for you, I'll make an exception. Garridan, let's show him no mercy."

There was a discord of footsteps as the three enraged vampires went for each other. It sounded like wild bears were fighting in the room. The loud growling and gut-wrenching thuds were deafening as they assaulted each other viciously.

They moved too quickly for me to keep up. Their movements were a blur, and the sounds of their bodies slamming against the walls and floors of the tiny room were terrifying.

"Hold him, Brother!" I heard Kazamir yell. "Hold him tight. I want to see the look in his eyes as I rip his head off!"

"Do you honestly think you can hold me?" Silas said, mockingly, through clenched teeth.

There was a sickening thud. Kazamir had punched Silas in the stomach.

"Shut up!" He growled.

I was able to eke out a small moan, and the room fell silent.

"Dani?" Silas gasped.

"What have you done to her?" he roared. Silas found some strength in his anger.

I watched as Silas spun from Garridan's grasp, twisting in a way that threw Garridan to the floor.

Garridan let out a strangled cry as Silas shoved the chair leg into his chest and through his heart.

Garridan lay, silent and unmoving, as Silas crouched over him, his shoulders heaving.

"Garridan!" Kazamir screamed. He was incensed. "First my sister, and now my brother! You will pay for this!"

Kazamir turned his attention to me. "You'll feel my pain as you watch your beloved human die before you!"

He took a few steps toward me.

Silas growled long and low. "Get away from her!"

Kazamir stopped and turned to look at Silas, his hands inches from my face.

He opened his mouth to say something, but Silas was already on him.

They fought and tumbled.

I saw Kazamir hit his knees with a thunderous crack before me, the floor boards buckled beneath him with the force. Silas was behind him, and he had him in a chokehold.

"Look at your sweet Silas now!" Kazamir said to me, his eyes were wild with panic, his voice was strained and came out in choking gasps. "Wach him now, girl! See his brutal temper come to life." A gurgle formed in his throat and he coughed around it before choking out, "He's the monster now."

His hands fought frantically against Silas's unrelenting forearm around his throat. The fear and knowing that his death was imminent was clearly written all over his face. Kazamir turned his eyes on me one last time.

"The only monster in this room is you, Kazamir!" Silas snarled.

'Where's your mercy now, Silas?" Kazamir was still trying to struggle free, and he was trying to hide his panic by keeping his bulging eyed stare locked on me.

"You deserve no mercy, Kazamir. You have lost everything in your quest for vampiric superiority. You wanted the world, and now you have nothing." Silas's voice was a low hiss in Kazamir's ear.

Silas's grip tightened on Kazamir's throat, and his face was twisted in apoplectic rage. "You sent your family out on a futile quest for glory. Their deaths are on your hands, not mine."

Silas's face continued to contort, and his fingers turned white as his grip tightened on Kazamir's neck.

Kazamir tried to make some sort of sound, but it was cut off in a grisly hiss as Silas's hands gripped even tighter.

"You'll get no mercy from me, not this time."

Suddenly, there was a loud snap, a wet ripping noise, and then silence.

Silas dropped something with a loud, smacking thud on the floor. It was Kazamir's head, and it had rolled to my feet. His blue gray lifeless eyes stared up at me.

My heart tried to beat quickly in fear, but it must have been too much.

I blacked out again.

"Dani? Dani? Can you hear me?"

Silas was talking to me, but it sounded fuzzy.

I tried to lift my head, but nothing was working; I was just too weak. I could feel him untying the ropes that bound me to the chair. The ropes were the only thing holding me up.

I slumped forward, and Silas caught me.

"Shit! Hang on, Dani, I've got you." I felt him lift me out of the chair and lay me on the floor.

"Silas? What's happening?" It was Leanne's voice, but she sounded far away, mechanical.

"It's bad, Leanne. She's lost a lot of blood, and her heartbeat is weak. She'll never make it to a hospital."

Silas turned my head and hissed. He must have been looking at the place where Kazamir bit me. "That bastard damn near ripped out her throat!"

He went silent for a second. "Leanne, I don't know what to do." Silas sounded so anxious and disturbed; it wasn't like him.

"Silas, put the phone next to Dani so she can hear me. Even if she can't, we have to try and let her know we are going to save her." Leanne was taking charge.

I wanted to let them know I heard them, but I couldn't even open my eyes.

"Dani, you're going to make it! Silas is going to make this all better."

"How, Leanne? I can't give her blood or get her to a hospital. It's all too little too late!" Silas held my hand.

"You're not thinking, Silas; save her the only way *you* can! Do you understand what I'm saying?" Leanne was begging him to comprehend.

"I do, but it's not her choice. I-I don't know if I can."

Silas gently brushed the hair from my face with his free hand; he was still holding my hand tightly with the other.

"Silas, listen to me! She chose you and all that entails. If you don't do something soon, you'll lose her for good. We both will! Dammit, be your usual selfish self!" Leanne was screaming.

Silas was quiet. He kissed my forehead and said, "I don't know if it will work. She doesn't have much blood in her veins, and her pulse is so weak. It might not be enough."

"Just try! You have to try! Save my best friend; save the love of your life, Silas Quinn!"

I needed to let him know I wanted him to do what he needed to. I dug down deep and somehow found the strength to squeeze his hand.

"Dani?" he cried out.

"Silas, what happened?" Leanne asked, quietly.

"She squeezed my hand," Silas answered.

"She must be trying to tell you something! Ask her permission! This may be your only shot!"

"Dani, is that what you want? Are you ready? Can you squeeze my hand again if that's what you want me to do?" Silas asked, expectantly.

I found my strength again and squeezed his hand.

"I'll try," was all Silas said.

After that, he must have hung up the phone because I never heard anything else from Leanne.

"I'm so sorry, Dani, for everything."

Silas lifted me up in his arms and moved my head, revealing the unruined side of my neck.

He kissed my neck first.

His lips parted against my skin, and then I felt his fangs bite down.

There was a warm rush, and I went numb as Silas released his venom. I felt nothing; it was a sweet release from the pain.

I felt Silas's fingers on my lips. He gently parted them and pressed something against them.

"Dani, I need you to drink. Please."

I could feel a cool and a viscous liquid fill my mouth. It was almost sweet and slightly salty. It begin running down my throat before my brain registered that it was Silas's blood.. My body did what I couldn't voluntarily, and I swallowed.

Seconds later, my heart lurched, and suddenly every fiber of my being was on fire. What was happening to me?

The pain was excruciating. I swear I could feel every vein

and nerve ending in my body, and they were all aflame. I wanted to scream, to cry out, to move; anything would have been better than this silent motionless hell. I was still aware of Silas in the room, he had never let go of my hand.

I convulsed once, violently, and then was still.

"I'm so sorry, Dani," he kept repeating.

Silas placed his other hand on my cheek. "God, you're so cold."

He placed my hand back beside me

A moment later, I felt myself being lifted. There was a rush of cold air that washed over me.

I felt Silas lay me back down. It felt like the back seat of a car. "Hang on, I'm going to get you back to the cabin."

After what felt like forever, I felt the car move, and every bump in the road or slight jostle began to send wracking pain through my body. I couldn't do anything but silently scream.

My heart began to try to race; it was irregular, and each palpitation sent burning fire through me. My heart lurched again, and then it stopped.

"Dani?"

CHAPTER
Forty-Six

IT'S a bizarre sensation to feel your heart stop beating. We've all felt our hearts race, palpitate, skip a beat, thud and thump; it lets us know we are alive. My heart stopped, and I was conscious of it. I could still feel the burning in my veins. That didn't leave, and I was beginning to wonder if it ever would.

I was still aware of being in a car, I could feel the movement of it and hear the tires on the road. I could also hear Silas, his hands gripping the steering wheel, his muttering about the slow pace we had to move due to the weather. His voice sounded so fearful and sad.

I wanted to speak to him and reach out to him, but my transforming body wouldn't allow it. I needed to let him know I was still here, but how?

————

The car finally came to a stop, and I heard the engine cut off. We must have been back at the cabin.

Silas gingerly gathered me up.

I could feel him carrying me up the stairs of the porch.

He opened the door and tried to step inside, but something stopped him. It felt like static and thick spiderwebs, and it felt like it was trying to push me back.

"Shit!" Silas cursed. He turned around and sat down on one of the chairs on the porch, cradling me in his lap.

I felt him jostling around for something, and then I heard him tapping on his phone. I could hear distant ringing and soon Leanne's voice answered.

Silas began talking over her. "Leanne, the transformation is working! I can't get in the house with her; you need to invite her in!"

Leanne didn't hesitate; I could hear her clearly over the speakerphone. "Dani, I invite you in!"

Silas rushed me back to the door, and the weird staticky veil was lifted.

We were inside the cabin.

"Leanne, I'll call you back as soon as I can." The phone beeped as he hung it up.

Silas rushed me up the stairs and into the bedroom, laying me down, gently, on the bed. "Dani, I don't know if you can hear me; I really hope you can."

I can, Silas; I hear you! Don't give up on me just yet.

"I'm going to get you cleaned up and out of those dirty clothes. They left you in a mess." Silas sounded so desolate and miserable.

"I have no idea if anything is working. It must be if Leanne had to invite you in. I wish you could speak to me. I'm scared, Dani, for the first time in a very long time." He was rambling, nervously.

I have never wanted to wrap my arms around Silas as much as I did right now, and I couldn't. Why couldn't I wake up?

I felt Silas remove my shoes and my socks.

He moved to my pants next. He inhaled sharply as he took in my damaged thigh. I had no idea how badly I was hurt because everything in and on my body was in agony.

Silas started unbuttoning my flannel shirt.

He sat me up and laid my body against his chest so he could pull it off me. He left the tank top on. It must have avoided most of the gore. Silas laid me back down on the bed.

"You're so cold, Dani. It's odd not feeling the warmth of your skin." He covered me with the quilt. "I'll be right back."

I heard him leave and go into the small bathroom next to the bedroom. He turned the tap on, letting the water run for a few seconds. I heard him rummaging around and then the door of the cabinet banging shut.

Silas turned off the water, and I heard his footsteps returning.

I felt the mattress sag as Silas sat next to me and then a warm and wet sensation as he washed my wounds with a warm washcloth. I focused on the gentle cleansing motions Silas was using to take my mind from the pain of the rest of my body.

I heard Silas unwrapping something. It was the sound of crinkling paper and soon the smell of some type of antiseptic filled my nostrils. The smell was sharp and almost painful.

He dressed and bandaged my wounds. Once he was finished he covered me with the quilt again.

"Now, we wait, I guess," Silas said, sounding unsure.

He got in on the other side of the bed and lay down next to me.

Silas stroked my face and twisted my hair through his fingers. Every now and again, he would reach under the blanket and feel my arm. "You're not warming up. Either the transformation is still working or you're..."

Stop it! Don't even think it, Silas! I'm still here; give it more time!

I wanted to scream. Not because I was suffering but because Silas was.

"Please, wake up, Dani. You are everything to me; I'm lost without you." Silas kissed my face and then my lips.

He laid back down and placed his head on my shoulder. He began humming.

Suddenly, he stopped, and I felt him sit up. "Something's changed."

I felt him lower his face to the side of my neck that Kazamir bit, and he inhaled, deeply.

"Yes, something has definitely changed!" Silas removed the bandage on my neck, and I heard him gasp. "It's healing!"

Silas threw back the covers and removed the bandage on my leg. "This one is practically gone!"

Silas placed his hand gently upon my cheek. "Do you hear that, Dani? It's working!"

I hear you, Silas! I just need to wake up!

I heard Silas leave the room and run down the stairs.

I could hear him downstairs; I could hear the tones on his cell phone as he dialed a number.

"Leanne? It's working!" I could tell by Silas's tone he was smiling.

CHAPTER
Forty-Seven

IT STARTED WITH A TOE WIGGLE. Then, my fingers began to twitch.

I heard Silas spring to his feet; he must have been sitting in the rocking chair in the corner of the room.

"Dani, you're moving!" He rushed to my side and flung the covers off me.

I tried to move more but couldn't muster up much more than making a fist or wiggling my toes.

Silas was beside himself. He grabbed my hand, intertwining his fingers with mine and gave it a squeeze.

I squeezed back.

"Haha!" Silas laughed, boisterously. "Easy now; just take it easy. Let your body adjust."

He caressed my face with his other hand, and I broke into a smile.

"There's my girl."

Silas's voice was so full of love and emotion; I needed to see it.

My eyes fluttered open, and his face was the first thing I saw. His green eyes were raw with emotion, and his smile lit up his face.

"Hi, there," he whispered.

I blinked in the suddenly too bright room and tried to get my eyes to focus. "Silas? I..." My voice was off; my throat was so dry and inflamed.

"Shh, you don't need to talk, not yet." His hands began to flutter over my body like he wasn't quite sure what to do with them. That was a first.

I tried to laugh, but it sounded weird, as well.

"What?" Silas questioned, a hint of amusement in his voice. "Are you okay? Do you want to try and sit up?"

I nodded and tried to push myself up.

Silas assisted me, and soon we were sitting face-to-face.

My senses were really starting to come around now. I could see so much more clearly, and I could hear everything. Except one thing. I lifted my hand to my chest and placed it over my heart.

Silas looked at me, sadly. "Yeah, you'll get used to that."

He moved his head and looked away from me, glancing out the window. It was still dark outside.

Silas stood up. "Feel up to standing yet?"

He held his hands out to me.

I wiggled my toes and began to move my feet. Rolling them around at the ankles.

Next, I tried moving my legs. I bent my knees and then swung my legs over the side of the bed. My movements were so fast and I had to really concentrate to slow them down.

I took Silas's hands, and with his help, stood up.

I stumbled a bit, and he wrapped his arms around me to steady me.

I rested my head against his shoulder, and that was when his scent hit me. Silas always smelled good before, but now, his scent was captivating.

I buried my face in the hollow of his throat and breathed in, deeply. He smelled like clean leather, bourbon, and fresh, salty sea air. He smelled like Silas, and in that moment, I knew no one else on Earth smelled like him.

I lifted my face away from him, and he looked down at me and smiled.

"My goodness, Dani." He laughed. "Your eyes are absolutely wild."

I looked up into his eyes, and I could see small flecks of gold I had never noticed before, and I could discern every one of his thick eyelashes. I was captivated by the myriad of colors his hair turned as the light hit each strand. His dark brown hair had streaks of auburn, black, and a touch of amber honey that my human eyes were too dull to notice. I took in the new wonders of his face and found myself wanting to reach out and trace all its features.

I didn't get a chance to; Silas gently turned me around to face the dresser mirror, and I stepped forward to look.

My reflection took me off guard. I was pale. I looked almost gray or ashen white. It was disconcerting.

I noticed my eyes next and saw what Silas was talking about. The dark brown of my irises had spread, almost completely darkening both eyes. My pupils had turned into small vertical black slits barely visible against their dark brown background. I looked demonic.

Silas walked up behind me, placing his hands on my shoulders and then letting them fall slowly to my elbows.

The sensation of his skin on mine was new. His fingertips felt warm and silky against my skin, they sent waves of pleasure through me like nothing I had ever experienced before. He kissed my shoulder.

The feeling of his lips on my skin nearly made me come undone. Every nerve ending in my body came alert and alive to his touch.

Silas was not unaware of my reaction. He smirked. "You look bewitching; you have no equal. You, my love, are beautiful."

I turned to face him.

"I love you," he said and he leaned in for a kiss. It was hesitant at first, soft and gentle but soon the sparks flew.

The sensations I felt were indescribable. The way his lips felt against mine, his skin on my skin; everything was heightened. I was on fire again, only this time it, felt amazing.

Our kiss turned hungry. All the fear and the tension of the last several hours left unspoken was released in that one fiery kiss.

We slowly stepped back from one another, both of us wild-eyed.

It was then, just as I was looking into Silas's vibrant green eyes, when I realized something.

I grasped my throat. The dry, burning rawness of it overtook everything.

I tried to speak, but my voice was gravelly. "Silas, I'm so..."

"Thirsty?" he finished with a knowing smile.

My body took over. My lips began to thin and withdraw over my gums, and I turned to the mirror in time to watch my upper jaw line change as my fangs lowered, white and gleaming and ready to feed. I panicked, and in my panic, I clutched at Silas's arm.

"Jesus, Dani!" he hissed. "That's quite some grip you've got." Silas began prying my fingers from his arm.

I quickly let go. "I'm sorry," I spluttered. "I panicked."

"Clearly." Silas laughed. "You need to feed; wait here."

"Silas, you're not going to..." I couldn't finish the sentence.

"What? Bring you a human?"

He shook his head and laughed. "No, I have blood in the refrigerator, remember? Just wait here and get dressed. I'll be right back."

He smiled at me and then went downstairs.

That was right. He had made a call to one of his contacts about getting some blood bags delivered here while we were hiding out. I never asked much about it because, honestly, I didn't care to know how he obtained them.

I found a hoodie and a pair of leggings and got dressed. I swear I could feel every stitch and thread in the clothing as it slipped over my skin.

That's when I noticed I could hear Silas downstairs in the kitchen, moving things around in the fridge. I began to take notice of other things I could hear, the clock on the mantle downstairs, the hum of electricity in the lightbulb in the lamp. The world was so loud now. That was going to take some getting used to. I could hear, see, and feel so much.

I walked over and sat in the rocking chair by the window. The night was fading, and the sky was beginning to lighten in the distance. I was noticing all the tiny imperfections in the glass and the brushstrokes in the paint on the windowsill, normally invisible to a human's naked eye, when Silas came back in the room with two blood bags.

I could smell them before he even walked in the door.

Gone was the metallic copper smell blood usually had, and in its place was a sweet, almost wine-like, fragrance. My head snapped toward Silas's location, and my mouth began to salivate as my fangs lowered. I could feel the venom dripping off them.

Silas approached me, slowly uncapping the tubing.

"Try to take it easy; don't overindulge." He handed me the first bag.

I took a small sip.

I was apprehensive at first, but when the first drop of blood hit my tongue, something else took over entirely. I couldn't get enough! Blood flowed over my tongue like velvet, soothing the aching dryness in my throat. The taste was euphoric. It took all I had not to moan with pleasure as the thick, sweet, ambrosia coursed over my tongue and down my burning throat.

I emptied the first bag in seconds, twisting and squeezing it to get every last drop.

I dropped it on the floor and held my hand out for the other one.

"Another!" I begged.

Silas smirked and handed me another bag.

I went slower with that one, savoring the smooth texture, the richness of it, and the way it soothed my parched throat.

Silas bent down and picked up the empty bag I had tossed on the floor and waited patiently for me to finish the second.

When I couldn't squeeze any more from the bag, I felt myself begin to anger.

I easily ripped the bag open and began licking it clean, trying to get all I could. It wasn't enough! "More!" I growled. I was surprised to hear that sound come out of me.

I shot up out of the rocking chair, sending it backwards into the wall with a crack.

I began stalking toward Silas.

"More!" I growled again. Something had taken hold of me, and I couldn't shake it. It felt like an extreme high from which I couldn't come down.

Silas hastily grabbed me up and wrapped me in a tight embrace. "Dani, you need to calm down."

A snarl escaped my lips as I tried to wrench myself free. I was so strong. I could tell Silas was straining and struggling to hold me.

He almost lost his grip on me.

His arms tightened around me, and he placed his lips close to my ear and began to speak in a low and soothing tone. "This is the bloodlust. You must gain control of it. Think of something else to distract you; focus on me. I cannot let you go until you do."

I tried to wrestle out of his grasp one more time and sank my teeth into the flesh of his shoulder.

Silas hissed and choked up on his bear hug.

"I mean it, Dani! I'll do this all night if I have to." He growled, and the sound brooked no argument.

I stopped and stood, deathly still, trying to find something, anything on which to focus. The room became too loud again, and my clothes began to feel itchy and restrictive.

I turned my face inward, buried my face in Silas's chest, and inhaled deeply. His scent invaded my senses with a vengeance. I could feel myself coming down.

I returned his embrace and found my hands wandering frantically at first, like I was trying to find purchase in something, anything. In doing so I ripped the back of his shirt.

Silas never moved; he just stood there, tightly hugging me to his chest.

"Take it easy. Shh, shh," he whispered, calmly, into my ear. His breath in my ear sent a new sensation through me.

My frantic movements slowed down, and I found myself running my hands under the now ruined back of his shirt, marveling at the feel of his skin against my fingertips. It was smooth, and his muscles were taut, but mostly I noticed he no longer felt cold to me. That took my attention away from my bloodlust, and I relaxed.

Silas noticed and relaxed his hold on me just a little.

"You're not cold anymore," I whispered.

"Did you just now notice that?" He chuckled. "I can assure you, I am. We both are, and if you're going to keep running your hands over me like that—"

Silas didn't get to finish his sentence; I shut him up with a kiss.

CHAPTER
Forty-Eight

THE SUN HAD RISEN FULLY and was sitting high in the late morning sky. We were sitting on the couch, listening to the fire crackle in the fireplace.

I was taking in the views from the floor to ceiling windows and was in awe of everything I could see now. It was all so crystal clear. I could even see the tiny dust motes dancing in the rays of the sun that came in through the windows. The needles on the evergreen trees outside danced on a light breeze, and I could make out each of their individual movements. It was a tad overwhelming, but I couldn't look away. I wanted to take it all in and see more.

But first, I had questions about last night.

"I need some questions answered," I began.

"I'll do my best to answer them." Silas laughed.

"First, how did you find me?"

"Oh, that's easy. I wasn't far when you texted you were ready, so I started back. When I came to the car and saw the open trunk and the spilled groceries, I knew something was terribly wrong. I found your keys on the ground, but no cell phone. I hoped you still had it on you. When I closed the trunk, it disturbed the air enough I caught a trace of the Brothers Grimm." He paused to see if I was following.

"Go on," I urged.

"I went into a fit of rage but ultimately calmed myself. I wanted to save it for them. I called Leanne to see if you two still had your location sharing turned on."

"That's right!" I butted in. "I had it turned on so she could keep track of our travels and I could share where we were."

"Exactly." Silas winked. "Luckily, it was still on, and Leanne was able to locate you and send me coordinates."

"Thank goodness for modern technology." I shook my head and curled up closer to Silas.

"They had taken you to an abandoned mining site. There was one of those old mobile office trailers there. That's where you were being held."

Silas and I were quiet as we reflected on the terror of last night. It was crazy so much had transpired in less than twenty-four hours. Everything had changed so much.

Silas wrapped his arms around me tighter, and I buried my face in his chest, inhaling the scent of him again.

Silas kissed the top of my head and finished his story.

"I guess you're wondering what happened next," he said.

"I saw most of it. I know I lost consciousness a couple times, so I guess I need those gaps filled in."

"You want to hear it?" Silas asked, sounding surprised.

"Yes! Every gory detail! I know they got what they deserved, and more!"

"Savage." Silas smirked.

"I kicked in the door and caught them by surprise. I grabbed one of the wooden chairs that was next to the door and broke off one of the legs. They came at me, and we fought. They were able to overtake me initially, and Kazamir got in a sucker punch. When I heard you and saw you tied to that chair, hurt and bleeding, all my pent-up rage came out.

"I was able to break Garridan's grasp, spinning around,

throwing him to the ground and staking him with the chair leg they had stupidly forgot to disarm me of. Kazamir was beside himself with rage. We fought, but I was faster. I was able to bring him to his knees, swiftly, snapping his neck and ripping his head off in the process."

"My hero." I hugged him.

I remembered almost all of it, but I wanted to relive it. I didn't let him know I had heard what he said to Kazamir.

"I only wish I were the one to do it!"

"The rest felt like an eternity, though it was only a matter of minutes. I did what I had to do and got you out of there, but not before finishing the job with Garridan and knocking over the oil lantern and setting fire to the trailer."

"So, the Boo Brothers are gone for good this time?" I asked.

"Yes, there's no returning from that," Silas answered.

"Good riddance," I spat.

Silas laughed. "Indeed."

He began running his fingers through my hair. "I was so afraid I was going to lose you. You were in a terrible state. The wounds on your neck and thigh were grisly, and you were so weak from blood loss. I could barely make out a heartbeat."

I sat up and looked at him, placing my hand on his cheek.

He leaned into it and stared back at me.

"You saved me; you didn't lose me," I said, softly.

"I was terribly conflicted about changing you. Leanne told me it was what you wanted, but I needed to hear it from you. How you found the strength to squeeze my hand, I'll never know." He shook his head.

"I'm glad you did, and she was right; it is what I wanted." I smiled at him. "But it's going to take some getting used to, that's for sure." I repressed a laugh.

"I guess it's a good thing we have all eternity to get it right." Silas did not repress his laughter; he never really did.

It was contagious, and I began to laugh along with him.

I nestled back down in his arms and said, "But Silas, I thought you said when you were changed it was just a little painful. What I experienced was agonizing torture!"

"I was wondering about that. I'm only familiar with my own experience, and your experience was a lot different than mine."

"What do you mean?" I coaxed.

"You had very little blood in your body to carry the venom through, not to mention a weakening heartbeat. You basically had pure vampire venom coursing through you with none of your human blood to buffer it. It's no wonder it was torture. I had no way of knowing if the change was happening; you were so motionless. Your eyes wouldn't even open. Then, your heart stopped."

He squeezed me to him a little tighter.

"All I could do was wait. I was hoping against hope the change was taking place. I didn't know it was until I tried to step through our front door. I could feel a barrier pushing against you. That's when I knew it had worked."

"I felt that. It felt like thick spider webs and static."

"That's exactly how it feels," he said. "I never knew quite how to describe that feeling, but you nailed it."

"It's an odd feeling, for sure. There's so much that is going to be different from here on out. I'm curious to see what else has changed."

"I'd like to test a few things out." Silas smirked.

"Test? Test me how?" I lifted my head from his chest to look at him and narrowed my eyes in suspicion.

"I just have a hunch about a few things, especially after you grabbed my arm upstairs and with how much I struggled to hold you during your bloodlust."

"Did I hurt you?" I asked, surprised, and looking at his arm.

"No, no," Silas laughed. "I was just shocked at your

strength. Look, it's nearly noon. Why don't we test out your new abilities and we'll see if my assumptions about you are correct."

He smiled, slyly, at me.

"But you won't tell me what those assumptions are?"

"Not yet." He grinned.

Silas stood up and made his way to the door. He placed his hand on the knob and said, "Shall we?"

CHAPTER
Forty-Nine

SILAS BEGAN with a warning before opening the door. "Brace yourself. When you step out into the sun for the first time, it might feel wrong or painful. It's different for everyone, but you'll definitely be uncomfortable."

He gave me an encouraging smile and held out his hand.

"But I've been in the sun all morning. It's shining through the windows." I gestured to the floor to ceiling windows that covered the front of the cabin.

Silas looked at me, thoughtfully. "That is true but, these windows are double-glazed. They do not let in the sun's UV rays."

"I see." I stepped back, hesitantly.

"It'll be okay, I promise. Your skin is mostly covered, so you'll mostly feel it on what's exposed, and if it's too much, you can step back inside." Silas smiled at me again and opened the door.

He stepped out and offered his hand once more.

I stepped to the threshold, willing myself to take that first step. I held my breath, closed my eyes, and reached for Silas's hand as I stepped into the sunlight for the first time.

The sun's rays hit me like a ton of bricks.

My eyes flew open, and I hissed through my teeth as my exposed skin began to burn, painfully.

"Silas!" I gasped. "It's too much, I can't..." I was panting.

Silas watched me warily and said, "Do you need to go back inside?"

I took a step back toward the house but stopped. I would get through this. No one said it would be easy.

"No," I hissed through gritted teeth. "I can endure it."

I tightened my grip on Silas's hand and walked determinedly to the middle of the porch.

I turned my face up toward the sun and let go of his hand.

I stretched my hands out, palms up, challenging the sun to do its worst and drinking in the pain.

Just like the night that Kazamir and Garridan attacked me, I embraced it. The pain let me know I was alive. I wasn't alive in the full sense of the word, but I was still here, and I was still standing.

As if sensing my acceptance, the sunlight's pain abated. I was already growing accustomed to the stinging sensation and was somewhat numbed by it.

I turned to look at Silas.

His brows were furrowed in concern, but as soon as our eyes met, I smiled at him and his face relaxed.

"You're amazing," he said with reverence.

My smile widened. "What's next?"

Silas pointed to the tree line. "Let's take a walk through the forest."

I took his hand again and allowed him to lead me toward the forest ahead and the cooling relief of its shady pine branches.

The trail meandered in and out of the trees and up into the mountains that surrounded our cabin. I was amazed at the fact trudging through the snow, climbing the hills, and descending the valleys did not leave me breathless. I kept expecting to grow tired, but it never came.

———

We walked for a long time, sometimes together, and other times Silas let me wander on my own, allowing me to take everything in on my own terms. It was during one of those slight separations when Silas tried to catch me off guard.

I heard it before I saw it. He was several paces behind me. I was distracted by the sights, sounds, and smells of the forest around me. I could hear the branches of the trees rubbing together in the breeze.

In the distance, I heard some elk crunching through the snow. I could smell them, too. They had a musky and a gamey smell, like a mixture of campfire and mushrooms.

I had stopped to watch the snowfall. I was astounded at the fact I could see the tiny details of the snowflakes that fell close to my face. I was also still trying my best to get used to the constant stinging and burning of the sun.

That's when I heard it, despite the distractions. Something was flying at me from behind. I could hear it whizzing through the air.

I spun around just in time to knock the rather large snowball away from me.

"Dang. I thought you'd be distracted enough not to see that coming." Silas was grinning, widely.

"I heard it well before I saw it," I said as I brushed snow off my hands and arm.

"You heard it?" Silas asked, bewildered.

"Can't you?" I asked, seemingly confused.

"Depends. Judging by how quickly you turned around, you had to have heard that coming as soon as I threw it."

He began to look excited. "Interesting."

"Why is that interesting? I thought all vampires had excellent hearing."

"We do. But Dani, do you realize how far away I was? I don't think I could have heard that coming at me until it was about fifty or sixty yards away. Not to mention the speed at which I threw it. I wasn't holding back."

He laughed. "You spun around and knocked it away like it was an annoying house fly."

"How far away were you? I mean, you seemed fairly close when I turned around."

He pointed down the trail. "See that lone pine back there? I was there."

But that had to be at least 100 to 150 yards away. I thought back to just seconds ago, trying to do the calculations in my mind. I know I heard the snowball whizzing through the air. Come to think about it, I also heard Silas running behind it.

"I heard you coming, too, but I was mainly focused on the snowball."

"This is amazing! You're amazing! Tell me what else you heard." Silas was as excited as a kid on Christmas morning.

I told him about the small elk herd I could hear and smell. "There is a small herd of elk, maybe four of them, moving around just north of us."

"Really?"

Silas got in front of me and inhaled. "I don't smell anything."

He stood, quietly, and craned his neck trying to listen. "I don't hear them, either. Are you sure?"

"I am." I nodded.

"Well, let's see if we can find them!" Silas stepped to the side and gestured for me to go ahead.

We trudged along in the snow for a bit, when the smell of the elk hit me again. This time from the northeast. They were on the move.

"This way." I pointed.

We walked in silence so I could listen for the elk.

"Wait a minute, I can hear them now, too!" Silas whispered.

"How far do you think we've walked?" I asked.

Silas looked at his watch. "We've been walking about thirty minutes now, so maybe a little over a mile or so."

We came to the top of a small rise, and there below us was the group of elk, four of them, just like I thought.

"There they are," I whispered.

"They're still so far away, and you detected them a while ago." Silas shook his head. "Dani, that's astonishing!"

"But what does it mean, Silas?"

He took my hand, and we sat down on a nearby boulder and watched the elk.

"It means something in your transformation made you better than me, that's for sure!" He laughed. "I'd love to put you to the test further."

I smiled at him and grinned. "Bring it on."

Silas stood up. "Can you pick up this boulder we were sitting on?"

I stood and walked around it. The rock was massive, at least four feet tall and as wide as it was tall. It was much larger than the one Silas had hurled into the pond just a few short months ago.

"I don't know," I said, doubtfully. "Can you?"

Silas set down his pack and squatted next to the rock.

He wrapped his arms around it and lifted it to about waist high before dropping it back to the forest floor with a resounding thud.

"Now you." He panted.

I mimicked Silas, squatted down next to the boulder, and wrapped my arms around it the best I could. I was silently doubting myself.

"Well? Come on! Show me what you've got." Silas taunted me.

I smiled, took a deep breath, and lifted the large boulder first to about waist level, like Silas. It was easy.

I laughed, exuberantly.

With a heave ho, I lifted it above my head and threw it

into the valley below. I sent it crashing through the trees, scaring off the elk and sending the birds of the forest into flight.

I turned to find Silas smiling, gleefully, at me.

"Show off," he said.

I rubbed my hands together. "Now what?"

Silas walked up to me and hugged me.

He kissed me, softly, and said, "Catch me if you can."

He grinned at me, and then he was gone.

Silas was fast, but I had a feeling I was going to be faster.

I waited a few seconds and lit out after him.

The trees blew past in a blur, and soon enough I had tunnel vision. All I could see was the trail in front of me. I caught up to Silas effortlessly.

I easily passed him, laughing as I mockingly said, "Catch me if you can!"

I put on an extra burst of speed and left him behind.

I was sitting on the front porch steps when Silas came running out of the forest.

"Took you long enough." I winked at him and blew him a kiss.

Silas joined me on the steps. "When I said you have no equal, I truly meant it. I've never seen or met another quite like you."

"About that, are you going to explain your theory now?" I asked, expectantly.

"Yeah, I think I can. Keep in mind, it's only a theory. I have no way of knowing if it has any credence until I talk to someone."

Silas looked out toward the tree line as he gathered his thoughts.

"Well, I'm waiting." I nudged his knee with mine.

Silas laughed and began. "I believe your transformation is what made you stronger. Most people who are changed have plenty of blood left in their systems and a much healthier heartbeat than you had."

Silas's face darkened just a tad. "You also had the remnants of Garridan and Kazamir's venom already in your system."

"Okay," I said, slowly, and with confusion.

"Hear me out."

Silas chuckled. "You were damned near dead when I changed you. With a barely perceptible heartbeat, your body had slowed down what blood you had left and had constricted your veins to try and conserve what was there. It also stopped the flow of the venom the brothers had left. When I bit you and released venom into your system, it joined with theirs and raced through your veins and arteries, burning up what little human blood you had left, speeding up your transition."

"Emphasis on burning." I cringed.

Silas winced, "I hate it hurt you so much. If I could have made it happen differently, I would have. I'm so sorry." He picked up my hand and brought it to his lips.

"I know that, but what's done is done."

I squeezed his hand and gave him a smile. "But you still haven't quite told me why my abilities are so much better than yours."

"I'm getting to it."

Silas smiled at me. "I haven't seen any other vampires with the abilities you display. Not anywhere in America, at least."

"What do you mean?"

"I have seen abilities like yours only in the old vampires of Europe. What we call The Old Ones. You just so happen to have had a small amount of some of the oldest vampire venom residing in your veins when I changed you."

My brow furrowed. "The Old Ones?"

"Yeah, the original vampires, the OGs, the first of the first, if you will. They are the purest form of vampire there is. Their abilities are uncanny and unmatched. I believe the manner of your transition made you the way you are.

"You had pure vampire venom coursing through you from three different vampires, two of which were extremely old, and I certainly didn't hold anything back. I practically depleted myself. I also gave you quite a bit of my own blood to seal the transformation. I'm pretty sure it made you more potent."

Silas grinned, wickedly, at me.

Could this be real? Was I an anomaly? It got me thinking. What else was I capable of?

CHAPTER

Fifty

WE STAYED at the cabin for the next few weeks, living off the supply of blood bags Silas had stocked up on. I was getting better with my control, but our supply was dwindling fast. I had even suggested we take to hunting animals a few days a week to make our supply last longer.

Silas warned me I might not like it, and boy was he right. The blood of the elk and the deer that were plentiful in the forest around us was too gamey, and the fur was gross. I could see how it would work in a pinch, but it was not worth it. Human blood was so much more delectable. I was scared to death of how I would react and of losing control when I tried to get it directly from the source.

That day came sooner than I expected. We were down to our last few bags, and Silas wanted to make sure I was well-fed before attempting reentry to civilization.

"A well-fed vampire is a happy vampire, and a happy vampire is less likely to snap." Silas was trying to make light of the situation, but I was petrified.

"We have no idea how I'll react. How can you be so calm about this?" I put my face in my hands and shook my head.

"I have faith in you." Silas placed his hand on my shoulder.

"I'm glad you do because I have none." I sighed.

"I have enough for both of us. If things get hairy, I'll pull you out of there. It's going to be fine; you'll see."

Despite Silas's reassurance, I could hear the traces of apprehension around the edges of his tone.

"How did you fare, your first time around humans?" I asked.

"Yeesh, you had to go there, huh?" Silas made a face and pushed his hair back. "You have to remember, it was different times, and I had a much different mentor."

"I know, but still..."

"I killed my first feed," Silas said, bluntly.

I cringed. "I don't want to kill anyone."

"I know that, Dani. I won't let you take someone's life."

"Why did Eliza allow you to do such a thing?"

"Eliza and her brothers had a much different outlook about humans. She didn't care about humans one way or another, but as I told you before, when she saw how much taking a human life began to bother me, she taught me how to feed without killing."

He sighed heavily, "I was hoping to never have to reveal this to you about myself but, when I was first changed I was extremely violent. The bloodlust took control over me in a way that was so completely terrifying I had lost who I was at my core. I could be antagonized and provoked into doing such awful things when the bloodlust hit."

His eyes went blank and he shuddered. "It wasn't just my first feed that I murdered. I killed several more after that. I ripped their throats out with such ferocity it was beyond animalistic, it was barbaric."

He hung his head as if it physically pained him to remember his past.

"There's a point right before the person dies that their

heart gives a sudden and last desperate few beats to stay alive. The taste of the blood changes, it becomes sweeter and it feeds the bloodlust even more. To me, it was highly addictive and caused me to go beserk. The final drop is the sweetest and is imbued with an esscence that's indescribable. It's what makes vampires become bloodthirsty monsters. You can control it if you choose to. You have to."

He got to his knees in front of me. "I won't let you do that. I won't let you kill or taste that final drop. I refuse to let you feel that guilt or change into a bloodthirsty monster. If you never taste it you'll never know the difference." He gave me a soft smile, lifted my hand to his lips and kissed it. "You're strong enough, I know it."

"I hope you're right about me." I sighed. "I wish I could just survive on blood bags. Then, I wouldn't have to worry about it at all."

Silas laughed. "We'll see how much we can get, but it's not something I generally care to do."

He paused and gave me a playful smirk "You'll find fresh is best."

I rolled my eyes and was preparing to argue, but my phone went off just then. I was thankful for the distraction.

"It's Leanne," I said, quietly.

"Are you going to answer?"

"I don't know what to say."

"Start with, 'Hello'; it always works for me." He smiled.

I took a deep breath, tapped *answer*, and held the phone to my ear. "Hello?"

"Hey, Dani, it's good to hear your voice. How is..." She paused "everything?"

I winced; the volume of her voice was ear-splitting.

I held the phone slightly away from my ear and turned the volume all the way down.

"I'm not sure how to answer that, Leanne. Everything is

just so different, and it's also the same. If that makes any sense at all."

"It does." I could hear the smile in her voice. "I miss you; it's not the same around here without you."

"I miss you, too, Leanne."

"Are you at least enjoying yourself, I hope? You're not getting into any trouble, are you?"

"Hmm, not yet." I laughed. "I am better at a lot of things than Silas is, so I have that going for me."

I winked at Silas, and he squeezed my knee.

"Well, that's good. He needs to be knocked down a peg or two."

Silas laughed. "I heard that."

Leanne and I shared a laugh at Silas's expense.

"Listen, Dani, I just wanted you to know I'm here if you need to talk. I might not understand everything that's going on, but I am familiar, more than most."

"I know."

"I'll always be your friend, no matter what's changed. Don't be a stranger, okay?"

"Sure. Thank you, Leanne."

"Oh, and don't worry about things around here. Jeff and I are holding down the fort. You all take all the time you need to adjust."

"Love you, Leanne."

"Love you, too. Goodbye."

"Bye."

Leanne hung up, and I wanted to cry.

Silas recognized the look and held open his arms to me.

I gladly let him wrap me in a hug. I hadn't even thought about going home until now. There was no way I could, not yet. Not without knowing how I tolerated being around humans.

"Silas, I want to try. How soon can we start?" I sounded a lot bolder than I felt.

"How about tonight?"

"Tonight?" I gulped.

"Don't worry," Silas laughed. "I've got you."

So far, my only experience with feeding had been blood bags and a few elk and deer. I didn't even need to bite the blood bags, and the other just tasted too bad to me.

"But how does it work? How will I know what to do?" I asked, timorously.

"Believe me, you'll know what to do. Your instincts will take over. It's stopping that's the hard part." Silas smirked.

"I'm glad you find this amusing." I sagged against the couch cushions, crossing my arms in frustration.

"Just leave everything to me. I promise; it'll be okay." Silas patted my leg.

"What if I release too much venom? What if I can't stop?"

I stood up and began pacing the living room. "What if I accidentally hurt someone, or worse?"

Silas stood and approached me placing his hands on my shoulders.

"You're overthinking this. I won't let you fail." He kissed my forehead. "I promise."

CHAPTER
Fifty~One

WE LEFT that evening for town. The ride was quiet. My mind was racing, going through every possible *what-if* scenario.

I turned on the radio to distract myself.

"Relax," Silas said, softly.

"Ha! Easy for you to say. You've done this about million times."

I began tapping my foot against the floorboard.

Silas pulled over on the outskirts of town.

"You're right, I have done this a time or two." He smirked.

"I'll make it easy for you. We'll just walk the sidewalks through town, and if it gets to be too much, we'll duck down an alley and get out. The smells aren't so concentrated outdoors. Nothing like being inside a crowded space. Not that there will be a lot of crowds in this tiny town." He chuckled.

I took a deep breath. "Okay, let's go."

I gripped the armrest, feeling the vinyl give way under my fingers and stared blankly ahead, attempting to steel myself for the unknown.

Silas pulled into the grocery store parking lot and parked the car. It was empty because the store was closed.

We got out ,and I held my breath.

"Breathe, Dani," Silas said, taking my hand. "Just don't breathe too deeply. Take it slowly, not all at once."

I squeezed Silas's hand for dear life and slowly breathed in the night air little by little.

I could smell the fumes from the car and the faint intermingling smell of the different foods inside the grocery store. Another small breath brought me the scents of the restaurants nearby. The smell of searing meat and smoke from barbecues were no longer appetizing to my new vampire palate.

I moved a bit farther away from the car.

Silas was walking with me every step of the way.

I caught the sound of a heartbeat, much too fast to be a human.

The smell hit me, making me wrinkle my nose. It wasn't appealing, whatever it was.

I looked at Silas, and he nodded toward the dumpsters.

"Something is alive in there. I can hear its heartbeat. Whatever it is doesn't smell edible, though." I crinkled my nose in disgust.

"Just keep listening and using your other senses to see if you can figure it out," he coaxed.

I turned to face the dumpsters. The smell of the garbage within was noxious, but my curiosity at the living thing inside was stronger.

I pushed past the smell and focused on the heartbeat.

Soon, I was able to pinpoint the smell of the animal. It was pungent, almost acrid.

I heard it begin to scramble as I approached. Its little heart was really beating now, and I could smell the sweet smell of the adrenaline it was pumping through its veins.

I ventured another step.

A cat, impossibly fast, jumped out of the dumpster,

landing with a hiss and a yowl and then sprinted away into the darkness.

"I think that poor cat was as surprised as I was." I laughed.

"Probably more so. Animals have their instincts and know we are predators. It's why the songbirds are quiet when we are in the forest. They know we're not human," Silas explained as we walked away.

"If only humans trusted their instincts more..." I didn't finish my thought.

"You would not be where you are now, and vampires in general wouldn't have easy meals," Silas finished for me.

We let that thought linger between us as we walked toward town. It was cold out, so luckily for me, most everyone was inside the buildings. I could hear their conversations and their laughter, but I could also hear their hearts. They were beating out a rhythm only Silas and I could hear.

Above all else, however, I could smell their blood. Some were sweet-smelling, others had a smoky smell, and some were floral or fruity.

I grasped at Silas's hand as the hunger began to take hold.

Silas turned me toward him, taking my other hand and placing us in the shadows.

His face was so close to mine our lips were almost touching.

"Stop breathing. Just for a moment. You don't have to breathe," Silas whispered, staring into my eyes.

If anyone saw us, they probably thought we were two lovers stealing a kiss.

I slowed down my inhalations, and soon stopped breathing altogether.

I held my breath, and instantly my mind cleared, and the hunger abated.

"Good?" Silas asked.

I nodded, and we stepped back out into the glow of the streetlights and storefronts.

I stayed silent, focusing on my breathing and taking shallow breaths as not to overwhelm myself again.

We continued walking and soon found ourselves near a bar.

The smells of cigarette smoke, beer, cheap liquor, and sick permeated the air around me. The sounds coming from the bar were loud and boisterous. Men's and women's voices shouted over the loud honky-tonk music playing. In the background, I could hear the clacking of pool balls and the sound of breaking glass and shouts. A fight must have broken out.

Silas found a bench across from the bar.

We sat down, and he said, "This ought to be good. Let's watch the show." His eyes twinkled with mischief.

I giggled, softly, and he squeezed my hand.

The sounds from inside the bar became louder as the miscreant, whom I assumed was the instigator of the fight, was tossed out, unceremoniously, by a very large and a very bald bouncer.

The bouncer spotted us and gave us a nod.

"Watch that one, now. He's trouble," the bouncer said as he closed the door behind him.

The man who was tossed out stood up.

He turned around and flipped off the bar with both hands. He was mumbling to himself, drunkenly and incoherently.

When he stumbled past us, I could smell the stale beer that permeated his being. But mostly I smelled his blood. It smelled rich and woody, like port wine.

I stiffened and began to stare the man down.

"Whaddya lookin' at?" the man slurred.

He looked at Silas, who was sitting there, calmly, with a sly smirk on his face. "Hey! You better get your bitch under control."

He hiccupped and looked as though he were going to

have trouble holding his liquor down. "I don't like the way she's lookin' at me."

He hiccupped again and began stumbling.

Silas just continued to stare at the man with that irritating smirk of his.

It only enraged him further.

I tried not breathing, but the damage was already done. I had already caught his scent, and I could feel myself changing.

The drunken man staggered and stumbled toward us. "I said, 'Whaddya lookin' at?' "

Silas stood up, placing one hand firmly on my shoulder. "I believe we are looking at dinner."

He moved quickly, knocking the man off his feet and dragging him into the alley behind us.

I followed swiftly, my fangs aching in anticipation.

Silas had the man pinned up against the wall. He had gone full vampire now, and the man was whimpering in fear.

The drunk spotted me and tried to scream, but Silas clamped a hand over his mouth.

The smell of urine hit me as I approached the man and looked into his eyes. He had wet himself and was nearly in tears. I wanted to pity him and let him go, but the hunger was too strong.

"Stop struggling," I growled.

The drunk man went limp, and his eyes looked dazed and glassy.

Silas relaxed his hold and looked at me, dumbfounded.

"Do not scream; you're going to be silent. Understood?" I said, calmly licking my lips and feeling my fangs begin to let down their venom.

The drunk nodded.

"Now, stand still; don't move." I kept my eyes locked on his as he froze in place.

Just as Silas said, my instincts kicked in.

I pulled the man's head to the side, opened my mouth wide, exposing my fangs to the flesh of his neck, and bit down. I felt my venom enter his artery, and the man went limp in my arms. I had no trouble holding him up, though.

My venom stopped flowing, and the warm velvet well of his blood rushed over my tongue. It was euphoric.

I groaned in pleasure; I wanted more. I began to drink deeper and deeper still. The man's heart began to beat frantically in a last ditch effort to save itself. The rush of blood began to turn sweeter. I have never tasted absinthe but judging from what I knew of it's history, this must be what it felt like to drink it. The blood was brighter, more fragrant, and it began to awaken something deep inside me. I sank my fangs in deeper.

Silas approached me, taking hold of my arm. "That's enough, Dani. You need to stop," he whispered fiercely into my ear.

I growled, it was low and menacing. I had never heard a noise quite like it issued from my own body. I placed a hand on Silas's chest and shoved him backward.

Silas flew back, hitting the brick of the building behind us, causing it to crack.

He stood up, shaking off the dust, seemingly unfazed.

"Dani, you're killing him! Let go!" Silas's face was dark with anger and worry.

I couldn't let go; I didn't want to. A primal instinct had taken over and wouldn't allow me to do what I needed to do.

"Dani, if you kill him, his blood will be on your hands and mine, not to mention Leanne's."

He grabbed my arm again. "I made a promise to you. You're not a killer. Find the strength and let him go!"

Silas growled at me; he was prepared to fight me if he needed to.

He was right, I was not a killer, and I didn't need that man's blood on my hands, or anyone else's for that matter. I focused on Silas, the feel of his strong hands wrapped around my arms ready to pull me away. I found the strength to push down the bloodlust.

"There we go; easy now," Silas said, calmly. His grip loosened on my arms.

I let go of the drunken man, and he crumpled to the ground.

I backed away, placing my hands over my mouth.

"What have I done?" I mumbled against my palms.

"Dani, it's okay. He's still alive."

Silas knelt next to the man and rolled him over. "Listen."

I got myself under control and listened. The man's heart was beating, and it sounded strong.

I sighed in relief, letting my hands fall to my sides. "What do I do now?"

"Give him a believable story to explain why he's passed out in an alley," Silas said, rationally.

I nodded and got down on the ground beside the man. I felt my eyes change as I began talking to him. "Look at me."

His head turned toward me, and his eyes found mine.

"You got too drunk at that bar and you passed out in this alley. Your neck was cut by the glass that was broken in the bar. You're going to get up in a few minutes from now, forget all about this, and go home to sleep it off. Do you understand?"

He nodded and closed his eyes.

Silas and I left him there in the alley and made our way back to the car.

Silas was deep in thought on the walk back.

"I'm sorry," I said, hanging my head and watching my feet.

Silas stopped in his tracks. "For what?"

"For pushing you the way that I did. I could have hurt you."

Silas placed his arm around my waist, and we started to walk again.

"Don't be sorry. It'll take a lot more than that to hurt me."

He held me tighter to him. "The bloodlust takes hold and does different things to everyone. You handled it beautifully and you were able to drive it down."

"Really?" I had my doubts and thought Silas was just being nice.

"Really." Silas smiled, but something else was bothering him.

We got to the car.

As we were pulling out of the lot Silas asked, "Do you realize what you did back there?"

"No." I shrugged.

Silas began to laugh. "You have no idea?"

"No, did I do something wrong?"

"Wrong?" He scoffed and shook his head in disbelief.

"Dani, I've never seen anything like it! You mind controlled that man just by looking at him. You hadn't even bitten him yet. It's the stuff of legends!"

He looked over at me with such awe I had to look away. "You're one in a million, Danica Jones; you truly have no equal."

CHAPTER
Fifty~Two

I DIDN'T KNOW what it meant to "have no equal," as Silas put it. I knew next to nothing about vampires, other than what Silas had told me. That meant, once again, I had questions. Having questions was beginning to be a running theme with me ever since I met Silas. My newfound ability was making it very easy for us to feed, and it even allowed me to be able to obtain blood bags. It was surprisingly easy to get people to "donate" blood, and I was able to order supplies online. No more guilty snacking for me.

"We make quite the pair, you know?" Silas laughed as he took stock of our refrigerator's contents.

"Why is that?"

"Well, there's me, who won't kill those I feed upon, and you, who feels guilty for feeding. It's virtually unheard of."

"Maybe we can start a trend." I winked at him, and we both laughed.

"Dani, I've been thinking." Silas leaned against the kitchen counter and crossed his arms.

I looked at him, expectantly.

"I think you're ready to go out in a crowd."

My eyes widened in shock. "Already? I'm still so new at this. It's only been a few weeks."

"I know, and you're doing so well. I'm constantly surprised at your poise and demeanor when it comes to humans."

"It wasn't that long ago when I was one. I don't want to be a monster. I don't like the way I feel when I feed on humans."

"Ahh, but I think you do like it, and that scares you," Silas said, astutely.

I looked away from him, averting my gaze to look out the window. I couldn't stand he was right.

I heard Silas push off the counter and his soft footsteps as he approached the couch and sat down next to me.

He reached out his hand and took mine in his.

"Dani, look at me," he said, softly.

I turned to face him but kept my eyes downcast.

He chuckled, lightly, and took my chin in his hand, lifting my face to meet his.

I met his eyes, and he regarded me, intensely.

"You are not a monster, nor could you ever be."

Silas dropped his hand away from my face and held my gaze. "We literally have all the time in the world to figure this out."

I smiled, doubtfully, at him. "I hope so."

Silas kissed me and grinned. "Now, what do you say we get ready and go out for a drink?"

I scowled at his distasteful joke. "Honestly, Silas?"

He laughed and gave me a hug. "I meant of the alcoholic variety. But if one thing leads to another." He nipped my neck.

I pushed him away, laughing. "You're incorrigibly wicked."

Silas leaned back on the couch, spreading his arms out across the back. "I've been called worse." He smirked.

I rolled my eyes and went upstairs to get ready.

I chose a dark pair of jeans, slipped on a teal corded sweater, and put on my boots. I loosely braided my hair and let it hang over my shoulder.

I grabbed my black leather jacket and bounded down the stairs to meet Silas. I hated to admit it, but I was actually looking forward to going out.

Silas hadn't changed, but he still looked like a million bucks. He was still in his dark blue jeans and fitted black T-shirt. The only thing he added was an olive-green button-up, his brown leather jacket, and of course, his favorite boots.

He gave my braid a playful flip and asked, "Ready?"

I nodded and smiled.

We headed out to the car.

"Where are you thinking?" I asked as the car bounced along the driveway.

"I thought we'd hit up that bar from your first night feeding." He was grinning ear to ear.

"That place seems a little rough, don't you think?"

"Exactly why I want to go."

"Silas, I don't know."

"Oh, come on! It'll be fun!" He laughed, darkly.

"That's exactly what I'm afraid of," I groaned.

———

I took advantage of the thirty-minute drive to town to ask some questions. I knew Silas led a mostly solitary life over the last century, but I also knew he had met other vampires during that time.

"In all your travels, you've never met another vampire with, um, abilities?" I asked, hesitantly.

Silas took a beat to answer. "Not really." He gripped the top of the steering wheel with both hands. "I've heard rumors, and I know Eliza and her brothers were always on the lookout for anyone special." He laughed.

"To think, they caught you and didn't even know what they had." He shook his head.

"But didn't you say my transformation was different? That's why you think I am the way I am?"

"Yes. Most times, people are changed when they are healthy, full of life and blood. And most people only have the venom of one vampire, not three. You were on death's door, drained of a lot of blood. When I bit you and released all my venom into your veins, there wasn't much blood or much of a heartbeat to pump it through. Not to mention your veins were already constricted to help minimize the blood loss. You basically had pure vampire venom coursing through your veins with no human blood to buffer or dilute it. It made you more..." he paused, searching for the right word, "potent."

"I guess that makes sense, but why did my transformation happen so quickly? You said it was overnight for you; why did it only take a few hours for me?"

"I have a theory, but I don't know if it's correct. Like I said, without much human blood in your system to soften the blow of the venom, it allowed for a more thorough transformation because there was less to change."

"So a half dead human makes for a stouter vampire?" I was really trying to understand all of this.

"Maybe. I'm not completely sure myself. I still have questions, too."

———

We sat in silence for the remainder of the ride. Both of us thinking about what all of this could mean.

Silas parked the car in the bar's parking lot.

He reached for my hand before we got out.

"No more questions or thinking tonight, all right? Let's just have some fun." He smiled at me.

I squeezed his hand and returned the smile. "All right."

CHAPTER

Fifty-Three

THE BAR WAS CROWDED. The handful of people outside smoking was nothing compared to what met me inside. I walked past the smokers outside easily enough. The smell of cigarette smoke was choking and helped hide the smell of the humans underneath.

Once inside the building, however, it was a whole other ball game. I tensed. The noise was overwhelming, and the smell of all those people, their heartbeats, all that blood, surrounded me.

Silas squeezed my hand.

"Don't breathe in so deeply. Find another smell and focus on it." He stepped in front of me.

"I'm focusing on your scent, for example. The sweet smell of magnolia flowers is much better than any of this." He waved his hand, vaguely, at the bar scene behind him.

I stepped forward, and he kissed me, breaking me from my deer-in-the-headlights stance.

I relaxed into it and took in his scent.

"Better?" he asked.

"Better," I exhaled.

"We need bourbon."

Silas smiled and led me to the bar.

We found one empty seat.

He offered it to me and stood behind me.

The bartender spotted us and came over. He was middle-aged, brawny, bearded, and covered in tattoos. He had a very no-nonsense air about him.

"What can I get you?" he shouted over the music.

Silas leaned forward, "Two bourbons, neat."

"Make mine a double," I spoke up.

The bartender smiled at me. "Coming right up."

He grabbed a bottle of Jim Beam Black, poured our glasses, and slid them across to us.

We started a tab, and with my drink in my hand I spun around on my bar stool to people watch and tried to enjoy the music.

The warmth and the burn of the bourbon helped to soothe the ache in my throat. The more I drank, the easier the smell of all those humans was safe to be around.

I began to relax, but I was starting to get restless. I didn't want to sit anymore.

"Let's dance," I said, downing the last of my drink.

Silas placed his empty glass next to mine and laughed as I led him out to the floor. There were a few people already dancing, but most everyone was seated at tables or playing pool.

Silas and I cut loose and danced like no one else were there. Our focus was intently on one another. I reveled in the way his hands felt on my body and how we seamlessly moved together.

My clothes began to feel constricting and itchy the longer we danced. Silas's scent was the only thing I could focus on, and I couldn't stop staring into his eyes. There were other hungers besides my hunger for blood, which I was still learning to control.

Silas smiled, knowingly, and it took everything in me not to kiss him in that moment.

When the song ended, we began making our way back to the bar for another very much-needed drink.

We were breathless and laughing as we weaved our way through the crowd.

A server was headed our way with a tray full of drinks, when a drunk guy stumbled into her, knocking her tray over and onto Silas.

"S-s-sorry," the drunk slurred and stumbled away.

Silas and I knelt to help the server pick up the glasses.

She was mopping up the alcohol with a towel.

"I am so sorry about that," she apologized. "You don't have to do this."

"Nonsense." Silas grinned at her.

The server looked up at Silas, and her eyes went wide.

She looked at me and then turned red. "No, really. I got this," she stammered. "Here's a towel for your arm."

She shyly handed him the towel from her back pocket.

"Thank you." He smiled at her again, and I nudged him, softly.

"Here you go," I said through my teeth. I handed her the two glasses I picked up. I was trying to ignore her sudden flush and rapidly beating heart. It was crazy how my body responded to it. I could feel my mouth begin to salivate and my teeth began to prickle in the area where my fangs wanted to let down.

I stood up, rapidly. Maybe a little too rapidly.

The server looked at me like I had appeared out of nowhere.

I looped my arm through Silas's arm and said, "We should let her get back to work."

Silas took one look at me and recognized the signs. "Let's get you another drink," he said, warily.

I heard the server mutter as we walked away, "Wow, lucky girl."

We sat back down at the bar, and I shook my head. "That was a close one. But you, sir, should really stop that."

"What?" He laughed.

"You know exactly what you're doing. That poor girl practically melted." I laughed and lightly shoved him.

"At least I didn't try to eat her." He got close to my face and snapped his teeth at me.

"Besides, I have to practice on someone." He shrugged. "Not all of us have mind control to our advantage."

He leaned forward and kissed me, quickly. "I'll be right back. I'm going to wash up." He came in for another quick kiss before heading to the restroom.

With a smile on my face, I spun around toward the bar and waited to catch the bartender's attention.

Someone sidled up next to me, but with it being a crowded bar, I gave it no thought.

"Hi," said a stranger.

I glanced at the person next to me and gave them a tight-lipped smile. "Hi," I said, shortly.

"Here by yourself?" he asked.

I turned to look at him. He was leaning across the bar and had a cocky look on his face. He was large, not fat, just large with big, meaty hands. His hair was long and wavy, and he was dressed like a lumberjack.

I rolled my eyes and turned away from him. "No, I'm not here by myself."

He looked around; he made a show of it, actually.

"I don't see anyone." He shrugged.

"I told you, I'm not alone. Now, if you'll leave me be." I sneered at him. I should have tried to use my control on him, but I was just hoping Silas would return soon.

"Aw, c'mon, sweetheart, at least let me buy you a drink."

He reached out a big, meaty hand and tried to touch my braid.

"Not interested." I leaned away from him and caught the bartender's attention. "Another double, please."

The bartender brought me my drink and eyed the beefy lumberjack. "You good?" he asked me, quietly.

I nodded. "I can handle myself." I smiled and took a sip of my bourbon.

The bartender patted the bar as if to say, "I'm watching you," eyed the lumberjack again, and walked away.

Once he was gone, the meathead started in on me again.

"It looks like your man has ditched you." He smiled at me with a big, stupid grin. He had a hand on the bar, and it was closed around something.

I could see him toying with it under his fingers. I hoped I was wrong about what I thought it was.

"There was probably just a line for the bathroom." I shrugged and pretended to look for Silas. I left my drink unattended on purpose.

Out of the corner of my eye, I saw Mr. Meat Face put something in my drink. I could smell the bitterness of it.

I brought my attention back to him and looked him square in the eyes.

I pretended to take a sip but never let the bourbon past my lips.

He smiled like a fox in a hen house. He thought he had me.

"You shouldn't have done that," I growled, softly. "Come with me."

I watched as the cretin's eyes glassed over.

He stood up and followed me.

I dumped out my drink in the pot of a fake cactus next to the bar and walked toward the back of the building. There was a hallway there that led to what I assumed were a couple offices and maybe a storage room. It was dark and empty, and that's all that mattered to me.

"Come closer," I demanded.

He stepped right up to me. I could smell his cheap after-shave and the body odor it poorly tried to hide.

"Don't move, and don't make a sound."

He nodded, and I stepped even closer to him. His heart was beating rapidly; he was nervous.

I smiled, wickedly, and then made my move.

My face and my eyes changed in an instant, and my fangs let down, dripping in venom.

I sank them into his fleshy neck. I wanted to kill him. How dare he try to roofie me? How many women had he done that to? I planned to take care of him and make sure he never did that to anyone again.

I felt him begin to sag, but I didn't care. Let him die. Bastard.

Silas appeared by my side just then. "Dani! What the hell?"

I let go of the asshole and dropped him to the floor. "He tried to roofie me! I'm teaching him a lesson."

I bent over and picked him up again, fully intending to finish the job, but Silas stopped me.

"Dani, you can't kill him."

"The hell I can't!" I snarled.

"No, you can't."

Silas took the man in his arms. "You're not a killer, remember? But that doesn't mean I won't have fun with him."

Silas looked ready to rip this guy's face apart. "Tell him to stand up and look at me." Silas was downright furious. He was trembling with the anticipation of beating the ever-loving crap out of that guy.

I roughly grabbed the man's face in my hand. His stubble was rough against my fingers.

I turned his face to look at me. "Now, you're going to listen to him. Stand up and face him."

I threw the man's face away from me.

The lumberjack wannabe snapped his attention to Silas.

Silas growled low in his throat and pushed him against the wall; the drywall gave a little behind the man's back.

There was the slightest whimper that escaped his mouth.

"You should be scared; you sack of shit!" Silas's face contorted with rage, and his fangs came out in a spray of saliva and venom.

He tore into the man's neck and drank, heavily. It was marvelous.

The man sagged against the wall, and Silas let go.

He dropped to the floor like a sack of potatoes.

Silas bent over him and roughly grabbed his face. "You will never set foot in this bar, or any other bar for that matter. You will never try to drug another woman again. Do you hear me?"

The big dummy slowly nodded, and tears escaped his eyes.

"If you do, I'll find out, and I'll come for you again. But next time, you won't survive." Silas's voice rumbled with threat.

He dropped the man's face, and the man's head hit the floor with a dull thud.

I stood over the jerk and stared down into his face.

I spit on him and then promptly stomped on his nuts, making him double over and cry out.

Smiling, I walked away, but not before I heard the crack of Silas's fist meeting the man's face. I could hear the breath leaving the lumberjack as he lost consciousness and passed out.

Silas caught up to me. "We have to tell the bartender."

"Why?"

"Because that asshat needs to pay for his crimes."

"Fine," I reluctantly agreed.

We approached the bartender together and told him what happened. We told him to look back at the security video footage and he would see the man slip something in my drink.

Silas admitted to beating him up pretty badly and leaving him in a heap in the hall.

The bartender grumbled something under his breath and apologized to me.

He flagged down one of the servers and had her take over bartending so he could go look at the video.

When he passed by one of the bouncers, he whispered something into the bouncer's ear, and the bouncer nodded.

He got out his radio, and I could hear him telling the other bouncers to keep an eye on the exits and to try not to let the guy leave.

It was then when it hit me; I might have screwed up big time.

"Silas," I whispered. I knew he could hear me, despite the noise of the bar.

He looked at me, one eyebrow raised in answer.

"I didn't even think about security cameras in that hallway." I placed my hand over my mouth, silently begging myself not to get sick.

Silas reached up, took my hand away from my mouth, and placed a kiss on it. "No worries, there are none in that hallway. I checked when I found you back there."

I slumped against him in relief, and he hugged me tight against him.

"Our secret is safe, but no more antics like that again. You hear me?"

I nodded against his chest. "Let's go home."

Silas and I were preparing to leave, when lo and behold, the meathead came stumbling back into view. His nose was obviously broken, and he was covered in his own blood.

"You!" He shouted across the bar and pointed at Silas. "I'm going to kick your ass!"

He started across the bar as fast as he could, yelling the whole time. "I don't know what kind of game you're playing, with your face tricks and whatever, but your ass is grass!"

The bar went almost silent; everyone had stopped to watch the spectacle.

Silas groaned, and I laughed out loud in astonishment. Could that guy really be that stupid?

Silas stepped in front of me, but I placed my hand on his shoulder and stepped back in front of him.

"Silas." I looked him in the eye. "Sit down. I got this."

A funny look came over Silas's face, and he sat down.

I turned to face the chucklehead. In my anger, I felt my eyes begin to change.

The man began laughing. "She's got you whipped, ol' son, but it's nothing like the ass whooping I'm about to give you."

When I looked at him, his face dropped, and he turned white as a sheet.

His mouth opened and closed. He reminded me of a fish.

"Shut up!" I hissed.

His mouth snapped shut.

"You are going to leave, and when you leave, you are going to go play in traffic."

His eyes glazed over, and he slowly walked away.

I watched him walk out the door, despite the bouncer's best efforts to hold him there. I turned to Silas. He was rubbing his eyes.

"Silas, are you okay?"

"Yeah, I think so." He sounded troubled. "Dani, I think you inadvertently used your mind control on me."

"What? No. There's no way."

"Yeah, I think so. You told me to sit, and like a dog, I did. I had no control over my own body; it was the most peculiar thing."

He shook his head like he was trying to clear his mind. "Let's get out of here."

Silas took my hand, and we left.

On the way through the door, we overheard the bouncer on the phone. He must have been talking to the police.

"Yeah, it's Lenny O'Brien. He's drunk and has started all kinds of trouble. They're saying he tried to roofie some girl, and well, I don't know."

He paused and rubbed a hand over his bald head. "It looks like he's playing in traffic."

Silas and I looked at each other and broke into a fit of laughter.

The bouncer raised an eyebrow at us and watched us leave.

CHAPTER
Fifty-Four

"TRY IT AGAIN! Something else this time!" Silas was making me give him commands; it was getting to be exhausting.

"Silas, I'm done. I don't want to anymore." I flopped onto the couch and covered my face with a throw pillow.

So far, I had made him do mundane things, like hop on one leg or bring me things. Each time I made a "request," I looked him in the eye and said what I wanted. His eyes would turn glassy, and he would do it. The only catch was he was able to break the hold rather quickly.

Silas lifted the pillow off my face and smiled down at me. "One more time? I promise, no more after that."

"Ugh!" I pounded my fist against the couch. "Fine!"

Silas rubbed his hands together. "Make it something good this time!"

I stood up and faced him.

I focused intently on his eyes and told him, "You are going to let this drop. You are not going to ask any more of me today."

I watched Silas's eyes glaze over, and he nodded.

He turned and took a seat on the couch and sat quietly for about five seconds before he shook himself out of it.

"Ah, c'mon! That's it?"

"I told you I was done. I think we've proven your point." I took a seat next to him.

"You're no fun." He chuckled.

"I could have told you to take a long walk off a short pier, but then you would have had to find a pier, and considering we're in the mountains..." I shrugged in acquiescence.

"Mmm, well it's a good thing I am able to snap out of it quickly, or else I may have been on my way to the beach."

Silas put his arm around me and drew me closer to him. "I still have so many unanswered questions about your abilities."

"You and me both," I huffed. "Is there seriously no one we can talk to?"

"I'd have to track down a few people who might know someone or something. I'm honest when I tell you I've never come across anyone like you."

He gave me a squeeze. "I did meet some older vampires when I was in Europe. They kept to themselves, mostly, preferring to live life in the old ways. Hunting and feeding at night, avoiding humans and daylight. Real Nosferatu types, if you catch my drift. I was intrigued when I heard about them. I arranged a meeting with them and stayed with them for a time, studying their ways. I was still relatively young at that time, for a vampire, and was trying to find my way."

Silas paused, and a secret smile spread across his face.

"What's that look about?" I asked.

"Well, I figured if you can't beat them, join them." He shrugged.

"I wasn't exactly the knight in shining armor you've come to love." He laughed, darkly.

"But I thought you didn't kill those you fed on?"

"I didn't, but that doesn't mean my friends felt the same way. They finished them off."

I looked at Silas in disbelief.

"I know, I know. Not my best moments, that's for sure. But don't worry, I didn't stay with them long. I couldn't abide by their way of life and ultimately left them."

"Why bring them up, then?" I shuddered.

"Because, while I was there, they told me stories and tales of the Old Ones. The primordial vampires. According to Dragos and Grigore—"

I interrupted him. "Wait! Their names are Dragos and Grigore? Do they live in a castle in the dark and stormy mountains?"

I was trying to hold back my laughter. Those names were such stereotypical sounding villainous names.

Silas smirked at my amusement.

"Actually, they kept a modest woodland cottage in the Carpathians."

"Close enough." I laughed.

"Anyway," Silas poked me in the ribs. "Like I was saying, Dragos and Grigore told me tales of the Old Ones, and many of their tales included abilities similar to yours. There were vampires who could shapeshift, hypnotize without biting, scale the sides of castle walls, slaughter the entire keep before anyone knew what hit them, and much more. There was even a tale about a vampire who was more incubus than anything else."

"Incubus?"

Silas laughed. "A demon who seduces women and impregnates them in their sleep."

"So there were half human, half incubus babies out there?" I asked, skeptically.

"Something like that. According to Grigore, the demon bastards were the first vampires."

"But they're just stories, right?" I asked, trying not to sound hopeful.

"I don't know. There's probably some truth to them. When I say Dragos and Grigore are old, I don't mean old by human standards. They're old, like thousands of years old."

"Oh," I said in a hushed voice.

"Yeah. It's been close to 100 years since I last saw them."

"Do you think they would have answers? Or be able to help me improve my abilities?"

"Maybe." Silas shrugged. "But if we decide to go to them, be forewarned, they're very different from you and I."

"I got it. They're the real deal, true vampiric monsters." I nodded, hastily.

"In every sense of those words. They are not to be taken lightly." Silas was very serious; they must have been bad. "If we're going to see them, we better start planning."

"For what exactly?"

"A trip to Romania, what else?" Silas laughed. "You want answers to what you've become? Where else better to get those answers than the supposed birthplace of vampire legends?"

CHAPTER
Fifty~Five

WE PLANNED FOR WEEKS. There was so much to prepare for. It was overwhelming, to say the least. Silas practically had his phone attached to his ear, calling his contacts in Europe and the people he knew there. He was trying to track down Dragos and Grigore. He spoke in languages I never knew he could.

"Any luck?" I asked as Silas hung up his recent call.

He sat his phone down and raked his hand through his hair. "Yes and no."

He sighed in frustration. "They're not easily found, and they don't want to be. Good news is they're still around, so I'll track them down, eventually."

Silas walked over and stood behind me where I was sitting at the kitchen table.

He began massaging my shoulders. "What are you looking into?"

"Places to stay, plane tickets, passports, car rentals. You know, all the fun stuff."

I leaned back in my chair, letting Silas work on the knots in my shoulders and neck from leaning over my laptop.

"Wanna take a break?" He started kissing my neck.

I turned my face to his and met him with a kiss. "It can never just be a massage, can it?"

Silas smirked and then laughed. "Guilty, I guess. Can't blame a guy for trying."

I shut the laptop and stretched. "There's still so much to be done. I don't even know where to start."

Silas pulled out the chair next to mine and sat down. "Start with plane tickets. We can figure the rest out when we get there."

"Ugh, the plane ride is the scariest part. Being in close quarters with all those humans. Silas, I don't know if I can do it."

"I can always stake you and fly you there in a coffin." Silas said, darkly. It wasn't a half bad idea.

"You might have to," I huffed. "Seriously, though, fifteen plus hours is a long time to be surrounded by all that."

"You worry too much," Silas chided me. "We'll get you good and fed before we leave and keep the alcohol flowing on the flight. You'll be fine; you'll see."

"I hope so." I rubbed at my temples. "You know what? A break does sound nice."

Silas smiled, mischievously.

"Not that kind of break." I rolled my eyes and stood up and stretched. "I need some air. Feel like a walk?"

I turned to Silas and held out my hand.

He took it, and we headed outside.

The air was cold and crisp; it was just what I needed to clear my head.

I inhaled, deeply, savoring the aromas of the land around us. There was the smell of pine and wet earth beneath the snow, as well as the gamey tang of a rabbit and some elk and deer in the distance. The sun was bright and made the snow glitter prismatically.

Silas squeezed my hand, and I smiled, brightly, at him.

Just as we were about to head into the forest, my phone rang.

"It's Leanne. I better take this."

We headed back inside as I answered. "Hello?"

"Hey, Dani, I hope I didn't catch you at a bad time. Do you have time to talk?" Leanne sounded nervous.

"Of course, Leanne. What's up?"

"Is Silas there? Put me on speaker so you both can hear me." She sounded nervous still, but was that happiness or excitement I heard underneath?

"Okay, you're on speaker, we're both here," I said.

"Great! Hi, Silas."

"Hello, Leanne." Silas smiled.

"Jeff's here, too. Say, 'Hi,' Jeff." Leanne sounded absolutely giddy now.

"Hey, guys." Jeff sounded cheerful.

"Spit it out, already!" I said, impatiently. There was nervous laughter from Jeff and Leanne.

Silas and I gave each other a knowing look.

Silas held his left hand up and pointed to his ring finger.

I nodded in agreement.

"Okay. Here goes nothing." Leanne gave a slight pause and then blurted out "I'm pregnant!"

Silas and I looked at each other in utter shock and speechlessness. That was not what either of us expected.

"Are y'all still there?" Jeff's voice sounded concerned.

"Oh, yeah, umm we're just a bit surprised. That's great, guys! You both sound really happy." I sounded a bit doubtful. Leanne had always sworn off children. I wonder what had changed.

"Oh, we are!" Leanne giggled. "This is really good news for you two, as well."

"Yes, it is Leanne, but why don't you go ahead and tell me why?" I asked and stared at Silas; he was looking smug.

"Well, the Keeper Legacy gets to go on. Now that Dani is a vampire, too, it's very important it does."

"Wait! What? Does Jeff know?" I was practically yelling.

"Hey, Dani. Yeah, I know. Leanne filled me in on everything. It's a little hard to believe, but it definitely helps explain a lot, too." He laughed.

I looked to Silas for an explanation.

He winked at me and gave me a little smirk. "Leanne called me not too long ago to ask if she could tell Jeff. She said some things had changed that made it imperative he know."

"I see. Well, in that case, I'm really happy for you two." I smiled. "This is amazing!"

"Yes, and if there's anything you need, please, let me know." Silas chimed in.

"Oh, don't worry, Silas. This baby is getting a full ride to college on your dime." Leanne laughed.

"You got it." Silas chuckled.

We congratulated them again before saying our goodbyes and hanging up.

"Wow," I said in disbelief.

"Wow, indeed." Silas laughed at my bewildered face.

"I wonder what changed. You know as well as I do Leanne didn't want kids."

"Isn't it obvious?" Silas placed his hand on my cheek and stroked my face with his thumb. "You did."

He pulled me into an embrace as I took in what he meant.

CHAPTER
Fifty-Six

LEANNE'S NEWS hit me hard. Of course, I was happy for her, but it made me face my own mortality, or immortality, I guess. I was always going to be this from now on; frozen in time. I would never grow old, have children, or grandchildren, and I would never die, but worst of all, I would have to watch those whom I love age and live their lives and eventually pass away.

Silas noticed my melancholy at once. "Are you okay? You're not yourself today."

Silas came up behind me as I stood staring out the window. He wrapped his arms around me and kissed my shoulder.

"How do you do it?" I exhaled and leaned back into him.

Silas held me tighter. "Do what?" he asked, confused by my question and my mood.

"Watch the people you love live their lives, grow old, and then pass away, while you stay like you are forever." If my new vampire body allowed me to cry, I know tears would have been streaming down my face.

"Ahh, I wondered when you'd come around to this."

I turned around to look at him, wrapping my arms around his middle and burying my face into him.

"It's not an easy question to answer. Losing my mother was hard, as you well know, but we also know, eventually, our parents leave us. Losing my sister and niece was the hardest thing I faced. I watched them all live the life I would never have. Marriages, families, babies, love, and death were all taken from me."

I loosened my hold on Silas and looked up at him. "You're wrong about one of those things."

Silas looked down at me and raised an eyebrow. "Is that so?"

I nodded. "You found love. That wasn't taken from you."

Silas smiled, sweetly, and lowered his face to mine to kiss me. "True, but I'm afraid that in doing so I have robbed you of the very same things."

"No, I wanted this. I want you. I just thought I'd have more time to prepare before it happened. It was all so sudden."

"I agree. I wanted you to do this on your own terms, and instead, I chose for you." Silas hung his head.

I placed my hands on Silas's cheeks and lifted his face. "I wanted this." I said, slowly and firmly.

"I know what happened that night. I might not have been able to verbally tell you, but I was screaming at you internally to save me, to change me. When I heard Leanne tell you to save me the only way you knew how, I knew she had accepted my fate. She could have just as easily told you to take me to a hospital and I would have died en route. You saved me, Silas; you didn't rob me of anything."

A sad smile played across his face. "I'm glad you feel that way, but why are you so heavy-hearted?"

I pulled away from Silas and walked over to take a seat on the couch.

He followed and sat next to me.

"I guess it's just the thought of losing my best friend. She's going to grow old, watch her child grow up and have a family of their own, and I can't share that with her. Not really. One day, she'll be gone for good, and that makes me incredibly sad. She's the only family I have left."

"I understand; believe me, I do. But I also know Leanne, and I know nothing will change between you two. She loves you fiercely and couldn't care less what version of you she gets as long as you are still here."

Silas smiled and laughed, lightly. "She told me as much."

"What do you mean?"

"Shortly after you awoke, I called her to let her know it worked and you were alive. Well, undead, but you get the idea. She was overjoyed and broke down in happy tears. She said she didn't care what type of monster you were, she only cared that you came back, and she could deal with the consequences come what may."

I laughed and felt a little lighter. "That sounds like Leanne."

Silas laughed with me and said, "It doesn't get easier to lose friends and loved ones, and I wish I could say you'll grow callused to it after a while, but you don't. I will say the best thing to do is to delight in their happiness because, sometimes, it's all the silver lining our kind will get."

It made sense, what Silas said. I had a lot to get used to and to learn about myself. Dwelling on the fact one day all my friends and loved ones would be gone wouldn't do anyone any good. I would spend my time cherishing the now and not worrying about the inevitable.

"Now, I guess the only thing left to do is get to Romania so I can get my answers. But first, I need to get home and throw my best friend a baby shower!"

Silas laughed out loud. "I'm glad to see you in a better mood, and the promise of a vampire throwing a baby shower sounds delightfully interesting."

"I am feeling better; thank you."

I took Silas's hand in mine and gave it a gentle squeeze. "Please, don't ever think you have taken anything from me. I decided a long time ago I didn't want children or the white picket fence life. I wanted something more for myself, to travel and to challenge myself in ways I never imagined. You gave me that, Silas. I'm getting to go on the adventure of a lifetime! And I'm going to do it with the one person I love most in this world."

For once, Silas was lost for words. "I don't know what to say."

We leaned in toward each other and shared a kiss. It was perfect.

Silas placed his hand on my cheek, and I gazed into his eyes.

I couldn't go home, not yet, anyway. But that didn't matter because home for me was with Silas.

Epilogue

LEANNE CALLED to tell us to be expecting an envelope; she said it would be important. It was delivered to my address. Leanne mentioned it was an international parcel and she had overnighted it to us. I wondered what on Earth it could have been. I certainly didn't know anyone overseas. I asked Silas if he was expecting anything, and he was just as confused as I was.

The envelope arrived the next day.

"It's here!" Silas said, excitedly, after he closed the door on the delivery driver.

"Well, what is it? Do you recognize the return address?" I asked, expectantly.

Silas wasted no time in opening it. Leanne had placed the original parcel inside an overnight envelope.

We both stared at the stark white envelope, taking in the international stamps and the elegant calligraphy of our names and my address. The envelope was sealed with red wax, and it had a strange symbol stamped into the wax. It was a crescent moon and cross and was encircled by a serpent eating its own tail, an ouroboros.

"Do you recognize that symbol?" I asked Silas.

"Not really." He shrugged "Shall we open it?"

"Yes! I'm dying to know what's inside!" I nearly yelled.

Silas broke the wax seal and handed the envelope to me. I opened it and took out the letter. The paper smelled like roses and there was a faint undertone of sulphur. It was a very odd combination. Silas's nostrils flared when the scent reached him and he stiffened. I didn't think too much about his reaction and read the letter aloud.

Dear Danica Jones and Silas Quinn,

It has been brought to my attention you are seeking answers to Danica's purported abilities. Though rare in most new vampires, it's not unheard of. I believe I might have the answers you seek. In this envelope, you will find everything you need to come find me. I have one of my private planes awaiting you. Call the number located in the information provided, and a plane will be sent to the nearest airport to pick you up. I trust you have your passports ready? Don't keep me waiting. I look forward to making your acquaintances.

Sincerely,

Lord Ambros

We both stared at the letter for several seconds before Silas dumped the rest of the contents onto the kitchen table. There was a phone number printed on a business card with the name Antony Constantin, and there were handwritten instructions on what to do when we reached the airport in Romania.

"Do you know who this is?" I asked, hesitantly. "How do they know about us?"

"I'm assuming my inquiries didn't go unnoticed. I just didn't expect them to reach this particular set of ears." Silas looked up from the letter; he seemed scared.

I took the letter from him and set it down on the table. "Silas, tell me who, or what, this is?"

Silas took a deep breath, and with a trembling voice he answered. "Lord Ambros is one of the Old Ones. He is in a small sect of vampires and other creatures who call themselves The Children of Lillith. He's not one to be trifled with, and I don't think we can refuse his invite."

"Lillith? As in the mother of demons?"

Silas just nodded.

I picked up the card with the phone number and instructions. I looked at the stark white card with the bold black letters and numbers for a long time before picking up my phone.

"What are you doing?" Silas blanched.

I began punching in the number on my phone. "You said yourself we can't refuse his invite, and I'd much rather fly to Romania in a private plane."

Silas reached for my phone, but I easily stepped out of his reach.

"Dani, you don't know what you're messing with here." Silas sounded scared.

I hit the *call* button on my cell.

After a few seconds, the other line began to ring.

THE END
(For Now)